REUNION

AMERICANS IN EXILE

Abby Mendelson

REUNION
AMERICANS IN EXILE

iUniverse books may be ordered through booksellers or by contacting:

iUniverse
1663 Liberty Drive
Bloomington, IN 47403
www.iuniverse.com
844-349-9409

Because of the dynamic nature of the Internet, any web addresses or links contained in this book may have changed since publication and may no longer be valid. The views expressed in this work are solely those of the author and do not necessarily reflect the views of the publisher, and the publisher hereby disclaims any responsibility for them.

Any people depicted in stock imagery provided by Getty Images are models, and such images are being used for illustrative purposes only. Certain stock imagery © Getty Images.

ISBN: 978-1-6632-2279-4 (sc)
ISBN: 978-1-6632-2280-0 (e)

Library of Congress Control Number: 2021909554

Print information available on the last page.

iUniverse rev. date: 05/13/2021

For Judy

Endless Inspirer

Hopeless Enabler

Books by the Author

Fiction

Reunion: Americans in Exile
The Oakland Quartet
End of the Road: American Elegies
Ghost Dancer: 21 Stories
Scotch and Oranges
Paradise Boys

Non-Fiction

Spirit to Spirit: A Portrait of Pittsburgh Jazz in the New Century
Arena: Remembering the Igloo
Voices from the Hill: A Celebration of Hill House
Pittsburgh Prays: Thirty-Six Premier Houses of Worship
The Steelers Experience
The Pittsburgh Steelers: Yesterday and Today
The Official History of the Pittsburgh Steelers
Pittsburgh: A Place in Time
Reckoning with Rainbows: The History of the Pressley Ridge Schools
A Century of Caring: This History of the Holy Family Institute
Pittsburgh Born, Pittsburgh Bred (Co-Author)
The Power of Pittsburgh (Contributor)
Pittsburgh Characters (Contributor)
Pittsburgh: Fulfilling Its Destiny (Contributor)

I would be remiss if I did not express my sincerest gratitude to all those helped create *Reunion*, including the many people who constantly asked, encouraged, emboldened me, Marylynne and Richard paramount among them; old and dear friends Jeffrey and Teddie, Kathy and T, who helped maintain my vision; porch setters Bob and Prentiss, Barry and Gerry, Robert and Michael, who smoothed out the edges; the myriad AbVets, and David and David, for shared dreams; and Larry and Ben, Bobby and Barbara, Alan and Alan, and far too many other absent friends to mention.

The debt I owe to my children, Jesse, Elie, and Tova Chaya, and their own families, far surpasses my ability ever to articulate or repay it.

Then there are the many people whose stories I have shamelessly stolen, adapted, recreated, sewn into this patchwork quilt of a book. In every case, their narratives gnawed at me, affected me, hounded me – especially those who have passed from Middle Earth. I hope that I have done right by them, and I humbly apologize for any errors.

For who can yet beleeve, though after loss,
That all these puissant Legions, whose exile
Hath emptied Heav'n, shall fail to re-ascend
Self-rais'd, and repossess thir native seat?
For mee be witness all the Host of Heav'n,
If counsels different, or danger shun'd
By me, have lost our hopes.

John Milton, *Paradise Lost*

Contents

ARMISTICE DAY

▼

WASHINGTON, DC

No, no, no, no. No notes. No tape recordings, either. You're not wired, are you? No? Good. I don't want to be a part of this. I don't want my name appearing anywhere. This is just two guys talking. Soldier talk. I want you to know about Harry Burns. James Harris Burns, III. Remarkable man, simply remarkable. Great solider, deep thinker. Great insights into America – American foreign policy, American imperialism, American history. As brittle as he was brilliant. Contrary to a fault. Difficult. Died a few weeks ago. Sad story. Tough story.

He's evanescent now. Will-of-the-wisp. In time, he'll entirely disappear. I didn't want that for him. I want someone to know what he was about.

What Vietnam was about.

Especially with Harry Burns and Les Six and the Black Flag Battalion and all of it.

In telling it, the story defies linearity, although I'll try. I'll try to piece it together, make it a kind of pastiche. A mosaic that will illustrate his character. And the soldier talk of survivors. And the armistice that followed.

Harry Burns might have pulled easy duty. A lot of guys did. But he, and a bunch of other Ohioans, were put in the Black Flag Battalion. From there we were siphoned off into six-man squads sent out to do – whatever was necessary. Whatever they wanted to keep off the books.

Our squad – tagged Les Six by the Frenchies who were still hanging around after their army pulled out – was an odd lot of guys. Armies are made that way. Men – boys, really – thrown together, finding themselves in harm's way, having to depend on each other to survive. To do extraordinary things. To do unspeakable things. Things they can never talk about except to one and other.

Nobody else wants to hear what happened. They say they do, but they don't.

Even if they're told, they won't understand.

They're civilians.

You weren't followed coming here, were you? You're sure? Good.

You like the place? Atlasta Lodge. It's my uncle's. Built the entire thing himself, circa 1940, with his own two hands. Oh, he had a little help with the plumbing and the electric – needed registered guys for the permits and all – but he did everything else, and I mean *everything* else, by himself. Cut all the logs from nearby forests. Cured the wood. Hung the windows. Laid the floors. Stained the walls. Even made the furniture. All local wood. Made the stone fireplace, too.

I inherited it. He had no kids, and none of my cousins or siblings were interested. My wife and kids don't come here, either. Too Spartan. Too remote. Hell, that's perfect for me. It's the place I get away to. Right, generally alone. Don't get me wrong: Ashtabula's a nice quiet place. Ohio, in general, is a lot more quiet than you'd think. Midwest. Friendly. Everybody minds their own business.

But sometimes the Neal Family Farm, with all its demands, can be overwhelming. All those triggers. So I come here. Generally alone.

Only exception has been Les Six. Brought them here when I thought we needed it. No way we could be overheard. No, never any families. Never any civilians. Weekends devoted strictly to soldier talk. To exorcise the demons. Or try to, anyway.

No, don't worry about what you hear on the roof. Not rats. Squirrels. They're fine. We're friends.

He was a Neal, my father's brother. I was named after him, Alvin C. Neal. But don't use that. Don't. *Don't.* Every so often I Google myself – just to see that I'm not there. Suits me fine to be invisible. It's jungle warfare. Leave no trace. If they can't track you, they can't hurt you.

They wanted to make me an officer, but I refused. Didn't want to be a lieutenant, especially in the jungle. Lieutenants were stupid. Lieutenants were responsible. Lieutenants got you killed – or got themselves fragged. Grenade in the sleeping bag. I wasn't going to go that way.

I'm no leader – no, never was. But in Vietnam I just figured out stuff faster. Not smarter – not smarter than Chadwick, certainly, who was noticeably smart. Not smarter than Harry Burns, who really understood history and politics. But quicker. Instinctive grasp of the situation. Bishop called it precognition, but I don't know about that. All I know is that I'd get a feeling about what was going to happen. Then figure out a way to deal with it. Kept us alive.

Funny, I never had that before or since. I'm a dairy farmer. I deal with the down and dirty: feed, farmhands, foot rot. Milk and manure. Details. The trees. Harry Burns saw the forest. He could have been a congressman. A judge. But Vietnam scarred him. Scarred all of us.

War will do that for you, Bishop said.

Having your life in danger, Reed Murphy said, *will turn your fuckin' head around*.

It was Harry Burns who tagged me Doc Neal because, he said, I could diagnose a war party like a doctor does a patient. Also, he said, *because you're* something *with a knife*. Well, sure. Sometimes you want to get by without firing a shot. I was good at that. All that Ohio farm training, field dressing deer, skinning rabbits, gutting fish.

Worked well in the jungle.

Now this is not a war story, an *in country* story, and don't tell it that way. But I think we have to start there. Because there are things that hang in the air for decades. For lifetimes, really. Paradigmatic moments from which everything seems to flow.

Of a thousand – ten thousand maybe – moments in country, one stands out as the lens through which you can see all our time there. And through which you can begin to understand Harry Burns. Tall, aristocratic, a leader. *He* should have been an officer, but he refused it, too. Saw too many parts of the puzzle, the good and the bad all at once. Clouded his judgment for details.

Despite his willingness to argue, to insist that he was right, he nevertheless made you feel he had your best interests at heart. Understood you. Made you feel you were the most important person in the world.

To jump ahead, it tells you everything about Vietnam, and our time there, that he came home and instead of doing something important, he spent the next 40 years stocking shelves for the kind of main street sporting goods store that no longer exists.

Let me give you one day in country, Fire Base Bravo, north of Khe Sanh, 1968.

The sweat and stink of the jungle was like a blanket smothering us. The stench of rotting things. The smell of raw fear. Small, frightening things, muffled sounds, fleeting shadows. We learned to see what wasn't there. To distrust the slightest flicker of light. To rely on subtleties.

That day we were in a clearing smaller than a phone booth. Reed Murphy was a monster back then. As massive as he was profane. Football player; lineman. Father owned the Ashtabula hardware store. A lot of guys didn't take to killing at first. Reed Murphy did; must have been born with a black flag in his heart. Looking off into the jungle, he said, "you always see the flash before you feel the explosion. And for that split second you never know if it's going to hit you or not. You're never sure. You always have that fear. That fear you can taste in your mouth."

That was two months before he got blown up by a concussion bomb and spent the next six months in army hospitals and rehab, Tokyo to Walter Reed – a fact, like his 57 confirmed kills, he never let us forget. But that was a moment, a place, of precognition. Which is why it was so important to Harry Burns.

At that point, Harry Burns was about five yards out, watching. Suddenly, he turned and said, "you see it coming, don't you, Reed?"

Reluctantly, Reed Murphy nodded.

"That's how war is," Harry Burns said to all of us. "Did Kiefer see it first? Did he hear it? He's dusted. So's Fredette. Muschweck and Bass and Burger. Raab and Sabol and Tucci. Jaworski. Poproski. Frank. All dusted."

"C'mon, Harry," I said, "it's tough enough out here. Let's keep focused."

"I am focused," Harry Burns said. "I am very focused, Doc. I am focused on all the guys who bought it in our first four months. Before we knew what we were doing. Now we're the last, the last of Les Six. The last squad in the Black Flag Battalion."

Before I could say anything, Rex came in. He was like that even then – you had no idea he was listening, or even in the room, and he'd answered faster than you could think. "Black flag," he chattered. "Black Label. Black Label. Mabel, Black Label!"

I don't know how he got into Black Flag, much less the army. Mistake, maybe. Rex was drafted like the rest of us, but he came in underweight and nervous. Pink, translucent skin. Chatterbox. The war just made things worse. Made him unravel. Rex was already given to OCD acting out, blurting, free associating all over the place. All it took was for me to mention Black Flag, and he just riffed off of that.

"It's OK, Rex," Bishop said. "As usual, he doesn't know what he's talking about."

"No," Harry Burns said, "maybe he does. Maybe it's more than Black Flag. It's Black Label for the country."

Harry Burns really was the best and the brightest. Big and brave and buff – at least at age 20. Here, a typical Rex riff got him talking about how the war really was Black Label, how it represented a complete failure of American policy. Of American vision. How American imperialism was a pitiful substitute for a viable foreign policy. "We're its tethered goat," he said. "Its sacrificial stalking horse."

Of course, none of us knew what he was talking about. We were kids, barely out of high school. Our global vision extended to drive-in movies and hamburger stands.

"Deep," Bishop said. "Harry Burns is always deep."

"Very fuckin' deep," Reed Murphy agreed.

"Everybody I mentioned," Harry Burns said, "was sacrificed on the altar of political ambition."

"Don't know about that," Al Gutierrez said. Good guy, black-rimmed glasses, Albuquerque. "Don't know about policy. Don't mean shit. All karma. No matter what you do, it's written. Written 1,000 years ago. Nothing can hurt you 'less it's written."

Whenever Gutierrez said that, there was always push back, notably by Bishop. I know you've seen pictures of Bishop now – weathered and wizened and weepy. Right; a wreck. But you should have seen him back in the day: he weighed about 165 and could run like a gazelle. His father owned a car leasing company, and Bishop would try to outrace the Fords and Buicks. He also had no patience for Gutierrez. "What's all this New Mexico live-in-the-desert-cactus-hugger stuff?" he said. Then, as now, Bishop never spoke a word he couldn't say in front of his mother. "It's not like that. Not like that at all. It's gravity: there's only so much death in the world. The more death you deal, the more you keep it away from you."

Bishop believed that. More or less, we all did.

"Right," Reed Murphy, said. "Kill 'em. Kill 'em all. Kill 'em first."

Which of course got Rex into full babble. "Right," he said. "Right. Kill 'em all."

"You got to be careful," Harry Burns told Gutierrez. "You got the sign on you."

Gutierrez didn't like being ragged, but who does? "Why don't you take your Zippo, Harry Burns," he waved, "and light 'em all the fuck up?"

Because aside from explaining the situation to any and all, what Harry Burns loved most was setting things on fire. He said that all he needed was his M16 and his Zippo. "Nothing like burning dinks to warm a soldier's heart," he said, deliberately not answering Gutierrez because he already had.

I saw something move, or thought I did; it amounted to the same thing. Time to get moving. "Gutierrez," I said, "take your karma and get on point. Ten yards out. Bishop, watch our backs. Harry Burns, right. Reed Murphy, left. Dinks. Watch out."

As we rose to move, Gutierrez didn't watch where he was going.

"What we did," Reed Murphy said at one of our reunions – just four of us some 20 years later, a sorry, sodden weekend, spring 1988, here, at Atlasta Lodge – "was waste 'em. Hit the ground running and waste 'em. And what we did, back home, they didn't see the iceberg. Not the tip. Not the fuckin' shadow. They didn't see it at all. We were as far away from *CBS News* and *The New York Fucking Times* as the Earth is to the Moon."

No, Reed Murphy wasn't drunk, not yet, but he was getting there. Gave over that athlete's body to bottom-shelf bourbon and barbeque.

"Remember that old man at the Quang Tri border?" I asked.

"I knew you were going there," Bishop said.

"Prisoner, right?" Harry Burns asked.

"Right. Motherfucker cursed us. Tough old bird. Even tied to a chair he cursed us. *You Americans are very rich*, he said. *But you've never had any attachment to your land, which you stole. Therefore you have no* chi. *And no culture, which arises from* chi. *So you will lose everything here. And everything at home.* Man, was he right."

"We sure as shit lost everything there," Reed Murphy said.

"Wasn't for lack of trying," Bishop added.

"Or lack of firepower," I said. "Or lack of will."

"*Will*, for us," Reed Murphy said, "was to be off the books. Away from the chain of command. Invisible. Deniable."

"It was a great operation," Harry Burns said. Harry Burns was still in shape back then, still saw the big picture. Far more balanced than he would become. "Took our orders right out of GHQ, Khe Sanh. Black flag was payback for five months of VC attacks. Mortars. Rockets. Artillery. Ground troops. Name it."

"I could cry when I think about that," Bishop said. He wasn't burned out yet, but was well on the way. "We had an answer for that. Hundred thousand tons of bombs."

"When that was over," I said, "they sent us in."

"By that time nobody was looking," Reed Murphy said, hoisting his Ancient Age. "Completely off the books. Records sealed to this day. Hidden. Never found."

"None of us existed," I said. "Who we were. What we did. Nothing."

"We ignored every border," Harry Burns added. "Like us, they didn't exist."

"Ignored every law, too," Bishop said.

"Was it two months?" Reed Murphy asked. "Running drugs for the warlords?"

"I personally packed more heroin than a Columbian cartel," I said. "Ran guys into Laos. Into China."

"Took sides," Bishop said. "Killed both sides."

"Fuck," Reed Murphy said. "Everybody was on the take. So we took 'em."

"Everything was tribal to those people," Harry Burns said. "And everything was 1,000-year-old payback. So we lined up – and hoped they stayed with us."

"Until they didn't," I shook my head.

I was surprised: Bishop actually laughed. "It was jazz, Chadwick said."

"Chad was right," Harry Burns nodded. "It *was* jazz. It was improv."

"Nobody saw the war like Chad," Reed Murphy said. "Fuckin' genius."

"Rotated in after Gutierrez got blown up," Bishop said.

"It looked all clear," I said. "Of course, it did. 'Til he stepped on that land mine. Blew him to pieces. At least there was enough so his family could have a funeral."

"Maybe he was right," Harry Burns said. "Maybe it was all karma. He was being *real* careful. Got himself blown up anyway." Harry Burns paused. "Where's Chad?"

"DC," I answered. "Not doing well. Maybe time for some search-and-rescue."

"Rex," Bishop said, starting to tear up. "Rex, too. Maybe the VA for Rex."

It was the next day. Harry Burns was contemplative, as always, trying to make sense of it all. Reed Murphy, trying to anesthetize all the old wounds, was nursing a hangover. Bishop stared out the window, wasted and weepy. For my part, I was worried about our other two surviving members, Rex and Chadwick, MIA out there in America.

"We displayed a certain craziness," Harry Burns said distractedly, spooning raw honey into his tea. I never saw him drink anything stronger.

"A certain innocence," I said. "Chadwick. Old Joe Clark. Gutierrez. Rex."

"Jimmy Two Feathers," Bishop added.

"Who?" Reed Murphy finally moved, reaching for another bottle of Ancient Age.

"Jimmy Two Feathers," Bishop repeated. "Never told us his real name. *White* name. Insisted on being called what he said was his *Native* name."

Reed Murphy shook his head, not surprisingly like a man after a bad night. "What the fuck are you talking about?"

"Jimmy Two Feathers," Bishop said. "You don't remember him?"

"Apparently not," Harry Burns said.

"Fuck no," Reed Murphy swigged.

"Showed up one day," Bishop said. "Started talking about the ghost dances – how bullets would pass right through him."

"You're making this shit up," Reed Murphy said.

"No, I'm not," Bishop said. "He lasted two hours. Took one right in the chest."

I said that I had no recollection of this. Still don't. But that's memory – spongy, never certain. Bishop, to the contrary, was *certain*.

"And the Jap who wouldn't speak to us," Bishop said.

"Now I *know* you're shittin' us," Reed Murphy said.

"He didn't last either. What was his name? I can't remember. Fujiyama? Hirohito? Something that sounded historic or fungible."

"Wait a minute," Harry Burns said. "Right. Firefight. Jap bought it right out."

"Right," Bishop said.

"What a war," I shook my head.

"At least you came out of it in one piece, Doc," Reed Murphy said. "I got blown up by a concussion bomb."

"To make someone else die is to cheat death," Bishop said. "Maybe that's why you lived through it. Those 57 confirmed kills."

Reed Murphy smiled. "It's like love. You always remember the first person you kill, where it was, how it was, who it was. His face. His posture. His situation. How he looked. How he smelled. Was it right away or did it take time? If he looked at you. His eyes – especially his eyes. His teeth. His tattoos. His clothing." Reed Murphy paused. "I had 56 more after that. Fifty-seven confirmed kills."

"Who first called it the Black Flag Battalion?" Harry Burns asked. Harry Burns was always interested in the big picture, the names and dates of things. We had eaten lunch – nothing fancy, something out of a box – and I was clearing the dishes.

"I remember that Rex loved it," Bishop said. *"Raise the Black Flag! Raise the Black Flag!"*

"We sewed black flags on our uniforms," Reed Murphy said. "Fuck the regs."

"It was the jungle," Harry Burns shrugged, "and our kill counts were stellar. What were they going to do, court-martial us?"

"A little *esprit-de-corps*," I smiled.

"Black," Bishop said. "Wholly black. Black Label beer. Johnny Walker Black. Beemans Black Jack gum. R&R in Saigon when we all got black flag tattoos.

"Sent us out in groups of six," Harry Burns said. "Why six? Four points of the compass plus up in the trees and under the ground? Magic number?"

"Nobody gave a rat's ass." Reed Murphy was drinking again.

"I think more to the point," I said, "we learned not to ask. Asking wouldn't have helped us stay alive."

"The Six Pack," Bishop said. "Six Pack of Death. When we hit the Six Pack of Satan things got out of hand. Old Joe Clark convinced himself that we really did work for Satan. Started speaking in tongues and doing weird incantations. Started to believe that none of us could be harmed because the dinks hadn't paid the Devil his due."

"I remember that," Harry Burns said. "I remember Old Joe Clark – he was fairly steady before that – going around the bend. He was going to get us into serious trouble. He was going to get us killed."

"I actually thought about cutting his throat," Reed Murphy said. "One day in the shit I came this close to putting one in his head, but some dink sniper did it first. Old Joe Clark never saw it coming. No one did. You know how you can feel someone looking at you? You couldn't with the dinks."

"Right," Bishop said. "They were invisible."

"They were magic," Harry Burns said. "No doubt about it."

"*Chi*," I said. "It'll get you every time."

It was dusk. The wind stirred up, and clouds massed in the west.

"Funny," I said, "the four of us came from Ohio, small-town sons of shopkeepers and farmers. Rex was from West Virginia. Bluefield. Chadwick, DC. We're the six who got to go home. The other guys couldn't cheat death."

"Al Gutierrez," Bishop said, "really sweet guy."

"Sweet guy," Reed Murphy said, "but shitty karma."

"Old Joe Clark," Bishop said, "Eastern Kentucky."

"The four of us," I gestured, "all grew up as bird hunters. Boots and flannels. Steaming coffee and runny noses. Trudging across stubbled fields, shotguns cradled in our arms. Pheasant and grouse. Ducks and geese. Wild turkey."

"Caps slung low over our eyes," Reed Murphy said. "Jaws set. Dealing death."

Did I tell you that I pay cash for everything? I never use credit cards. No one can track me. I even set a tripwire around the farm. No one's going to sneak up on me.

One thing or another it took me the better part of 10 years – 1998 or so – to get them back to Atlasta Lodge. By that time I had managed to bring Rex up to Cleveland and got him into the VA – he was in pretty bad shape, having hallucinations and paranoid episodes, and his family wanted no part of it.

Then there was Chadwick – I had to tell them about him. Chadwick was cool. Precise. Until he wasn't. Arguably brighter than Harry Burns, he was from the Washington, DC, black middle class. Father was a lawyer, or a professor, or both. Mother worked in the State Department. Or Treasury. Somewhere. Chadwick had Ph.D. written all over him.

"I thought Gutierrez was bad enough when he talked karma," Reed Murphy said. "Then Chadwick came out with all that *feng shui* shit. *Feng shui*? We got fuckin' landmines out there and he's talking about arranging rooms to achieve some sort of universal harmony? Was he for fuckin' real? In *Vietnam*?"

No, Reed Murphy didn't get Chadwick. Chad was too cerebral for him. Clean. Measured. An absolute clock.

Until the torture did him. Sure, we had warned him not to go past the perimeter – but you know Chadwick. *I got it scoped*, he said. Well, he didn't, did he? It's a miracle we found him – down some dink hell hole; amazing what those assholes could do with bamboo slivers. They were having fun, all right. So we killed them all and brought Chad back. But he could never focus after that. Couldn't get time right.

"It's a miracle he survived," I said.

"Some fuckin' miracle," Reed Murphy said. "Survived for what? As what?"

He was living at home, and I'd call him every month or so, just to check in. Finally, his mother said he was no longer there. Something about life with them being too regular, too regulated, too something. No, she didn't know where he was. But if I found him.

I got in the car and drove through the night. It took a little detective work, but I found him all right, a DC dumpster diver. You can't imagine the stench. And the rats. Chadwick? Unkempt and unclean. Ghastly, gaunt, gap-toothed. A troubled, tortured soul living large in hell and looking it.

"You ask him how all that *feng shui* shit was working for him in his dumpster?" Reed Murphy said.

"You ought to ease up on him," I said. "That's Chadwick we're talking about."

"Right," he said, mollified. "Sorry."

I tried to get him cleaned up and into a shelter, but he wasn't having any of it. I came back a few times. He surfaced, sank, surfaced again, then drowned. I found out too late to go to an Episcopal funeral he would've hated.

The other three? Bishop is a bit less focused than he used to be, but he's mostly OK. These days, he spends most of his time at the Vets Center. Couldn't focus on all the new regulations and taxes involved in car leasing. Reed Murphy is more or less hanging in the hardware store, mostly in the back where he doesn't have to deal with people. Why? Here's an illustrative anecdote. "The other day in Canton," he said, "there was this little traffic dust-up. Bit of a disagreement about a parking spot. Everything was cool 'til the guy put a finger in my face. Not smart. So I had to break his hand. I imagine he drove himself to the hospital. If he couldn't, too bad. Probably taking Advil today. Probably has a cast the size of a football."

Harry Burns? Seemed fine – at least in '98. "Rainy morning," he said, "our CO – remember him? Jacobson. Officious little dick with a big head and bristly mustache."

"I remember that jerk," Bishop said.

"Said he was sending us to Saigon for R&R. When we said we didn't need it, he just glared. *Those are orders.*"

Saigon was loud and offensive. Shell games and clip joints. Dinks probably pissed in the drinks. Most of us didn't take the place seriously, but Rex, well, Rex was really OCD by then. Sure, we all got our weasels greased. That's what GIs do. But Rex, Rex was giggling, damn near drooling. Spent three days in some wretched little place. We had to drag him out. Wound up getting the clap. Penicillin cleared it up.

When Reed Murphy nearly killed some dink over a bar bill it was time to go.

"We were *Time*'s Man of the Year in '65," Harry Burns said. "The world was our oyster. And everyone wanted to give it to us. But we couldn't handle it. We fell victim to Vietnam. It was *our* war, ultimately, and we didn't deliver.

"So if you ask me: am I proud of what I've done?" He shrugged. "Pride is not part of the equation. I served my country. I did what my country asked of me."

To which Reed Murphy added, "and my family disowned me."

There was a lull, then something bubbled up out of memory.

"Remember that VC?" I asked. "The one we chased for two weeks?"

"Hell, yes," Reed Murphy said. "*Man* that was some hard travelin'!"

"He terrorized the countryside. Burned whole villages to mask his escape. When we finally caught him I actually thought about cutting out his heart and eating it. To assume his strength and spirit into mine, give me more power."

"Good night," Bishop said.

"Right," I said. "I didn't do it. But I actually thought about it."

"That's the difference between you and me," Reed Murphy said. "I always thought you thought too much. I just would have done it."

"Thinking kept us alive," I said.

"As much the luck of the draw as anything else," Harry Burns said. "No, what kept us alive was our ability to kill everything. Remember that village chief, in that long valley, as dirty as the day was long. Cache of arms under his hootch. VC had his kid."

"Sure," I said.

"We shot him," Harry Burns said. "Shot his whole family. And one stalwart American Zippo lighter burned down his whole village."

"I remember that," I said. "Flushed out the VC. They ran – and we chased 'em all the way into Laos. Killed 'em all. Families, too."

"Then we flew the Black Flag," Bishop said.

Harry Burns breathed hard – and I was surprised to see that. "It could have been that one," he said. "It could have been any one. But Rex was never the same after that. Couldn't take it anymore. Started talking to himself."

"I love all this shit on the news now," Reed Murphy said. "Torture. Torture? Fuckin' civilians. They wouldn't believe what's done in their name. We *lived* off torture."

"We could have won," Harry Burns said. "*Should* have won. The army with the *will* to win wins. Not intelligence. Not morality. Not power. *Will.* We didn't have it. They did."

"We had everything else," I said. "Supplies. Weapons. Troops. Firepower. But no stomach for it then, no stomach for it now."

"It wound up ruining us," Harry Burns said. "Turned us into a nation of failures."

"How can we tell these stories and stay sane?" Bishop asked.

"Rex couldn't," I said.

"Neither could Chadwick," Reed Murphy said.

"Neither can America," Harry Burns said. "Kennedy took one in the head in '63. Johnson didn't run again in '68, died five years later. Nixon resigned a year after that, in '74. It was as if the *chi* of Vietnam rose up and destroyed them. Tainted them forever." He paused. "They tore America apart – and paid the price."

"I remember back home they had body counts every Thursday," I said. "Numbers invented to assuage the American public – those who were listening. None of it had any relation to reality."

"Ike wouldn't have lied to us," Bishop said. "Ike *didn't* lie to us. Kennedy did."

"Kennedy," Harry Burns said, "was a pretty boy skirt chaser who screwed up his dinky PT boat – then had the nerve to strut around like a hero. Shit. Ike was a *man*. A *man's* man. Ike knew what it was like to command troops in the field."

"Fuckin' McNamara," Reed Murphy said, still relatively sober, "would not be dissuaded or dismayed. Not how they worked at the Ford Motor Company. Not how they won World War II. Punish the enemy. Destroy the enemy. Drive the body count so high they'd *have* to surrender. What that slick-haired piece of shit didn't understand was that it was *our* body count – and *they* would never surrender."

"Jungle," Bishop said. "Couldn't see 'em. Couldn't hear 'em. Couldn't find 'em. Couldn't identify 'em if we did. Melted into the landscape – and not only in villages and tunnels. They *disappeared*. Invisible people. Lived in trees. Underground."

"I don't blame them," Harry Burns said. "It was *their* landscape used to best advantage. Booby traps. Ambushes. Fire fights. McNamara *should* have heard that, but didn't." He paused. "At the cost of our lives.

"It was our generation's failure of character," Harry Burns added. "Born during *Pax Americana*, victorious, optimistic, peaceful, prosperous. We were exceptional people, and there was nothing Americans couldn't do. No problem we couldn't solve, no law of nature or physics we couldn't alter, ameliorate, or amalgamate."

"The fuckin' newsies didn't lose it," Reed Murphy said, "though they tried. Main Street didn't lose it. The colleges didn't lose it. Washington certainly didn't lose it – bunch of fuckin' empty suits. *We* lost it. *We* didn't do what we had to. *We* flinched."

"And got repatriated with no detox time," Bishop said. "Day One in the jungle. Day Two back in a world that despised us. Blamed *us*."

"Like when I had to deal with Rex's family," I said. "Nobody in Bluefield wanted him. Nobody available to be his keeper. PTSD. Combat fatigue. Shell shock. Real men don't get it. Hollywood myths don't get it. Gary Cooper. John Wayne. Made-up names, made-up people. The stories we tell ourselves."

"Civilians don't understand," Bishop said. "They *never* understand."

"They don't know what it is to shit through a new asshole," Reed Murphy said.

Every Monday morning I Google myself – just to see that I'm not there. There's no record of me. No one can find me. I'm invisible.

By early 2008 Harry Burns wasn't OK. The rages, the fights, the night sweats and the nights I had to calm him down. He dreamed of dead people. People long dead. People maimed. People voluble and mute and living in a demon-infested landscape.

He dreamed of a jungle looking back at him.

Bishop and Reed Murphy and I were back at Atlasta Lodge trying to piece together what we were going to do about Harry Burns.

"*All you need,*" Reed Murphy said, "*is your M16 and a Zippo lighter.* Harry Burns said that."

"Harry Burns was King of the Zippos, all right," Bishop said. "Could burn down a hooch faster than LBJ could lie. Then he'd say, *don't need all that hearts-and-minds stuff if they're all dead.*"

"Harry Burns always hated commendations," I said. "Said we were decorated for failing. At best, for waxing dinks. What's the bonus in that?"

"Wax or be waxed, motherfucker," Reed Murphy answered. "Harry Burns called it good old fashioned fatalism dressed up like a mai tai with some zipperhead name, a frozen cherry on a plastic skewer, and a paper umbrella. It was same-old when-your-number's-up. Nothing more, nothing less."

"I talked with Harry Burns last week," I said. "He told me that his daughter Doris had all his mail routed to Delaware; she said he lives with her, which of course he doesn't. He's sure she's forging his signature. Stealing his VA checks."

"Why doesn't he do something about it?" Bishop asked.

"I asked him that. He said, *my daughter's no damn good. And my son's worse.* Meaning he's helpless."

"Fuck," Reed Murphy said.

"Right. To top that off, Harry Burns is becoming more infirm by the day. Living in a world reduced. Spends his time talking about the military's role in American life."

"Never liked blood the way I did," Reed Murphy added.

"Well, who did?" I asked.

Reed Murphy tipped his bottle at me.

"The last thing he said to me before we hung up was *the only true reflection of a country's stamina and moral fiber, the highest expression of its national character, is its armed forces.*"

"That's wrong," Bishop said, "and we all know it."

"We know it a lot more than a lot of people know it," I added.

"This is a big fuckin' country," Reed Murphy waved, "with a lot of moving parts."

"Right," I said, "Harry Burns didn't take into account Chadwick and

Rex and Gutierrez and Old Joe Clark and their families and their friends and the million other casualties of war. But for Harry Burns, with his two busted marriages, estranged son, Dragon Lady daughter, it's a comfortable field of vision. His three years in the military, and eleven months overseas, all occurring in his 20s, take on increasing importance."

"The rock upon which he's built his church," Bishop said.

"Defining for him the parameters of life," I added. "Not only his sin, seemingly enormous, unforgivable --"

"He should talk to my fuckin' family," Reed Murphy said. "No, on second thought, he shouldn't."

"-- but also his expiation, his redemption."

"War," Bishop said, "its healing fire, its healing blood."

"I could hear it in his voice," I said. "It wasn't just a military or political discussion. This is the end of the line for Harry Burns. Harry Burns is seeking salvation."

"A false concept if there ever were one," Bishop shook his head.

"A way to tie things off," I shrugged.

"He won't get it," Reed Murphy said. "Chadwick didn't. No more than Gutierrez or Old Joe Clark did. Or Rex. None of us will."

"Not in this lifetime," Bishop added.

An hour later. Reed Murphy had finished one bottle and started another. Bishop, starting to make himself a sandwich, quit halfway through.

"We need an action plan," I said. "Not Doris, the Dragon Lady of Delaware. Not Edwin, his son. I met him once."

"I met him, too," Bishop said. "Never cared to repeat the experience."

"I don't know a single human being with whom Harry Burns did not have a significant fight," I said, "including his children. Most people more than one fight. Sooner or later he found fault with everyone. And even if he didn't, I can't count the number of times he said we would do something, or he would show up, and didn't. Never mentioned it afterward." I paused. "Harry Burns was a hard man to befriend."

"Every time we sat down to talk about something," Bishop added, "and it was always something *he* wanted to talk about – he lost interest halfway through and floated into another George Patton story."

"Despite all that," Reed Murphy said, "we owe him. We *all* owe him."

"Amen to that, brother," Bishop said.

You know that they're reading everything. Monitoring us. They'll be monitoring our thoughts next, if they aren't already. They'll figure a way. They always do.

That's why I have to be so careful these days.

That's why we had to be so careful about Harry Burns.

We set it aside for a week. Then it was a month. Then it was five months. Then I got Bishop and Reed Murphy back to Atlasta Lodge. Bishop was thinner than ever, but Reed Murphy had gone clean and sober. While he hadn't veered away from all his bloodthirsty talk, he had switched from Ancient Age to Maxwell House.

"Harry Burns said we could have won that fuckin' war," Reed Murphy said. "Invade the North. Crush Hanoi. Unite the country. Then we would've lost the peace. The South was so inept, so corrupt, it wouldn't have lasted 10 minutes."

"Right," I answered. "Harry Burns saw it all. Concerned about soft-on-communism charges, instead of dealing with Vietnam as a self-contained conflict with a socialist overlay, Kennedy, Johnson, Nixon, that unholy trio of murderers, plowed on."

"Until it took their lives," Bishop said, "their honor, their legacies."

"Losing a war," Reed Murphy added, "especially a highly unpopular war fought for no good reason, will do that to a Commander-in-Chief – who has nowhere to hide the buck." He shrugged. "All the napalm and bombing runs and body counts brought us was Tet. Drug lords. Assassinations. Tribal murder. Me, I got a Silver Star. My nation's gratitude for getting blown up, coming home an outcast and a cripple."

"I'll never forget the sound of Old Joe Clark getting clipped," Bishop said. "It was like slapping meat. No cries. Then the silence of death."

"Pain," Reed Murphy said, "pain is something else. Pain is like going to another country. When the pain is there, there's nothing else. No negotiating with it."

They were veering perilously into feeling sorry for themselves, but Harry Burns was the situation, and we had to get back to him.

"Harry Burns," I said, "told me he felt his memory departing, rolling backwards like a sardine can. About three weeks ago he managed to drive himself to Walter Reed – don't ask me how – but on the way back his daughter somehow snagged him. Don't ask me how that happened, either. Harry called me, I presume from her house, because I heard some banshee shrieking in the background. Said he'd see me in October. But he never made it. I called again, but Dragon Lady wouldn't answer." I paused. "I can only presume he is more or less a prisoner and that she stole his stash."

"We can't leave the troops in the field," Reed Murphy said.

"I hate leaving Ohio," Bishop made a face.

"We need to spring Rex for this mission," Reed Murphy said.

While there was much to mitigate against bringing Rex, I thought that maybe it would be good for him and Harry Burns.

"Right," I agreed.

"What's he do all day in the VA?" Bishop asked.

"I don't know," I answered, "other than read books in his room."

"Rex?" Reed Murphy asked. "*Can* he read? I mean --"

"Civil War," I said. "Antietam Creek. Who knows what goes on in his head."

"Harry Burns is going to be all right," Bishop demurred.

"For the time being, maybe," I said, "but I don't like what I'm feeling."

"You always did have that way, Doc," Bishop said.

We had planned to go that weekend, but back to precognition. Something told me to call. Sure, Dragon Lady didn't pick up. But, surprisingly, Edwin did. "Didn't you hear?" he asked. "No, I guess you didn't. Dad died. Two nights ago. Family memorial in Delaware. Day after tomorrow."

Within an hour I had the other two in my Dodge Caravan, then stopped at the VA for Rex. You know the drill: institutional walls, institutional terrazzo floor. Lot of guys in pajamas and bathrobes. Since I had brought him in and was registered as his caregiver I had no problem signing him out for a couple of days. While Rex stared and nodded a lot, he seemed fine. Said goodbye about 14 times to the desk clerk – a large, smiling black woman – but that was normal.

Ohio flatland morphed into I-70 East in Pennsylvania, the road dark and hilly, dipping and swaying all over the place.

"Harry Burns," Rex stared out the window, rocking back and forth. "Harry Burns. Harry Burns. Harry Burns." Then softer. "Antietam Creek. Antietam Creek."

At first the war was good for me. Off the farm, away from Bluefield. First time I ever had my own gun. First time I ever had shoes. Army of Northern Virginia, on the march, heading for Antietam Creek.

"With that Zippo lighter," Reed Murphy said. "Harry Fuckin' Burns, all right."

"He was something to look at," Bishop added. "Before he let himself go. Tall, rugged, Sam Shepherd retooled as a lumberjack. Scots sumo wrestler. Caber tosser. Shock of white hair. Features like the Old Man of the Mountain. Ramrod posture."

I hit the turn signal and steered around an 18-wheeler. "He was a mass of contradictions, but maybe we all are. A self-effacing man – *why anyone should take me seriously is laughable* – who nevertheless expounded on everything and always insisted he was right. Generous and kind, he also picked fights – bitter, unforgiving, lifelong battles. For Harry Burns, the closer the relationship, the deeper the enmity. The greater the betrayal. For some reason I escaped unscathed. I was his DMZ."

Reed Murphy tapped his fingers restively on the armrest and stared at the headlights. "As Harry Burns aged, and more was taken from him, he reached back, reached deep, and dredged up more courage. Played the Vietnam Vet, wore his battle ribbons, medals. Then got miffed when so few people paid attention to him, and so few seemed to care. Or honor his sacrifice. Trotting out his signs and symbols and service record at every turn, Harry Burns became the elephant in the room, impossible to ignore, impossible, one way or another, not to address."

Bishop shrugged. "Maybe Doris the Dragon Lady didn't snatch Harry Burns. Maybe Harry Burns was coming to her, coming home to die. Like the guys in the VA, Harry Burns was broken, bereft of spirit, mind and body and soul worn away. Torn like a tired muscle, while everything else in his life, every other construct, had burned away. Only the old was familiar, formative. His family. The military."

Rex muttered his name.

In a war of schizophrenia – we were all Americans, after all; all had the same revolutionary heroes, our militaries went to the same school, served in the same wars, even roomed together and traded girlfriends – Antietam Creek was the psychotic breakdown. The bloodiest day in an unspeakably bloody war, Antietam Creek was like some frenzied beast tearing at itself in a paroxysm of blind rage and senseless hate. With every reason to stop, to call a sensible cease fire, we steamed full ahead into each other's innards, choked with gun smoke and cannon shot, flush with musket fire and fixed bayonets – not stopping until the carnage became complete.

"I don't know about you guys," I said, "but this drive to Delaware is good for me. I've spent the past six hours trying to frame a cogent response. I've had too much caffeine but not enough to kick in. So I'm not going to say that Doris the Dragon Lady killed him. Smothered him with a pillow. It's just that there are a lot of survivor benefits. So I don't know how pro-active she was in getting him the best VA medical treatment – or any medical treatment at all."

"Let's put it this way," Reed Murphy said, crumpling his empty Starbucks cup. "We all knew Harry Burns, what his body was like, what he was about. He wasn't going to live long anyway. So if she didn't outright kill him for his pension and insurance, Dragon Lady certainly didn't delay the process."

"Dragon Lady," Rex said, clicking his teeth. "Dragon Lady. Dragon Lady. Dragon Lady. Dragon Lady."

Antietam Creek became white noise. Ordinance. Rifle fire. Bullets thudding into trees, dirt, flesh. Bodies falling.

Antietam Creek became a silence unto itself.

Antietam Creek reeked with the stench of dysentery and dismembered body parts, puke and piss and limbs piled outside makeshift hospitals.

"I remember when Dragon Lady came east to go to school," I said. "Liked Delaware, or so Harry Burns said. Settled down at the Wilmington Opera House. Good at fundraising. Good at getting along with major donors, especially the Du Ponts."

"I remember a lot of kids," Reed Murphy said. "Collected them. Multiple kids by multiple fathers, plus waifs and strays. Harry Burns helped pay for them."

"He still is," Bishop muttered.

Took us the better part of a night and a gray, overcast November morning, but we pulled into the little town of Ellendale, Delaware, looking for the Willow Street Congregational Church. Bishop said to ask for directions.

"No," I shook my head, "I don't want to ask directions. I don't want to look it up. They'll be shadowing us. They'll know. And the less they know, the happier I am. I found my way out of the jungle. I found my way back to Ohio. I can find a church in Ellendale, Delaware."

"It was not the fog of war," Reed Murphy said. "It was not stupidity. Or cupidity. It was a fifth column. Enemy agents. Enemy agents all around us. Infiltrating us. *Infecting* us. Our victory was deliberately stolen from us."

"November in Delaware," Reed Murphy added. "Cold, rainy motherfucker."

"Let's keep it together," I said. "I'll find it. Small clapboard church."

"Fuckin' snake handlers," Reed Murphy said.

"Off the map," I said. "Off the grid. Kind of place Harry Burns would've liked."

"Fuckin' crazy daughter liked it more," Reed Murphy answered.

Reed Murphy pointed out a slight, white building. "Is that it?" he asked.

"Got to be," I muttered, and pulled over.

"Looks very dark," Bishop peered out.

"I'll have a look," I said, and jumped out of the car.

A minute later I was back. "Doors locked. Missed it."

"We don't leave the troops in the field," Reed Murphy said. "We should get him."

"No," I demurred. "He belongs with his family."

"They're accidents of biology," Bishop disagreed. "They don't deserve him. *We're* his family."

"He belongs to us," Reed Murphy said.

We found the funeral home – pillars, lights, unpronounceable German name – only to discover that Harry Burns, somehow true to his name, had been cremated. Ashes spirited away by the family, as expected.

"Against his wishes," Bishop said. "Of course."

"Dragon Lady probably flushed them," Reed Murphy said. "She hated Harry Burns. Hated all of us. Only took him for his benefits."

"The good news," Bishop said, "is that he was probably too sick to know what was going on."

"Harry Burns," I said. "Best of us. No remains. No records. No remembrances. As if he'd never existed. A blissful oblivion. Maybe he'll find peace."

"Maybe," Reed Murphy said. "Dragon Lady couldn't be bothered with Arlington, which is what Harry Burns wanted."

"I remember that," Bishop said. "Harry Burns saying, *Arlington or nothing.*

"He got nothing all right," Reed Murphy answered.

"Arlington," I said. "What vet doesn't want that? Barring that, the Ohio family plot, or a nice spot in the Blue Ridge Mountains. Harry Burns loved it there."

Out of nowhere, Rex started to babble. "Salute the flag. Salute the deck officer. Salute the flag. Salute the deck officer."

Antietam Creek was a sunny morning, soldiers rising out of the cornfield like mist, ghostly figures in blue and gray, men with malevolence in their hearts, Blue Bellies white with fear, Johnny Reb jabbering like monkeys.

Antietam Creek was the nation and its wars, flies ubiquitous and incessant, jackals gnawing through mud- and blood-encrusted uniforms to devour dead flesh.

Antietam Creek was ignoring sense and self, gorging on primitive lusts, blood rising like floodwater.

Antietam Creek was the mountain fog we faced every day.

"Tough story," I said. "In Harry Burns' decline, and dementia, he wound up with her. Doris the Dragon Lady. The Witch of Wilmington. For Harry Burns, it was sanctuary. Safe haven. He took it, not matter how cut-rate. And she bled him white."

"Harry Burns will forever be MIA," Bishop said.

"MIA," Rex chattered, rocking back and forth. "MIA. MIA. MIA. MIA."

Antietam Creek began at dawn, September 17, 1862, with Joe Hooker's attack at Hagerstown Turnpike. His complement: 8,600 men. His objective: Dunker Church. His opponent: our great hero, Stonewall Jackson, arguably the war's most brilliant, resilient, and feared general, commanding 7,700 men.

Glimpsing our rebel bayonets in the church's adjacent cornfield, Hooker halted his advance, hauled up four artillery batteries, opened fire. Advancing under the hail of cannon shot, Blue met Gray in the cornfield, where both armies fired into each other. Virtually impossible to ascertain who or what or where, control of the cornfield changed hands more than a dozen times.

Does this happen to you? The post office is diverting my mail. They're after me.

Back in the van. After the hell-for-leather ride out of Ohio, we were quiet, deflated, wondering what to do.

"Another fuckin' SNAFU," Reed Murphy groused.

"SNAFU," Rex babbled. "SNAFU. Situation normal all fucked up. Situation normal all fucked up."

Antietam Creek was an All-American firefight. With bullets whining, thick enough to see, cutting the foliage like a scythe, cornstalks simply exploded. The man next to me — a boy, really, no more than 16, from a farm near Richmond — tried to speak, but his cheek was shot out. With blood gushing from his mouth, he collapsed in a heap.

As acrid gun smoke settled into the corn like a black snow squall, the malodors of flesh, vomit, urine, and feces filled the air. It was Antietam Creek. Thierry Woods. Anzio Beach. Khe Sanh.

"We got to do *something* for Harry Burns," Bishop said.

"The Memorial," I said.

"Right," Reed Murphy said. "The Wall of the Union Dead."

"Union dead," Rex picked it up. "Union dead. Union dead. Union dead."

At Antietam Creek's Bloody Lane, I lay down just below the rim of the dry, sunken road, waiting for the Yankees to rise above me, waiting with musket ball and bayonet. I kept my face on the ground and tasted dirt.

Suddenly, they were upon us. As I fired, a Union bullet grazed my head. Even though I didn't feel it, the shell knocked me down. Before I could move, bodies began falling on me, faster, then faster still. At first I couldn't breathe: their weight was overpowering, and the stench of sweat and vomit, diarrhea and urine, were overwhelming. Then I was soaked with other men's blood dripping through the corpses.

I started to struggle, then stopped. Northern soldiers were walking on the fallen, bayoneting anything that moved. I was too low to be nicked by Yankee pig stickers.

I was saved.

"It was a real shootin' war," I said, steering the Caravan around Washington, looking for a place to park. "But nobody wanted to call it that."

"I took an oath – an *oath* – to protect and defend the Constitution of the United States of America," Reed Murphy said so loudly I thought he would break a window. "So did they. But they didn't keep it. They lied. They murdered."

"They were small and mean and mean-spirited," Bishop said. "Reductive. As if Hemingway had Steamboat Willie tell the story of the Spanish Civil War."

"The rolling black flag campaign rendered Rex insane," I said. "We were children. Look at what they took from us."

I parked four blocks away. As we got out of the car – Reed Murphy with his cane, Bishop watery-eyed and distracted, Rex so disoriented I had to hold on to him – I said it was hard to believe that Harry Burns was gone.

"He was sick," I added, "anemic; his red blood count down to virtually zero."

I was surprised to see Reed Murphy stop and smile. "He was quite the sport back in the day. Climbing broadcast towers. Racing motorcycles. Nearly got himself killed more than once. Dared the devil to take him."

"The devil got his due," I answered.

"Let's tell the truth," Bishop said. "We loved the war. It was the greatest adrenaline rush of all time."

"War lovers," Rex picked up. "War lovers. War lovers. War lovers."

Lincoln and his war of attrition.

In Antietam Creek's Bloody Lane, where I hid beneath dead men, the firing continued unabated for more than three hours, bodies bloody and dying, piling atop each other, more than five thousand over 800 yards.

"I have to agree with you," I told Bishop. "Nothing's made me feel so alive since."

As if on cue, we stopped in reverence before Vietnam Veterans

Memorial black slab, cold and dark, early morning, November 11. There were candles and flowers and tattered, weeping men. Bishop started to cry.

"All these names," he said. "So many names."

"Harry Burns won't be here," I said, "although the war killed him. Chadwick, too."

"But we can find Gutierrez," Reed Murphy said. "And Old Joe Clark."

"Names. Names. Names. Names," Rex said.

"Right, Rex," Reed Murphy said. "Lotta fuckin' names."

"Some of these names saved my life," Bishop said.

Mine, too, I thought.

"Sorry we didn't bring candles or flowers," Bishop said.

"We brought us," Reed Murphy shrugged.

"All the way from Ohio," I said.

"O-HI-O," from Rex. "O-HI-O. O-HI-O. O-HI-O."

Antietam Creek. That cornfield was our first taste of the jungle.

Antietam Creek. We fired in fright, fired in fury, fired until nothing was alive.

Antietam Creek. We fired until all wars, all times, all lines of carnage and blood and murderous rage became one.

Antietam Creek. Once the violence was unleashed, everything died.

As the last shots echoed, and the marching feet receded, and the black smoke dissipated, a stillness like dusk settled on the bloody, tortured earth, the rocky shore, the troubled waters of eternally blood-stained Antietam Creek.

"C'mere," Bishop said. "I found Old Joe Clark. Joseph Haden Clark. Touch it. Feel that buzz? That's his spirit reaching out to us."

"Alberto Ramon Gutierrez," Reed Murphy said, running his hand across the marble surface.

"Time to lay it down," Bishop dabbed his eyes. "Time to be a civilian."

"You're right," I said. "Time to be a civilian. Harry Burns would've liked that."

"Time to call an armistice," Reed Murphy said.

Standing back from the wall, we let the enormity of the loss sink in.

"Walking here at night," I gestured, "I hear foot falls. I hear twigs snapping."

"I got'cher back, cap," Reed Murphy clapped his hand on my shoulder. "Fifty-seven confirmed kills."

"Kills," Rex picked it up. "Kills. Kills. Kills."

It's the law of unintended consequences. It doesn't matter what you intend. You broke it, you bought it.

In the end, in Northern Reconstruction, the Yankees were vicious. They were relentless. We were Americans *they defeated. We didn't like our faces pushed in it. Didn't like the usurpation of our Southern heroes – Washington, Jefferson, Madison. Of our Revolution. Didn't like the destruction of our culture.*

We needed heroes. Hence the beatification of Robert E. Lee, Stonewall Jackson, martyrs to the cause. Hence the creation of the Ku Klux Klan – a wholly foreseeable equal and opposite reaction to the Carpetbaggers and Scalawags.

Because nobody likes being taken to the woodshed. Especially over time.

"Harry deserved better," Bishop said. "Ashes scattered to the winds. To the fields. No burial with honor."

"We were children," I said. "*We* deserved better."

"It's Armistice Day," Bishop said.

"Armistice Day," I said. "November 11, 1918. Eleven in the morning. When the war to end all wars stopped."

"But we can't stop fighting," Reed Murphy said.

"*Won't* stop fighting," Bishop said.

"Church bells rang when that war ended," I said. "Ours ended with a helicopter's whine and a wounded man's whimper."

"And some nameless jungle bathed in blood," Bishop said. "How many? How many were murdered there? Through the wars and hatreds and a thousand blows on human dignity?"

"All the blows cry out," Reed Murphy said. "The betrayals. The beheadings. The blood that soaked into the ground and never left."

"The Armistice brought stillness to the torn lands and bloody fields where war-weary soldiers put down their arms, crawled out of the mud, and sought a way home," I said. "But not in the hollows of their souls where dark dreams never die."

Bishop put his arms around us. "We remember Chadwick and Harry Burns."

"We remember Gutierrez and Old Joe Clark," Reed Murphy said.

"Old Joe Clark," Rex said, a wisp of memory from far away.

"We remember Harry Burns," I said. "The best of us. A true American hero that nobody knew."

"But we did," Reed Murphy said.

"Maybe that's enough," Bishop wept.

"Enough," Rex rocked back and forth. "Enough. Antietam Creek. Enough."

Do you see it? Do you see it now? That's why I want you to leave me out of this. Because I'm not important. The story is. Harry Burns is, all that talent, all that potential, wasted, lost. That's what war does to us, takes from us. Turns us into. Rex and Bishop and Reed Murphy. What they were and what they became. Their troubled thoughts of war and home. For Rex Antietam Creek. Thoughts skittering in the wind.

Men – a world – desperately needing an armistice. An Armistice Day.

BRIDEY

▼

BLOCK ISLAND, RHODE ISLAND

In my line of work there's things you can prove and things you can't. And if you can't live with the difference you find another way to make a living.

Here's one I learned to live with. I can't prove a lot of it. But it's all true.

It was supposed to be an easy one. Mail it in and walk away.

Because I know Art Beckham – known him 20 years. They don't come any better. Honest. Thorough. Decent. And there was nothing special about this case. No nicks, no anomalies. As open-and-shut as you get. Space heater gone south, two monoxide deaths. Happens all the time. Still, paperwork is paperwork, and deaths like this, in townships like New Shoreham, need state oversight. So there I was, on the chilly morning ferry to Block Island, to confirm Art's finding of accidental death.

Like everyone who lives in Newport, I spend the occasional day or two on Block Island – nice place to get away. One of the attractions is that the weather is as changeable as the water itself. The Sound and sunshine, sometimes balmy breezes. But fog, too, so thick you can't see the car's hood through the windshield. Storms that flood houses, bring down trees. Winter snow squalls that race parallel to the ground, blind everything, ground airplanes. Gale-force winds that stab your face like a fork. Sleet that covers the Mohegan Bluffs and Corn Neck Road and the Great Salt Pond – everything on the unprotected rock outcropping – and lasts for days.

One January, when the mercury never topped freezing, gas lines quit, diesel generators died, and pipes burst everywhere. By the time everything thawed, the home-repair guys made out like bandits.

As the ferry thrummed within sight of the Island, and the cold bit at my legs, I thought about John Russell, instructor at the Academy. Tall, tweed jackets, half-glasses perched on the end of his nose. Spoke in a conspiratorial half-whisper, oddly accenting a word's final syllables. Triple threat: taught evidence, forensics, criminology.

I smiled. Straight up. Tough grader. His crime scenes – *man!*

I learned a lot from him. A lot. What I learned most was, sure, anyone can present the obvious story. Everyone *loves* the obvious story. The captain loves the obvious story. The state's attorney loves the obvious story. The governor loves the obvious story. *You* love the obvious story. Because you close cases with the obvious story. The SA gets convictions with the obvious story. The governor gets re-elected with the obvious story. Once in a while, you even get promoted with the obvious story.

"Great!" Russell clapped his hands. "Now prove you're worth something and get the not-obvious story. The hidden story. The hidden story is the one you can't prove. The hidden story is the one you tell everybody about – or not. Because sometimes it's so hidden, and so hot, you can't discuss it. But the hidden story is vital. The hidden story keeps you sharp. Keeps you from missing some key point or detail – which sometimes gets you the real conviction. Or keeps you from getting killed."

I opened my notebook, felt the ferry jounce over a wave made by a fast-moving pleasure boat. Harold "Hap" Leahy, white, 38, decorated Iraqi war veteran, tank commander, sand devil, burly, florid man, pronounced limp from firefight shrapnel. Always dressed in army surplus, his own. On the Island for two or three years, no one certain. Like a lot of marginal people, Leahy more or less showed up one day, hung around. People found it hard to remember when he *wasn't* there. No police record. Jitney driver of his own antique Checker: cab rides, tours, ferry pick-ups, airport runs, shopping for shut-ins. Lived on the Weber estate, whatever that was.

Susan Reyes, white, maybe 50, maybe more. Panhandler, homeless before shacking up with Leahy. Spent time at a couple of Newport shelters before working as an off-the-books stock clerk. Hard not to see her as another piece of flotsam washed up on Block Island for tourist season.

Some come to beg, others to waitress, clean rooms, *au pair*. Like everybody else on the Island, make a buck off the tourists. By all accounts, Reyes was pleasant, quiet, missing most of her teeth, slight speech impediment – stroke victim, maybe, the way the left side of her face was a bit slack. Could've been a fall or a beating. She never said. "We don't give the panhandlers physicals," Beckham snorted over the phone. "No one complained about her, so we let her be. Lotta people down on their luck these days. Lotta loose change on the Island. You know that, Augie."

"I do indeed," I told Beckham.

My great-aunt Bridey was baptized Bridget Halloran, a 19th-century Irish farm girl. The seventh of eleven children, she grew up in a shack, heated by peat fire, the lone room stinking of piss, pig shit, and puke. Sleeping three to a lumpy, cold, frequently wet straw ticking, her life was dirt, squalor, and hunger. By the time she was 16, in the first flush of womanhood, Bridey hated the farm, hating being a potato farmer's illiterate daughter.

The next step up was gutting fish in the market.

Because there were too many for her family or her parish to support, she was given a steerage ticket to America – it was cheaper to put her on a boat than find a place for her in the county workhouse. Before she could think, Bridey and her sack of patched clothes were on their way to Cork, a sprawling, dirty city full of oily, fishy smells, scalded iron, blacksmiths' fires. Casting in with Deidre, a year or two older, freckles, tangled red hair, from a rich Englishman's estate, Bridey found her way to the docks.

There to encounter great crowds. Flimsy paper ticket in hand, shoved into the bowels of a great iron ship, she found the stench of sweat and shit overwhelming.

There were nearly 1,000 people in the bottom of that ship, hundreds in one compartment alone, stacked like corn in a crib, little light, less comfort. Feverish, vomiting, in calmer moments she ate a dreadful soup, doled out of a washtub-sized kettle, accompanied by bread as hard and dry as a wooden plank.

Exhausted, Bridey heard stories about Tessie Fair, an Irish miner's daughter who married a millionaire. That's America for you, *someone said;* Bridey prayed it was so.

Still, Bridey spent most of her week crossing the Atlantic perilously sick,

Deidre bathing her brow, bringing her broth, sharing the bread she'd cribbed from the estate kitchen and tucked into her bag.

Bridey told Deidre about her family. When she asked in return, Deidre darkened. Until she was 14 she thought her uncle was her father. Then her mother's story kept changing. Landlords, rich folk, priests, Deidre had no idea. What she did know was that as a bastard girl out of County Kilkenny, it was easier for her to leave then to try to marry decently, with the blessings of the church, and create a happy life.

By the time I got off the ferry the morning fog was burning off in gray, windy sheets, smoke from shipboard gun volleys.

New Shoreham PD was a clean, one-story concrete-block building on a low rise above Water Street. The building spelled Art Beckham: clean white walls, paperwork neatly stacked, wood- and metalwork recently shined. Big and black and genial, Beckham's ministry was largely sweeping up drunks, stopping bar fights, and preventing domestic escalations. There was the occasional robbery, sure, and burglary, but by and large Block Island was easy duty – especially given home security systems.

"Mild and gentle," I stuck out my hand, "like the Island."

You'd think that a man Beckham's size would have more difficulty getting out of his chair, but 30 years later Art still had a lot of the scholastic athlete in him.

"You know the drill, Augie," he smiled and shook. "Tourists come here for a good time. Locals come here either to cater to them or to retire and be left alone."

Art waved a white paper cup at me and I nodded.

I knew the story. He would've played more ball, but blew out a knee in high school. He was good at Providence, arguably the best down lineman the school had ever seen. But he wasn't a big-enough-deal prospect to merit high-fallutin' surgery. So, sure, he can walk. Can even run on a good day. But not well enough for the gridiron. So he went into law enforcement and made a nice life.

"I haven't seen an accidental death like this one – faulty space heater – in 15 years," he rifled a sheaf of papers.

I shrugged. "Routine that someone from state reviews the work of your hands, sprinkles holy water, and blesses the results."

"I'm a lapsed AME Zion, Augie," he laughed. "All that papist mumbo jumbo don't cut much around here. You being a simple statie is enough for me."

"You sent it over, Art," I said, "and I read the file. Anything worth adding?"

"It's all there," he said. "Cold spring – is there any other kind on the Island? Space heater. Unvented. Pilot light out." Beckham shrugged. "Checks out. Happens more often than we'd like to admit. Hundreds of people die in this country every year from space heater accidents. This was two more."

"Tell me a little about them," I prompted.

"Not much to add to the case file. Leahy'd been here a while. Iraq seems to have messed him up a little. Well, that war messed most everybody up. Maybe all wars do. Anyway, he was sober and stable enough."

Beckham turned a hand.

"Earlier this year he adopted a panhandler named Susan Reyes. Don't know much about her. Clean, polite, presentable."

"You didn't roust her?" I asked.

"On what charge, Augie? Vagrancy? Well, sure. But I prefer live-and-let-live here on the Island. Innocent until you've really broken something. Besides, we still have a little freedom left in this country. So it's just fine for a clean, decently appointed, middle-aged woman to ask perfect strangers for gifts. Why not? She stood there, holding up a hand-lettered cardboard PLEASE HELP sign. Neither aggressive nor intrusive, an exercise of free speech. So said the town council in a 3-2 vote."

"Didn't anyone complain?"

"Of course they did. This is Block Island, remember? I told them it wouldn't hurt them to extend themselves a little to the less fortunate – and be grateful for the blessings they have. Good lessons for their kids, too."

"Anybody buy that?"

"Most everybody. The others, well, they're the kind who complain when the weather's too perfect. I don't let them bother me. To your point, Augie, Susan Reyes was personable, respectful, grateful. Everything that a good panhandler ought to be." Beckham paused. "Some of them fluctuate back and forth. Clean rooms. Waitress. Cut lawns. We try to make sure they're relatively safe and sanitary."

"Where'd she stay before she moved in with Leahy?"

"Where do any of them stay? Necessity is a great teacher. And they're very resourceful. We have a lot of nooks and crannies. They find 'em. Anyway, Reyes was quiet. Found a shed, or something, to stay in. Before I got any complaints she hooked up with Leahy. Two damaged people found each other. It's a beautiful story."

"Right," I muttered. "Weber estate, you said. I need to see the place."

"Go north. You can't miss it. Brick-and-iron wall. R.A. Weber, USN, ret."

When I raised an eyebrow, Beckham just smiled.

"Care to join me?" I asked.

"Doesn't need two of us. I'll let them know you're coming."

In Boston, Bridey and Deidre burst into the blinding sunlight. Without so much as a how-de-do, the two were sized up by a woman – broad-shouldered, rough-handed, hair cut short like a man's – who inquired if they wanted work.

Before Bridey could say anything, Deidre asked what kind.

"Service," the woman said, "working in a great house. Room and board and clean clothes. Six dollars a week."

Although Deidre said she's had enough of fancy folk and great houses, it sounded good to Bridey, disoriented by the crush of people, the noise, and the sheer size of the dock and Boston harbor. Inside and clean sounded like heaven.

Bridey had no idea what dollars were, or what six of them meant, but that sounded good, too.

"It's a proper posting for a couple of illiterate colleens like you," the woman added, using a stick to poke at their hair and lift their lips to look at their teeth.

"Ye be treating us like plow horses," Deidre objected, but Bridey said nothing.

"Can't have damaged goods for the Vanderbilts."

While Bridey had no idea what that meant, Deidre demurred.

"You don't want to end up on the streets," the woman prodded.

While Deidre was deeply offended, Bridey knew what that was like from market days in town, and said immediately, "if you please, ma'am, thank you, ma'am, yes."

"Name, child," the woman demanded.

"Bridget Halloran," Bridey said, curtseying like the schoolgirl she never was, "but everyone calls me Bridey."

"Well, Everyone-Calls-Me Bridey, the Newport train leaves in 15 minutes. See that you're there."

"Yes, ma'am," Bridey said, curtseying again. "Thank you, ma'am."

"Ye may be wiping the arses of the rich," Deidre said, "but ye be living in a beautiful house by the sea, and ye won't starve to death."

Tearfully kissing Deidre goodbye, Bridey went into the station, a hot building with high windows and immense brickwork, then down the stairs to the Newport train.

Stuffed into a seat, nearly suffocated by an immense woman who slid in beside her, Bridey suffered the jouncing, crowded car that gave her a blinding headache.

Finally, the journey was over. The mannish woman, who announced herself as Mrs. Poole – Bridey was convinced that, as in Ireland among the higher classes, the Mrs. was merely an honorific – ushered her and a half-dozen other Irish girls onto the platform and into a waiting carriage.

When Bridey started to ask about when they might eat, Mrs. Poole put her finger to her broad lips. "Hush, girl," she said. "You'll soon be home."

Shortly, the carriage swept up a wide, curving drive, then swung around to the back of a great house – indeed, Bridey had never seen anything so grand or so big.

Bigger, even, than St. Brendan's back home, and that was the biggest thing she'd ever seen. This was a grand, immense building, a palace, by the look of it.

"Does the Queen live here?" she asked one of the other girls, who giggled and said America had no queen.

The house, an oddity on Block Island, was not standard-issue gray clapboard but instead a rambling sandstone neo-colonial. Through the black iron gate, down a gravel drive, past a wide expanse of lawn. View of the water. Garage, in matching style and stone, in the distant back. I presumed the departed were discovered there.

Weber himself opened the door. A tall, trim man, he still wore a clipped military mustache and enjoyed a thatch of light brown hair. Nobody that age – I put him above 50, easily – is in that shape without many miles on the stationary bicycle.

"Detective Sergeant Joseph Daugustino," he smiled, extending a hand.

"Actually, sir, D'Augustino, if you don't mind. But Augie works just fine."

Well, Detective D'Augustino," he continued the smile, "what can I do for you?"

His hand had a slight tremor.

"Captain Weber, thank you for taking the time."

"That's what I have most of these days. Time." He paused. "You caught that, detective. Parkinson's. Early onset cost me a promotion to admiral." Weber motioned me to follow him through a large, wood-paneled living room with overstuffed chairs and hunting prints to a smaller room on the side of the house outfitted in nautical themes – ship's windlass, barometer, antique maps of the Seven Seas, captain's chairs.

"That's not false or sour anything, detective," he continued. "I was in line. Commanded the *Nellis*, a 6,000-man aircraft carrier. Stepping stone to admiral. I had the time in, the ratings. Then this," he waved a hand, "drydocked me.

"Was a time, when I was 25 and a hotshot lieutenant j.g., I could piss up a rope. Now I'm lucky if I can hit the bowl." He smiled. "Parkinson's more or less under control with medication, although only a stopgap. Degenerative condition. Only a matter of time. As we say in the military, the situation."

I listened politely.

"You need perfect health to command a ship, any ship, especially one as big and complex as an aircraft carrier."

Weber moved over to a cocktail cart.

"Married well – Marte's a member of the Danish royal family. Where she is now, celebrating spring. Invested better. Enjoy the company of two wayward daughters – four marriages, so far, no progeny.

"They keep moving the time on me," he smiled. "Eight bells keeps getting a little earlier every day. Can I offer you something, detective?"

"I never drink on duty, sir," I said. "Personal as well as procedural rule."

"Wise," he nodded. "And you can belay that *sir* business, detective. I'm not your commanding officer. Not anybody's CO these days. Haven't been for a long time."

"I understand, captain."

"Not captain, either, not any longer."

"You earned that rank serving our country. I believe in honoring your service."

"Thank you, detective. Is that the proper title for you, who serve as well?"

I nodded.

"Good. Having said that, I hope you don't mind if I –"

"Not at all, captain. After all, the sun is over the yardarm *somewhere*."

"I like the cut of your jib, detective," he winked at me and hoisted a cut-glass bottle. "Man after my own heart. Gin. Sailor's grog. And I have the vermouth nearby, ready to wave across the glass if need be.

"Please have a seat," he gestured.

Weber started to pour, but the tremors in his hands became too intense. Putting down the bottle and matching tumbler, he breathed a bit, then picked them back up, poured, silently saluted me, and drank.

"Strictly a landlubber now. Worst of all, no sailing. I did sail racing sloops for a bit, but like my commission had to give that up. You race by touch. Not by sight. *Never* by sight. Can't do that anymore."

"Why not crew?" I asked. "Or simply go along for the ride?"

"Never sailed, have you?"

I told him I hadn't.

"Not the same. To feel the boat – to *control* it – is exhilarating beyond words. To be in the boat and have someone else do it," he shook his head. "Oh, I can still sail well enough to get to Newport and back. Montauk on calm days. But that's not racing. That doesn't get the heart going.

"Anyway, detective, you hardly came here to talk about me."

"Well," I took out my notebook, "Three questions. What can you tell me about Harold Leahy and Susan Reyes? Why were they living in your carriage house? Was there anything that would lead you to think this wasn't the accident it appears to be?"

Seeming surprised, Weber asked if Beckham didn't cover all this ground.

"Yes, he did," I allowed. "And he's a good man. A *very* good man. Knows his job. If he says this is an accidental death, I'm sure it's an accidental death. But procedure demands that someone from the state come out for a look. Make sure the I's are dotted and T's are crossed. Matter of routine."

"You've never been in the armed forces, have you, detective?"

"No," I answered. "Is it that obvious?"

"No, just a guess. From the outside it seems all rules and discipline, barked orders, by the book."

I shrugged.

"But it's very different on the inside, especially from the standpoint of command. On the *Nellis*, I never saw my crew as 6,000 sailors. I saw them as 6,000 individuals, each with particular talents, wants, and desires. Histories. Strengths and weaknesses. A great part of my job was making sure that they would all function in concert, strength, and harmony. To do that, they needed to be encouraged and inspired, to perform difficult, dangerous, demanding jobs upon which lives depended. All done in close quarters: men and women. Different races and classes. A great deal of sweat and not a few collisions. A successful leader has to handle it all. While no captain can know all 6,000 sailors under his command, I had to size up as many as I could as quickly as I could. I couldn't afford to be wrong. Not clipping along in the Atlantic headed for Iran."

Weber paused to drink.

"The way I met Hap Leahy – he preferred Hap to Harold or even sergeant – was prosaic enough. I took the ferry back from Newport – had some appointments in town – and found my car battery dead. Needed a ride home. Leahy drove a cab, black Checker, *Baghdad Betty* in cursive on the left front fender. He was wearing military garb: beret, uniform shirt, sergeant's stripes, service ribbons, and so forth. When I got in I asked if he'd mind telling me his story, that I was retired military, too. He said he was from Eastern Massachusetts, coastal folk, Gloucester, Lynn, somewhere like that. Operation Iraqi Freedom. Purple Heart. Couple of others. Commanded a tank. After Iraq had trouble. Mind wandered. Down on his luck. Drifted down here. Jitney driver.

"'Your quarters, sergeant?' I asked.

"'Catch-as-catch-can,' he said. 'Sometimes I just lay down inside ol' Betty here.'"

Weber paused to look out at the Sound, spotty blue in the early afternoon sun.

"I began to object.

"'No big deal. Been in worse places. Winter I get indoors, one way or 'nother.'

"No military man can abandon troops in the field. On the spot I offered him the use of the carriage house – a made-over garage for the estate caretaker. We outsourced that job years ago. Rooms were lying fallow. Told Leahy he could live there rent- and utility-free. Least I could do for a decorated veteran. Only requirement was I would inspect his quarters every Sunday morning before church."

"Which one?"

"Is that germane, detective?"

"Simply curious."

"St. Ann's by-the-Sea. Episcopal. Good healthy walk. Pretty little place."

"Leahy didn't mind?"

"Not at all. Seemed to welcome it."

"Did you go?"

"Every week. Amusing," Weber smiled. "Leahy stood at attention when I entered his quarters, snapped me a proper salute."

"And?"

"Everything shipshape. Every week."

"How long?"

"Two years. Bit more."

"And the woman? Susan Reyes?"

"Just showed up one day. She was homeless, begging by the docks and hotels. Leahy was a decent sort. Felt sorry for her. Brought her home. They kept separate bedrooms. His relationship to her seemed paternalistic, perhaps brotherly. He was caring for her, I think. Nothing more. You see this aboard ship. Of course, the crew couldn't have pets. But sailors adopted families in various ports, cared for stray animals on shore leave. Like all of us, they have a desperate need for connection. To feel good about themselves doing good for others. Leahy was no different.

"I remember when he introduced me. 'This is Susan,' he said. She nodded. That was all. Nothing more than that. No indication of any kind of intimacy." Weber sighed. "Sadly, many of the Navy's men and women come from broken homes or difficult domestic relationships. They look for the military to heal them, to provide them the structure that they don't have. Many of them perform extraordinary acts of kindness. Of loyalty, often to those who need it most. Susan Reyes was one of those. Leahy's adoption of her was just that: an extraordinary act of kindness.

"I remember one story about her. One afternoon, I asked Leahy to drive him me from the ferry, which he did, then asked if I minded if he brought along Susan, who'd been out in the sun all day and was feeling a bit peaked. I didn't mind at all.

"'Well, little lady,' I said, 'how was your day today?'

"Whereupon Susan grinned in her toothless way, said how happy she was that this beautiful community had adopted her, then talked about an older man, white hair, white beard, who always had time to visit with her, and who always put some folding green in her cup. 'Today,' she smiled, 'it was a double sawbuck. Mr. Andrew Jackson himself! We got us some good eatin' tonight!'"

Weber smiled at the memory. "She seemed so proud of herself. So happy. It was her daily victory. Leahy seemed happy, too, happy for her.

"Then she said, 'People don't know what desperate is. What it is to be abandoned by your family, by everyone you loved and who you thought loved you.' She gestured at the crowd. 'Five people a day believe in me. Five people save my life.'"

"Thank you," I said. "This helps. Makes them more than merely cadavers."

"Thank you for taking the time, detective. Leahy was proud of his service. I told him I admired him – in part because sergeants and CPOs get things done. Officers generally gum up the works –"

He smiled, and I did, too.

"– but non-coms, they're the ones you count on."

I asked how Leahy responded.

"Just grunted. Leahy was not a garrulous man. One day, as he drove me home from the ferry, I prompted him to tell me about his time in Iraq.

"'Well, cap'n' – that's how he pronounced it. 'Cap'n. The thing I keep thinking about, the thing that I can't get out of my head, are the times we took fire. Took plenty of fire, us sand devils. Funny, cap'n, it was frightening but, looking back on it, it wasn't dangerous. There was a lot of 'em, a *lot* of 'em. Felt like Saddam drafted his whole country. And they kept comin'. But they couldn't fight. None of 'em. No strategy. No tactics. They wasn't smart. And they wasn't trained. So we cut 'em to pieces.'

"Then he paused.

"'But what killed us, cap'n, what really laid us out, was them IEDs. Miserable bastards. They was everywhere. Scared the shit out of us – pardon my language, cap'n. Never knew what when where. One time, oh, hell.'

"'Take it easy, sergeant,' I said. 'You don't have to say any more.'

"'That's all right, cap'n. Anyway, one time, we were riding herd on some armored personnel carriers, and the one right behind *Baghdad Betty* hit one. Blew half the side off. Tough scene, cap'n. We scrambled out to help – there was nobody, nothing around – and started pulling guys away from the truck. I had a man bleed out in my arms. Nothing I could do. Nothing anyone could do. Hard to get over that, cap'n.'

"He was shaken, detective, shaken to his core. I told him that I could never stand in his stead, that I saluted his service, and he thanked me."

"You identified the bodies."

"Yes," Weber said. "I had seen them Sunday – morning inspection and all."

I nodded.

"Everything seemed fine. *Was* fine. Shipshape, detective. Leahy and Reyes were clean, sober, presentable. I didn't think twice about it.

"It rained Monday – rained hard – and Leahy didn't take the car out. Well, why should he? Precious little money to be made on a dismal, rainy Monday. Not a lot of ferry trade. No tourists. Not a market day. Perfect time to stay below decks.

"Tuesday, however, was gorgeous – beautiful blue sky, white fleecy clouds, nice breeze. The kind of day that people come to Block Island to relish. Still, no movement, not from him, not from her. OK, I thought, this is who they are. Take another day off. Why not? Sleep in. We all need money, some of us more than others, but given their limited desires perhaps they had enough for the short haul. Stay at home. Mend the nets. I thought it odd, wasteful, but it was their choice, not mine.

"When Wednesday dawned the clone of Tuesday, and Leahy's Checker still hadn't moved, I thought I had better take a look. After all, given their work ethic – hustle ethic, if you prefer, detective – I couldn't imagine that they'd abandon both of these days." He shrugged. "Make hay when the sun shines."

"Right," I nodded, writing it all down.

"I knocked, got no answer, used my key. While the odor of gas had largely dissipated, there was still a trace of it. I left the door open and opened all the windows. There were Leahy and Reyes, both in their beds as if in a child's dollhouse, neatly tucked in, still seeming to be asleep." Weber shook his head. "It was hard to see, detective. He was in the bedroom, she in the spare bedroom – more of a storage closet. He'd made up a bunk for her. Small, but serviceable. Anyone in the navy has slept in smaller spaces. They were as chaste as pilgrims. Faulty space heater."

"No trouble?" I asked.

"Nothing that I ever saw. Did Leahy suffer from PTSD? I don't know. Some men need the discipline, the order, of the military. Or prison, sorry to say. Some men are ill-equipped for freedom. Was he? I don't know. But I would have thought – *did* think, in fact – that he always conducted himself in a controlled and respectful way, and the fact that he took responsibility for that woman added immeasurably to his life."

"Might I have a look?"

"Certainly, detective."

Confused, dazed, Bridey was hustled onto the back stairs, then whisked into a tub – a glorious, wonderous, far-too-quick bath – then into a black uniform with a white apron. The head housekeeper, a Miss Duff – steel-rimmed eyeglasses, fistful of keys at her belt – showed Bridey to her room, a Spartan affair with a bedstead, nightstand, and wash basin, then told her it would be servants' supper in a half-hour. Bridey, immediately grateful, realized she hadn't eaten all day.

"There are four unbreakable rules of service," Miss Duff told the new girls after supper, "aside from all those found in the Bible."

"First, the good servant is invisible. You never speak, or even look up, unless invited to or spoken to first.

"Second, the good servant anticipates. You must know what your mistress wants – before she wants it.

"Third, the good servant is clean. Mrs. Vanderbilt, and all the other grand

ladies, expect no foul odors, dirty clothes, and certainly no lice. Any one is grounds for immediate dismissal.

"Fourth, the good servant is chaste. No profligacy, no flirting, no co-mingling will be tolerated. The slightest hint of promiscuity will be grounds for immediate dismissal. And any dismissal comes without references.

"Finally," Miss Duff added, "your employment at The Breakers is for the summer only. Some of you may be asked to attend to the family upon their return to New York, or none of you. In either event, there are no guarantees."

Miss Duff did not bother – never bothered – to ask if they understood her. She simply presumed that they did. Anyone who didn't would be given a second chance – they were charitable people, after all – then summarily dismissed. There was only so much they could do with sub-humans, and The Breakers was not a settlement house.

As we walked down the gravel driveway to the carriage house, I felt as if I were on an English country estate.

"I'll vouch for him, detective," Weber said. "Having thought about it since his passing, he was clearly chief petty officer material. Perhaps even an adjutant."

Weber opened the door, ushered me in.

"Old carriage house," he gestured. "Unfortunately, neither well heated nor well ventilated. I should have been more careful in its outfitting. Propane heater. Unvented. No detector. I never paid much attention to it. People never plan to have an accident."

I nodded and looked around. Neat, as promised. Early 1960s furniture. Small desk, small television. A few books of military history. Walls with framed paperwork and medals. Presidential Unit Citation. Honorable Discharge. Purple Heart. Distinguished Service Cross. Bronze Star. All in the name of Sergeant Harold Leahy.

Photos, too. Somebody younger and thinner, blue jeans, work shirt, half-bending away from the camera. Tank crew, someone looking very much like Leahy, helmet, sunglasses. Trademark splotchy skin.

Nothing of Susan Reyes. Not surprising. Nothing much survives homelessness.

The bedrooms revealed nothing. What wasn't military was standard JC Penney ready wear. Reyes had a few sleeveless T-shirts. Plaid shirts.

Blue jeans. Socks. Underpants. No brassieres. I'd seen the body: she didn't need any.

"Of course, we haven't moved anything," Weber said. "Won't until we get the all-clear, from you or Beckham."

"Right," I said. "Regulations require that we call this a dormant crime scene until the case is cleared. Shouldn't be very long. So if you would, please leave the premises untouched until Captain Reynolds signs off on it."

"Not a problem. Not as if we need the room. Take all the time you need."

"Thank you, captain," I said. "Thank you for understanding."

"If anyone understands going by the book," Weber smiled, "it's a military man."

As Bridey later discovered, The Breakers was hardly alone. In 1895, when she arrived in America, ten percent of Newport, 2,000 of 20,000, were servants. Over half of them emigrated from Europe, and in any given summer cottage, as these mansions were euphemistically called, half the staff was Irish.

Bridey had never seen anything like The Breakers, the 70 rooms, the gold-and-marble fittings, the halls and stairs and passageways like a rabbit's warren.

It was a mystery to Bridey where all this money came from. It all seemed like a dream – so much so that every morning she was surprised at where she was. Had she awakened on her straw ticking back in County Cork, she would not have been surprised, given her sudden new life at The Breakers.

Working under a woman named Adele Stohlmeyer, Bridey was assigned to Mrs. Alice Vanderbilt, Mistress of The Breakers. Amazed, Bridey marveled at the four closets that housed Mrs. Vanderbilt's seven clothing changes a day, more than 100 dresses in all, entirely different outfits for her varying roles: Morning gown. Riding habit. Luncheon dress. Afternoon promenade. Afternoon tea. Dinner dress. Ball gown.

Quickly learning how to navigate the back passages, Bridey contented herself with laundry and pressing while dreaming of those moments when, as in an Arabian Nights fantasy, she could attend the balls, hearing the music, watching her lady and the other women dance with impossible beauty and grace. Sometimes, Bridey would swell to the sight of the moonlight off the sea, imbibe the salt air, revel in the time, the swells in their clothes, the riches of the walls and floors and ceilings. The music alone seemed to come from Heaven. Poor peasant girl, she had no words for it.

Throughout, the work never stopped, except Sunday for church, which Bridey never missed, praying that the Holy Mother would smile upon her.

Every other day, up at six, at work by seven, Bridey retired only after her mistress did, often not until after a midnight swim.

Yet Bridey, brought up to think of life as work, was glad of it. Clean, happy, polite, she was glad that people were not as crude as they were at the market back home. That they did not shout and curse. That they had manners, and morals, not like the grabby-handed farm boys she knew.

Certainly, she was not a Vanderbilt, nor ever would be, but in some distant way Bridey felt a part of the family, the clean clothes, roof over her head, good meals – thick, rich bread, meat every day, fruits and vegetables she had never before seen.

I didn't like it, and I told that to Reynolds.

Captain Nate Reynolds – more familiarly cap – was genial enough. White hair, white uniform shirt. A big man who never seemed to sweat, no matter how hot it got, and could tell you to the day, hour, and minute how long it would be until he retired.

Not that he preferred fishing to police work.

Regulation government-issue gray office, regulation gunmetal gray desk. Never wanted anything fancier. Photos, citations, on the wall – a career well spent.

"So?" he asked. "What do you have for me?" His standard opening gambit.

Told him. Faulty space heater. Exactly what Art Beckham found. As clean and clear as you get. "Neat," I said. "Too neat."

"Right," he drummed his fingers. "And these folks? Leahy and Reyes?"

"Nobody knows about him, other than Iraq. She was homeless. Two clicks away from John and Jane Doe."

"This kind of thing does not make me happy," Reynolds made a face.

"I know, cap."

"Two cyphers. Interred at public expense. That may come back to haunt me."

"Right."

"They had to leave some kind of trail. Don't take a lot of time on this, but take another look, will you, Augie?"

I nodded.

"Take those famous instincts of yours and see what you can find. Maybe some of Leahy's fellow cabbies know something. Maybe Susan Reyes bunked with someone before Leahy. Maybe they're more than what washes up in beach towns."

"On it, cap."

"Excellent, Augie. Excellent."

There were days when it was all a breathless blur, all Bridey could do to keep up. Doing the laundry, bringing fresh linens, servicing Mrs. Vanderbilt's two daily baths, she thought how hard it was, how keeping everything straight made her head hurt, how good it would be to quit.

Then she thought of how warm it was to live inside, how well she ate.

How nothing smelled like pigs or peat.

How she never had to face that endless gnawing devil, hunger.

That hunger was Satan himself.

The cabstand was simply a corner of the parking lot where the men – and they were all men – lined up near the ferry. In good weather they stood outside smoking and drinking coffee. In bad weather, they huddled in a building not much more than a shed with a few broken chairs and a telephone. Whoever picked it up answered 851, which everyone on the Island knew was the code for cabs. It seemed to be 50-50, asking for drivers by name or simply asking for a cab. Not advertised, not regulated, they were part of the Island's underground economy like the waitresses and cleaning crews.

Gypsies, jitneys, they kept prices down – and kept the Island moving.

There were a half-dozen of them when I went, all white, 25-55, give or take. Roustabouts and regulars. Summer help and lifers. Two of them writing the Great American Novel. Usual chatter about the weather (good), politics (bad), Red Sox (ugly).

I waded into the crowd, raised both hands in a peaceful gesture, took out my badge, and before anyone could move, said, "this is strictly routine, guys. Hap Leahy. State requires someone like me to take a looksee after someone dies. Nothing more than that. So I'd like to ask you a few questions."

Shrugs all around. *Sure. Why not? Whatever you say, detective.*

"Thanks," I said. "Tell me about him."

They all looked at each other.

"For next of kin, if any."

"Suspect something, detective?" This from a Viking, short and round and red.

"Not at all. As I said, just routine. Tell me about Hap Leahy."

A wary man with a Fu Manchu mustache shrugged. "Good-enough guy. Not always so crisp, you know. PTSD. Talked about IEDs. Somebody named Jones."

"James," a longhair corrected him.

"Right. James. Somebody important to him. Never got the gist of the story."

Heads shaking all around.

"Must have been hell."

"I'll bet," I offered.

"Right," he said, and others nodded. "Sometimes he'd be saying something – could be anything. Could be how the Red Sox were doing –"

"Or weren't doing," a heavy, unshaven man said, and they all laughed.

"Right," Fu Manchu said. "In the middle he'd stop, as if the past kicked back in."

"Nothing more than that," the Viking said. "Nothing to make us think Hap was ill."

General agreement.

"He ever talk about home? Family? Anything other than Iraq?"

A lot of muttered *no's*.

"Susan Reyes," I asked.

"Was that her name?" the heavy man said.

I nodded.

"We really didn't know her," the longhair said. "We don't deal with panhandlers."

"They work their side of the street," Fu Manchu said, "we work ours."

The wind had picked up, a sure sign of a squall out on the Sound.

"Anything else?" I asked.

They shook their heads.

I thanked them.

For all that, for all her new previously unimaginable life, Bridey longed for home. Missed the village, the hills, the sea. Well, there was a comfort – from the rooftop walkway she could see ships and salt water. Close her eyes and think of home.

Bridey was hardly the only one. All the girls – under housemaids, scullery maids, undercooks – all seemed to be Irish, all seemed to jabber at once about the farms, the shanties, the unremitting stench of farming and fishmongering. About the boys – the brothers, cousins, beggars on the street – with their fidgety hands, their restless fingers.

As they spoke, she thought, no, she didn't love home, with its filth, nor did she love her family, including her sisters. But she did miss the village, and the familiars.

"I left a boy there," her roommate, a cook named Edna, said, "a nice one, a cute one," she smiled. "I think about him some times."

"And you?" a scullery maid named Agnes prodded Bridey. "Did you break some poor Paddy's heart when you got on that ship?"

Bridey smiled and shook her head. "I was too busy working," she said, "sewing and cooking and cleaning. Watching after the young 'uns. Drawing water and tending the fire." She paused. "Now I'm here. Oh, I'm sure I'll meet someone, sooner or later. Right now, I'm trying to fit in." She shook her head again. "Right now, I'm trying to eat."

And finding out that not only was invisibility required, but also perfection. One day, Bridey laid out a pair of Mrs. Vanderbilt's shoes, one with a slight smudge on it. Upon inspection, Miss Stohlmeyer rose in fury like a sudden and savage storm.

"Impossibly stupid Irish colleen," she howled. "Get out of my sight!"

Bridey wept all the way to her room.

"I saw one of the swells today," she told Edna, undressing for the night. "Don't know which one. They all look alike, you know. Boater. Mustache."

"Don't you worry about who's here," Edna warned. "Belmont or Astor or Whitney. You work for Miss Stohlmeyer who works for Miss Duff who works

for Mrs. Vanderbilt. That's all you need to know. You're an under housemaid, a laundress, and you had better know your place. And not know anything else."

I checked DMV. DOD. DOJ. Prints. Dental. DNA. Called in a few favors and used the fancy photo-matching software at Providence.

Whoever Harold "Hap" Leahy was, he didn't exist.

Not a soldier. *Never* a soldier.

The limp from shrapnel? Money on the table, he got drunk, fell down a flight of stairs, ankle never set right, concocted a story.

Why lie? Why disappear?

What was he so desperate to leave behind?

Why construct this fictional Harold Leahy, decorated combat veteran?

And why create all that fake documentation on his walls?

For Weber?

For himself?

Susan Reyes was a different matter. Took a little detective work for her.

With that dead white skin and natural blonde hair she was a tad pale to be Latina, but no matter. There were a lot of other questions here. Missing teeth – something took those uppers. Maybe pyorrhea. Slight limp, slight weakness?

First, I returned to her last known whereabouts: Rhode Island homeless shelters, where the portrait emerged of a woman who kept to herself. Never much referenced anything. Well, that's the m.o.: most have deep scars or deep shame, and don't want to say who they are or how they got there. Creatures who scurry away from the light. Susan Reyes was one of them. Seemed like something had wiped away her past. Never talked about a spouse, children, parents. Simply arrived. Then left.

I visited two shelters administered by harried, well-meaning men and women permanently rumpled and exhausted. Church basement. Older apartment building. Good Shepherd. Mother of Mercy.

"I barely remember her," Good Shepherd's Rich Taliaferro glanced at her photo. A rank man in work clothes, he took a second look. "We get so many in here."

"Accidental death," I said. "We're trying to piece enough together to notify any family. Assuming there is any family."

"If I'm remembering her correctly, she was a quiet, relatively clean woman among the tattooed outcasts. With limited resources, only so many hours in a day, and the constant turnover, we wind up paying more attention to the squeaky wheels, the needy ones, con men, and predators. The quiet ones generally fly under the radar, by design or not. Susan Reyes was one of those."

Mother of Mercy was run by a caffeine-addicted nun named Sister Juliana.

"Do you get visions, too?" I asked.

"Depends on how much Wild Turkey is in the glass," she answered.

"A nun after my own heart," I smiled.

"Detective," she asked, "what can I do for you?"

She brightened when I showed her Reyes' photo.

"Sure, I remember her," she said. "Just showed up one day. Well, they all just show up. No records, no nothing. People disappear, re-appear. Happens all the time."

"She gave her name as Susan Reyes," I prompted.

"You could say anything, detective. *They* generally do. We feed, clothe them. Get them rudimentary medical care. And don't ask too many questions. They rotate in and out all hours of the day and night. Some – many – are uncomfortable being around other people. In institutions, even one as low-maintenance as this one. They prefer sleeping under bridges, if you can believe that. Susan – if that's what you say her name was. Maybe someone told her the oatmeal was hotter at Good Shephard. Or there was a good bunk in someone's backyard. Or she went out for a walk and couldn't find her way back. The level of mental illness – untreated, unrecorded – is staggering."

Sister Juliana paused to refill her Patriots mug. "We try to keep them safe, at least for a bit. We find placement for some. Others just disappear. The woman you know as Susan Reyes was one of those."

Sure, I thought, driving away. Mental illness. Walkabout gone south.

But maybe she got tired of being one person and became another.

And told the story often enough she wound up believing it.

After all, America is a land of re-inventing, re-imagining, transforming ourselves.

Last stop, last known whereabouts, Calley's Discount City, family-owned store outside Newport proper, where she stocked shelves.

And where America had magically transformed Carlo Calabrese, grandson of illiterate immigrants, into Chuck Calley, successful American entrepreneur.

And possible distant cousin, 'cause our grandfathers were *paesani*, knew each other in Calabria, may have been cousins of some sort, back in the hills and hollers.

"She was fine, Augie," Carlo-Call-Me-Chuck said after our standard hug-and-back-slap greeting. We had grown up side-by-side in Cape Cod cottages in Newport's Italian working-class section. Same stumpy profile, Mediterranean tan, receding hairline. "Never said much. A little slow – retarded, maybe. Oh, I'm sorry. New nomenclature. Challenged. Maybe a stroke. Maybe one too many beatings."

"Right," I nodded, "I thought of that."

"Anyway, I had no idea who she was. Name adopted? Stolen? Invented? I don't know. Didn't stop to ask. I don't do background checks on the people who bottom feed. Didn't ask where she stayed, either. Did her job, moved boxes from here to there, opened them, stacked shelves. Lowest rung on the ladder. You know."

"Right."

"And, sure, Augie, I paid her under the table. No social security number. Said she didn't have one. I needed a pair of hands. She needed a couple of bucks, not paperwork. Didn't want to have income tax and fica and state and what all taken out of the little she was making. How many of them like Reyes are out there, Augie? Day workers and care workers and housecleaners paid under the table and out of Uncle's reach? Couple of bucks here, couple of bucks there. Hand money. Difference between hamburger and hamburger helper. White bread and something to put between two slices of it. Said her name was Susan. Could have been anything."

"You could have," I began.

"I could have what? In a $20 trillion economy, the underground – under reported, kept-in-a-jar-under-the-porch economy is 10 percent – or more. That's two trillion dollars' worth of Susans and Sylvias and Santiagos not cutting in Uncle. And let me tell you something else: they couldn't afford to live if I had to slice their paycheck 14 different ways to accommodate every apparatchik who wants his skim off the top. Then, if I had to add all that surcharge to what I charge – money, by the way, they're never likely see again – I couldn't afford to stay in business.

"Then one day she isn't there. Simple as that, Augie. Happens all the time. These are day workers. They bounce in. They bounce out. They get lucky. They get stoned. They get somethinged. Shack up. Blow up. Bust up. You know."

"Thanks, Chuck."

"*Arrivederci, mio fratello,*" he bowed, hand over his heart.

Of course, Bridey was invisible. Of course, Mrs. Vanderbilt did not look at her, and certainly did not know her name. Quick as a ferret Bridey was, too, in and out of her mistresses' room before anyone took notice. And in the odd times that she was in the room with Mrs. Vanderbilt, the grand lady spoke as if Bridey weren't there. It was the oddest feeling, for Bridey not to be acknowledged, even with a nod, much less a thank-you, but that's what servants were for. To do.

Standing mute while Miss Stohlmeyer helped Mrs. Vanderbilt dress, Bridey gaped at the sheer number of clothes she wore. Although she had no expectation of ever rising in The Breakers hierarchy, Bridey feared she would never keep all the clothing, all the arrangements, in any semblance of workable order.

It was all too overwhelming.

Of course, Bridey was invisible. But that does not mean that Bridey was not seen. She was. By a perfect scoundrel named Porter Curtis, rumored to be the Master's bastard son, there to spend the summer in the so-called cottage.

Although Bridey could hardly have known it – the gossip didn't spread that far down the family chain – Curtis was a ne'er-do-well whose immense wealth kept him out of the most awful scrapes, many of them unspeakable.

It was on a fine summer morning, as Mrs. Vanderbilt was out riding, that, lurking along the servants' corridors, he caught a glimpse of the Irish housemaid.

That's all he needed.

Enflamed with desire, Curtis knew he must have her. He would not be denied.

Choosing his time carefully – his hostess would be returning soon from her ride, and would want her bath – he knew that Bridey would be alone in her lady's chambers, running the water to heat up the tub. Sneaking in behind her, capturing her, arm about her slender waist, strong hand clasped upon her mouth, Curtis told her he meant to have his way with her, and that if she cried out now, or spoke later, he would swear that he had caught her stealing and would have her turned away from the great house.

Petrified of his words, never having been in a man's powerful embrace, Bridey pushed against him. But Curtis was faster and stronger, had her down in a trice, and took her maidenhead more quickly than she had ever imagined that it could happen.

Bridey wept from the pain. Felt the hot flow of blood down her legs. Heard a hog's grunt. Then knew it was over.

"I will see you again, my girl," Curtis threatened. "Say nothing."

Crying for shame and for pain, Bridey snatched a handtowel to stop her bleeding and fled.

Curtis may have been a beast, but he was as good as his word, stalking Bridey, finding her at vulnerable times, and lonely places, having his way with her.

She had to be somewhere.

I scanned missing persons reports and tests for blood and bone. No fingerprints on file anywhere. No DNA. Dental records, but you have to know where to look.

Then I ran her photo through the URI crime lab. Added a few teeth, a few pounds, shaved off a couple of years.

And hit paydirt.

It couldn't be. Susan Reyes, homeless panhandler, was the long-missing-and-presumed-dead Seattle heiress Patricia Hulings. There she was in countless publicity and meet-and-greet photos: same hair, albeit longer and nicely styled, blue eyes, firm chin. Cutting ribbons, hosting luncheons, standing with hard hat and sheaf of plans. Patricia Hulings, of Hulings Holdings, the 150-year-old Pacific Northwest dynasty. Disappeared a decade-and-a-half ago, give or take. Search parties, favorite mountain trails. Former boyfriends hauled in for questioning. Family nearly prosecuted.

Declared dead. Memorials held. Wings of museums and hospitals dedicated in her memory. Science lab at UW.

Enshrined. A saint.

Something caused that memory loss. A little dirt, a few missing teeth, she barely resembled the society doyenne. Besides, as any detective will tell you, we see what we're looking for. We don't expect to spot Seattle's Woman of the Year eating table scraps at truck stops or clutching torn bags of belongings at homeless shelters.

No one expected to see Patricia Hulings cleaning toilets or waiting tables for tip money on I-90. What head lice and torn clothing will do for you.

Did she run? If so, was it something far more dark and malevolent than mere wanderlust? All my instincts told me no. From every account, Patricia Hulings felt responsible for her family's wealth, for administering the foundations.

And what would the family and foundations think if they discovered that the great benefactress Patricia Hulings had morphed into the ragged beggar Susan Reyes?

I couldn't imagine they'd be grateful. They had long ago accepted their loss and moved on. Built their monuments. Canonized her.

Now this sordid ending?

Would it not be kinder to let the departed remain that way, in peace?

I sat by the harbor and looked out at the sunset, a yellow smear across the sky, great gobs of color knifed across a faded blue canvas.

The day sighed.

Two people so broken, so unhappy with themselves, and their pasts, invented entirely new personae. Fit the character, play the role until the mask becomes the face.

When they closed that door, did they continue to lie to each other?

Did they lie to themselves?

An odd feeling, one she had not previously experienced. Could there be something growing inside her? It was too early to be certain, but she was. Women know, she remembered her mother saying. Women know.

Perhaps not. In the quiet of an early morning, Bridey questioned Edna, mentioning that her monthlies had ceased. "Am I working too hard?" she asked.

Outside the tiny village of Balineed, County Cork, when Bridey's monthlies came unannounced and unbidden, her mother told her it was visited on all women for Eve heeding the voice of Satan. Her mother had never discussed cessation of what she had called the curse.

"A better question would be," Edna giggled, *"are you doing the dirty deed?"*
Bridey blushed.
"Who? Not that cute footman --"
Bridey interrupted her with tears. *"Mr. Curtis forced himself on me."*
"Oh, my dear," Edna began.
Bridey hung her head.
"Did you tell?"
"Who could I tell? He threatened to put me out."
"Oh, you poor child."
"Do you think?"
"Oh, yes," Edna nodded.
Bridey was genuinely perplexed. *"Don't you have to be married to have babies?"*
Edna shook her head. *"Don't you know?"*
Bridey looked blankly at her.
"Didn't your mother ever tell you?"
Flushing, Bridey told Edna that her mother had said that babies came only through the sacraments of the church, through the ministrations of a priest, a man, a woman, and holy water. That since this union was neither of her own wanting or desire, nor was it blessed by the church, she could not be with child. A man took her, but she did not desire him or wholly understand the act. She knew only that it hurt.
Edna sat silent.
"This was not a holy union," Bridey protested. *"I cannot be with child."*
"Men exist to get what they want," Edna began slowly. *"And what they most want is a young girl's privates. The Vanderbilts and their families and friends are no exception."* She paused. *"You're hardly the first. And you won't be the last. Nelly Fane and Gracie Wilson – you didn't know them."*
Bridey looked quizzical.
"After they were dismissed it's as if they never existed. They're shadows now.
"This is America. There's no recourse for an Irish girl."

Even for April it was abnormally cold as I got off the ferry. The horizon was gray on gray, and a chill rose off the water itself. The rancid diesel odor clung to my pea coat.

Something still wasn't right, but the thrumming engines and the screeching gulls distracted me. A bit more caffeine would help me think straight.

At least, I had my cover story straight.

During the day, when Bridey had to run for her labors, she did not have time to consider her position, although her worries made her miss a lot of the servants' chatter at meals. But when she lay down, panic set in. She had a little one coming: what could she do?

She certainly could not tell him. Or Miss Stohlmeyer, who had never exhibited anything but a venomous hate for Bridey. Perhaps Miss Duff. Yes! Miss Duff might be stern, but she was also fair, wise, and understanding. She would help Bridey. She would know what to do.

Sniffling, twisting her fingers in her lap, she tearfully told Miss Duff that Mr. Porter Curtis had his way with her. "Now I've a little one coming," she wept. "What can I do?"

Flying into a rage, Miss Duff berated Bridey for being a wanton, a harlot, an illiterate fishmonger who needed to gather her things and leave.

"But," Bridey began to remonstrate.

"You are not my concern or the concern of this house," Miss Duff snapped. "You're nothing more than a common streetwalker. Get out."

"Welcome back, detective." Dressed in a heavy sweater, Weber opened the door.

"Nice to see you again, captain."

'Not that I mind in the slightest, but I thought this was only routine, the case virtually closed, your inspection merely a formality."

"Correct, sir. But there are two things. First, Sergeant Leahy's personal items. His family would like them returned. I said I would do that."

"Very kind, detective."

"Will you need an inventory of what I'm removing?"

"Not at all. None of it belongs to me anyway."

"Thank you. Second, well," I smiled, "you know how captains are. My captain detests loose ends. The woman, Susan Reyes, is a loose end. Her trail dead ends, and we can't find identification of any kind. It's what my captain calls a floater. He asked me to take a second look at their quarters, to see if there's anything I may have missed that would reveal something about her identity."

"What do you think you'll find?"

"I have no idea, which is how I work every case. Keep an open mind. No pre-judging anything. That way I'm not likely to overlook anything. Not likely to dismiss an anomaly out of hand – because I don't know that it would be an anomaly."

"Always open to the situation."

"Yes, captain, that's right."

"Good man." He smiled. Here are the keys. Take all the time you need. Let me know if you find anything."

"I will, sir," I lied, then paused. "I can assure you, captain, this will be the last time anyone from the state police will bother you."

"No bother at all, detective. If you don't mind seeing yourself there? Thank you. I'll see you when you're finished."

Trudging into town, Bridey looked for work. Taking pity on the poor thing, a heavyset laundress named Emily Smith took her in, allowing Bridey to sleep next to the washtubs. Although the hand-scrubbing was hot, oppressive work, and the food minimal, at least Bridey had a place to stay. Shortly, with her slender frame, Bridey began to show, yet she was able to keep it hidden. Until one day when the laundress happened upon her bathing and saw the unmistakable bulge. "I'll have no trollops here," she seethed, "to give this establishment a bad name," and put Bridey out.

Desperate, Bridey returned to The Breakers, begged at the servants' entrance, only to be threatened with arrest and turned away.

Confession? Perhaps a priest could wash away her sin – and direct her to a better life. It was a hot August day, even hotter in the stuffy wooden confessional. A coffin, really. "Father," Bridey told the priest, "I have nothing to confess. He took me."

"You must have attracted him," the priest remonstrated.

"No, I didn't. I never even looked at him."

"The sin of Eve is upon you," the priest said. "The Serpent fornicated with our Mother and taught women to lie and to tempt. Surely, you have. You are wicked, and you bear the fruit of your wickedness upon you."

"Father, I am not unholy," Bridey began to cry.

"St. Mary's does not need any Irish street trash coming around here. Go to Boston and find a home for unwed mothers! Begone, girl!"

It was exactly as I had left it.

No signs of a struggle. No history of violence. No one would expect Art to toss the place. *I* wouldn't toss the place, except for Reynolds' concern about loose ends.

One floater, why not? Look at the population. But two? Something wasn't right.

And with such elaborate cover stories.

Takes a lot of work to hide that well.

Why is that?

Maybe Reynolds wasn't wrong.

Maybe the answer was here.

Everything was absolutely right. And something was very wrong.

Both of them, flat on their backs, covers neatly tucked. No thrashing. No troubled asleep. No moment of realization as asphyxiation took hold.

No, I didn't tear up the floor boards, but I did a thorough search. I began with the walls, framed paperwork and medals. Presidential Unit Citation. Honorable Discharge. Purple Heart. Distinguished Service Cross. Bronze Star. All in the name of Sergeant Harold Leahy. They looked official as all get-out. But the paper was wrong, the printing from pdfs, no raised seals. All of them forgeries.

In the small, wooden desk, newspaper circulars. Empty address book. Telephone directories, Newport and Block Island. Underneath I found it, a lined school notebook, standard issue, mottled black-and-white cover, *Bridey: A Tale of America, By Harold "Hap" Leahy.*

Round, school-boy hand, every indent, every syllable break correct. OCD or the nuns? My guess, the latter. I smiled. I could feel that steel-edged ruler.

I began to read, then quickly said, no, this was no middle-school student. The themes were far too knowing, far too adult, for an early teen.

When I was done, I wondered if it was real or an entire fabrication like his life.

But if *Bridey* was real, it explained everything.

It was a beautiful day, the kind for which Newport is justly famed. As the sun began its lugubrious rise in the sky, Bridey walked along the fabled Cliff Walk. Looking up at the grand house behind her, then out at the deep, inscrutable water, Bridey wept and said "America," and hurled herself onto the rocks below.

In the winter, in the cold, in the drop from 20,000 summer soldiers and sunshine patriots to 1,000 bundled-up residents, there was little for Leahy to do. He could have gone to Florida and managed a motel – he had friends who did that – but he liked being in one place. He'd make do on Block Island.

And he'd take care of Bridey.

Surviving on standing orders – pick-ups at the ferry, trips to the market, even shopping in Newport for a hopelessly arthritic man who placed monthly orders – the free quarters, and, at Island prices, even freer utilities, made the difference.

One day, when the world was crusted over in a sheath of ice, he smiled and told Bridey they were sweating out the winter.

Peering through the frozen mist, he saw the lights throb at the airport, heard the foghorns lowing. Face ruddy and scarred – wind, sun, the vagaries of rosacea – Leahy was housebound, afraid to slide to his Checker, there to stutter-step down the road to the market. Settling in, he handled nothing more strenuous than jiggling the rabbit ears on his little black-and-white TV and writing in his schoolboy hand.

Seen through the lens of the Irish girl, real or imagined, it was easy to reconstruct the Leahy/Reyes relationship. The way Russell demanded that we think at the Academy.

Were they running from someone – or something? No, they didn't have that feel to them. Too measured. Too easy, in their own way.

No edges of witness protection. No elaborate cover stories, at least not for her. Leahy seems more an adopted identity than a story. And nothing for her.

I sat at the small kitchen table, closed my eyes, spread out my hands. An old habit: in the darkness I could feel who and what they were.

Reyes out in the rain, small, soaked, holding her hand-lettered cardboard sign. PLEASE HELP.

He saw her, a tiny woman, with a dirty PawSox ballcap, worn jeans, plaid shirt.

Leahy gave her two dollars, for which she thanked him.

He said, "you look like you could do better."

She shrugged and made a web of her fingers. "The pieces don't match. I can't think right. I'd rather beg than wash dishes and live in a shelter." She grinned, and Leahy saw her missing teeth. "Been there, soldier. Need to get back on my feet."

"How?" Leahy asked.

"Get some rent money, sewing machine. Used to be a seamstress. Do it again."

"I know the gig," Leahy grunted. "Why here?"

"Figured it was right. People feel good here. I can live on the cheap."

"Have to hand it to you – "

"Susan," she said. "Susan Reyes."

"Have to hand it to you," he said. "You got the right idea – and a good attitude."

"Thank you, solider," she said. "I appreciate the kindness."

"By the way, where you from? Not around here. You ain't got the twang."

"Oh," she smiled, and Leahy counted but six teeth, "here and there. You know."

"I do, Susan Reyes," he nodded. "I certainly do."

As he drove he thought about her. He knew her, knew her straits. Regardless of her name, knew the bone-white Irish skin – blue through her wrists and below her eyes. Leahy knew the price of failure, knew how much she needed the money.

Knew she could be his relative.

Knew she could be Bridey.

Rain fell so thick that it completely obscured the landscape. Leahy could barely see the road. Better to pull over and wait.

Seeing her up ahead, he drove the Checker, rolled down the window, asked if she had a place to stay. Shaking her head *no*, her fringe of wet hair below the PawSox cap sprayed water back and forth.

"Get in," he said.

When she hesitated, he insisted. "C'mon, Susan, get in."

Grabbing her dirty rucksack, she hobbled into the back seat.

With nowhere else to go, Leahy took her home, through the great iron gates, down the drive, past the lawn and the garden, to the garage behind.

"You live here?" Susan asked, incredulous.

"Only the carriage house," Leahy laughed. "The owner took pity on me."

"Both of us," Susan gestured. "Two pitiful creatures."

Inside, she stripped off her outerwear, her torn ski jacket, threadbare PawSox cap. Leahy saw the blue jeans hanging off her bony hips, ill-fitting flannel shirt, both of them obviously scrounged from a shelter box. Small, slender, flat-chested, Susan had a body like a boy, a 50-year-old boy. Blonde hair, cut short. Missing teeth. Trouble standing straight, left side lagging behind her right.

Dinner by Chef Boyardee, quick clean-up, early sleep. After Leahy said goodnight to her, and moved off to his bedroom, Susan lay in the dark, thinking.

Perhaps then, perhaps many nights later, she arose, stripped off the worn blue cotton nightgown she'd gotten from St. Vincent de Paul, then quickly, silently, moved into his room, peeled back the covers, and embraced him, needy and weeping.

Leahy, for a big, gruff man, understood, and was surprisingly gentle, as if the whole world entire depended on this one act of love.

Later, gently caressing her tiny, flat chest, her bony ribcage, he found a knot in it, a bad break, clumsily set, if it were set at all. Maybe, Leahy thought, it knit on its own, painfully, in the back of a bus or the bottom of a boxcar.

Were they lovers after that? Unclear. But they had that intimacy between them.

I heard the conversation that Weber chose not to share with me.

"Iraqi Freedom, cap'n," Leahy said, one Sunday when Weber came to inspect the quarters. "We called it Scorpion Shit from Hell. You know soldiers. I joined. I trained. I went where Uncle Sam sent me. To Iraq. It was hot. Then hotter. We took fire. Returned fire. A lot of fire. Then a lot more fire. After a while, nothing got near us. Four-man, M1 Abrams. Tough little monkey. Fast. Strong. Maneuverable. Lot of firepower. Strange as it seems now, I always felt safe in it. Felt it could protect me from anything the ragheads dished out. *Baghdad Betty*, after my gunner's desire for a little RnR in the free zone, with a cold Bud and a hot babe. Plenty of that around."

"Sailors do love liberty ports, sergeant," Weber nodded. "I understand fully."

Leahy told his firefight stories, his shrapnel story, so often that he believed it himself. More real than the reality from which he was escaping, whatever that was.

Two weeks later Susan began to cough. She wouldn't speak about it, and so he didn't either, but Leahy was concerned. Sinus infection? Maybe. But as the coughs wracked her tiny body, and blood skittered into the spittle around her lips, Leahy saw Susan wipe it up quickly, then hide the tissues. At first it was dismissible, but as the situation worsened, Leahy was heartbroken – he couldn't stand to see her suffer. Whatever other suffering he'd known, he'd conflated into a dying GI and an illiterate chambermaid, both of his own invention. Now they'd become this bleeding blonde beggar.

Somehow Leahy has to destroy the village in order to save it.

Stroking her cheek, smoothing her hair, Leahy smiled at Susan, then kissed her.

Headlights pierced the blackness, ships' horns mewled in the distance, and the cold crept around him. The chilly spring had made the world disappear.

They were inalterably alone.

Beyond pleasure. In the bogs and hollows and the endless water before him.

Stop thinking. Smooth out the edges.

Make it stop.

Expecting the worst, Leahy rendered his own diagnosis: esophageal cancer, particularly virulent. No cure. Pain of meds, radiation, chemo. No money for it anyway. Even if they had the money, it added up to nothing, delaying the inevitable by very little.

The chilly spring showed no signs of warming.

I can't watch cancer take her, he thought.

I can't watch another woman fall to her death on the stony cliffs.

That night, he made certain she had an extra glass of wine at dinner.

"'Night, Hap" Susan said, as he tucked her in.

"'Night, Bridey," he answered, but she was already asleep.

Then Leahy blew out the pilot light, made his peace, and lay down.

Was any of it true? I don't know. What I do know is that the past surrounds us, grips us, even if we haven't lived it.

Even if it isn't true.

Leahy. Reyes. How real were they?

How real is anybody? The selves we present to the world? Or the selves we become when we close the door?

Twenty years as a statie and I'm still grappling with that question.

Susan Reyes? Hap Leahy? Two lost souls seeking expiation. Redemption. Salvation. Perhaps their former lives were so scarred, so horrific, that both had to escape, and in escaping, found each other, and knowing that, in their own tortured Gotterdammerung, there was nowhere else to go, and they had to end it themselves.

Perhaps Weber had it right: people who had experienced terrible things were often most loyal to the weak. To someone, or something, they could save.

Because they could not save themselves.

Reyes, as battered and broken as she was, was all Leahy needed to save. Then he couldn't.

Like his dying soldier in Iraq, like Bridey, Reyes was beyond his power to help.

Meaning she could no longer help him.

And when that portal closed, life was no longer worth living.

Time to turn on the gas.

My great-aunt's story didn't end there. Instead, it spread like an oil slick, like cholera, from The Breakers to the other Gilded Age houses. One by one, they all closed, choked to death by their own morbid obesity, millions upon millions of dollars poured into empty monuments, lavish displays of their own rapacious wealth.

The Vanderbilts should have learned the first time, after the first Breakers burned down in 1892, but they didn't. Taking two years, they built and opened the second Breakers in 1895, the year Bridey came to America.

The season: ten weeks. The staff: forty.

The sins: uncountable. The tragedies: legion.

Innocents rise from the grave to strike down the wicked.

In 1896, a year after Bridey's death, Cornelius Vanderbilt II – who employed his own son to procure him pliable maids – suffered a stroke which rendered him an invalid for the last four years of his life.

He and Alice Vanderbilt – Bridey's Mistress – had seven children. Two died young. He disinherited his namesake for marrying a woman whom he believed wrong for their family. Another son, Alfred, was sued by his wife for adultery. He lost her, $10 million, and a son. In 1912, he wisely did not sail on the doomed Titanic. *However, in 1915 he did sail on the equally doomed* Lusitania, *torpedoed in World War I. His brother Reginald died a hopeless drunk, age 45, in 1925.*

Patricia Hulings. Patricia Hulings, of all people. Patricia Hulings died with a fraud, a cypher, in a borrowed caretaker's cottage house 3,000 miles from home.

Hap Leahy. Weber believed in him. We all have to believe in something. We all need land to reclaim. Lost ships to raise. People to resurrect. Even near-admirals who marry well, invest better, and have two wayward daughters.

I went back to the main house.

"I'm officially closing the case, captain. With your permission, I've taken all of Sergeant Leahy's citations and uniforms for his family."

"Of course," Weber nodded.

"You can dispose of the rest of their gear. It's no longer an open investigation."

"You're taking the remains up to Gloucester, you say."

"Having them transported, yes."

"Maybe I'll drive up there one day, pay my respects."

"I'm certain that Sergeant Leahy would like that, captain."

But I knew Weber would never go. He was not a well man, Leahy was another piece of military detritus, and Gloucester was a long way away.

"I would like to do something for his internment."

"All taken care of. His family saw to that. They're very proud of his service."

"I should imagine so." Weber paused. "Thank you, lieutenant."

"Sergeant," I corrected him.

Weber smiled.

"I still have a few friends back on the mainland" – he nodded in the direction of Newport – "and a few favors I can call in. Don't be surprised if you receive a promotion soon. Public service needs more men like you, and men like you should be rewarded. Men who serve their country. We're a special kind, you and I. And Hap Leahy."

"Thank you, sir," I said.

"Don't mention it."

"Permission to speak freely, captain," I began.

"You hardly need it, detective," Weber waved.

"Captain Reynolds won't appreciate it that you've gone over his head."

"Good man. Respect for order. Rank. Chain of command. Good man. Could have served on the *Nellis*." He paused. "Captain Reynolds will be proud of you."

Sure, I joked about having to bless the work of Art Beckham's hands.
Maybe I needed someone to bless mine.
Confession, penance, absolution – without the booth and the screen
I needed to get my thinking straight.
I needed to see the Padre.

A sad and shabby bar, the Red Door is underlit, with a faulty jukebox that nobody plays, and ancient windows that couldn't pass code.
Probably dangerous.
Probably nailed-shut dangerous.
Probably Triangle Shirtwaist fire dangerous.

This property *should* be condemned. But it had the two essential ingredients to staying open and being profitable: consistent clientele and political *proteksia*.

Everybody came to the bad, butt end of Newport to cool off and calm down. Judges and journeymen, senators and steamfitters, pols and padrones, reporters and reprobates, intelligentsia and insomniacs showed up any hour of the day or night. *An opium den*, one visitor snorted, and the assembled sleepily agreed.

Even Norman, the owner, bartender, and *spiritus loci* who washed glasses, *did not mix*, and muttered inanities all night, would have agreed. Proudly.

Even more important, the Red Door was a true DMZ: what went on there, orally or physically, stayed there. That was the one hard rule, and everyone played by it.

Restive, restless, I walked in, waded through the layered cigarette smoke and chatter about the profoundly inept Red Sox, found Bob Wolf at the bar. Central casting for the *Globe*'s Rhode Island bureau chief: corduroy jacket, loose tie, scuffed shoes, fingernails and beard in desperate need of trimming. His weekly column, Wolf Bane, in which he frequently lambasted pols, was required New England reading.

He was also the newsie's newsie: he knew how to keep his mouth shut.

With a fondness for Jim Beam, Wolf said it got him where he needed to be.

Wolf also doubled as the Padre.

He nodded; I nodded back.

Catching Norman's eye, I gestured for two Beams iced-down like a reliever's arm, a refill for the Padre, a starter for me. I could have used a Number-Ten Washtub, but I settled for a regular ration.

"How are you, Augie?"

"Fine, Padre. You?"

He ignored my question. "No, you're not fine, detective. You look troubled."

I shrugged.

"It's the wise shepherd who knows his flock." He paused. "Tell me about it."

"This is off the record," I began.

"That's why they call me Padre, Augie. You know that. Because what I hear here goes in one ear – and stays there."

"I mean off the record for the next 20 years."

"Augie."

I told him about the floater, the Jane Doe who called herself Susan Reyes. I told him how the trail deadended at Calley's.

"Man," he nodded, "I'll keep that one to myself."

"You're a living hemorrhoid. Don't you have a vice charge I can nail you for?"

He signaled to Norman for two more Beams.

"So I do a little research. A *lot* of research. Not going to let this thing beat me."

"Right," he agreed. "Not the ever-vigilant Detective Sergeant Joseph D'Augustino, statie-of-the-year five years running."

"No prints anywhere. No DNA. Go to URI-Providence, use facial recognition software, run it around the country, match it up with this and that, and *bingo!* discovered she's really Patricia Hulings."

"Oh, wow." He drank half the Beam. "Whozat?"

"Of the Seattle Hulings."

"Whozem?"

"One of Seattle's grand families. Arguably the grandest. Donated a couple of parks back in the day. Hospital. Museum. University campus."

"Oh, *those* Hulings."

"Right."

"And she --"

"Right."

"How?"

"I have no idea. Your guess is as good as mine. Probably better, since I don't have one. What I do know is that Patricia Hulings, who matches Susan Reyes' age, height, build, coloring, did indeed disappear 15 years ago. Missing, presumed dead. Dead enough for surviving family members to divvy up the loot. Donate another hospital wing, museum wing, and UW science lab in her memory."

"What are you going to do?"

"That's the question, isn't it, Padre? Does the family want to hear that she was homeless, a vagabond who couldn't even keep a job stacking shelves? That she died from an overdose of faulty, unventilated space heater? Or would they prefer their version of the story? That she died in the wilderness. Far more romantic."

"Never let the facts get in the way of a good story."

"Right. The Hulings family expended every effort to track her down, as far as I can see. Then had her declared legally dead. Had their ceremonies. Even have a marker for her in the family crypt. So I figure: let it alone. Leave the dead buried. And the plaque burnished." I drained my glass. "They wouldn't thank me anyway."

"Got that right, my son."

Wolf raised three fingers, made the sign of the cross. "You are without sin, my son. Go in peace."

I kept Leahy straight for Reynolds, left Reyes a floater.

"Good police work, Augie," he said. "Can't win 'em all. Red Sox taught us that."

"Bottom line, cap, I don't see any reason to challenge Art Beckham's findings. Autopsies? I don't see why the taxpayer should pay for autopsies. Two more-or-less homeless people, John and Jane Doe, died of carbon monoxide asphyxiation. Faulty space heater. Happens all the time. Nobody's asking for more. Let it alone."

"Potter's Field?"

"I don't see why not, cap. Nobody's coming to look for them. Not even Weber, who says he will but he won't. Weber thinks Leahy is real. Why bust his bubble? I told him Leahy's family in Gloucester is going to bury him with full military honors."

"Keep Leahy's con going."

"Why not, cap? Let Weber have his war hero. He won't look for the grave."

Reynolds drummed his fingers.

"Couple of bodies washed up on the beach."

"Draw the line," I prompted. "Sign the order."

"You'll take care of it?"

"Absolutely."

"Excellent."

It's as if I were committing a crime – but if it were, what was lost? Who were the victims? The Hulings family? Weber? Hardly. Nevertheless, I wanted it tied off, to make it rest in peace without a trace.

Nobody would ever follow up on the burial, but just in case I had the remains cremated. I had the paperwork, transported the bodies myself to a family funeral home just outside of Newport, cut myself a money order.

"No next of kin," I explained to the assistant director, a slow, sanguine man named Wilkerson, hair dyed black, liver spots on his meaty hands, "Homeless folks."

"Odd, isn't it," he asked, "cremation? Doesn't the state use Potter's Field?"

I shrugged. "I'm just the delivery boy on this one."

"AIDS?" he asked.

"Not that I know of," I turned a hand, "and the paperwork doesn't reflect that. Been on the force 20 years now, Mr. Wilkerson. Sometimes you pull strange ones." I smiled. "I've learned to follow orders. Not ask too many questions."

"And – a postal money order?"

"Computers are down. Or so they tell me. Let me ask you, sir, do you want the job or not? I can go across town --"

"No, no, no, it's fine."

Wilkerson helped me roll the two body bags out of the police van. I watched as he slid the first into the oven. At first I had planned to remain, that someone should perform a vigil for these two lost souls. But the thought was too depressing.

"Do you want to stay?"

"I don't need to, no."

"Should I dispose --"

"No, I'll be back for the ashes in the morning."

Perhaps before she died, Bridey cursed them. The family, the house.
Perhaps it was the Furies.

Perhaps it was Divine Justice, vengeance for Bridey, and all those like her, who perished, one way or another, at the hands of these callous, careless people who demanded servile invisibility to maintain themselves.

Eventually, The Breakers, the grandest American summer cottage of them all, became a museum, where common folk could walk through and dream about what life was like in a time of unlimited wealth, of overworked, underpaid servants like Bridey who, fearing for their lives and livelihoods, satisfied their masters' every want and need.

The Breakers may be their memorial, but they remain invisible. There's no mention of Bridey – or any like her – in The Breakers. Or on the rocky shore below.

There's a coda to this story. If 20 years as a statie has taught me nothing else, it's that there's a coda to every story – if for no other reason that there are always consequences, that stories tend to travel forever, one way or another.

I took two days off and combed every immigration record on the East Coast. There is no record of a Bridey – or Bridget – Halloran coming through Boston Harbor in a 10-year period, 1890-1900. Like everything else, Leahy fabricated it from whole cloth. Why? Somehow it didn't matter if she existed. Someone like her, someone with a different name, assuredly did. And he needed to remember her.

It took me six months to get to The Breakers. A lieutenant's schedule is far more complicated than a sergeant's. Sometimes I think this white shirt is too tight on me, that it isn't worth the paperwork.

Early autumn, wind on the waters, leaves turning. Parking a block or so from the grounds, I walked off the path, worked my way around the cliffs below the grand house, where Leahy claimed that Bridey – pregnant and alone and afraid – had thrown herself.

While the water lapped at the rocks' edge, I took the lid off the container and poured, a steady gray stream into the unsettled current. "Goodbye, Hap," I said. "Goodbye, Susan. Patricia." I paused. "Goodbye, Bridey. May you all rest in peace."

Codega; or, The Seven Ages of *Nikki!*

▼

VENICE, ITALY

Prologue: A Discount on Your Sins

Of the myriad stories written about Nikki, no one got her right. Sure, she was a fashion icon, and that may have been the problem. Because no one ever saw my cousin as a three-dimensional human being. So no one could explain her disappearance, her subsequent self-exile to Venice.

They had no quarrel with her meteoric rise – that made sense. Nikki was so right for her time, for that bizarre, quirky age. And so right to leave when it was over. And, later, so right for Venice. Venice, with its unsettled landscape, its pervasive decadence, its shifting moral compass.

I chose it – she didn't. I chose it. But she adopted it.

And made Venice her own.

By the time she called me from France, destitute and distraught, she had burned through her peripatetic past, felt constricted by her imprisoning present, had to go *somewhere*, she said.

Hearing that in her voice – and I knew that voice as well as I knew my own heartbeat – I knew that returning to Minnesota, even to America, would have been toxic for her. Too many clucking tongues. Too many triggers. Nikki needed anonymity, a geographic halfway house. Six months, perhaps a year away, then back to something, or someone else.

Certainly away from Nikki. From *Nikki!*

I did think twice about it, of course. Because going to Venice to re-calibrate your self is akin to seeking sobriety at a tail-gate party. But at that point in her life, that kind of queasy environment seemed right for her.

A little step-down treatment. A warm shower as opposed to an icy bath.

In all the twists and turns, the watery by-ways and shadowed alleys, perhaps she'd find herself.

Of course, I had my doubts – who wouldn't, given what she'd been through? I did think about the prairie, which she knew, and the moors, which she didn't. Neither would have worked. Nikki needed more – more noise, more contrasts. Venice was better. Better than the American prairie, with it gentle undulations, a kind of geographic mother's ululation. Better than the English moors, with their darkness and foreboding, a nightmare come to life. Venice was better for Nikki's geographic primal scream therapy. Better for the blinding light of day balanced by the blinding darkness of night.

Where only a codega could find his way around both.

And offer absolution from the relentless, creeping water. The heavy, clotted air. The history of perdition and seduction. Of destruction and disease.

From the echoes of the Black Plague and the Red Death.

Only a codega could give you a discount on your sins.

Nikki! Age One: Lindstrom, Minnesota

She's my first cousin, Nicolette Dubray. *Du-bray*. Hardly a sturdy Norwegian name. Her father, Henri, was, as you might imagine, French. Alsatian, actually, who got lost. Heading for Chicago, he slept through the station, got out in Minnesota, wound up marrying into our mothers' grand Scandinavian family. Our mothers, two of the five Lindvig girls. My father an Aagaard. So Nikki and I grew up with different last names but the same genetic code, including raging acne. A source of great amusement to our high-school classmates, it left our faces pitted and scarred for life.

Two years my junior, Nikki was more or less raised as my sister. Adjoining houses, family vacations. From the time she could talk, she'd stretch out her arms for a hug. "Cuz," she'd say, or demand, and there I was.

Norman Rockwell tomboy. Overalls. Back pocket sling shot. Thin build, Scandinavian skin, duck down-blonde hair cut very short. Cross-country runner. Later, when she became a fashion icon, wearing those stark white outfits with hints of primary colors – which one wag at *Women's Wear Daily* called the feminine equivalent of white-washed A-frame houses, or Louis Kahn with pipe cleaners – her looks made her instantly recognizable. Overnight, Nikki became her own brand.

She became ***Nikki!***

Before that, though, before New York and Paris and Venice, life was this side of rustic. Our great-grandmother had a small farm about 20 miles out of town. Hand water pump in the kitchen. Wood-burning stove. Stream in the basement to keep the preserves cold. Barn, collie, crab apples.

At home, Nikki'd say, "love you, Cuz," and I'd answer the same back. We'd cuddle on the couch, eat popcorn, watch old movies on the fuzzy black-and-white TV. It was all very innocent.

Played ball, went fishin', shared secrets. Same soul, different bodies.

She joked about Peter the Bobblehead, my habitual moving back and forth, my ambivalence. Maybe that's why I chose Venice for her; nothing seems to stay still.

Although our great-grandmother owned that small farm, we weren't farmers. Instead, we were townspeople. Shop keepers. School teachers. Lindstrom is a little town outside Minneapolis, and Nikki and I grew up before malls, before supermarkets even. We shopped at hardware stores and family groceries. Other people shopped at Lindvig's Sporting Goods, the store for hunting clothes and fishing gear, which our grandfather founded. As a proud first-generation American, Grandpap always unfurled a special awning for the Memorial Day Parade and hung bunting for the Fourth of July. Nikki and I stocked shelves from the time we could walk.

Our mothers followed their mothers and grandmother, putting up summer fruits, pickling onions, beets, and cucumbers.

The town movie theater was the Shadowland, and it seemed that Deborah Kerr played there every week.

It was as unremarkable as you can get, and I never wanted anything else.

I don't remember how it began, but Nikki loved the idea of making her own clothes. Encouraged by her thrifty Norwegian mother, she seemed to spend every minute of those endless Minnesota winters at the sewing machine. Tutored and encouraged by Home Economics teachers, and getting the idea that she was good, or at least unique, one day in high school she announced that she wanted to trademark everything with *Nikki!* – a demand that was met with typical Lindvig smiling indulgence. I thought the idea would die quickly, and so was surprised when she was supported by Grandpap Lindvig, who knew how dry goods worked. "You never know what sells," he said. Everyone chuckled but went along – especially when he said he'd pay for it.

Of course, no one knew it then, or could have, but by indulging Nikki's schoolgirl whim he wound up making her a fortune.

The family lawyer, a proper Norwegian with the improbable name of Winslow – lanky, stiff-backed fellow, name doled at Ellis Island by an immigration clerk who either had a sense of humor or more likely simply misheard Wiland – was good at his work and liked it. Made the *Nikki!* trademark iron-clad. Set up trusts, too, for any income that might accrue from it. "Not worth doing unless you do it right," he said. "I owe your grandfather that much." He paused. "And more."

As a senior at Chisago Lakes High, Nikki entered a *Vogue* fashion contest, again encouraged by the family. Enabled her, but believed the odds were against her. "Someone from a New England finishing school will win," my uncle said. Quietly he added, "sure, let her get it out of her system. Better to have New York reject her than her own kind. That'll bring her around to her senses. And marry that Dahlberg boy who keeps hanging around. Or teach school. Nothing much else on the horizon for a small-town Minnesota girl."

Until Nikki won, of course.

Nikki! Age Two: New York, New York

The famous Diana Vreeland gushed over her, beckoned her, and Nikki went, to pose for photos and collect her prize. We thought she'd be home in a week – two at most, if she took in the Statue of Liberty, the United Nations, and a Broadway show. When my Aunt Henrietta asked Ms.

Vreeland if her daughter needed a chaperone, Ms. Vreeland assured her that she herself would take care of Nikki. Thus assuaged, Aunt Henrietta bade her daughter goodbye.

Although Nikki wanted to take the train, to see the country, Ms. Vreeland insisted that she fly – first class.

Leading the contingent at the Minneapolis airport, her lone suitcase stuffed with homemade togs, Nikki waved good bye, dashed back for a hug, then boarded the flight – first Chicago, then New York.

I stayed home, of course. Took a few courses at a local business school, learned my way around a balance sheet, and went to work full time at Lindvig's.

For Nikki's part, well, I admit there's a lot I don't know. A lot I don't want to know. Because in retrospect the less said about her profligacy the better.

Suffice it to say, I wasn't there.

Predictably, her mother fretted, and her father fumed, and threatened legal action, but Winslow wisely counseled patience. "Granted," he said one night in their parlor, "Nikki has not yet reached her majority. But there's very little we can reasonably do about her extended out-of-town stay. Ride out the storm," he added. "She'll be back home before you know it."

Of course he was wrong.

Who could have predicted it would be the last time we'd ever see her in Minnesota?

Back home, it was a growing, bustling time, with various arrivals and departures in our voluminous Norwegian family. While Nikki was duly invited to all of them, one way or another she found excuses not to attend – a fact of life we all found a mite tiresome. Finally, when she passed on her own mother's funeral – some conflict, she muttered; I don't know that it was ever clearly specified – the notifications dwindled, then stopped altogether.

Nikki no longer belonged to us.

Clearly, she had become something – someone – else.

Her pale appearance, her wispy blonde hair. With the right lighting, and a little pixie dust, her skin seemed translucent. Luminescent. That's what the camera caught, a kind of shimmering luminescence. Eileen Ford swooned. Helen Gurley Brown applauded. Suddenly every magazine on

Fashion Avenue had to have Nikki on the cover. *Vogue, Cosmo, Harper's* all loved her. The gamin look, bone-white skin, chopped-off cornsilk hair. That androgynous quality in her. Something about that bisexual maleness in women – Louise Brooks, Marlene Dietrich, rivals Edie Sedgwick and Twiggy – captures the eye. And once the eye is captured, fashion follows.

Nikki – *Nikki!* – parading her own branded outfits was everywhere all at once, or so it seemed. They called her Prairie Flower. American Natural. Ghost Dancer.

She couldn't get enough of it.

New York couldn't, either. Three big-name manufacturers got into a bidding war to put her line into production. The results were stunning – every major department store had *Nikki!* displays in their windows. To give him credit, Winslow, hard-headed Norwegian that he was, never lost touch with her, her manufacturers, distributors, and outlets. Associating with a New York law firm, he insured that Nikki got every cent – which set her up for life.

What gave Nikki her power? Her allure? I'm still not certain. Of course, her timing was spot on, for no longer were models ravishing, alluring creatures. Sirens, leading men to their ruin. To the contrary, they were lanky, bony, boyish. Nikki.

Plus Nikki was not pretty, not in a classical or even sensual sense. She had no curvy cheeks or bee-stung lips. No deep-set, come-hither eyes. She was plain and ordinary. She was acne-scarred, although make-up and airbrushes smoothed out her skin. She was the girl next door – if next door was a dry goods store or a lunch counter.

Prairie Chic, Downhome Darlin', Homespun Honey – the headline writers worked overtime for her. *Women's Wear Daily* alone was consumed by Nikki for months on end. One week *The New York Times* dedicated an entire Sunday magazine to fashion, Angela Taylor writing that "these days, *couture* reigns supreme in three places – Carnaby Street, Fashion Avenue, and the Minnesota Prairie," adding that Nikki's designs were vertical versions of Frank Lloyd Wright's low slung Prairie School.

New York sold her then sold her some more. Sold her as glamour and sold her as romance. Not sex. Never sex. Sex is wet, musty, rank, distasteful, hurried, animal, sweaty, an act requiring post-coital cleansing and absolution. Romance, to the contrary, is illusion. Myth. Perfect for airbrushed little Nikki, who was all art and image and press agentry.

There was the famous *Cosmo* cover, "New York Fashion Summit: The Gorgeous Gamins Who Rule the Rag Trade," Edie, Nikki, and Twiggy, all smiles and snuggles for the camera. Secretly, of course, they were hellishly competitive, insanely jealous, and simply hated each other.

Fashion shoots. Openings. Couplings with rock stars – furtive and fetid, nothing more. Later she said, "I always loved *you*, Cuz," and I believed her. I still do.

Flirtations with faded European royalty, as suave and continental as they were debauched and penniless. They had castles – but neither heat nor indoor plumbing.

For Nikki, it was fun. It was exhilarating. It was life to the brim and spilled over. Overnight Nikki had gone from stocking shelves to being wined and dined and whirled about New York in white stretch limos. Hard to keep your head on straight.

Impossible, really.

Gene Smith took snaps of her at his flower factory. There was a poster, later rendered into a postcard, of Nikki and Warhol mugging fiercely for the camera, Edie Sedgwick glowering behind. When I asked Nikki if she took to Warhol at all, she just shrugged in her deeply feline way. "He used people," she said. "Endlessly." She paused, a cat shaking water from its back. "Edie needed him so desperately. So she couldn't see that." A pause. "I didn't need him, so I saw him for the vampire he was."

"All that" – I searched for a word – "power?"

"He was banal," she said. "I thought he was a fool. An incredibly wealthy celebrity who conned everybody. Everybody but me."

Fame raced after her. It was widely believed that John Phillips' "Trip Stumble and Fall" was about her – the lyric "you've no respect, you see it you grab it/you've got yourself a very bad habit" seemed to sum up her life – but it was also said about many others at the time. At least Nikki was famous enough to make the rumor mill!

Attribution aside, she did get herself a very bad habit. A few of them, actually, largely amphetamines to keep her weight down, to keep going. Faster and faster and faster – plus good old New York City FOMO, fear of missing out.

I visited her, just once. I did take the train out, liked the countryside, was awed by the size and swank of New York – but didn't much care for Nikki's friends. Or what she'd become.

A lot of money. *Lot* of money. Lot of people surrounding her, using her. A lot of – cacophony. At one point, her agent – a loathsome, lanky, drawling Hudson Brahmin – asked me if I'd like a complete run of all her photo shoots, including framed covers. I demurred. It was all fakery. Nothing like the girl I grew up with. Nor was Nikki, not any longer.

I went back early. Standing on the sidewalk outside her Downtown loft, she held her arms out and hugged me. "I love you, Cuz," she said. I pulled back and looked at her quizzically.

"Maybe that's what New York has taught me," she smirked. "Love is love. And sex is – sex."

"Maybe, Nikki," I touched her cheek. "Maybe."

"Sorry, Cuz," she kissed me, hailed a cab, and waved.

Nikki! Age Three: Paris and Biarritz, France

As fast as it came, that's how fast it evaporated. Fashion's insatiable, monstrous appetite went elsewhere, and *Nikki!* was no more.

The crowd moved on. So did she, before it could kill her – one way or another, as it did so many others back then.

Truth was, Nikki got bored, bored playing an anorectic teenager for insipid photo shoots. Tired of being a two-dimensional image. "It has nothing to do with me," she told me one night on the phone.

Finally, after a stay in Bellevue which made national news – it was billed as nervous exhaustion, but I knew it was drugs – she was gone.

It took a while for Nikki to land.

It was some dinner, and the Prince was genial, suave, impeccably dressed. Cravat, sport jacket, pocket square. Exuded immense calm and endless charm. Came with his own string of what the press called polo ponies, two or three on each arm, but seemed to dote on Nikki. So it was hard for her to resist. What woman could?

Was she in love with him? Infatuated? Bedazzled? Hard to say. Taken with him? Sure. Why not? More than that? Not certain. But the Prince was just what she needed at the time. A good transitional figure. Then the Prince and his continental lifestyle came to a grinding halt. A moment of – not terror. Not disgust. Maybe just stubborn Scandinavian. Time to pack up the Conestoga and push on.

But that was later, that was in Biarritz. That's when she called me. Home? Oh, no. After New York, and Paris, she couldn't come back to Lindstrom. Who could? Who *can* come home again?

First she had to leave New York, and the Prince – some title reaching back to the Second Empire – had promised her Paris. Sure, she smiled.

Later, she told me that she got out of New York just in time. Nikki escaped the clubs, Studio 54 and CBGB; the graffiti artists, Haring and Basquiat; cocaine and AIDS. Heroin and Punk. The blank androgyny of her ur-successor, Debbie Harry, her demented sexual itch of "One Way or Another." Her post-coital ennui of "Heart of Glass." New York had degenerated from play and freedom into a dull, thrumming place for ginned-up ganglia. Nikki had had enough.

Paris, for her, was calmer, at least at first. With her *Nikki!* line still selling she kept designing, serving as least as the figurehead of her empire.

But France wasn't America. Despite her French name she did not speak the language – certainly not well enough to please the notoriously difficult Parisians. In America, she was a prairie girl who was forgiven any social *faux pas*. In France, she wasn't. How quickly the diamonds turned dirty.

Perhaps a resort town. Away from the soot and snobs of Paris. The rain and the rules. More water, more sun. The Prince had a place in Biarritz. Well, of course he did. Who didn't? Ocean front. She sent me a photo, Nikki alone on a balcony, back to the ocean, huge dazzling smile, sunlight dancing off her deep black sunglasses.

Couldn't fool me.

As it turned out, she spent a lot of time alone – all those polo ponies. Penicillin, too. She swam. She listened to quiet jazz. Miles Davis and Stan Getz. Dave Brubeck and Paul Desmond.

She grew restive.

Back home I was under a lot of family pressure. I married a town girl, an oncology nurse at the local hospital, nice young lady from good stock. But it didn't take. The more we tried to make it work – and it got pretty desperate – the worse it became. Finally, we divorced quietly.

Because it was always Nikki. No one else ever measured up.

"Nikki," I finally called her.

Of course, she knew what I was thinking. "America is so," she reached for a word, "tawdry. So obvious. I'm not coming back."

"Nikki," I said.

Pushed, pulled, exhausted, she finally said, "Oh, Cuz. Oh, Cuz, Cuz, Cuz, Cuz. Take me away."

I caught the next plane.

Nikki! Age Four: Spring, Venice, Italy

There was a certain inevitability to it. Venice. *Venice.* Venice or nothing.

Venice. Orson Welles' *Othello*, where the heat and humidity drive everyone mad, where lies become truth, fever defeats everyone, and murder befouls the air.

We got there that spring, early April, the sun already hot and strong, Nikki thinner than ever, bandaged and bundled like some small, wounded animal.

Spring, the season of comedy. Of abandoning reason. Of happy endings.

Blinded, Nikki hid from the light.

We had hoped for salvation, or redemption, re-birth perhaps, but would have settled for simple catharsis – not that catharsis is so simple, but at least it leaves room for new beginnings.

We had eschewed all her contacts for the obvious reasons, but I had a letter from a friend of Winslow's who knew a Signora Umberto, "as discrete as the day is long," he said, "who has a nice, private, *way* out of the way pension on a back canal. If it's available," he added, "she prefers long-term leases. No questions asked."

Intrigued, I called her from Biarritz, and after a bit of picking our way through two languages, I committed to three months. Top floor, two bedrooms, large living/dining area, no balcony, no view to speak of.

"I don't care," Nikki sighed when I told her. "Just get me out of here, Cuz."

Signora Umberto was a pleasant surprise: tall, stylish, given to crisp, starched blouses, orange scarves, and gracious smiles. It was clear that she had no idea who Nikki was, which pleased Nikki no end. Signora Umberto also found it odd that we were neither lovers nor gay. When I tried to explain that we were cousins, she simply put her finger to her lips.

While I did not know what to expect, I feared that our time together would be endless therapy, Nikki hashing out her various conflicts in Minnesota, New York, and France. To my surprise, and great relief, she never mentioned any of it. If she hadn't developed the proverbial thick skin, she had at least constructed watertight doors, effectively closing off one part of her life and never revisiting it. She never discussed the past. Life was all *here*, all in the present.

It's how she survived.

There was morning fruit and coffee in our pension, the odd breeze or echo entering the windows. Jazz on the Bose, all those junkies played soft and low, Bird and Billie, Pepper and Baker. Nikki took her afternoons in Piazza San Marco, white clothes, white skin, enormous black sunglasses, enigmatic smile. The bustling crowds, she told me, the fluttering wait staff, the strutting pigeons all calmed her.

Her nights were different. With Venice an Expressionist play, Nikki was fearful of the shadowed light, odd angles, unsettling sounds. Darkness visible. Darkness lurid and disorienting. Darkness deadly and destructive.

The Red Death and *Death in Venice*. The heave and pitch of tides.

She shopped, determined to add ornament to the pension's Modernist furniture and white plaster walls. Masks from balls, grotesque, with elongated hawk noses and opaque bird eyes. Black, like pitch, like Satan. A codega lantern, hand-blown Murano glass, translucent with a single jagged red scar. Like fiery blood.

By the time her first spring in Venice had passed Nikki had a reserved table in the crook of the buildings. More reclusive than imperious, she had instructed the waiters to keep the celebrity hounds away. Especially the paparazzi, who shot her from afar anyway.

Sitting in the Piazza, sipping demitasse after demitasse, Nikki was silent, celibate. I never saw anything more beautiful.

Occasionally, without seeming stimulation, she'd touch my arm and ask, "how you doin', Cuz?" My answer was always a smile and she'd return to her reverie.

She began to read about the place she was gradually adopting. About Casanova. His licentiousness. His courtesans. His 120-odd lovers.

About the water. The Grand Canal, churning, choppy waters, where none of the rules apply.

About the peasants, taken, bathed, powdered and perfumed, their pungent, earthy aromas, their musty, feminine odors, their rancid reminders of manure and menstruation scrubbed from them. Taken young, they were like the masks no one could penetrate, the codegas leading the sightless and confused through the back alleys. Nikki found her doppelgangers there; I saw it.

It was Venice, and it was Nikki. Not glorious, imperial Rome. Not sunny, benign Florence. But dark, brooding Venice. An old whore selling gauzy memories and faded riches.

As the weather turned warmer, we found ourselves walking at night. Of course, we got impossibly lost in the endless Venetian maze – 118 islands, 400 bridges, 170 canals, all crowned with innumerable alleys, all of them dark, all of them seeming dead ends. Hiding from the groaning, shuttered churches, we ignored an army of beggars, disfigured, crippled, limbless. Hopeless, we happened upon a codega, a boy with a lantern, who said he would lead us back to our pension.

As light splintered across the pockmarked walls, the water's uneven surface, shadows scurrying furtively, we heard the echoes of Venice, distant music, lovers' groans, motor launches' guttural complaints. Holding hands tightly, Nikki and I were glad for our codega. Lightning quick, he knew all the alleys. At one point, he turned, and Nikki and I were shocked to discover he was blind.

"How?" I began.

"The light?" Nikki gestured at the lantern held aloft.

"For you, Signorina," he said. Touching his head, he added, "I know everything here. *Everything.* People get lost. I save them from their terror."

Nikki! Age Five: Summer, Venice, Italy

It was summer in Venice when she came to me.

Summer. The season of excess, of solipsism and surcease.

Of consummation.

Summer in Venice. Even the water seemed to be on fire.

Only the mornings were cool, under the gray, pre-dawn sky, the wind rippling off the ocean, driving off the smells of sweat and sewage. Across the city, windows were drawn down, sealed, cauterized with ubiquitous green shades to keep out the heat.

To keep in the sin.

One afternoon, as Nikki eased behind her table in Piazza San Marco, there to graze on espresso and biscotti, to stretch and turn and cross her legs, a pretty little girl sunning herself, she spotted, through the gathering crowds, through the blinding light, standing out against the white chairs, the white table cloths, the fluted lines of white marble, the very blankness claustrophobic and choking, a beautiful blond boy no more than 20. "Let's pick him up," she nodded. "Take him home. We can both seduce him. Share him," she smirked, then laughed in her hollow, throaty way. "Discard him."

"Nikki," I began.

"Way too pedestrian," she laughed again. "Way too cliché."

The air was very still that night, carrying the faint odor of wet laundry. Lightning licked the horizon.

Keeping the windows open even on the steamiest nights, Nikki didn't like air conditioning. She preferred the heat.

She preferred to sweat.

That night it was as if she had awakened from a months-long sleep. Slow and somnambulant, a creature bestirring itself in its animal desire, she crept into my bed.

It was something we had felt from our earliest moments.

We were incestuous – we could feel it, could feel we both shared the same body, as if we were fraternal twins, as if we were a double helix consuming itself.

And we were insatiable, rivers of fluids running back and forth, soaking each other, soaking the sheets, even soaking, it seemed, sodden Venice itself.

"Hi, Cuz," she'd smile in her sleepy way.

We spent days – months – in bed, sour, rancid, needing a codega to find our way out. The steam of sweat, the sluice of sex, the stench of the canals. Acrid, pungent, sweat and semen, vinegar and vagina. The summer stupor of Venice, the rotting walls, sewage seeping into the canals. The ebb and flow of tourists and thieves, penitents and pickpockets, bella donnas and beggars.

The rancid air of the canal permeated our room, and we tasted ourselves on each other. On the clammy sheets. On our sweat-sheened bodies.

So aroused again to life, Nikki looked for a larger cause. She wasn't political – was *never* political – so did not want to hook up with some organization that was going to embrace the righteousness of some aggressor over another.

The World Wildlife Fund had at her – a former lover, or series of former lovers for all I knew, made the connection. She did think about it – after all, Bardot had done well with it. In the end, while animal rights seemed clean enough, she wasn't sufficiently wed to the cause.

Children's safety? She dismissed it as too much Princess Di – and since she had none of her own, nor did she plan to, Nikki felt wholly without credentials.

Restoration of world cultural treasures! Artworks, cities, and so on. She could be involved by making appearances, raising money for urban spaces, including her own adopted city of Venice, where the rising waters threatened the health and safety of, oh, every living thing. "A definite maybe," she said, laughed, then put the request on the proverbial back burner. Or deep freeze.

Journalists still had at her. "Someone must have ratted me out," she groused one morning, salving her acne scars. "Signora Umberto!"

"Absolutely," I laughed.

"Right," she nodded.

I managed to keep them at bay – I and Signora Umberto, who denied any knowledge of any Nikki living in her pension. I and the waiters in Piazza San Marco, who shooed them away with dark looks and snapping towels.

The lone exception who nearly penetrated the curtain was the chief fashion writer for London's *Financial Times*, a persistent woman who called and wrote excessively. Finally, when I got on the phone to issue a final **no**, she verbally elbowed her way in. "Re*g*ina Frost from the *Financial*

Times," she said, as if I had asked, "long *I* on the second syllable not long *E*. I wonder if --"

I demurred, politely, telling her that "Nikki really isn't giving any interviews, and, really, Ms. Frost, you're wasting your time." I wished her a pleasant day and hung up.

Not to be denied Ms. Frost showed up at our door the next morning, a worn, leathery woman with canvas shoulder bag and matching notebook.

Nikki considered going back into the pension, but held her ground. Turning, she looked at me.

"Reg*i*na," I said. "Rhymes with --"

"Thanks, Cuz," Nikki smirked. "I got that." Standing, swathed in white sheath and dark glasses, Nikki shrugged *why?*

"She's tenacious," I said. "I'll give her that."

"My editor would love for me to write a story about Nikki and *Nikki!*," Regina ran full-speed-ahead. "Anniversary of *Pop!* in post-Carnaby fashion. And your line still sells. So --"

"Barely," Nikki muttered. "I have nothing to do with it anymore, or very little. It's all licensed to Sequential, and what they do with it," she turned a hand and shrugged.

"Yes," Regina said, taking out a pen, "but don't you think – ?"

Taking a deep breath, Nikki turned toward her. "There's nothing for you here, Reg*i*na-with-a-long-*I*-on-the-second-syllable," she said. "I know you're just trying to do your job. And I'd like to help. But I'm not that person anymore. Haven't been for a very long time. Maybe I never was. Maybe I was just someone people like you made up. Anyway – and don't print this, please, this is just for you, for your persistence, just" – and here she flashed that famous *Nikki!* smile – "between us girls, everything from back then seems so fabricated, as if it happened in a movie. As if it happened to someone else. So much of what I did was scripted, choreographed, directed. There was very little room for improvisation. There was very little room for *self*. It was never about *me*." Nikki paused, suddenly weary. "It's all so very long ago."

Nikki! Age Six: Autumn, Venice, Italy

One autumn afternoon an engraved invitation arrived. A masked ball – a real one – The Masque of the Red Death at the Palazzo Espagna on the Grand Canal. Costumes, masks, midnight pick-up. For Nikki only.

Autumn. The season of overreaching, of not knowing oneself. Of not heeding and suffering the consequences. Ultimately, of epiphany.

"Wonder how they found me?" she asked, then laughed in her hollow way. "Wonder why they want me?"

"Who's it from, anyway?" I mumbled, not looking up.

She flipped the invitation over. "Some Italian," she laughed.

"Of course you're not going," I objected.

"Of course I am," she shrugged, looking at me sideways.

I set down my coffee cup. "You've spent – how long is it now? – seeking sobriety. Hiding from, well, everybody and everything. If you've talked to three people since we've gotten here – including me – it's a lot."

"Reg*i*na," she smirked, "with an I."

"Four," I said, "fine. And now..."

A sly smile. A bit of recidivism. "Oh, it'll be fun," she stretched.

"Unchaperoned?" I asked. I was arch, but Nikki knew I was concerned.

"Don't worry, Cuz," she laughed, "I'll be careful."

"Nikki," I said.

"Why, Cousin," she said in her best Minnesota school marm, "I do believe you're jealous."

"I'm always jealous, Nikki. And if the truth were to be told, I always was. But that's not what's at work here. It's..."

She stopped my mouth with kisses, and there went the morning.

Half the afternoon, too.

I objected again, more than once, but Nikki was having none of it. "The Masque of the Red Death," she giggled, waving the invitation. "Oh, how droll."

"Oh, how disgusting."

"No, it's Orlando," she waved a hand. "He was always nice to me." Shrugged. "Tracked me here from Paris."

"C'mon, Nik," I shook my head. "I thought you were done with those people. That life."

"I am, Cuz," she touched my cheek. "You know that. But Orlando was nice, at least most of the time. Sometimes he was a dear. And I'm curious to see what time has done to him."

Orlando. Ariosto's relentless knight. Woolf's time-traveling, gender-shifting 30-year-old. Madness and fantasy. Sex and death.

I looked at her, naked, holding up one skimpy outfit then another, putting an enormous black feathered bird mask in front of her.

"Once more, Cuz, with brio." She shrugged.

"You're an alcoholic, Nikki, you know that. You can't go back."

"Not a little one for nostalgia?" she smiled.

"You know better than that."

"Well, I'm going."

I wanted to say *be careful*, but she had already read my mind and mumbled about being a big girl now.

When the water taxi came for her – white gown, white plumage, that hideous black mask – I did not see her out.

It was like the old days, all right. Greeted at the door by liveried servants, Nikki – and everyone else, the crowd pushing forward eagerly, expectantly – was dosed when she walked in, no doubt from the seemingly innocuous punch given her. Given Nikki's size, the drug hit her quickly, as did the impossibly rococo room, all its ornate cornices and ragged flocking and burning candelabras swirling about her, a cyclone she could neither stop nor control.

Hellishly thirsty, she kept dipping her cup in the enormous, ornate punchbowl, kept drinking, the music – a Renaissance orchestra slightly out of tune, quarter tones off, tempo off as well – insistent and insinuating, a beetle eating her brain.

Suddenly at her elbow Orlando – he seemed a full eight feet. Eyes burning, he spoke to Nikki in a seductive whisper, conspiratorial, as if she were the only person in the world worthy of his great cosmic insights. Of parsing life's unfathomable dichotomies, fornication and celibacy, sin and redemption, death and resurrection. Steering Nikki to an inner chamber, the music growing louder, he showed her murals on the walls and ornate reliefs on the ceiling depicting the night's entertainment, a lurid, highly suggestive retelling of *The Book of Revelation*.

The Book of Revelation, Orlando whispered. Where everything is revealed. The Great Beast. The Red Dragon. The Whore Babylon.

Where *you* are revealed, Nikki.

As the walls began to melt, above her the white-haired Son of Man, eyes a river of fire, brass feet burning, spoke, his voice, like Venice itself, the sound of many waters.

"I have the keys," he said, "of hell and death. I gave you space to repent, but you did not. And therefore before you ride Four Horsemen: conquest, war, pestilence, and death."

The white-haired Son of Man raced toward Nikki, she cowering, burying her head under her arms. Orlando grew taller and laughed loudly.

To her left arose the great Red Dragon, seven horrible heads, ten horns, seven crowns. Although she closed her eyes, Nikki could stop neither the Dragon nor the Archangel Michael from doing furious battle, defeating the Dragon and naming it Satan.

Where he proceeded to stride the Earth triumphant.

The floor disappeared beneath her, Nikki hanging suspended between seven Angels who held seven plagues and bathed her in fire and blood.

As she gasped for breath, the Beast of Blasphemy rose up, swallowing her, its heads inside out, accusing her, then vomiting her out in her own filth.

Drowning, frantic, Nikki glimpsed a woman atop the terrible beast, a woman like her, her mirror self, holding aloft a golden cup of excrement.

Babylon the Great, Mother of Harlots and Abominations of the Earth.

Venice the Great, Mother of Harlots.

Nikki! The Great Harlot.

Nikki saw herself, saw the Woman drink the blood of saints and martyrs.

Nikki saw Venice fallen, **for all nations have drunk her sins, and the kings of the earth have committed sins with her** the Woman said.

Nikki saw Venice like herself drowned in blood and burned in fire, and while the kings of the earth, who had committed fornication with her, bewailed and lamented her, they were helpless to save her – Nikki, who retched up the burning sea of blood.

When it was over, many hours later, they brought Nikki home, and waited until a groggy Signora Umberto answered the bell, then gathered up her battered charge like so much ocean-borne detritus and took her inside.

Nikki did not need to say what her eyes told me. That there's a price to be paid for peering into the abyss.

There's a price to be paid for knowledge. For catharsis. For epiphany.

Thunderstorms rolled across Venice the following day, the weight of the weather matching the heft of the great Venetian wealth, or its remnants, built on conquest and carnage.

For days Nikki lay bruised and feverish.

For days I sat by her bedside. "You need to listen better, Nik," I said, but she couldn't hear me. "Past the voices in your head."

But she couldn't. And neither could I. Beggars. Burn victims. Masks. Masques. Canals poisoned, redemption and salvation beyond our reach.

I saw the blind boy holding the lantern, twisting in the alleys. We couldn't keep up, got lost in the darkness.

Eros and Thanatos. The Woman receives, lives. The Man gives, dies — dies in her arms. In her urge to live she believes she is immortal.

"The blind codega will save us," Nikki said in her delirium. "He will lead us to safety. We will know him by his footfalls, and he will light our way to redemption."

Nikki! Age Seven: Winter, Venice, Italy

It has been many years. We barely speak about the past.

Winter in Venice. Season of scherzo. Of satire. Of irony. Of joke.

Of temperatures that flirt with freezing, of quiet times that presage floods.

After a brief but virulent illness, silent, smiling Signora Umberto passed and was succeeded by her severe, sulking son Ennio, who offered to sell us the building. Nikki and I considered it, briefly — "we could be *landowners*, Cuz," she hugged me and laughed — then considered the endless upkeep, the impenetrable Venetian tax code, the labyrinthian labors of hiring staff and/or an agency to rent out the other floors and provide services. Then we wisely decided that owning the pension would be too much like work. Instead, we left it in Ennio's tattooed hands and signed what amounted to a lease-in-perpetuity for the top floor.

The canals began to rise, then rose some more, the water rotting foundations and first floors all across the city, the rot lingering like malaria.

Nikki, still collecting royalty checks, was fine, then she wasn't. One night, as we lay together, she took my hand. As I turned toward her, I felt tears. "I'm the queen of vaginal atrophy," she said quietly, then turned away.

As much as we loved each other, we never slept together again.

Diabetes – undiagnosed and untreated – robbed Nikki of her sight. Osteoporosis stunted and hunched her spine. Still, we still went to Piazza San Marco every day – she insisted on it – although there were days when she could barely hobble, or when water covered it, and we had to turn back.

On dry days she sat, a husk in heavy blankets in the bright Mediterranean winter sun, her cornsilk hair now bone white but still cut in the same signature bob, her acne-scarred face seamed and furrowed.

"Here we are, Cuz," she said over coffee, "in Venice, in the winter, and there's ice in the Grand Canal. What a joke. What a bitter, bitter joke."

Waiters stayed discretely away from us.

"I was unfaithful to you, Cuz," she said.

She couldn't see my shrug.

"It's a life badly lived, Cuz," she said. "A bad life."

"Maybe just bad drugs," I answered.

Her blind eyes stared ahead.

"A few weeks ago," I said, "completely out of the blue, I received a package from Eddie Egeberg. Remember him? He shot pictures of you out on the prairie."

Nikki smiled briefly at the memory. "You didn't tell me," she complained.

"It didn't seem important," I answered. "He told me that it was the sole surviving contact sheet from that Saturday at our great-grandmother's farm. I hadn't heard from him in decades – had no idea he knew we were here.

"I knew, of course, that the two of you were an item for a brief time, but had no recollection of how that happened. For all I remember, I introduced you. Did I?"

"No," she laughed, low and throaty. "I jumped off that cliff all by myself."

"I do recall at least one photo he took of you," I said. "*Not* on the contact sheet. Nikki in the nude. Nikki with her tiny nipples erect and pointed. Nikki with her *mons veneris* bushy and inviting."

"Cuz," she remonstrated, "I'm too old to blush."

"Unfaithful? Memory? It gets more unreliable every day. It's notoriously tricky, shape-shifting, altering the stuff of life we swear is true. Like a muddy river bottom. Like Venice, Nik. We're really not certain. What we do know is that the past hangs on us, clings to us like a shroud. Who are you if you can't remember stuff? But what if you remember stuff that never happened? Vapor trails, Nik. Here, bright and vivid, then just as quickly they're gone."

She asked where this was going, but I ignored her.

"I remember eating lunch with Eddie a few times," I said. "I remember that he liked to eat well."

She smirked.

"When you were in New York, I knew, somehow, that he had left town. Then I knew he was back after a divorce – where was it? Maryland?"

"Yes," she sighed, annoyed, "and I only know this, Cuz, because he continued to contact me over the years. I never answered him. The thing that we had ended badly. They all did, Cuz, except you. And Eddie was a giant creep for which he has been trying to atone all these years. I don't need or want his apologies or friendship. Like all my former lives, that one is completely closed."

Pigeons fluttered about. Nikki instinctively ducked, although she could neither sense nor see how close they might be.

"Men get obsessive about women, Nik," I said. "I don't know your history with him. I knew for a time you were an item. Then you weren't. If I knew more then, I don't recall it. One thing's for certain, though. I don't want to open wounds. Or pick at scabs. Or refresh bad memories."

"I don't mind, Cuz," she said. "Actually, it's good for me to know where he is at any given time, since he has a habit of surfacing unexpectedly – which still makes me cringe."

"Unfaithful?" I asked. "I don't know what that means, Nik. The past is just that – past. Memories may or not be true. Even photographs lie.

We have each other now. We always have. That's all we know now, and all that matters."

She thought for a moment. "We're here, Cuz," Nikki said. "We're here, in Venice. It's endless summer." She smiled. "And when it isn't, I'll put on a sweater.

"It's winter in Venice, Cuz. A good joke."

Epilogue: Feast of the Epiphany

As I look back on it, on life's mediation of polar opposites, of dark and light, water and land, sin and redemption, I think that's why Nikki liked Venice so much, why she stayed. So much of her life was in flux, so much surprising and unpredictable, that she required a recalibration, a redefinition of character at every turn. Like Venice's endlessly shifting surface, she had to deal with the new Nikki every day.

Of course, there's always a more mundane way to look at things. Perhaps Nikki simply saw Venice's choppy waters as the liquid equivalent of the Minnesota prairie. Nothing more profound than that.

At her best, she dealt well with her own dualities, the dichotomies in her life. The frivolity and the fastidiousness, the passivity and the purpose, the ennui and the activism. Along the way, she created her own version of *kronos* and *kairos*, the dreadful march of time like an invading army versus the sensual moments that seem suspended like motes in the air. I suspect the latter is the real reason she so loved Venice. The timeless, museum-like quality to it – so unlike the life hurtling pell-mell she had known. She relished Venice's dead air, saw it as Edgar Poe's M. Valdemar, or Oliver Sacks' living statues – people in suspended animation. In Venice, she looked at the crumbling walls and saw Valdemar's putrid face.

For time had transformed Nikki, into a blind, crabbed creature, scuttling about the back alleys of Venice, far from the long-legged girl who once raced across the prairie, from the fashion doyenne who captivated New York. Now, far more like the blind codega, Nikki was a haggard, acne-pitted crone prey to the pimps and pickpockets of this watery landscape, true sister to the rotting city of Venice herself.

DIANE: THIRTEEN WAYS
OF LOOKING AT AN ICON
▼

BAYSIDE, NEW YORK

I

A governess and language tutor on grand Russian estates prior to the Revolution, Tatiana Lutoshnikov emigrated to America after the First World War. Still carrying her Old World bearing, gray hair pinned in a careful bun, she sits straight in her high-backed chair, a remnant of grander days in her Upper West Side apartment. Cameo prominent on her high-collared burgundy dress, wire-rimmed glasses *just so*, she speaks in precise, unaccented – and decidedly unsentimental – tones. Only a slight thickening of *th* sounds betrays her country of origin.

"Miss Nemerov was a spoiled, willful child. Unwanted, clearly unloved, she was not unlike the aristocratic children for whom I cared in Russia. The pattern was quite familiar: her father was flagrantly unfaithful, never bothering to conceal it. He was a disgusting person, and the less said about that absent, philandering man the better.

"Either as a result of his behavior or her own pathology, Miss Nemerov's mother was distant, frigid, the latter in every sense of the word, especially with for her own children. Given the culture and the time, she felt that children were necessary, but only as trophies, something to be displayed and then ignored.

"Both Nemerov children grew up feeling they could connect only with each other. Certainly, from an early age they loved each other very much. And that love quickly became sexual. For Miss Nemerov sex became the substitute for every emotion.

"This was as painful as it was obvious.

"No, this is hardly speculation. Of course I knew. How could I not? I lived there.

"Why did I say nothing? To whom should I have spoken? It was a different era. Such things were not discussed.

"To be more candid, I also needed the job. I was an emigré, with neither friends nor funds. To be dismissed by the Nemerovs – and I certainly would have been dismissed – with no reference, or, worse, a bad reference, would have meant my ruin.

"Throughout it all, I did the best that I could. Miss Nemerov was a bright, brittle girl given to long silences and unfinished sentences. Very smart, very depressed, even as a child. Her sessions with her brother calmed her down, fleetingly, as did her nightly masturbation. And of course we all knew about that as well.

"Yes, Miss Nemerov lived in a dream world. But she didn't know anything else. Life, for her, was a kind of movie set. She never looked behind it. She was sheltered, separate, and believed that everything she had and did was perfectly normal. Later – and this was after I had moved on to another posting – when she realized how different her life was, she was shattered."

II

Pulitzer Prize winner, Poet Laureate, professor, Howard Nemerov is as solid as old metal; a man who exudes wisdom and success. In plaid shirt and khakis, he sits comfortably in his book-lined Washington University office, smiles, spreads his hands as he speaks.

"No, this isn't special pleading. No, I don't think so. No, not at all.

"So, no, don't use that word, please. Incest. It's so squalid. Poets have only words to work with, to define worlds, and I object to that one. It wasn't, no, it wasn't.

"What was it? It was fine. It was rarefied. It was like the biblical version of primordial man – hermaphroditic. We were two halves of a single whole. We shared the same soul. We were our entire world. We were one.

"Diane was such a fragile creature. So small. So frail. Nearly invisible.

"As a result I always felt that I had to nurture, to protect her. So for a time when she was very young we were everything to each other. Everything. Always.

"One way or another she was the one love of my life. Certainly we knew we had to share each other with others – and we did – but in ways that were different and did not affect us.

"So that Allan – and Marvin, and the others, the many, *many* others – were only surrogates for me. For *us*. I knew that. And accepted it.

"I still know it.

"How many of my poems are about Diane?

"In one way or another, all of them.

"Let me read you 'Young Woman' and you'll see what I mean.

Naked before the glass she said,

"I see my body as no man has,

Nor any shall unless I wed

And naked in a stranger's house

Stand timid beside his bed.

There is no pity in the flesh."

"And 'I Only Am Escaped Alone to Tell Thee.'

I tell you that I see her still

At the dark entrance of the hall.

One gas lamp burning near her shoulder

Shone also from her other side

Where hung the long inaccurate glass

Whose pictures were as troubled water.

An immense shadow had its hand

Between us on the floor, and seemed

To hump the knuckles nervously

"You see that, don't you? I see her still, young and slender and coltish, in the halls and closets and bedrooms of that grand New York City apartment."

III

She's older now than when she lived across from the Nemerovs, heavier, more vain about her appearance. A neighbor in the same apartment building, Mildred Levy sent her husband off to work every day, encouraged her sons to enlist in the armed forces, listened to radio dramas, and watched Diane grow up. Dressed in a dark blue dress and blonde wig, speaking clearly and directly, she is fierce in her judgments.

"I'm no voyeur, you understand. Never was, never wanted to be. No, I am *not* a voyeur. But that little vixen, touching herself in that way. With those big eyes staring right at you. At *you*. Same time, same place, every night. She knew *exactly* what she was doing, and the effect it would have on people.

"That child – and that's what she was, a child – had a way of capturing your eye, your attention, and holding it, making her most simple movement or gesture just riveting, impossible not to look at, and once looking, to devour.

"That's her freak photography, too, isn't it?

"Anyway, yes, she was a teen – young, slender, small-breasted.

"Of course I knew who she was, the Nemerov girl, from the family that owned Russeks, a very fancy Fifth Avenue department store. *Very* fancy. When fancy department stores were the thing.

"Diane came into the bathroom every night, nine o'clock or so, just about the time I took my evening shower. She left the lights on, of course, so the entire world could see. *Would* see.

"She *knew* we were looking.

"It was always a bravura performance, one worthy of Sol Hurok or Saint Subber. Rubbing. Writhing. Teeth gritting.

"When she'd finished, she would continue to stare at us, turn out the light, and leave the room.

"It was the oddest thing I'd ever seen.

"Until I saw her photographs.

"When I saw some of those truly horrible, *unnecessary* pictures, I thought, these are exactly what she used to do. Put us into a sealed room, repulsive and forbidden and seductive all at once. *Demand* that we look.

"Demand that we look at the dreadful, the impossibly unwatchable.

"That we steal other people's secrets.

"Then I thought of her obsessive sexual behavior, seducing strangers, forcing people to look when, out of kindness or courtesy, they would otherwise have looked away, but instead sharing her guilty secrets. It was a pathology as profound as her so-called art was deviant. As her needs were perverse."

IV

We don't have much of Roger Caldwell – a tall, well-spoken young man whom his fellow Beat poets called Babbitt for his Main Street, grain merchant roots, for his insistence on short hair and clean clothes – in part because he died at age 25 of a heroin overdose. Legend has it that he wrote reams of poetry; the same legend has his angry older brother arriving in New York to collect the remains, refusing to speak to any of Roger's friends, and burning all his manuscripts. The few scraps that survive – hand-typed, yellow-foolscap, 25-cent broadsides sold in Washington Square – present an angry young witness clearly in the school of Ginsberg, but without the rhythmic drive, the depth, the wit. Clearly, Caldwell knew Diane and her work.

"Study in Black, White, and Blood"
the crabbed, freaked life
the boy
shrieking claw-handed
clutching the grenade
the lives stunted, distorted
the twins
the dwarfs
the doppelgangers
the shrieking claw-handed boy clutching the grenade
the rooms that become smaller and smaller
the rooms that become a bathtub
the voices that crowd in
the shrieking claw-handed boy
the shrieking

the shrieking
the shrieking

the world becomes the room
becomes the bathtub
becomes the razor
becomes the boy
becomes the hand grenade
becomes the shrieking
becomes the shrieking
becomes the shrieking

the boy shrieking

V

Diane's older daughter, Doon Arbus, serves as executor of her estate and manager of her art properties – a considerable holding of books, collectibles, and museum-quality prints. Perched beneath a veritable reef of tangled black hair, she bears traces of her mother and father in her face, the habitual weariness around her eyes of one, the gentle, soft-spoken mouth of the other. Overall, a sense of fatigue drapes her like a shawl – the hard memories, the stress of being the child of famous parents – a fatigue reminiscent of the pose and posture of her mother, especially in her last days. Bone-wearying fatigue, like that of a storm victim, which in a way she was. Zealous guardian of her mother's legacy – and legend – dressed in a dark silk blouse and worn blue jeans, Arbus sips espresso in a small Italian coffee shop in Lower Manhattan and speaks in an affected Upper East Side drawl.

"Sometimes I think I'm the key to my mother, me as an embryo, anyway. There she was, 22 years old, pregnant with me, photographing herself naked, or nearly so. It's a theme she returned to her entire life. Nudist camps, orgies, voluminous lovers, Diane found that naked was the fiercest mask of all, the ultimate hiding place.

"Because she was hiding in all her photos. I knew that. The boy with the grenade? He was Diane. You see that, don't you? That rage. That hysteria. The strap unbuttoned. The hand grenade. The *danger*. Having told the world about herself, how much better, how much more in character, that her narrative concluded with an exclamation point.

"As an artist, as a physically ill woman, Diane simply burned out. Felt the spigot had turned off. She was hardly the first person that ever happened to. Hardly the last. We all spend so much time growing, developing a mature vision. Then so much time repeating ourselves. Then going away.

"For her part, Diane said everything she had to say and then left. At least she left before she became crabby and querulous, sputtering out, not being able to judge when she was good and when she was making a fool of herself.

"I was young, and people were always buzzing around. And I was in competition with her. Isn't every daughter? What girl doesn't want to sleep with mommy's boyfriend? And Marvin, well, let's just say that Marvin really liked girls a lot. A *lot* lot. So, well, sure.

"So with Diane flitting about all hours of the day and night – driving all over New York in that ratty little Renault – I was the mother, really. There's a lot of my father in me; he's very giving, very paternal, very organized. So I was mother to Diane – there were times when she reminded me of a kitten with dysentery – but also to my sister Amy, who really did need a mother. And Diane was mostly absent, one way or another.

"From what I understand, Diane was really like her mother, who was never around. Always out. Diane was always leaving us with someone. Sometimes she'd disappear for days at a time, then return, spent, weepy, whiny. Smelling bad. She complained that her body was revolting against her. The body she always despised for its neediness. The body she used to connect with others.

"Westbeth Artists Housing? There's a memory I've been desperately trying to repress. What an insane place. All those neuroses. Like trying to douse a fire with gasoline. It was the worst thing that ever happened to her – short of finding Hubert's – Ed Sanders, Robert DeNiro, Sr., Moses Gunn. What a crew!

"Here's a secret about Diane. She'd hate me for telling you this, but what's art without betraying somebody? She never liked the *art* of photography. The beauty, even the uniqueness of the image – as arresting as her images are. Photography, instead, was the means to an end. To expose herself. And other scarred souls we would normally reject. She forced us to see them. To see *her*. Diane had that power."

VI

As might be expected, Alan Alda is a bright, sensitive, articulate man. Taller than he appears on television, hair gray and stylishly long, he is far less zany or forced than his characters. Studied and careful as he speaks, Alda is nothing less than an elder statesman. Writer, director, actor, he is proud of the fact that some of the more heartfelt episodes of *MASH*, his signature show, came out of his typewriter. Dressed in a gray pinstriped suit and muted purple tie, Alda sits in a far corner of the Plaza's Oak Room, crosses his long legs, and smiles sadly.

"I've thought a lot about this over the years. Funny, how these things work. She called him Swami – that was the first adult role of his life. Allan, being Diane's Swami. Pygmalion. Shaping her. Directing her. She was a lonely, confused teen – Girl, in their parlance, a role she never really relinquished – and she demanded that he tell her what to do. What to think. Sounds a lot like Sidney Freedman, doesn't it?

"Look at what he did previously – nothing much, really, nothing with any depth. Now look at Sidney, for which most people remember him. There was a lot of Allan in Sidney Freedman. A kind, thoughtful, helpful man. Most of all, he tried to help Diane.

"She'd been gone for two years before he came to *MASH*, yet he still mourned her. There was a sadness about him. A stillness that only profound loss can engender.

"It was a wound that couldn't heal.

"There's a lot of down time on TV shows. Set up. Take down. Fix the lights. Break for lunch. Allan and I got to be friends. At first he didn't want to talk about her – he'd wince a little when someone brought up her name and deftly change the subject. Like Joe DiMaggio, who never discussed Marilyn. Or Jack Kennedy, for that matter.

"After we got to know each other he opened up about her. Teenage romance. Fantasy life. Servants. Later he found out she'd been abused.

"Diane's demons. She slept around. Slept with friends. Slept with subjects. Slept with strangers. Allan was devastated. As she – unraveled may be the best way to put it – he couldn't keep her. Broke his heart. He carried that with him, that sorrow, that loss. As an actor – a consummate actor, by the way – he was able to transform it into the wise, caring psychiatrist who could empathize with every soldier's pain – and help him or her through it. As I think about it now, losing Diane, as difficult as that was, made him part of our ensemble. In some ways, we became the family he didn't have.

"Over the decade he and I were on *MASH* Allan told me he tried to help her all his life. He said he knew how damaged she was when he met her. A kid. A young teen. Even then, he thought he could cure her. It's a particular delusion we both share.

"He put up with her. *Really* put up with her. Eventually she spun out of control – and hurt him. Hurt him badly – wittingly, of course. She knew that. But she couldn't – or wouldn't – stop. I'd go so far as to say that she was deliberately trying to destroy him because he was the best part of her.

"Please understand that it gives me no joy to say that. But I honestly believe that's how it was.

"And if Diane couldn't stop, Allan couldn't either. He was constantly enabling her. To the point that he often referred to her as if she were still alive. Often he wondered aloud if there could have been any way he might have saved her. Of course there wasn't, and he knew that, but still.

"Suicide does that, doesn't it? Leaves everyone else to wonder, grieve, pick up the pieces. Spend the rest of their lives wondering how they failed. Desperately trying to put Humpty Dumpty back together again.

"Marvin. She wanted his love and attention – *all* his love and attention. Well, she picked the wrong horse, didn't she? She was good at that. Marvin was married, profligate, narcissistic. Marvin slept with her daughter. Allen Ginsberg has a line, 'will you be my angel?' She wanted Marvin to be hers. And he wouldn't. And when you're as fragile as Diane, that hardly helped.

"Poor Allan. Poor, poor Allan, trying to hold onto some sense of normalcy, decency, the memories of the smart little teenager he married. His question haunted all of us: what transformed a mannered, pretty, perfectly coiffed scion of fashion and wealth into a dirty little urchin with chopped-off hair who displayed herself incessantly; who slept with everything that moved? It tore Allan up. A sweet, decent, caring man. It tore the life out of him. What she put him through."

VII

A large, balding man, Richie Shirkes wipes his hands on a rag and steps away from the offset press he operates in a New Jersey industrial park. Nodding to his helper to finish the job, he gestures to two metal chairs in the corner of gray concrete-block walls.

"I was a six-foot, one-inch, 185-pound pulling guard in high school, and I enlisted in the navy the day I graduated. Well, we were a navy family, weren't we? Grandpap Bill saw action in the North Atlantic in World War I. My dad, Bill, Jr., served at Midway under Bull Halsey. My turn was Vietnam. I didn't need a war; I would have joined up anyway. That's just how my family rolled.

"It was also time to get out of the house and see some of the world.

"So there I was, sworn in two days after my 18th birthday, June 29, 1965.

"For the first part of my hitch I was stationed at the Philadelphia Naval Shipyard, able-bodied seaman, doing this and that. And being 18 years old, I more or less had a permanent hard-on. Who doesn't at that age?

"Weekend passes I'd go home, Greyhound to North Jersey. Sometimes into the Port Authority, New York.

"No, I don't remember where I heard about it. Probably on the base. You know. Sailor talk. Last seat, back left as you face front. Free sex. The freest of free sex. The easiest of easy lays.

"How often did I do that? Seaman/semen, you know. Every chance I got.

"No, I didn't know any of them. Never asked names. Never spoke, in fact.

"Sometimes they were hot, giggling numbers. Kids. Teenagers looking for some quick-'n'-dirty. Sometimes Puerto Ricans. This one. This one was different. You said her name was Diane? No, I didn't know that. I didn't know she was famous. How could I? I didn't know anything about her until you told me.

"Well, yes, she was memorable because she was so different. So quiet, so still. So sad. It seemed like she was punishing herself instead of simply having it off.

"Right. She seemed bewildered, desperate.

"No, she didn't speak. Most of them didn't. It was too fast. She seemed exhausted. And she smelled bad. Sour. Maybe I did, too. Maybe they all did. But her odor made the news. She was small and dirty. She smelled rancid, like rotten food.

"Of course that didn't matter. We had an itch and we scratched it.

"She drew up her legs and opened them. Wasn't wearing any underwear, if I remember right. Sweaty. Gasoline fumes and bus exhaust.

"I don't think she ever looked at me. Looked out the window.

"After Philly I wound up pulling duty on an aircraft carrier. Vietnam, for me, was a liberty port. Navy bars. Clip joints. Dose of the clap. You know.

"Finished my hitch, went to work installing elevators. Always work in New York. People are forever building or repairing or retrofitting something. After a while got to be too much for my back so I rotated into printing. Quieter. Indoors. Out of the cold.

"What else do I remember? Two things. I remember glancing back, and seeing the stain spread from between her legs onto the seat. She didn't seem to care. And I remember a particularly ugly part of the Jersey Turnpike, Secaucus, and the stench of the oil plants, thinking that was somehow fitting.

"I mean I was 18, and liked getting my rocks off, but part of me thought I'd never feel clean again."

VIII

A distinguished woman given to designer dresses and colorful scarves, initially Dr. Helen Boigon chose not to be interviewed. Long retired, her office closed and files sealed, after due consideration she relented, saying that she felt it her duty "to separate fact from fiction, life from legend. And Diane had plenty of the latter." Meeting in her apartment, a few floors up from Columbus Circle, she is gracious and precise, warm and welcoming.

With a glass of wine in one hand, and a sheaf of notes in the other, Dr. Boigon begins by listening.

"I always love to hear the street. To feel its rhythms. It's an old habit, and old habits are the hardest to break. New York is so – alive!

"Would you like a glass of wine? It's an indifferent chardonay, but it's potable. No? Well, then, your good health!

"Here's a telling detail. Maybe they're *all* telling when it comes to Diane, because she was really out there, really all over the place. Talk about no filters! She met Allan when she was 14. They were married four years later. And she wore his underpants.

"There's no harm in this now, I suppose. All the principals have passed, their legends are all burnished, and virtually everything I have for you is public domain anyway. If the public actually cares.

"While I have no objection to show you my notes, they probably won't help you. Both my code and my scrawl are pretty much indecipherable. There's a lot of jargon, too, which won't help you, either. I can translate excerpts for you, if you'd like? Good.

"Diagnosis? I'd rather talk in lay terms. That'll make things easier for you.

"Diane suffered from a witches brew of risk factors which resulted in dangerous self-abuse. As a child she was undoubtedly abused. Neglected. Angry – which, like all depressed people, she turned against herself in an avalanche of desperate, self-destructive behaviors, not the least of which was a dangerous profligacy. Then there was her anemia, exhaustion, early onset of menopause, hepatitis. She was dirty, disheveled, down to 100 pounds. For a normal person the combination would have been overwhelming. For Diane, it was entirely debilitating – and eventually fatal.

"I don't know that calling her manic-depressive will help. Certainly, she acted that way – at least from time to time. Yes, there were times when Diane sat and barely mumbled. Near-catatonic. Sprawled on the floor, sobbing, sniffling, self-pitying.

"Then there were times when she'd literally bounce all over the room, nearly Tourettic, touching, twitching, blurting, free associating.

"Howard, yes, Howard. I must say that with all Diane's talk about sex – compulsive, bisexual, promiscuous, the more degrading the better – she never once admitted to having sex with her brother. I think that she did, that there was something in her past that created or abetted her pathology, but I never isolated or identified it. Something deep, dark, pathetic, profound.

"There was a shadow that marched across her face at any mention of her family, but that simply met the profile of childhood trauma, perhaps repeated, perhaps not. She did have an absent, uncaring, adulterous father. A distant, deeply depressed mother.

"That all turned to sex. I did not – *could* not – say this at the time, but it was a wonder that she didn't get killed. Perhaps her survival instinct was too keen for that.

"Yes, she picked up sailors. She said she did it to make her feel more alive. Of course, it had the opposite effect – sedative, numbing. It made her feel more dead, as if she had left her body, as if it was not Diane who was actually there. Put her deeper in the hole, just where she wanted to be.

"Obviously, Diane suffered from extremely low self-esteem – about as low as you get, given what she did.

"By the time she was 14 – still a child; you *must* see that – Howard, in whatever form, had abandoned her, and she quickly replaced him with Allan, a beautiful, charming man; older, like her brother. Attached herself to him like a barnacle, and he became her Father, Brother, Husband, Lover, Friend. Always taken to the limits – and beyond. Ever the abettor, Allan was always available, always dropping everything, and everybody, to fly in from California, to advise, comfort, repair, regulate her. Yet once having had him, she cheated on him, flagrantly, repeatedly, with strangers, but also with friends, guests, subjects.

"Then there were barbiturates – and who knows what else? She couldn't sleep, then she could, days at a time, her lethargy and somnambulance overwhelming her.

"Her art? I'm hardly a critic and would prefer not to comment on it, except for two points. First, that 1967 MOMA show. The critics got it all wrong – her work, her world, her myths, her masks, worst of all her motives.

"It was the mask Diane was documenting, not the grotesque. They saw it as voyeurism and exploitation, but it wasn't. That misreading disturbed her enormously.

"Second, she embraced *Untitled* because of the complete blankness of these institutionalized people who had no masks. No hidden lives. Then Diane rejected it – because she had found nothingness at last. After a life of *eros* she found *thanatos*. *Untitled* was the suicide note that survived.

"Unless it's her 'Albino Sword Swallower.' There's a self-portrait! Here's this woman enslaved by her art, crucified by her obsession. Sexually aroused – nipples poking through her blouse. Monstrous phallus shoved down her throat. It's Diane screaming to be unshackled.

"Hers was the unbearable weight of being. She was 48, and the thought of getting old terrified her. After years of looking like a young girl, she had started to age. She was drying up, literally and figuratively. She was wearing makeup to hide her wrinkles. Her girlishness, which had served her so well for so long, had become garish.

"In some way, suicide, for her, was the ultimate orgasm. The ultimate release. Finally feeling *something*, if only everything ebbing away.

"I could be poetic and say that Diane died of an overdose of the '60s, but that wouldn't fit the bill. She died of an overdose of being Diane. Like all suicides.

"Did I see her suicide coming? I don't know that anyone ever does, or wants to, because there's always the hope that the patient will turn the proverbial corner, but no, I didn't. Diane had so many things on the other side of the balance scale that I felt she would ultimately right herself. Her daughters. Her lovers. Her art – which was painstakingly created and formidable. Her teaching, in which I believe she took some joy, although with Diane it was hard to decipher, because her self-hating rants were always so virulent, at least in my office. The community where she was living. Even, ultimately, Diane herself – smart, feisty, stand-your-ground. Worth living for.

"I thought, OK, she's exhausted, depressed. Let's adjust her meds and take a look in a month. She'll be fine – well, if not fine, at least functional. What we work toward. So, no, I didn't see her leaving all that. She didn't seem – so used up.

"Do I feel that I failed? No, not at all. I did my job, and, frankly, did it well. Some patients are ultimately beyond us. Diane was one of them.

"Does that hurt? Of course it hurts. I'm a clinician, not a robot. Suicide hurts everyone in the room, one way or another. Therapists especially, given how intimately we know these people.

"Would I do things differently? Certainly. Medicine is an evolving science – some would call it an art – and both the therapeutic models and the medicines are different. How different? That's a complicated question, and a good one, but I haven't given it sufficient time to frame a cogent answer. You – and she – deserve better than an off-the-top-of-my-head reaction to possible emerging treatment methods for a patient decades departed.

"I hope I've helped you, but I'm afraid I haven't. I don't think I've said anything particularly revealing or profound."

IX

A large woman with short hair, square shoulders, and a fistful of keys attached to her waist, Rose Klobucher is the head of New Jersey's Vineland care facility, Diane's last sustained project. Sitting in the linoleum-floored cafeteria, mug of black coffee in her hand, she stares into the past as she considers her subject.

"Our challenge – *one* of our challenges – at an institution like Vineland is to see our residents as human beings, as individuals, however challenged, and then to facilitate meaningful social interactions for them.

"They are very special, in many ways very fragile, and since they have almost no natural defense mechanisms, we have to be very careful about with whom they interact.

"So at first I was hesitant about Diane – who wouldn't be? I didn't want to let her in. I didn't want her around our people. Because I'd seen her photographs. Bizarre poses, brain-damaged people. Freaks. Transvestites. Tattoos. All those beds. I was naturally afraid she'd exploit our residents. But she was so persistent. And, frankly, she seemed so *harmless,* that I thought I'd allow it on a trial basis.

"I felt uneasy when she arrived, but I still couldn't see the harm. I couldn't *define* a harm. So I let her have free reign of the place. Because our residents have no sense of self to cut them off from raw, albeit stunted, emotion, I felt that, ultimately, they couldn't be exploited.

"It was remarkable, really. Diane interacted wonderfully with them. Since they have no artifice – the personae we create for ourselves – she was able to see them, in their depth and their dignity, for who they really are. And they loved her! Loved when she came, loved posing, for that big boxy camera she carried. It was so big, and she was so little, I always felt she would topple over.

"The photos she showed me were wonderful – she seemed to capture our people with all their virtues.

"She told me that *finally* she'd found what she'd been searching for, people with no masks. No facades. No secrets.

"Whether or not I agreed with her diagnosis – our patients as a kind of tabula rasa, a flat, banal canvas – I never saw anyone so happy, so animated. She established an incredible rapport, a *kinship*, with our residents.

"So, yes, I was surprised – very surprised – when Diane stopped coming. There was no warning, no word. It was like Peter Pan: one day she simply never returned.

"Our residents were upset for a bit, but they do not possess great memories, so in rather quick order they forgot her. Much like the world, I think, which has forgotten her photos. I happen to like them – I'm no art critic, you understand, but I like her work. I know I'm in the minority, but I like it. Her photos force us to confront and accept people we usually avoid. That's important, I think. In that way, Diane had a great gift.

"No, I certainly can't speak to her suicide. I'm hardly an expert on the subject, and I really didn't know enough about her. But if I had to hazard a guess – and this is strictly a lay person's surmise, mind you – I would say that here at Vineland she found the end of the line. Obsessively, it seemed to me, she had returned, again and again. The more Diane came, the more I think she saw our residents as lost, and lonely. Trapped in childish minds and stunted bodies. Was this a vision of herself which she embraced at first – and then with which she couldn't live? I really don't know.

"What I do know is that she seemed restless, impatient with the mendacity of daily life. She said as much to me many times. I think she thought she'd find something else here. Which she did, for a while. Then, apparently, she didn't.

"I think she looked at these people – and saw herself. Found the nothing she always feared was there. So I was not surprised that she took her own life.

"I find myself thinking about her a lot, more than I thought I would.

Looking back on it, she reminds me of Hemingway in Idaho, a troubled man looking for peace of mind.

"He didn't find it there, either."

X

A frail, fussy man who fidgets endlessly with his pipe as he speaks, Arthur Sutherland seems to sink into the folds of his armchair. Considered by many as the most significant critic of post-World War II American photography, he has written landmark studies of such artists as W. Eugene Smith, Richard Avedon, Robert Frank, and Annie Leibovitz. Clearly made uncomfortable by the subject, Sutherland frequently glances out the windows of his book-lined Turtle Bay condominium.

"I know I'm the minority here, but I don't care for her. Never did. Not then, not now. Nothing's come along to make me change my mind. That's why I've never written about Diane. Just to puncture the balloon? Not worth the candle. Because she was *not* technically proficient. *Not* interested in anything more than superficiality. Diane's entire *raison d'etre* seemed to be to besmirch human beings – humanity, really – to present them in their worst light. Why? Poe's Imp of the Perverse? Milton's Satan's 'myself am hell'? I have no idea. I'm an art critic, not a detective or a psychologist.

"Ambitious? Competitive? Can you write that all in caps? I'll say she was. All artists are. That mousy little facade – the little-girl voice, the hesitancy – that was all an act. A come-on. To make her appear less threatening, less invasive. To put people completely at ease so that she could seduce them – sometimes literally. Strip them bare. Get them to show the side, or sides, that they kept hidden.

"Sleep her way to the top? Certainly, she slept with some of her editors; who doesn't? In that business it's SOP. But she also slept her way to the bottom. Look at the smug, self-satisfied looks on some of her subjects, male and female. How do you think she got them?

"Ultimately, for Diane photography was not about art. Certainly not about technique; she had virtually none, not in shooting, which was primitive, not in printing, which was non-existent. So while, yes, art is artifice, some is more false, more forced, than others. Think Ansel Adams:

there's far more darkroom than daylight in his work. It's brilliant, of course, but the finished product has nothing to do with his raw material.

"I dismiss her work as *faux* realism, as fictive as her fashion shoots, the *pretense* of the street. Her portraits are as moving as a car wreck – and about as deep.

"I still find it fraudulent that some disheveled kid in the park suddenly became the symbol of Vietnam, of angry, insane American militarism. Absurd!

"Maybe that's what killed her – all right, I *am* straying far afield, but nevertheless. The darkness, the artifice, the *un*reality of it all. Gene Smith's *Dream Street may* come true – there's despair in his landscapes, but there's also hope. *Always* hope. Not with Diane: there's only despair. Think of the ugly, stunted twins. Penelope Tree. Ultra Violet. *Everyone* complained that the portraits were *not* true. So while to some extent all artists photograph themselves – they are narcissists after all – Diane gave us all those perverse images. Because all she ever photographed was herself.

"Finally, she was lionized for all the wrong reasons. Oh, how she *suffered* for her art. She would have appreciated the irony. Yes, she was depressed, but what artist isn't? Yes, she hit an aesthetic dead end, but what artist doesn't?

"It was said that the '60s killed her. That Diane was a martyr to all that decade's exuberance and excess. There were other incredibly stupid things that were said as well, but very little of it was on point. Artistic burnout? Maybe. Possibly. I don't really know. But martyr to her age? The story is absolutely bogus. Like her so-called art.

"I think she left the world when there was no one left for her to manipulate."

XI

Lee Santos taps the bar for a refill, nods as the burly barman replaces his Rheingold and moves some of his money around. Easy-going, mid-sized, in a blue work shirt and tan windbreaker, Santos was a New York City detective for 35 years, the lead officer investigating Diane's suicide. These days he drops by Maurice's afternoons at 4:00 pm.

"It was the luck of the draw. I took the call that day – captain gave it to me. Unknown woman, suicide. 'Go down there and make sure it's all done by Hoyle.' That sort of thing.

"Of course, it was all wrong. We saw that the minute we walked into that ratty Westbeth apartment. We? Me and Johnny Romo – my partner. Polish, not Italian: Romanowski. Died about 10 years ago; heart attack.

"So we went in there, and there was this tiny little woman – couldn't have weighed more than 100 pounds, if that much. Coughing and choking and puking all over the place. Took barbiturates – enough to make her sick, not enough to kill her. And there was blood – she cut herself, enough to make her bleed, but not enough to make her die. There was somebody with her – the man who called it in. On the phone he had said she was dead, but she clearly wasn't. Not even close.

"Johnny Romo and I looked at each other.

"Right, the suicide failed, like most of them do. For teens, only one in 200 make it. By the time you're a senior, it's one out of four – the more frail, the easier the gig. Not her. She was what, 50 or so? Not enough *umph* to off herself. Didn't know enough about barbs to take a fatal dose. Or enough about cutting to do herself.

"That guy there – some sort of relationship to her, not sure what. After about 12 seconds I didn't care. He said that she did want to die, but that more than that she wanted to disappear, to be left alone. And couldn't we see our way to *saying* that she was dead – and letting her disappear?

"Johnny Romo and I looked at each other.

"'I will make it worth your while,' he said.

"Do you have any idea what a New York City detective made in 1971? Barely over $20,000. With a wife and four kids and a three-bedroom house on Staten Island. After taxes took a bite out of it, my take-home barely covered the mortgage, the groceries, and the '64 Rambler we held together with duct tape.

"These people – no, I didn't know who they were, and didn't ask – had money. A *lot* of money. Who approached me? Within five minutes there was someone there. A suit. Family lawyer, he said. With a lot of money – a lot more than I would have figured, given the way she was living. Anyway, there was enough money to take care of the people who needed to be taken care of, and there a lot of them. The suit wanted it done right; the suit wanted it to stick. And it stuck.

"A lot of guys had to be taken care of, and they were taken care of. I made sure of that. Because I didn't want this coming back two years later to bite me and Johnny Romo on the ass.

"You have to remember something. This is New York. You can accomplish a lot if you spread enough money around. It's not that everyone's on the take – we're not as corrupt as all that. It's just that things cost a lot here. A little folding green helps grease the wheels, that's all.

"So they paid me to write it up as a successful suicide. Why not? She wanted out. So me and Johnny Romo helped her go out. What did we care? What did the guys at the morgue care? A form here, a seal there. Do you have any idea how many stiffs the City processes in a day? So, sure, cremation. No body. No burial. Got the papers to prove it. Great. Go find the ashes in the East River.

"The woman's family carried it the rest of the way. To give them credit, they never broke cover. Played it perfectly.

"I mean, here was some obscure *artiste* with ugly pictures. So, goodbye.

"How much did we get paid? I don't recall. But it was a good payday. A very good payday. Christmas came early that year.

"No, I have no idea where they hid her. I couldn't care less. I took the envelope, fabricated the report, and forgot about it.

"She was dead, wasn't she?

"Let me ask *you* a question: who got hurt? Not the family, because they set it up. Not the insurance company, which didn't pay a nickel because it was a suicide.

"So where was the harm?

"Nobody got cheated on this one. Everybody got well."

XII

Despite having lived in New York City for six generations, the Hastings family still affects its Virginia roots. Given to long hair and floppy hands, Denver Hastings IV, current proprietor of Hastings Art & Artists: Representing the Finest in the Fine Arts Since 1851, is both mannered and Southern. Wearing a wide, flowered tie, matching pocket square, and a light blue suit with a white chalk stripe, he sits smartly behind his Chippendale desk on the second floor of his teak-lined 57th Street office, sips jasmine tea, and speaks largely from the wrists down.

"There are two Dianes, really. The first is more or less a worthless blip, a piece of '60s nonsense that is easily ignored for lack of honestly, non-existent narrative, anything approaching technique. The second, of course, is the suicide, the presumed tortured artist whose brief creative life lends brio to everything she did. Like Sylvia Plath, whose suicide wildly inflated her value as a poet and writer – the poetry is flat, *The Bell Jar* unreadable – Diane's dramatic departure has made her family a fortune.

"That dreadful daughter with the awful hair!

"Oh, the pathetic artist *always* sells. We just *love* that story. And Diane sells well. Those original prints? Worth a fortune. Better than blue-chip stocks and, given her lack of darkroom skill, easy enough to duplicate forever and pass off as originals.

"Oh, did I say that?

"Her MOMA show wasn't all that she wanted it to be. Whatever is? And the charge – and it really stuck, by the way – that she was little more than an artless voyeur – that *really* stung her. Poor little rich girl. She didn't have what you'd call a thick skin, and the art world is vicious. As I imagine you know.

"She railed. Her *subjects*. Her *stories*. Her *composition*. How could these cretins possibly miss what was so obviously there?

"She was angry, depressed. Felt alone. Felt abandoned.

"What artist doesn't?

"What she didn't see was what everyone else did: the absurd and abusive side of a very disturbed person. In that anger – in that undisguised angst – lay her power. But no one can sustain that anger and make art. Much less great art.

"On top of that, every artist has a limited palate. For her, Hubert's was the paradigm. Hubert's repeated over and over again. The deformed. The repulsive.

"You can't make great, sustained art of that, either.

"Permit me to put it another way. Those images. Those – *creatures*. Jack Dracula. *Jack Dracula?* Are we supposed to take that *seriously?*

"I do love all the irony. 'Child with a Toy Hand Grenade' – a perfectly normal kid mugging for the camera (and the strange lady behind it) – became *the* symbol for the murderous dementia of the '60s. This was a fraud worthy of the maestro himself, Andy Warhol, Master Illusionist, who, A) exemplified Mencken's great line about no one ever going broke underestimating the taste of the American public, and B) absolutely perfected the art of making something from less than nothing.

"Then there was Diane's supposed last crusade: all that poking about at Vineland, an artless hodge-podge of images of the helplessly retarded. Somehow, it was magically transformed into *Untitled*, which was about right, because it had neither vision nor subject matter.

"She left as a photographer who never met an image – or person – she couldn't distort. A barely interesting practitioner of the Ashcan photographic school. By the time of her passing her photography was largely ignored, largely forgotten.

"Put a different way, the '60s had turned into the '70s, and she was suddenly out of step, out of touch. None of the images she was making made any sense. She herself seemed queer, in the old sense of the word. Nobody got it anymore, the twins, the transvestites, the dwarfs, the giants.

"Editors tired of her – her stuff drew too many complaints. Too many friends were offended. She turned everyone, and everything, into something alien, bizarre. Inherently false. Flat out *ugly*. Not what art directors wanted. They wanted *illustrations* not nightmares.

"Access conditional, access denied.

"Just as well. Diane hated taking direction, found the work boring, insulting.

"As Oscar Wilde said, divorces are made in heaven.

"She told people she'd burned out of shooting. Had had enough. Didn't miss it. Well, I can understand that. How many sword swallowers can you stomach – literally? Why be a relic? Why not just disappear? Which she did.

"Let me put it another way. A lot of people find living in the persona they've created for themselves a burden. They want to slip the surly bounds of being and become pure nothingness. Masks off, like her Vineland folks, and – *nothing*.

"Diane found a way to do that.

"The art world, fickle as ever, had moved on. And her career was essentially dead. What Diane needed was value added. She got it with suicide. Feminist icon, all that obiter dicta that had nothing to do with the minimal value of her images. But with that story? *Pow!*

"She wanted more than the 15 minutes she'd been allotted – and death gave it to her in a way that life never could.

"Suicide: the perfect marketing tool.

"All the sisters embraced her for all the wrong reasons – don't they always? Never let the facts get in the way of a good ideology! A sister who takes her life *has* to be righteous. *Has* to be oppressed and worthy of the pantheon. To say otherwise is to be eviscerated for terminal callousness, for unfeeling and unfettered gender bias.

"Suicides are Housman's athlete dying young: they don't get old, become bores, nags. Renounce free love, free sex, free art. Turn racist or Republican.

"So the whiny, needy, self-loathing little girl became the icon for the New Woman. What a joke!

"Suicide: anything to sell stuff. Just like her grandparents' department store. It's all about sales. Repeat business.

"No suicide? No myth. No books. No prints selling in the serious six figures. Instead, if she'd be remembered at all, it would be as the little weirdo who exploited the deformed and degenerate and then faded from the scene.

"In the end, what a picture she must have made. Slumped in the tub, bathed in her own blood, eyes staring, mouth agape, a mess for someone else to clean up, the greatest performance art of all. Her triumph, face twisted into a grotesque mask, a *risus sardonicus*, her sneering goodbye."

XIII

A small, gray-haired widow, Emily Nathanson appears to have taken up permanent residence in her housecoat. Sitting on a worn couch in her Bayside, Long Island, garden apartment, she sips hot water and lemon from a 1964 World's Fair glass.

"I don't spy on my neighbors. In the warmer weather I take a folding chair outside, sit in the shade of the building, read the newspaper. *Newsday*. So, yes, from time to time I saw Mrs. Nemerov and her visitors. Other times I saw her when she and I happened to be at the mailbox or the supermarket. That's all.

"Short, slender. Thick hair, entirely gray. Army surplus chic, if you know what I mean. Khakis. Fatigue jackets. That sort of thing. Nothing stylish. Nothing flattering. No make-up. As if she wanted to look unattractive. Masculine, even.

"Camera? No, why?

"We had a nodding acquaintanceship. Nothing more than that.

"Sometimes we'd pass in the street, or see each other in Bohack's. 'Good morning, Mrs. Nemerov,' that sort of thing. No, I never did know her first name. Not even the initial. It was NEMEROV on the mailbox, that's all.

"Did I know she was married? No, I just assumed so. She had that way about her. Didn't seem like a spinster. Women know these things. When I called her Mrs. Nemerov she never corrected me. And the young woman who visited her seemed like her daughter.

"Over the time we lived in that complex she had two visitors that I recall. One was that younger woman. Yes, could have been her daughter. Looked like her. I'm a mother, too, and I know how it looks. The woman had a huge nest of black seaweed hair – she couldn't think that was attractive, but who knows with young people these days. That's about all I remember. There was a man, too. He also looked like her. A bit older, very affectionate. Could have been her brother. What did she call him? Something with an 'H.' Harvey? Henry? Howard? That was it. Howard.

"I remember when they walked together she took his arm.

"I did take them for brother and sister, yes. No, I never asked. It was none of my business. Whatever she wanted to say she would say. Which was nothing.

"She was quiet. Kept to herself. Seemed sad.

"Whenever I saw her she'd nod. Not rude. Just quiet. I can't recall her saying anything other than 'good morning, Mrs. Nathanson.' It's a long time ago, though, and I didn't pay much attention.

"I had no idea who she was – or wasn't. She wasn't Mrs. Nemerov? I don't know anything about that. As I said, I called her that, and she never corrected me.

"What happened to her? I don't know. I don't know if I moved out first or if she did. As I said, I didn't pay much attention. I left in the fall of 1988 – I fell, broke a hip, and moved in with daughter in New Rochelle. She and her husband fixed up a beautiful apartment for me in their basement. Since they got divorced I'm back on Long Island.

"No, I never saw Mrs. Nemerov again. Never heard about her, either. Why should I?

"No, as I said, she never talked about herself. A polite *hello* at the mailbox or the market. That's all. Not even a smile.

"Not even the ghost of one."

DIRTY DIAMONDS

▼

PRAGUE, CZECHOSLOVAKIA

"No, Bulldog," Aunt Charlotte took my arm as we strolled around Old Town Square, "it's not about me. It's *never* about me. It's about you. About you remembering when it's over the only thing you'll have is choice and the consequence of choice."

Prague is a city of storms. Of Masaryk hurled from a window, Russian tanks rolling into Wenceslas Square, Jan Hus burned at the stake.

First posting: Junior Officer, Foreign Service, Consular Division, Prague, Czechoslovakia, November 1968. Prague Spring barely buried, luck of the draw.

After all the prerequisites – Yale degree in international studies, foreign service training, two years shuffling papers in Washington and the field, wardrobe of white shirts, rep ties, three-piece wool suits – my two-minute pre-flight briefing came from a lanky, officious, handball player named Jon Breen, "preliminary contact for visa requests and passport problems," he said. "Chief of Staff Bill Gerard. Head of Office Roger McLaren. Papers, tickets, itinerary at the front desk. Due there end of week. Git."

Doing my homework on the flight over, I found that before the Spring and the Russian tanks, the history of Prague is the history of murder. Beginning with Good King Wenceslas – who a thousand years ago, when he was merely Prince Wenceslas, was murdered by his own brother. Charlemagne and his Holy Roman Empire – which was none of the above. Central Europe's first university, 600 years ago, whose first rector, the heretical Jan Hus, was roasted alive. Reformation; blood. Counter-Reformation; more blood. Old Town Hall 400 years ago, 27 Protestant leaders executed.

The Hapsburgs. The Thirty Years War. The Nazis. The Russians. Jan Masaryk. Prague Spring, the Russians, the murder of 100 protestors. Books taken from libraries. Plays unproduced. Radio shows silenced. Films unshown.

Prague betrayed, then betrayed again. Prague, a gussied-up version of bombed-out Berlin. Sold out by Europe, defenseless against the Wehrmacht. Possessed by First War memories, the Czechs capitulated, saving both the city and the country – at an incalculable price in human life. Under the Russians, Prague, with its past and its dreams and its soaring music, its folk dances and fairy-tale architecture, became Checkpoint Charlie *mit schlag.* Everyone came to the American Embassy – for everything. With the Red Army came the Soviet influence – insistence – that everyone spy on everyone else, inform on everyone else, sell out everything and everyone else.

As good a place as any, I thought, to join the Foreign Service, overseas edition.

The American Embassy, housed in a four-story building, stood stern and severe, serious and stone, befitting a world power, the real victor of World War II.

Inside, the embassy was serviceable enough. Large rooms, plaster walls, ornate molding, big latched windows gawking at the street. The centerpiece was a large, ornate ballroom in the Empire style, frieze creeping up into ceiling – fauns and cherubs and the like – and a trio of blindingly brilliant chandeliers. With obligatory American flags hanging at both ends, it was Ambassador David Willoughby's favorite room for hosting parties. Meaning that he could drink publicly and get away with it. Easily seating 350, it could host as many drunks as could list safely from starboard and port.

After I presented my credentials to a middle-aged woman, she gestured me down the hall to the right. Two offices in, interior side, Roger McLaren, Senior Officer, Consular Division was embossed on the doorplate. Surprised to find no one around, I walked in, nosed into an interior chamber, and found McLaren standing with a big girl who had her blouse off and --

"Oops," I smiled and backed away.

Waiting in the outer office I thought, sure, some women like back-seat moves from a 40-year-old with longish hair, buck teeth, and bad skin.

Nonplussed and not apologetic, McLaren strode into the room.

"Con Jacobs," I stuck out my hand.

Ignoring it, he came on Southern, which he wasn't, and cliched, which he was. "Howdy, Junior. Come with your cardboard suitcase and hayseeds in your hair? First rodeo?" He looked me over. "Young, personable, good-looking. Well dressed, trim, intelligent. Well educated, well connected, hard working. You'll make it a point to learn every applicant's name, speak to each as a person not as a suspect. That right?"

I nodded.

"You won't last long. So many scam artists in Prague, so little time." He turned, gestured. "Order of the Day, all day, every day," he walked ahead of me, "tread lightly."

Turn to the left, flight of stairs, basement. Research, Tom Ruhle, Prop.

"Surprised they ever let you see the light of day," McLaren greeted a bulky man rising from his desk. "We feed him vitamin D and provide him a sun lamp to offset his pink skin. Sunglasses requisitioned for the odd trip out of doors."

Ruhle smiled and gripped my hand. Apparently, he had read – and memorized – my resume. "James Connelly Jacobs," he recited, "goes by Con, age 26, height 6-1, weight 185. Graduated Phillips Academy, 1960; Yale, 1964. Skull & Bones. Football team, lineman. Recruited Foreign Service. Training, Consular Division. Shakedown cruise, two years at State, two years in field, first foreign posting here – aren't we the lucky ones? – just in time to help pick up the pieces after Prague Spring. Thought we'd have it easy for a while, that the Russian bear had settled in to hibernate. No such luck. Welcome aboard," he smiled. "Enjoy your time here."

"In dark, dank Prague?" McLaren shook his head. "Never."

"Don't mind Roger," Ruhle said. "Got up wrong side of the bed. This decade."

"I've noticed," I said. Ruhle laughed; McLaren didn't.

Up two floors to the Chief of Staff's office. Foreign Service lifer, Bill Gerard was short, stocky, dirty blond hair chopped off farm style; tough like industrial sandpaper with a voice and face to match.

Standing when I came in, stuck out his hand, grunted something in a language unknown to man, then motioned me to sit. "Kansas Democrat and proud of it," he said.

"Pennsylvania Republican and profoundly ambivalent," I smiled.

"Said you had a sense of humor," he nodded. "That should do you well here, as crazy as it gets."

McLaren smirked.

"Officially, this ship is captained by Ambassador Willoughby, a harmless-enough member of the white-shoe set. A man who excels at party and Party. The former as in pouring drinks – he never met a cocktail shaker he didn't like. The latter as in raising significant contributions from his wealthy friends in South Hampton and Steamboat Springs. Very successful; rewarded for his efforts. And for not sleeping with the First Lady. Or *for* sleeping with the First Lady. Depending on which way the wind's blowing that day." Gerard had a laugh as coarse as his Kansas haircut.

"His job is largely ceremonial. We do the heavy lifting – *all* the lifting, really – and tell him what to do. He's good at it, too. Stands on his mark. Finds his light. Says his lines. Does not offend the locals or their overlords. Never takes sides; walks right down the middle of Main Street. Neither ambition nor vision. In college he majored in golf. In two years here, the most profound thing he's said was 'it's five o'clock somewhere.'

"While the flow chart says I work for him, he works for me. That's not ego, that's fact. I monitor him, where he goes, what he does, what he says. I'm more finely attuned to our role here, our policies and protocols, than he'll ever be. Gets in the way of his charm – and the Parliament speaker's wife, or whoever he's pursuing this week.

"So. You do not work for the Ambassador. You *never* work for the Ambassador – unless he's Averill Harriman, who actually knows something. If Willoughby ever approaches you – he won't, because you're too far down the food chain to be noticed – get someone senior to handle him. If it is somehow an emergency, you never give him what he wants. Give him what he needs. You'll learn to distinguish between the two."

"Yes, sir."

"Foreign Service Officer, Junior Grade, Consular Division."

"Yes, sir."

"We represent the United States of America."

"Yes, sir."

"We protect our fellow citizens."

"Yes, sir."

"But what we really do is avoid risk."

"Most certainly, sir."

Prague is a city of secrets. Of whispered words, furtive gestures, lives erased.

I didn't remember her first visit to the embassy. The days were long, the lines endless, and she was another in a dizzying array of supplicants braving the weather and the Secret Police to apply at the American Embassy for asylum, for escape from shuttered, Sovietized Prague. The Paris of Central Europe now closed for business.

People who came in off the street were sent to me. I manned – not a desk, a counter, where I stood all day. *Flat*, Gerard banged his hand, *like a Kansas wheatfield.*

They stood, too. That way, people without appointments, friends, or proteksia would keep their supplications brief and get out. Encouraged – commanded – by Gerard to keep approaches to no more than three minutes, *like a good soft-boiled egg*, he said, staffing the counter meant acting fast, making quick judgments.

Still, my job made me uncomfortable. I had to be polite, yes, and courteous, and paradoxically curt and callous. While I'm certain the regimen was designed to toughen me up – to think and react by regs and not by reason – I found myself wanting more information, looking for ways to help, thinking of how to make exceptions.

If I felt that I was betraying so many people – confused Americans, lost Czechs, even the odd Hungarian or Russian – at least the encounters were brief: no valid papers, no credible story, no contacts. *Sorry, no possible help. Next, please!*

So I didn't notice Elena Moravec the first time she came – a shy, skinny waif, page boy black hair, round glasses, frightened manner; Czech national, passable English. Of the hundreds I saw that day, she was both pitiful and indistinguishable. Later, when I looked back, my notes indicated that she had no papers, story, contact. She thought she was in danger, but nothing concrete. She needed help, had nowhere to turn. Perhaps not, but as a presumed Czech citizen there was nothing we could do.

"C'mon, Junior," McLaren grabbed my arm, "let's grab one."

Given McLaren, I didn't know if he meant a girl or a gimlet – probably both – but it had been another long day so why not something interesting after work?

"What's her name?" I asked.

"Jill," he said, shrugging into his overcoat, "but you can't have her. At least not yet. She's mine. Nurse who works at the American hospital."

"Drinks, then," I said.

"Right," he threw a scarf around his neck. "Prescott Club."

"Sure," I said. I hadn't heard of it. Like a country club, you needed to be taken. Properly introduced. Reserved for high-ranking Americans and members of the diplomatic community. Closed door, password. Pavel sent me. Or some such.

Leaving the embassy, we passed the Today Show, the endless demonstration against the war. *America out of Vietnam!*

"Stalwarts," I smiled.

"Mosquitos," McLaren said. "Pests. The Czechs love it when we take the heat."

Three blocks away, the Prescott Club, tarnished bronze plaque outside a standard office building door, was home to the post-work pour. Recognized right away, McLaren breezed through a set of carved wooden doors, then blast doors two inches thick. "I feel like I'm being sealed in a bank vault," I said, taking off my coat. Looking around, it met all expectations: woody, clubby, 19th Century. The selection was simple but effective: martinis, pilseners, Chivas neat. "Never sissified mixed drinks," McLaren said. "Order one of those, they suspect that you sleep with boys. Subject to blackmail. Do all sorts of reprehensible things. Sell yourself and our secrets to the Ruskies."

"Can we talk here?" I asked, joining him in a bucket-sized martini.

"Why?" he asked. "Is there something we need to talk about?"

"No," I demurred. "Not at all. Just wanted to make sure it's safe."

"Safe as milk," McLaren said. "Safe as the embassy. Safe as American soil." He paused. "Or maybe not. With the Ruskies in town, who knows? One in three Czechs will sell out their mothers, and usually do, so be careful about what you say."

Noticing a pixie-ish cocktail waitress, I asked, "easy pickings here?"

"Yes and no, Junior," McLaren signaled for a refill. "The Czech girls love us – rich Americans, possible life in America. But despite all his mewling about being a Kansas Democrat Gerard is a New England Puritan. Strict non-fraternalization rule. More than one junior officer has been sent packing because of it. Take some advice, Junior. Look for home-grown heifers. Plenty of them around, embassy and elsewhere. Next week is Willoughby's Thanksgiving party. Prime place to troll for good nookie."

Willoughby's annual extravaganza, his non-denominational Thanksgiving party, doubled as his end-of-year farewell. With many people taking off for Christmas vacations, it was a nice gesture, a gathering for staff, visitors, ex-pats of significant social standing.

Hot, crowded, noisy, even in the large ballroom there were far too many people stuffed into one place – and stuffed into last year's clothes. My job, as a junior officer, was to stand, smile, be happy, sober, attentive. *Did I say sober?* Gerard demanded.

With good reason. Of course, the *hors d'oeuvres* were scrumptious (*try the cheese balls, Junior,* McLaren said, *perfect the way the drop of Tabasco creeps up on the Neufchatel and pineapple and only slightly elbows aside the chopped pecans.*) But the *piece-de-resistance* was Willoughby's signature egg nog. More nog than egg – *far* more nog than egg. Bit of brandy. Ration of Havana Club rum. And nothing less than a jeroboam of Mr. James Beam himself. Wave the egg above the rim.

So oiled, the visitors' vastly amusing *bon mots* were worth a Top Ten:

1) "It's lunacy to think we'll spend that kind of money to put someone on the moon. Kennedy's folly won't be Nixon's." Young American Hospital resident, brown suit, losing his hair, glass of nog in each hand so he wouldn't run out.

2) "If Vietnam isn't over by year's end, it'll certainly be before the '70 midterm. Nixon can't keep the Congress if the war continues." Small, roundish man, nasal in all the wrong places, wearing a paisley tuxedo.

3) "You can carp all you want about Tricky Dick. At least Landslide Lyndon's gone. In my grandpappy's day they would've strung him up as a horse thief." Slender, slightly soused Southerner clutching a woman not his wife.

4) "Mark my words, now that Lyndon's out of office, his damn Civil Rights Act will be found both unenforceable and unconstitutional." Short bleached blonde equipped with too loud a mouth and too big a jiggle.

5) "The Czechs may make a brave face of it, but they're inherently weak. The Russians'll be here for the next 1,000 years. They're conquerors. It's in their blood." Tall, vacuous man who found himself infinitely amusing.

6) "These hippies are filthy, disgusting, foul-mouthed, anti-Americans. Time to lock and load." Long nose, long hair, aggrieved self-righteousness.

7) "You're right that Nixon's a bastard. But it's a tough world out there, and that's what you want in the White House. A bastard – who'll stand up to all the other bastards." Tall man, horn-rimmed glasses, hands in his pockets. *Get him a drink!*

8) "King. Kennedy. Who's next? I wake up every morning wondering who was shot the night before. And the riots! Good time to be out of the country for a while." Small, dark man, too much hair, too little Nehru jacket.

9) "Don't let anyone fool you: Mao Tse-Tung *is* the Great Wall of China. And if he isn't, Nixon is. We'll get nowhere while either one of them is alive." Distracted man, international trader, cracked voice, ill-fitting suit.

10) "The Paris Strike simply encouraged all of De Gaulle's royalist tendencies. Where's the guillotine now that we need it?" A large man in tight, faded suit and tie, burping his way through the evening.

"You're a cute one, aren't, you?" A voice at my elbow. Sixty? More? Faded red hair, gray highlights. Ebony walking stick. Lovely frock – deep blue, necklace of sparking stones. Not diamonds, but lovely, restrained elegance. Middle height, trim.

"Big. Strong. Fresh. Fetch your Aunt Charlotte a flagon of Willoughby's famous egg nog, would you, Toots? Then let's talk."

I smiled, nodded, found Tom Ruhle stirring the concoction. "Who is *that?*"

"*That*," he said, doling out drinks to doyennes, "is Charlotte Russell. Codename Charlotte Russe. Aunt Charlotte to everyone. Our resident fossil. Born 1907. Came to Prague '37, no reason given, just in time for Europe to sell out the Czechs to the Nazis. Chose to stay. American agent? Not certain. Worked for the Czechs. Underground railroad getting people away from the Nazis, out of Europe. Survived the Soviets, too."

He poured me a glass of egg nog.

"If cover it is, Con, she's perfect. Ran a salon like Gertrude Stein in Paris, more or less played Beatrice Lillie – dotty, outrageous, *splash of color at the throat.*"

"Beatrice Lillie?"

"Before your time. Flighty, lightweight, high-pitched. Cover for cunning, bravery, brilliance, dedication. Repeatedly put herself in danger. Or so the story goes.

"Knows everyone. Seems to walk between the raindrops – hell, between the blizzards – and emerge whole and dry. For all I know, she walks on the River Moldau. She's funny – and worth knowing. Out to pasture now. She's more than earned it."

"None for you, Toots?"

"Not on duty," I smiled. "If I got sloshed, Gerard'd have my ass."

"Not if I don't have it first," she drank. "Got to know how to hold your liquor if you're going to make it in the Foreign Service, Toots. Didn't they teach you that at –"

"Yale."

"Bulldogs! Were you a Bulldog by any chance, Toots? You look big enough."

"Indeed, I was. Lineman, played both ways."

"Oh?" She raised an eyebrow.

"Only on the gridiron," I assured her.

"I'm glad, Toots. You're too hunky to lose to the other side."

I smiled.

"Another one for your Aunt Charlotte, if you would, Toots? When you return I shall dub thee Bulldog in honor of Old Eli Yale."

Going, returning, I handed her the egg nog. "Tell me about Aunt Charlotte."

"Charlotte Russell. Charlotte Corday. Charlotte Russe. Charlotte Bronte – Currer Bell, if you prefer. I'm a lot of Charlottes. The Universal Charlotte. Signorina Carlotta. And you, Bulldog, another 26-year-old who thinks he knows everything? So tell me. What do you want to do when you grow up? When you achieve your majority?"

"I don't know how to answer that," I admitted.

"You wouldn't. Scion of wealth, scion of privilege, pushed along like a leaf in a stream. Never had to make a choice. Enough *umph* to graduate Yale. Get in Foreign Service. Good in bed, aren't you? Must have had practice; you're a Yalie. Don't blush, Bulldog, the girls must like you. But what about *you*? Who *are* you? Who's inside? What do you want out of life? When you realize that you don't know everything?"

I just smiled.

"These are hard questions, dear. Maybe the best answer is like the famous Prague strudl. Or the slivovitz. Lovely, tasty; can I have some more?"

It was much later in the evening, the guests having all departed, Willoughby having stumbled off to his quarters, that the staff was helping clean up.

"Well," Ruhle asked, "how did it go with Aunt Charlotte?"

"This and that," I said, "Told me to call her for a good time. Pinched my bottom."

"She does that," Ruhle laughed. "Enjoy it. It's a compliment. A come-on, should you ever need her, although I can't imagine how you would. But if you do, don't hesitate. She's got incredible resources. And a Rolodex in her head that covers three continents." He winked. "For all her flamboyance, she's discrete as hell."

Prague is a city of sighs. Of inhaling and exhaling, of Reformation and Counter-Reformation, of repression and resistance.

The second time, Elena Moravec was more pitiful, tiny, shivering; thin fingers holding the coat buttoned up to her chin, saying she had nowhere to go and was in danger.

With her wisp of an accent she was not quite American but not un-American, either. Almost a speech impediment. I remember thinking that she could easily pass.

"America," she said hesitantly, "is good. America can help me."

I should have said no, told her to leave as I had. She reminded me of that.

"Please," she said.

Passing behind me, McLaren tugged at my coat. I should have listened to him.

"Miss – Moravec?"

"Elena Moravec," she nodded.

"Miss Moravec," I said. "You're not an American citizen. For whatever reason – I know what you said – you don't even have Czech papers. There's nothing I can do. You have to understand that. Please. I have to take the next person in line."

Grasping the counter with both hands, tears rolling down her narrow cheeks, she told me about how happy she'd been during Prague Spring, then how fearful when the tanks came. How devasted when her brother, her only sibling, was shot for being on the wrong side of a barricade. "He was such a boy," she wept. Still, she said, she thought they could survive, she and her parents. But the Russians had lists, she said, and her parents, who were close to Dubcek, were marked as dissidents, sent to a labor camp. Had she been with them during the round-up she would have been taken. Going into hiding, she was able to write to them. When their letters stopped, she inquired about them, for which she had her passport and identity papers confiscated.

"Jacobs!" McLaren, glaring, pointed to his watch.

Seeing him, Elena whispered, "meet me, Wenceslas Statue, eight tonight."

I began to say that I couldn't, but she had moved off.

No, I shouldn't have gone. But I did.

It was dark, crowds flowing up and down. I was early; Elena was already there.

"Thank you," she said, small and demure. "I was afraid that –"

"I came because I wanted to tell you that there's nothing I can do."

Taking my arm as if we were tourists out for a stroll, she began "let me --"

"Miss Moravec," I tugged.

"Elena," she held me.

"Elena," I said.

"Come," she held me tightly, and I felt the electric shock up my arm.

Small, crowded place, students, stains on the walls. She ordered two coffees.

"Your parents," I began. "Do you want me –"

"No," she said quickly. "They are dead. I can feel it."

She drank, then quickly, furtively, head bobbing like a bird pecking at seeds, Elena said that after she found her home being used as a Russian barracks, she stayed for a bit with an aunt outside the city. But when too many cars slowed down to peer into her windows, Elena was invited to leave. Staying a day or two at a time with friends, she knew she needed to leave Prague. "I would very" – it came out *wery* – "much like to go to America. James," she added, faint echo of *Ch* at J. "Please."

"Your English is quite good, by the way. Why is that?"

"I studied it in university. American literature. Edith Wharton. Zane Grey."

"What would you do in America?"

She moved her cup about. "I don't know. I just know I can't stay here."

"You could pass. As an American. If you had the right papers –"

"Could you?" she brightened.

"I don't see how."

"Black market?"

I looked around, furtively and foolishly. "No. You don't want forged papers – passports, visas. Too easy to spot. You'll be in prison for the rest of your life."

"Then how –"

"You'd have to have a real set. Even if you had your own papers we couldn't."

"I can pay."

"How is that?"

"Not here," she shook her head, "not now."

Holding my hand in both of hers, she wept again. "You're saving my life."

"C'mere, Junior," McLaren gestured before I got my coat off.

"Hm?" I said.

"Over here," he pointed to an alcove near the coffee room.

"What's up?"

"I'm only going to tell you this once, Junior," McLaren poked me in the chest. "Stay out of student cafes with skinny little locals who come on to you at the counter."

"What?" I was dumbfounded. "Were you spying on me?"

"Absolutely, Junior," he said, "and it's for your own good. Keeping you on the straight and narrow. So many ways to get lost in Prague. Stray down the wrong street."

I started to protest, but again his finger was in my chest.

"What tale did she spin? No, don't tell me. Let me tell you. Big bad Russian bear chasing Goldilocks. Daughter of dissidents. *That* chestnut?"

"No," I lied.

"It doesn't matter. There's *always* a story, Junior, always bogus. You do not want to walk down the garden path with the first pretty native who appeals to your every altruistic instinct and sings you a tale of woe. You want to stay as far away as you can. You want a piece of ass? You can have my little nurse. Gratis."

"It's not about that," I protested.

"Right. It's not. The minute you tell me it's not, Junior, it is."

"Roger."

"You've already have fallen for her! No. They fall for us, we don't fall for them. Little girl lost playing up to the big brave American. You'll protect her and save her – and at best she'll walk out on you. Disappear like smoke from a campfire. At worst, she'll deliver you to the Russians in return for her junkie boyfriend or her rotten, lazy family." McLaren squeezed my head. "Think of who we are and what we're doing here.

"Bottom line, Junior: Gerard gets wind of this, you're on the first plane back. Kiss Foreign Service goodbye. Which would be good for you, because you don't want to wind up in a federal prison. Or worse. No, Junior, don't thank me."

Of course, I didn't listen.

Because suddenly there was nothing else.

Smart enough not to come into the embassy again, two nights later she stepped out of the shadows as I left for the night.

Putting her finger to her lips, she steered me off into a shadowed side street, then another. After we were certain we weren't being followed, she took me to a tiny flat that she said belonged to a friend.

Leaving my coat on, I demanded that she tell me the story. "Your family. How they survived the Nazis. Russians in '48. Czech purges. What happened."

"There's a lot I don't know," she said, "that happened before I was born or when I was a young child. Did they collaborate with the Nazis? I don't know. They did manage to keep a nice flat, a summer cottage, and a textile business. The Russians? I don't know that, either. Who does, as a child? The dacha disappeared, but my father managed to stay afloat. We were not rich, more like petit-bourgeoise, but many were. The Russians were largely political, not economic, so we were left alone."

"Now?" I demanded.

"My father was a good friend to Dubcek. He thought Prague Spring would last. Now Dubcek is in disgrace, my brother was shot, and my parents," she teared up, then lifted her head and smiled bitterly. "Now that my parents are bourgeois recidivists, and I've been spotted entering the American Embassy, I'm being followed. I –"

She didn't finish, but she didn't have to. No longer able to resist, I took her in my arms. We made love fiercely, desperately, as if each were afraid the other would vanish. Later, Elena held me. "I have diamonds. They ought to be worth –"

From beneath the mattress she withdrew a small velvet bag, opened it, poured the contents into my hand. Magnificent: a dozen, perfect ring-sized stones.

"I have no idea," I rolled them back and forth. "I'll do what I can."

Prague is a city of shadows. Of endless persecutions, eternal deportations, egregious murder.

She answered the phone on the fourth ring.

"Aunt Charlotte?" I asked. "It's Con Jacobs."

"Who?"

"Bulldog."

"Bulldog! I knew you'd come around. To what do I owe the honor?"

"I need to ask you something."

"Right. I hear *that* in your voice. Where are you calling from?"

"Pay phone. Wenceslas Square."

"So it's that, hm? Smart. Someone put you up to this?"

"No. I'm on my own."

"Intriguing, Bulldog. Sexy, even. I know it's not because you can't have a good time with someone your age."

"I –"

"Not on the phone, Bulldog. *Never* on the phone. How soon can you meet me?"

I told her now, and she said Café Milano, near Old Town Square.

"It's as safe as safe gets, Bulldog," she promised. "Biscotti and *caffe corretto*. You won't be on duty, so you can drink. You did learn how to drink at Yale, didn't you?"

I assured her that I did.

Italian-themed, as if Milan had been filtered through Munich; Aunt Charlotte was already *en scene*, chatting with the waiter, a, dour, older man. "My nephew," she introduced me in Italian. "Jean-Claude. The latest," she laughed, "in a long line."

The long-faced man smiled despite himself.

"*Due*," she gestured.

Molto bene, Signorina Carlotta, he said.

With an old-lady's mustiness covered by perfume and powder, Aunt Charlotte's aroma was not offensive, but not entirely attractive either.

"They speak very highly of you at the embassy," I said.

"As well they should, Bulldog. In my day, I was the best. Better than the best."

"Still in the game?"

"No," she shrugged. "It's for young people, no matter how much ice you've got in your veins. And I'm no chicken. Well, in some things, sure. But not that.

"No, Bulldog, I'm very retired – and too tired to spend all night at the ball. Balling, maybe, but not *at* the ball. Besides, the Russians," she shuddered. "To call them bears is to speak badly of bears. They're less than human, less even than ursine. I know this sounds odd, but at least the Nazis had culture. At least they could be charming. These," she waved. "They're simply brutal. Kill then ask questions. If at all." She paused. "Maybe I have arthritis of the soul and am not as nimble as I once was."

I began to speak, but she waved me off.

"I recognize how important this is, Bulldog, or you wouldn't be here. It's a desperate time now. Prague like Berlin, like Vienna, is a transfer point, as a pass-through is more volatile than ever. That's why you're here, isn't it? East to west? No one ever went the other way. Why don't you begin by telling me her name."

I looked around.

"Oh, come on, Bulldog. Who do you think you're dealing with? It's safe here."

When I was done, she laughed.

"Bulldogs and beer blasts and good old Eli Yale. Now you're risking life in prison – or being shot by Russian agents – for some girl. First posting in the Foreign Service, and you're breaking every rule in the book. Is this love or obsession?

"Truth-telling time, Bulldog. Start with, how much of her story is true?"

I shrugged.

"Can you prove any of it?"

I shrugged.

"I was afraid of that. On a scale of one to ten, how much danger is she in?"

I opened my mouth, then closed it.

"I was afraid of that, too."

"She says she needs to get out of the country, and I believe her. My guess is that she'd have to leave as an American. She knows English well enough to pass – it would take a good ear to hear the slight thickening of *th* sounds, the elongation and echo in the vowels. Her lack of knowledge of America – she needs help there. Where to go, what to do. And, of course, a valid passport. I think I can get her one."

"Tall order, Bulldog, how's that?"

"She has diamonds. I've seen them. I'm no judge, but they look pretty good."

"Diamonds. Are they dirty?"

I shrugged.

"You bet they are, Bulldog. How dirty are her dirty diamonds? Let me count the ways. Digested and excreted. Stolen. Bribed. Slathered over in blood. *Mit schlag? Nein, mit blut.* A very great deal of *blut. Der grosse blut.* The blood of every subject people of Europe is all over them. Shot, strangled, starved, gassed. That's the question, isn't it, Bulldog? Does the *blut* ever wash off?

"What's more, Bulldog, diamonds like horses and show dogs need a pedigree. If they don't have one, no reputable dealer will touch them. So you'll have to go to the black market. They'll take 50 percent off the top – assuming you can find someone you can trust, someone who won't just slit your throat and dump your body in the river." She paused. "You need to understand this, Bulldog. Those diamonds are as dirty as dirty gets. Cursed. Bathed in blood and scorched by Satan. They can only buy destruction."

I didn't know what to say.

"You're asking me to come out of retirement, is that it, Bulldog? Help you get those diamonds sold, get this girl out of Prague, get her safely to America?"

I shrugged.

"What's in it for me?"

"Saving a soul? Satisfaction of a job well done?"

"You can't be serious, Bulldog. You're not that naïve. Now I don't mind helping a girl in trouble. These days I'm so far under the radar I could be underwater. The Russians don't know who I am, will never spot me. I'm the perfect courier. And by the time I'm done with her, this little girl could disappear in a crowd – or a telephone booth.

"No, there's a price to be paid, and I want it upfront."

"How much is that?"

"Not how much, Bulldog. What."

"OK, what?"

"I am, Bulldog. A weekend with me. My little in-city *pied-a-terre.*"

"The diamonds?" I asked.

Aunt Charlotte laughed. "I don't want any part of your dirty diamonds, Bulldog. I don't need your dirty diamonds. No, Bulldog, I want *you.* That's the price. Do *not* pity me, Bulldog. I am neither old nor desperate nor lonely. I am just fine. We girls just want to have fun. You want me to come out of retirement? A little fun is the price. You up to that, Bulldog? Weekend off? A little wine, a little bubble bath, *et moi*? Not such a high price to help your friend. A lot less than it's going to cost to unload the diamonds.

"You and I will spend a luscious 48 hours together, a lovely weekend retreat, during which you will satisfy my every desire. Afterward, I will employ all the cunning at my command, Bulldog, and spirit your friend out of the country. Can you live with that?"

"Sure, Aunt Charlotte. I can do that. But can you?"

"Just watch me, Bulldog. Just watch me."

Aunt Charlotte lived in a five-story building on Old Town Square, upscale dress shop at ground level, graduate students on the top floor – a garret where they seemed to be practicing the caber toss. "Clumsy," she laughed, "or awfully frisky." For her part, Aunt Charlotte owned floors two and three. Building owner, Czech cardiologist, floor four.

Her space was simply soaring; the second and third floors were one room, its own cathedral. One entire wall held bookshelves floor to ceiling accessed by a rolling ladder. There were no rooms, no walls, instead a series of sliding wooden partitions that could separate areas – cooking, reading, bathing – the latter an outsized tub raised on a platform like an altar. "By the time you're done with the bath salts and the bubbly," she caught me looking, "the wine and dinner and me, you won't feel a bone in your body. And you'll never sleep better in your life."

Per the latter, she gestured at a bedroom loft on stilts, accessed by a circular iron staircase – "scavenged," she said, "from a derelict church outside Prague. My architect and contractor are brothers," she said. "Corsican Brothers; they think like one person."

Crossing to the bath, she turned it on, poured in some sort of lavender powder which smelled like a sweet shop. "Takes a while to fill," she descended, gave me a glass. "Slivovitz in the meantime, Bulldog. Warms you, gets you in the mood."

Aunt Charlotte was as good as her word. Dousing the lights, she lit scented candles all over the room – a ghostly, ecclesiastical feel. Stripping into a bathrobe, she gestured that we should ascend to the bath. "Don't be bashful, Bulldog. Just relax."

As she took off her bathrobe and stepped gingerly into the tub, I looked at her old woman's body, flaccid and swaying. As she saw me looking, she turned to me, displaying herself. "It's easy, Bulldog," she smiled. "Just let it happen."

Lying in the bath, Aunt Charlotte stretched and fondled me. "Nice," she said. "Room for expansion, Bulldog. First, tell me about yourself."

"Difficult to concentrate now," I protested.

"You're a Yalie, Bulldog," Aunt Charlotte insisted. "Give it that old college try."

With the candles and the plum brandy and the bath making me dizzy, I had to close my eyes. "James Connelly Jacobs, dba Con, never Jacobs, never Jim.

"Family 19th-century Germans. Came to America, harness makers to trucking to transportation. Married Connellys, Irish, scows to tugboats to shipping. Staten Island to New Jersey, hauled freight for a century. Sold out. Safe, long-term investments. Moved to Bala Cynwyd. Republican. Ivy League. Country club. Learned to play golf.

"Played ball for Yale, simple and direct – two steps this way, stop the other guy so our halfback could get through. Or our linebacker. Nothing complicated, no finesse.

"Skull and Bones. Dad a member; sure, why not? Recruiting station for State, Foreign Service, CIA, all the quiet wars. Some things above board. Some not. My entire credential, other than not being expelled from Yale. Don't know why Skull and Bones, drunk frat boys with chamber pots on their heads, qualifies us, but perhaps they have standards that I don't see. Breezed through my interviews – American political theory a strong suit – took the training course. After two years of paper-shuffling and coffee-fetching in Washington, I was sent on the road. Domestically, then here, just in time for the pupa of the Russian winter to become the chrysalis of Prague Spring. Then back to another Soviet crackdown, steady stream of people of all party, politics, and persuasions snaking into the embassy seeking Uncle Sam's sanctuary.

"I'm a junior-grade Foreign Service Officer, Consular Division. Staffing not a desk but a counter, there to speak politely; write down names, numbers, and nominal desires; send the seekers to the requisite office – or back to the street."

"Why aren't you in Vietnam, Bulldog? You look big and strong enough to whup them thar entire Viet Congs yourself."

"Four-F. Messed up my knee playing ball. Besides, deferments are easy to get. Foreign Service. Connections. My father owns a Congressman and half a Senator."

Flickering all around bathtub, the candles' light reflected off the walls' dark wood. At dinner, too, white table cloth, wooden cabinets (caged from a monastery, she said), dark windows, the candles gave the room a hall-of-mirrors effect. The light flattered her, as she no doubt knew. As did Janacek's *Glagolithic Mass* playing softly as background.

Lobster bisque, sauvignon blanc, langostino, cobb salad, Bordeaux, chateaubriand, port, brie.

"And you?" I asked. "The legendary Aunt Charlotte?"

"Later," she smiled. "First, more of us.

"Nice and slow, Bulldog," she lifted the covers. "Make it last."

Aunt Charlotte woke me in morning with French press coffee, some rich, exotic blend from Africa. I had never had anything like it.

With the buildings across the Square, shrouded in fog, Old Town Square looked like distant memories.

"Over easy or over hard?" Aunt Charlotte smiled at me.

"You?" I asked. "Me?"

"Your eggs, Bulldog. With fresh dill, camembert, French bread, chardonay."

"All yours," I said, coming around the toilet partition.

"The space," she asked, "or what's coming out of it?"

"You're pretty good, Bulldog, you know that?" Aunt Charlotte raised herself onto one elbow. "Let's see if we can make you better. Many unnamed females, will thank me."

"Again?" She snuggled against me.

"What we said on the gridiron. Always fight in a 'dog.

"Good puppy," she patted me.

Saturday night, after slivovitz and sausage, a delicate weisswurst.

"OK," I said, putting down my napkin, "I told you my story. Now it's your turn."

"Bulldog's going to lead on the dance floor," she laughed. "Nice to see you assert yourself. OK. Montana, Big Sky country, where the silence is endless and winter really turns your head around. Miners. Range riders. Part of the one percent who struck it rich. I got lucky twice. First, I inherited a piece of a modest copper mine, enough to keep me in *strudl undt schlag*. A quarter, actually, the proceeds split between four of us. My daddy had four children. He inherited the mine from his daddy, who found it and worked it. Four of us, equal shares. Second piece of luck: an uncontested will. We all got equal shares and nobody fought about it. Meant if I was circumspect, I'd never have to work again in my life. And I haven't.

"We grew up friends. Funny, how money can drive you apart. One of my brothers – my older brother, George – did try to steal it all. That's what lawyers are for. My sister Anne – well at some point I committed some unspeakable crime, or at least she thinks I did, for she no longer speaks to me. What was the crime? I have no idea. That's what makes it unspeakable. Then there was my little brother Bobby. Poor Bobby. Bobby always loved being a hellraiser. Loved being a cowboy – literally. Rodeo rider. Too many broken bones. Too much self-medicating. Bobby died young.

"I got away from those people. Had to. I was 30, had to leave. Europe in the '30s. Sure, there was danger, and things were changing – often too fast for anyone to control. But life was cheap, and I met a boy – not here, in

Paris. He was beautiful, like you, Bulldog. Czech, wanted to come home. We came home, lived in a garret. Very romantic. It was time for him to move on. But I stayed. Prague is so --"

"Full of shadows," I offered.

"Very good, Bulldog. All that high-priced Ivy League education hasn't gone entirely to waste. Shadows. Plato. Never see the reality, just what plays on the cave wall. Sure. Maybe that works when the Third Reich isn't here – and they were here soon enough. Anyway, could have left. Maybe should have left. But I liked it. Liked my new life. The Europeans smelled money, so I had many offers of marriage. Turned them all down. Had a fine time with my lovers. Had a salon. Gave English lessons.

"Storm clouds gathered. Could have returned home after the sell-out and before the war, but chose not to. Why not? Inertia? I don't know. Maybe I was just young, foolish, romantic – like you, Bulldog. I felt immortal. I bet on the Czechs – and won. The war never did come here. OK, the Nazis did, and the deportations, and the Resistance. It was dangerous, Bulldog, I won't deny that, but it was also thrilling. Made the heart beat fast. A great aphrodisiac, Bulldog, not that I needed one," she laughed.

"Made a good courtesan – got laid for the cause. Many, many stories, Bulldog," she stretched, an aged feline, "for another time. The Nazis loved screwing me – I was an Aryan, real German blood. Their exotic, red-haired, Aryan-American. What a hit I was! Flamboyant. Best cover of all. Nazis, epitome of narrow, one-track minds. Couldn't possibly see me as the False Duessa. Hardly had to work at cover. Misdirection. They never would think of an agent like me. They never figured out that a little Prague pillow talk had anything to do with a Brno troop train blown to bits.

"An army has many weapons employed for the cause, including that tasty little Charlotte Russe. *Mm-hm.* Oh, don't look so surprised, Bulldog. My code name: all those luscious red strawberries. All that scrumptious whipped cream. Men can't think when it comes to that, anything below their belts. Remember that, won't you?

"I knew them all. Heydrich. Very impressed with himself. An odd mixture of charm and cruelty. Cut an impeccable figure in that tailored uniform. Stunning, really. An absolute monster. I had to work hard not to shiver when he touched me."

She drank and poured and drank again. "The Germans were so cultured, intelligent, charming that I could almost forget who they were and what they were doing." She paused. "The music, the medals, the meals – all exquisite. So were the people who disappeared. Neighbors. Friends. Lovers. Stores changing owners overnight. Flats going empty, new neighbors the next day. It was a terrible time.

"I learned quickly not to ask leading questions, not even to look. Followed the dots – or let my control do it. Made a good courier, too. Knew how to feign innocence, minor outrage at being questioned. Dropped the right names. Knew how to stare down apparatchiks. How to be nimble, improvise, be fast on my feet." She smiled. "Because these were Nazis, after all. They were good at their work and they liked it. They liked cleaning out Prague. They liked killing what they couldn't understand or control. They also liked the buildings, the arts, the Kultur, which is why they kept it all. Unlike the Russians, who seem to hate everything and appreciate nothing. Would have torn down the entire city except the end didn't seem worth the effort. Resistance never abated, but the Russian bear – a truly slow-witted creature – never seemed to get it.

"Anyway, Bulldog, yes, I was a stop on the underground railroad, then, in '48 and after. Of course, I knew Masaryk. Not well, but I knew him. Small country, and I travelled in the right circles. Still do. In '56 helped the odd Hungarian. Many, *many* of them found their way into Prague. I did what I could."

Aunt Charlotte smiled. "Got a couple of medals around here somewhere. Made me an honorary citizen. Means they like having me around, but not enough to let me vote. Apparently, they can't either, not these days, not in any meaningful way.

"To sum it all up, Bulldog, I loved faking them all. Women learn to fake a lot of things. Not with you, Bulldog. You're the best. Or will be when I'm done with you."

It was Sunday, after what she euphemistically called matins, after French toast and Greek olives and Italian coffee. And prosecco.

Time to talk business. This time after a stroll through Old Town Square, to a small café where the men scraped their chairs and rose to let an older woman in a flaming red scarf and black walking stick walk magisterially to the last table in the rear.

"It's all right, Bulldog," she said. "We can talk here."

After the young African waiter carefully placed two *cafes mit schlag* and two honey-laden *marlenkas* before us, Aunt Charlotte took a sip and smiled. "Life's always better *mit eine bissel schlag*, don't you think?"

She pulled her chair closer and spoke quickly. "If Elena's everything you say she is – don't look that way, Bulldog, I don't doubt you. I doubt *her*. You must be very careful, very circumspect. Otherwise, you'll get her shot. You have to understand these people. They're not like us. They're heartless. They'll shoot her and not think about it.

"It's good that she has diamonds. Because she's going to have to pay cash for everything – no paper trail. You can sell them – I still have contacts – for half their retail price. From that fifty percent, you'll have to pay for her papers. Wardrobe. Tickets. Room and board. Emergency fund sewn into that black coat you said she always wears. She won't have much left when everybody takes their cut, but that's all right. Aunt Charlotte will take care of her until she gets settled – where?

"Right now, I don't know, so don't ask, Bulldog. If she's ever traced to you, you won't have any answers. With a valid American passport, and no one on her tail, we can build her a new identity. You need to understand this: the first price you paid was a heavenly weekend with your Aunt Charlotte. It was heaven, wasn't it, Bulldog?"

"You bet, Aunt Charlotte."

"Good boy. You'll go far with an ability to lie like that. The second price is that you can't communicate with her for at least two years." She squeezed my forearm hard. "*At least two years*. Once she's clean and clear you can see her. Don't look so downcast, Bulldog. She's not all that special and you know it. This is what passes for a shipboard romance in Prague. You'll find she's a different person once she doesn't need you. Trust me, Bulldog, I know every dodge in the book. Including all of hers.

"It's better for you. If anything blows up, you'll have complete deniability.

"Come on, Bulldog, you're a good catch. Some hot chick will get you."

Pausing to look at the famous clock – its gears and levers, signs and statues, wheels upon wheels inexorably grinding out the time and the seasons and the sway of the planets – Aunt Charlotte took my arm again. "Elena will need guidance in America," she said. "Hence the need for Aunt Charlotte to take her. We can't simply dump her – with a forged passport and no place to land – and hope she'll survive. She won't. At best she'll be spotted, sent back, and imprisoned. In all likelihood shot – like the rest of her family. I'll figure it out. I've got some ideas, nothing concrete. Montana's nice this time of year. OK, maybe not," she laughed. "First I'll get her a hearing aid."

"Hm?"

"A fake one, but that'll account for her linguistic slowness and slight accent. It's great cover – no one thinks to question the handicapped. Tricks of the trade, Bulldog."

"Clever," I said.

"Yeah, ain't I?" she said. "It's been 15 years since I've been back. 1953. A long time. My mother's funeral. Tough old bird, lived to be 83. Crippled. Arthritis. Lost all 10 toes to frostbite. Montana winters are *not* for the faint of heart. Enjoyed being back in Big Sky country – for a day. Shopped at Marshall Field in Chicago. Came right back.

"Find someplace to keep her 'til we get our arrangements together. You cannot stash her in my flat, Bulldog. I don't want her tailed to my place. I don't want the KGB or CIA sniffing around my door. Find somewhere else – and keep her under wraps."

I nodded.

"Don't worry, Bulldog. I've spent my life dodging the bad guys. Nazis. Ruskies."

Aunt Charlotte squeezed my hand. "You're sweet, Bulldog, don't lose that." She reached up to kiss me on the cheek. "You must love her very much."

Then she was gone.

Prague is a city of silence. Of statues torn down, streets renamed, people exiled.

It was not symbolism; we chose one of Prague's many cemeteries because we could easily spot anyone around us. And we knew we couldn't be overheard.

Carrying flowers to place reverently on a random grave – the names all alphabet soup to me – we walked beneath a canopy of leafless brown trees.

"First," I said, "we're going to change your name. Elena is now Eleanor. Moravec is now Moore. You should practice until it becomes second nature."

"Eleanor Moore." She spoke hesitantly, English a distant second language.

Stopping, she put the flowers on a grave and slipped the bag into my pocket.

As we turned around, I glanced at the gray stones, fallen trees, scattered leaves. Beyond us, dark hills, gray sky, vast silence. As we walked, I knew I needed a way to make her case compelling. Headstones. Of course. The rules applied – except when they didn't. Bereavement moves you immediately to the top of the pile, generally no questions asked. Oldest dodge of all. Easiest misdirection. Death in the family.

Aunt Charlotte told me to walk slowly and circuitously, to check for tails. Nearing his door, I moved swiftly down the three steps. "I'll let him know when you're coming," she had said. "He'll know you. You can trust him. More important, he'll trust you."

Ostensibly selling printed material – postcards to pornography – the little shop was dusty and deserted. Looking up from the magazine he was reading, a thin man, round glasses, weedy mustache, unbuttoned vest, rested his cigarette on the rim of an overflowing ashtray. "Sparta chain smoker," she told me. "Filthy Czech cigarettes."

"You're he," he said, a statement not a question.

"Yes," I nodded. "You are –"

"I change my name as often as you change your shirt. Don't ask my name."

Sweeping aside his magazine, he deftly laid a black cloth on the desk top.

I gave him the velvet bag.

Card shark in another life; dealing diamonds paid a lot better. Taking a jeweler's loupe out of one pocket, tweezers from another, he looked the stones over quickly, then each one, individually and slowly. Finally, he took the loupe off his glasses and put down the tweezers. "Good," he said. "Cut well makes them better. Matched makes them best. Not antique, but pre-war. Where'd your friend get them?"

"I really don't know." I paused. "I didn't ask."

"Better that way," he nodded.

Quickly, he took out a small notebook and a pencil stub and did his sums. "Call it two carats apiece," he said, "at $12,000 a stone, that's $144,000. Premium for a matched set. Turn-of-the-century. Call it $200,000. Half equals $100,000. American."

"Done," I said. I had barely gotten the words out when he began twirling the knob of a small safe hidden beneath the desk.

With a highly active – and effective – black market in passports, papers, and visas, some were better than others. Prime beef was something real, especially from a country with the power to back it up – like America. So it is hardly an overstatement to say that we were deluged with requests. Of course, Willoughby had nothing to do with it; it fell to Bill Gerard, who took a dim view of everything. Everyone, every request, every story required not only triple paperwork but also extensive personal interviews.

Which meant I had to be severe in initial data collection, because if I sent someone up the line who eventually bilged out, I was reprimanded for wasting his and the embassy's time. As Gerard put it, for every failure he'd cut me a new one.

Normal channels wouldn't work; they required opening a job jacket for every approach. Color codes – dots affixed to upper right-hand corners – for likelihood, danger level, veracity. Records had to be meticulous – a bean-counter's dream.

Elena Moravec, first approach duly noted, rejected. Second approach, file amended, duly rejected. Case closed.

Of course, that's not where it ended. It proceeded. Off the books.

Why not plead her case? No papers. Not an American. No chance to intercede. Gerard? His entire life was spent avoiding risk. Ruhle? He'd smell a rat – and try to flip her into a spy. Or burn her to the Russians in exchange for something he wanted.

That left Jack Kirchener, and dealing with him would be tricky. I had thought about slipping the request in the pile, but he'd kick it out and demand documentation.

Instead, I forged an entire file. I had filed enough of them to know how to do it, so I simply invented who Eleanor Moore was going to be.

If Ruhle, in his basement listening post, was a raffish fellow – bright, charming, bending the rules this way and that – Kirchener, in his fourth-floor aerie, was slow, controlling, officious. Ex-Navy, refugee from an aircraft carrier, Kirchener had run his ship's press – daily menus to the daily newspaper. A gnome, he had badly cut red hair, thick glasses, aprons and arm guards over shirt-and-tie. The glasses, magnifying his eyes triple fold, gave him a perpetually puzzled look. Perhaps he was.

In a world of cheap ballpoint pens, scuffed linoleum floors, and scratched gunmetal desks, Kirchener oversaw three assistants in his print shop, producing everything from handbills and circulars to visas (a premium now that so many Czechs and others were trying to depart the premises) and passports, the latter for those foolish Americans who had lost theirs or had them stolen. Of course, to receive a replacement these Americans had to have the requisite paperwork – or wait for it to be shipped from the States – a process that normally took weeks.

The November morning was still dark and cold when I pushed Eleanor Moore to the front of the queue. "Morning, Jack," I said. "I have the odd request."

"Hm?" He didn't look up. Couldn't be bothered looking up at a junior officer.

"Passport," I said, speaking in bullets so he'd understand me. "American. Stolen. Needs to get home. Mother passed. Sudden. Funeral. Iowa. Bereavement."

"Paperwork," Kirchener demanded.

"Can't. Stolen. I believe her."

"I believe in paperwork."

"So do I. But isn't there provision for citizens who need to get home?"

Finally looking up, he blinked. "I don't know what they taught you at Yale, Jacobs, but here's what they taught me in the Navy. By the book. Get it in writing and get it right, sailor. Maybe they don't believe in that in the Ivy League. Maybe they believe in fudge factors and fairy godmothers. I really don't give a good goddamn what they believe. Get the paperwork, Jacobs, *all* the paperwork, or get out." He paused, and his outsized eyes seemed to eat the entire room. "And assuming you do, I'll be back to you in twelve days. Best I can do."

"Two problems. Funeral end of the week. Purse snatched. Wenceslas Square."

"Highly irregular," he objected.

"We work in a highly irregular business, Jack. Highly irregular time."

Kirchener took off his glasses and rubbed the bridge of his nose. "So I'm supposed to run up her papers on a wing and a prayer. On her say-so."

"Since you put it that way, Jack, yes."

"And why would I do that? It violates —"

"I know what it violates, Jack. I'll vouch for her."

"You're a junior officer, Jacobs. A *very* junior officer. Probably screwing this chick. Who are you to vouch for anyone? Besides, it's my ass if this goes south."

"I'll make it worth your while."

"Jacobs, are you —"

"Let me put it this way, Jack. I mean no offense about anything. I just know the kind of expenses you have. Wife at home. Very special friend with very expensive tastes who very much believes that every American is very rich. I could help."

"You bastard."

"Actually, Jack, my parents were very much married when they birthed me. But we're not talking about me, we're talking about you."

"I ought to turn you in."

"Of course you should. But you won't. Because I can help you."

He put his glasses back on.

"This passport is worth fifty thousand dollars. A third now, Jack, to get you started. The remainder when you produce it. Tomorrow."

Before he could answer, I put sixteen thousand dollars, in one-hundred dollar bills, one at a time, on the table in front of him.

Kirchener looked down, looked up, looked down again, and swallowed.

"Greed, self-interest trump rules and regs. That's what they taught me at Yale."

The trolley was crowded and slow, so I was late getting to the small Catholic cemetery on Prague's outskirts. As I came into the stone chapel, plain and musty and long unused, Elena was kneeling at an altar before a statue of the Holy Mother. Whispering, she crossed herself, kissed her fingers, and rose.

"I was afraid you wouldn't come." Holding me, she began to weep.

"We should walk," I said. "With a purpose. Visit a particular grave."

"Yes," she took my arm. "James – " again, it came out *Ch*ems – "do you –"

"Yes, I have your passport." Elena slipped it into an inner pocket of her coat.

"It's going to take three things for this to work," I said, holding the door for her. "First, I need some article of clothing you're not going to want back. Underwear, preferably. Something you've worn but not yet washed. Some hairs from your brush. And something, even a small wash cloth, with your cologne."

She looked quizzically at me.

"Red herring," I said.

"What?" She was genuinely confused.

"False scent." Literally, I thought

"Hm?"

"I'll plant them. If they're following you, they'll think you were there. They'll waste watchers on it, looking for you in the neighborhood. But you'll be elsewhere."

"Where?"

"Second, pack a single suitcase and move out of your flat. Tonight. Go out the back of your building. Try not to be seen. Move in with your friend on Smetana Street. Don't go out. Don't use the telephone. I'll come and see you tomorrow night, get your underwear, give you final plans. There'll be someone to take you. You'll be her niece."

"You're not coming with?" she quivered.

"No," I said. "It won't work. We'd be spotted." I paused. "Third, I won't be able to see you for a while."

"Two weeks?" she began to cry.

"More," I said. "Much more."

"No," she said. "I will miss you too much. I won't be able to live without you."

"You can," I said, "and you will. We have to make certain you're completely safe. I'll know where you are, and when its safe I'll come."

"How long?" Elena asked, but I put my finger on her lips.

"No more questions now. One thing at a time."

I had no idea if anyone was following me – I hadn't been trained at spotting a tail, and had missed McLaren in Wenceslas Square – but I was hardly furtive as I went to the embassy's safe house where they stashed folks being smuggled out of the country.

A word over coffee, a word in the lunch room, and it was easy enough to find where it was. Nice little place, two stories, cozy mews, well-tended flower garden with sentimental statues and a concrete fountain. Could have been a cottage in Sussex.

Key where it was supposed to be – beneath the flower pot on the porch. Small, homey, Czech provincial – wood floors, low ceilings, white walls with white trim, sentimental renderings of the nearby countryside, lights off, cupboard bare. Small attic; good for a second couple, guards, children.

Mussing the bed, putting her hairs on the pillow, I tossed a damp towel on the bathroom floor, wiped her cologne on the dresser and sink, dropped her panties behind the closet door. If McLaren finds them – if McLaren it is – he'll be proud of himself.

Completing the cover, I washed a coffee cup, put it in the dishrack, turned on a couple of lights, drew the curtains, snuck out the back. Through the vegetable garden, between a brace of cottages, into the next street, and gone.

I made a point of going to the airport, bought a plane ticket in Elena's name. For the time being it would draw them there.

They'd be watching the airport – the obvious way out. Elena couldn't leave that way, but Eleanor could. Except. They'd give her American passport the once over, then again, then trip her up. They were pros; it'd be easy.

So Aunt Charlotte, along with her freshly minted niece, would be taking the train, not to Vienna, which itself was the more obvious transit point, but to Venice, where they'd use their American passports, board a nonstop flight for New York. Nobody'd think to look for her in Italy, so they wouldn't.

Little bit of Bulldog razzle-dazzle. Misdirection of a good football play. Never know where the ball is – until it's 15 yards too late. I was a lineman; all I had to do was open a hole. Gale Sayers said, "just give me 18 inches of daylight." That's what I did.

Predictably, McLaren was furious.

"Where is she?" he demanded.

"Where is who?" I asked, feigning innocence.

"You know who I mean. That little Czech cooze who got her hooks into you."

"Roger," I said, "you told me to stay away from her. I followed orders. To answer your question, I have no idea where she is."

"You're a liar."

"Now you're getting personal. And why is this little Czech so important?"

I knew, of course that Elena Moravec didn't matter one iota to America, the American Embassy, American intelligence. What she mattered to was the Russians. Which meant these were deep waters indeed, ones in which I did not want to swim. McLaren as Russian agent losing face with his handlers because he lost this easy prey. McLaren as Russian ally returning a favor. McLaren as American agent swapping Elena for person or persons unknown. And so on. The scenarios were legion.

"Where is she?" he demanded.

"You said she'd disappear," I shrugged.

Prague is a city of shrouds. Of church bells tolling the dead, funeral processions, bodies bobbing in the River Moldau.

When Aunt Charlotte's letter arrived, Tony the mail boy whistled. I just smiled.

Dear Bulldog, she began.

Surprised that I'm writing like this? You must have read Poe's "The Purloined Letter" in some American Lit course at Yale – when you weren't chasing coeds, that is. Best place to hide is in plain sight. Nobody looked for me all those years. Nobody's looking now. Pink, perfumed stationery, purple ink. How's that for cover, Bulldog?

Sit down, Bulldog, you'll love this. Your Aunt Charlotte was hornswoggled.

I coached her. When we get to passport control, look them in the eye – they want to match the picture with the face. Act as if there's nothing the matter, that it's nothing more than going to the post office. That you've done it 1,000 times. When we get to New York act as if you belong there – you're an American. You have a sense of entitlement. When they say *welcome home, Miss Moore*, smile and say *thank you*.

At first, I was afraid: she seemed such a frightened, vulnerable little creature. Demure Czech girl. Then, relief! I have to hand it to her, Bulldog. When it came time, she was good. Damn good. So good I should have smelled a rat. I didn't.

She played her part all the way, train, passport control, plane, JFK – there's a third-world country! Fitting memorial to that monumental screw-up of a President. Right through passport control – *welcome home*, the exhausted, overweight INS clerk grunted at us. He barely looked at her. Why should he? American passport and all.

Story writ small, Bulldog, is that I lost her. Within 10 minutes of collecting our bags. After I stepped aside to powder my nose, and other delicate parts of my anatomy, she was gone. Vanished. I didn't overdo it, Bulldog. Didn't make a fuss. Looked around a bit – she might have gone to the newsstand – then left straight off.

Sure, maybe she wandered off and couldn't find her way back. Maybe she was snatched. But I don't think so. Not enough time to set it up, and far too public. Maybe she got squirrelly and ran – where? Maybe she was picked up by her Russian handlers in New York. Maybe she had a pre-arranged rendezvous point. Maybe she was an American who needed a new, laundered identity and conned us out of it. Maybe maybe maybe. My favorite five-letter English word. That's how I survived the last 30 years – on maybe. With a little bit of cunning, I'll keep going for the next 30. And more.

In any event, Bulldog, she's gone. Skedaddled. Your job: let it go. Looking for her, in any way, will only draw attention to you. At worst you'll attract some KGB assassin – you'll never see him coming, Bulldog. At second-worst, you'll find the Feds – aiding and abetting. Twenty years in lock-up – with a 300-pound cellie named Bubba.

I know what you're thinking: you have friends in the District. That they'll help you. Maybe they will. But I lived through McCarthy, Bulldog. I've seen friends lie and jump ship and switch sides faster than a cockroach on a hot griddle. Friends evaporate, Bulldog. You do not want to become an example, Bulldog. You do not want them to go after you. You have no idea what havoc they could wreak on you – and your family.

Find another girlfriend, Bulldog. And when you sleep with her, think of me.

I'll be back in a couple of months. Maybe less. I'd ask you to water the plants, but by that time you'll no doubt be gone. Better for you. They'll suspect you, but don't let them humiliate you. You're worth the lot of them. You just don't see it yet.

Don't feel too bad. She had me fooled, too, and I'm pretty good at it.

Think of her as your Dirty Diamond, Bulldog. You're better off without her.

Bottom line: you can never look for her, Bulldog. *You can never look for her.*

Burn this right away. *Subito.* Flush the ashes. Be done with it. Forever.

As for me, Bulldog, I'm at the famous Plaza Hotel – Scott and Zelda, more American Lit. Shopping galore – Saks, Bloomies, name it. Met an absolutely scrumptious Mexican named Manolo in the Palm Court. A doll – at least for the time being. He promised me washtub-sized cocktails at Trader Vic's. Who could resist?

Who'd want to?

TTFN

XOXO

Aunt Charlotte

Gerard did not take long.

He waved me to a chair, grunted. "I'll eschew the preliminaries," he began. "It would only insult your intelligence and waste both our times. I can't prove anything. And I don't care to. Too much time. Too much energy. I'm not firing you. I don't need the backlash. The lawsuits. The reprimands from a Republican administration. I'm telling you that I don't think this service is right for you. The Foreign Service has a chain of command. We need all hands on deck. Not loose cannons who follow their own agenda. Make us look like we can't run our own ships. Get the rest of us in trouble. You didn't, here, but you will, sooner or later, and the results – well, they may be slight or they may be severe. You don't want to be around for the latter. You were in way over your head on this one and got away with – beginner's luck. But luck has a way of leveling out, and you won't be so lucky next time. Law of averages.

"We don't like being made fools of," Gerard laced his fingers over his vest. "But the Russians *really* don't. We'll slap your wrist and send you to bed without supper. They'll shoot you in the back of head and dump your body on the embassy steps."

Gerard was hardly finished, but as he belabored his point, I thought, McLaren, of course. Couldn't have been Kirchener; he was too vested. Ruhle couldn't have known. No, McLaren either plays by the rules or caught the Russian disease and informed just to inform. Maybe he promised her to his Russian counterpart – call him Vassily. Vodka nights together. Trading girls. How McLaren got away with it was a mystery. Perhaps everyone traded across the barbed wire. Perhaps proteksia on top of proteksia.

I couldn't blame him. McLaren was the farthest thing from bright, didn't have many resources to help him up the ladder. He'd *have* to step on people.

"There's no I in team," Gerard was saying.

"They used to say that when I played for the Bulldogs," I smiled.

"I know all about your family's friends. You can play that card if you want – I'd be a dirt-farm Kansas Democrat up against all those blue-blood Pennsylvania Republicans. Sure, you could wind up in Venezuela or Honduras or the Philippines. Or I could make a big fight. And I'd win. Blackball you. With everything else going on, Hugh Scott won't go to the wall for you. But more than that, I don't think you're cut out for this kind of work. I don't think you'd do well over time. Aside from being a lone rider and ignoring protocols, your heart's on your sleeve and your head's in your pants. Sooner or later, that'll cost you. It'll cost all of us." He paused. "Never get in a fight you can lose."

"We ought to think about that in Vietnam," I muttered.

"That may be, Jacobs, and regardless of military policy and your undoubtedly expert take on it, I think you should resign. If you do, now, no black mark in your service jacket. Nice letter from me." Gerard paused. "I don't know if you learned about price in Bala Cynwyd. And I don't care, because it's a valuable lesson you're learning now. There's a price to be paid for everything.

"You'll do well elsewhere. You've got connections. You're solid, responsible."

"Down lineman, sir."

"Put those skills to work. Just not for Uncle Sam. Refugees tug at your heartstrings? We're not going to run out of refugees any time soon. Red Cross. UN. No, not the UN; what a waste. Resign. Say it's not for you. Refugees not right? Go back to Bala Cynwyd. I don't think you're right for the law, but you might surprise me. Sell financial packages. Real estate. Jaguars. You know the right people."

No, I thought, not Bala Cynwyd. A little too clubby. Not long enough legs. Connecticut's better. Along the coast. Old Saybrook. Guilford. Learn to sail.

Earn a master's in history, get a high school teaching certificate. Wear bow ties and sweater vests. Become Mr. Jacobs. Coach football. Basketball. Track and field. Not baseball. Never got the subtleties. Needed something with more strength, more ball. Shotput and the shotgun not the squeeze play. Marry well – blonde, gung ho wife and mother, PTA, station wagon, raise soccer-playing children. Barbecue on Sundays.

Standing, Gerard walked away, swiveled, growled, "I hope she was worth it."

You can never look for her.

Prague is a city of sorrows.

FRANKIE IN PRISON

▼

MEINERT, PENNSYLVANIA

By the time he goes on trial, dead to rights and field-dressed like a deer, Frankie in Prison has no more clout, no more political capital to spend, nothing left to trade to make his case easier or more sympathetic. Instead, Frankie in Prison is going to go away, and everybody knows it. Everybody. Everybody from the Mayor, Bill Roland, who more or less engineers it, or least doesn't prevent it, down to the least literate laborer on the public works lobster shift. Entirely out of options, broke, bereaved, bereft, there's nothing the once-powerful Frankie in Prison can do about it.

Two months prior, still living in hope, Frankie in Prison ducks into Jerry's Shoe Repair, hoists himself onto one of the old wooden chairs, and beams. *Get a shine*, he says, *change your luck*.

Of course it's true, and of course it works. Just not the way he wants.

Baptized Francis Xavier Halloran, Jr., Frankie in Prison never knows his father, who buys it in the navy, thereby ensuring that his son will never be called Junior. Raised, more or less, mostly less, by his overworked mother, Frankie in Prison grows up on his own, in South Oakland, the southern half of Wrightsville above the river, running every hustle in the book – pop-bottle return to grocery hauling, snow shoveling to car parking. Calling himself X, he switches when a 13-year-old Central Catholic classmate tells him about Malcolm X. Immediately becoming Frank, he says, *leave it to the coloreds to cock up a good thing*. Later, as he gains both physical girth and political stature, he takes the diminutive and more familiar Frankie.

Finally, he becomes Frankie in Prison, a name he never shakes.

Antipathy to African Americans is also something Frankie in Prison never shakes. When he's first proposed for Council, he finds to his relief that Council District Four, its gerrymandered border skittering about like a pole dancer, contains virtually no people of color. Rather than lump them with the Irish and Italians in Four, they've been placed in District Three, where they can vote as a block – and of course can be controlled. Quite openly, Frankie in Prison expresses true joy over this discovery, despising what he calls *those* people. Considering them unnecessary evils, Frankie in Prison describes them as both uneducable and ungovernable.

Later, on Council, Frankie in Prison is civil to all his colleagues regardless of race, makes common cause when he has to, but will go no further. Standing on principle, he refuses to attend their churches, dinners, or picnics. He invites none to his.

Still later, in FCI Meinert, Frankie in Prison stays as far away from them as possible, barely speaking to them in the kitchen, the unit, the yard.

What Frankie in Prison calls a dapper man who claims to be a reverend, and who is doing a bit for receiving a small ocean of stolen goods, all of which he claims are legitimate contributions to his ministry, is not fit to appear in a family publication.

Barely surviving Central Catholic High School, Frankie in Prison goes to work for the City's Parks & Recreation Department – really a Party recruiting station. Virtually everybody is vetted at Parks & Rec, where kids like Frankie in Prison are tested for ambition and alacrity, allegiance and alertness. Taking orders, running errands, anticipating the Party's needs, he proves his mettle by staying both silent and stalwart.

Judged by a series of harsh, alcoholic taskmasters whom Frankie in Prison generically dubs *death warmed over*, he matriculates with straight A's.

Tagged as an up-and-comer, Frankie in Prison enters politics for two reasons: being in government beats working for a living, and that politics floats on a sea of loose cash. There's *always* something to skim, Frankie in Prison sees, and he wants it all.

Invariably smooth, always ingratiating, Frankie in Prison remembers names, needs, relationships. Even Bill Roland – no slouch – says he has a real gift.

Frankie in Prison also has a real gift for doing people favors. Then for reminding them that they can do him favors in return. An even greater gift is that he never overdoes it, is never out of line. He's glad to be of service, equally glad to collect.

Considered a natural, when old man Jowers – the legendary Bull of Bates Street – retires, Frankie in Prison is put up for City Council. Of course he wins handily.

While Frankie in Prison's District Four takes in a half-dozen city neighborhoods – from the river north to just this side of the silk-stocking district, and to the west of the African Americans – his base is South Oakland, a warren of narrow streets populated by immigrant families, miners and millworkers on Dawson and Semple Streets. Tailors and tavern owners on McKee and Bates. Bakers and bar keeps on Ward. Greengrocers and shoemakers on Halket. Butchers with fresh rabbits and river fish on Park Place.

Assuming office, Frankie in Prison quickly realizes --- meteoric learning curve here – that everything is tuned. Everything. Nothing is static; everything is active. Everything exists for taking advantage, for looking good, for accruing political capital. For the all-important daily victory.

For the re-election campaign that begins the day after the election.

Roland knows all that, of course. So does the FBI. But they can't account for how quickly Frankie in Prison spreads his nets. Because what his case file should say, but doesn't, is that Frankie in Prison is a small-timer from a world of small-timers – adult newsboys and school janitors and ballpark ushers, people with too much month left at the end of their money. People with hustles going on the side, something to stretch the cash, something to keep them away from the number and the vigorish and the short-term loan-shark money. People cutting hair in their living rooms. Providing day care. Driving jitneys. People with a stash hidden away for the proverbial rainy day. Maybe even a go bag for the day the rain comes down in sheets.

People who keep everyone else away from their hustle.

So when Frankie in Prison goes away, they more than forgive him. They understand him. Because he's who they are.

So they come to him for help because they have nowhere else to go. They don't know anyone – and couldn't afford it if they did.

And they come to him because government is not about fairness. Progress. Public policy. Social justice. Whatever the current jargon might be. Instead, government is simply a bigger hustle. A way of getting some of it back to people who need it – and remember who it comes from. And take the time vote him back in office.

Frankie in Prison never takes their money. He takes Other People's Money. And brings it back to them.

And if getting some of that involves Frankie in Prison taking some of it for himself, that's just the price of doing business.

And if business means getting pinched and doing a bit, well, such matters are understood. Everyone in South Oakland has someone inside. Everyone, sooner or later. No shame. Part of life. Rite of passage, inevitable, like the army or death.

In South Oakland Frankie in Prison is like everybody else.

Largely indifferent to Council Chambers, Frankie in Prison barely glances up at the grand arched ceiling, the romanticized mural depicting Guyasuta welcoming George Washington with corn stalk and peace pipe, William Penn gesturing westward, Sieur de la Salle kneeling in prayer.

Never got me a single vote, Frankie in Prison shrugs, *so what do I care?*

Indeed, the title, setting, historicity – none of this matters to Frankie in Prison. Just so long as his neighborhood gets its fair share – and maybe a little more.

And that the balance sheet – *his* balance sheet – is in the black.

Taking his seat, Frankie in Prison is the perfect Party apparatchik, voting Roland's agenda, barely speaking, introducing neither legislation nor initiatives.

Supporting his fellow Councilmen, the Party, and the Mayor, Frankie in Prison makes sure that what's needed gets done – snow removal, water and sewage problems, police and fire protection, domestic disputes kept off the police blotter and out of the public prints.

Given his standard three Councilmatic aides, Frankie in Prison rightfully considers them Roland's spies, tells them nothing, and replaces them as soon as possible with three South Oakland lads loyal only to him.

Also awarded his share of perquisites, including a car, Frankie in Prison spends as much time in the district as anyone – more, really.

Really does his job, Roland's amanuensis Garth Childress grudgingly says. *Not much we can hang on him.*

Frankie in Prison also makes the acquaintance of every department head who could possibly acquire and/or approve goods and services for the City. Inspectors at the Bureau of Building Inspection. Appraisers at Lands and Buildings. Purchasing agents at Parks and Recreation. And all their counterparts at Water and Sewer, Public Safety, Housing, Emergency Medical, Fire, Environmental, anyone who can buy, rent, or borrow so much as a pencil.

The acknowledged master, one newsie writes, *of the silent, inside game.*

The other side of that inside game is that in the city – any city – there's an endless array of people offering goods and services. Everything from pens and paper to temps and tires. Paving and painting and parts replaced. They all need entre. Introductions. Sometimes they need a price tip-off or a bid rigged.

Sometimes they're willing to render a gratuity for such services.

Sometimes said gratuities find their way to Frankie in Prison.

Throughout, Frankie in Prison knows the delicate balance of potlatch, of symmetry, of give-and-take, of favors granted and obligations owed, of knowing when to collect a debt and when to forgive it. When to fight a wrong and when to forget it. When to take Normandy and when to retreat at Dunkirk.

At first, that's where Frankie in Prison's artistry shines. The Cezanne of Council. The Stravinsky of South Oakland.

Sure, Frankie in Prison believes in transparency, in public scrutiny, just as long as scrutiny means the tip of the iceberg, the top 7th, leaving the remaining 6/7ths out of sight and as far away from the public as is humanly possible.

It's Frankie in Prison's first Easter on Council when he realizes that he needs extra cash – a *lot* of extra cash – to stay in business. With the tidal wave of requests – demands, really – as immense as it is incessant, he simply cannot say no. Churches, schools, lodges, charities – everyone is having a spring dinner, ad book, raffle. Easter basket.

Everybody.

And everybody comes to see Frankie in Prison.

And when he goes to see them, he has to cover meals – including generous tips. After-hours bar tabs. Bottles of liquor.

Plus taking care of the down-and-outers who need an irregular hand-out or regular meal. Bags of groceries for the shut-ins. Even a new suit for little Jimmy to wear to his First Communion.

Doing his sums one night, Frankie in Prison pours himself two fingers of John Jameson, then another two, and rewrites his marketing plan.

First, Frankie in Prison reconsiders public office. *I've had it wrong*, he thinks. *I don't work for the public. The public works for me.* Meaning that unless there's a compelling personal reason to move on anything – money to be collected, favors to be cashed in, votes to be counted, good press to be garnered – the standard operating procedure is to do nothing. *I do nothing*, Frankie in Prison says, *until they make it worthwhile: campaign contributions to contract kickbacks to outright bribes.*

But there's a limit to everything, and at first Frankie in Prison understands that. Discretion. Carefully culled clientele. Nothing electronic, especially the telephone.

Then he doesn't. A trickle here, a rivulet there, and pretty soon it's a full-scale flood. Frankie in Prison's finely honed sense of entitlement – greed, if you prefer – finally gets the better of him. Drowns him.

It's not one toke over the line, Childress says. *It's the whole damn kilo. It's a banana republic's GDP – and then some.*

As part of his myopia, Frankie in Prison never takes Bill Roland's point that successful politics is win-win – everybody gets a piece, everybody goes home happy. Which is why, in part, there are numerous Wrightsville buildings named for Roland.

Understanding that Council – and his access – could go away at any time, Frankie in Prison has a garage full of cigarettes, a backyard beer garden, even parking spots that he rents. A nice tidy sum on the side. No scrutiny. Certainly no taxes. Just a little of this and a little of that.

He hopes that it will put him in good stead for life.

The best-laid plans being just that, when the time comes Frankie in Prison has to sell everything – even his house – to pay his fines, court costs, and legal fees.

Meaning that by the time he's back after five years away, Frankie in Prison is more or less destitute.

Make that more.

Taking his ease, Frankie in Prison desperately loves taverns, Cozy's and Coyne's and especially Jimmy O'Hara's Emerald. Frankie in Prison especially enjoys strolling in, nodding to Patsy, big-bellied and beaming behind the bar, barking *Irish whiskey, neat, and take one for yourself.* Which Patsy does. Two full pours, clink, nod, knock back.

Always happy to give back, Frankie in Prison becomes legendary for his annual picnics – summer Sunday, pavilion in the park, cornucopia of corned beef, cabbage, coleslaw. *The goal,* Frankie in Prison says, *is to spread around a little largesse – and make certain that our less stable brothers make it home safely. They vote, too,* he adds, sanctimoniously, *sometimes more than once.*

Perhaps Frankie in Prison's most notorious moment – other than his arrest, trial, conviction, and incarceration, of course – comes at an otherwise routine City Council meeting, at which Paul DeFazio, an effete, flower-wearing dandy from the North Side, proposes opening offices in every city neighborhood. Meaning budget-busting additional staff, real estate, upkeep, transportation, and so on. Roland doesn't like it, so Frankie in Prison doesn't, either.

While the proposal eventually fails, it is still in play when Frankie in Prison mutters, *more hacks and queers on the payroll.*

Hm.

As Councilman DeFazio's blood pressure visually spikes – high enough to wilt today's pink carnation – he dares Frankie in Prison to settle matters outside. To his credit, Frankie in Prison takes the proverbial high road and uncharacteristically keeps his mouth shut. But that is hardly sufficient for the newsies, who, like cicadas, thrum on Frankie in Prison's *bon mot* for a solid two weeks, excoriating him for gross insensitivity, hate speech, dreadful homophobia, and assorted other crimes against humanity.

Which is all fine, laughable even, because with Council elections entirely by district it hardly matters what anyone outside of Frankie in Prison's district thinks of him.

In South Oakland, Frankie in Prison, hailed as a hero, is more popular than ever.

Having been carried by Roland and the Party the first time, the re-election means that Frankie in Prison is on his own. Indeed, one of the many reasons that Frankie in Prison remains unrepentant – head bloody, certainly, but unbowed – is that he comes to understand that politics is not merely costly but is indeed the black hole of American life. Aside from the regular pay-offs – dinner tickets, ad books, sports banquets, seasonal baskets, and so on – there are campaigns. Literature. Lawn signs. Media. Posters. T-shirts. WAM – Walkin' Around Money – to pay for gas to ferry people to the polls, donuts for the poll workers, lunch for them that needs it.

All cash. All up-front. All union rates.

How am I supposed to generate this, Frankie in Prison asks his friend John Jameson, *on a City Councilman's salary?*

Sitting with his aides – three hungry Irish lads – on Election Night, Frankie in Prison, cheaters perched on the end of his nose, is tallying votes.

Got all but five votes on Semple Street, one young man – his name matters far less than the fact that he's Ward Chair Ed O'Hanrahan's nephew – says admiringly.

Pausing, setting down his paper, looking at each young man in turn, Frankie in Prison simply says, *get me the names of them five sons of bitches.*

So at a time of his life when he's old enough to know better, Frankie in Prison really falls in love with money – and the power to get it.

Of course, there's a price to be paid for his chrysalis, but, in deep denial, Frankie in Prison ignores the very idea of consequences.

Charging for access, macing contractors, shaking downs builders for permits, Frankie in Prison is suddenly swimming in money, Bill Clinton selling nights in the Lincoln Bedroom.

As Frankie in Prison brags, enjoying an afternoon draught at the Emerald, *a little larceny is good for the soul. Sharpens your wits. Makes you work a bit harder.*

While Frankie in Prison has come to believe that he's larger than life, he doesn't have the shoes for it. Real larger-than-life guys get a pass on their misdeeds because they are, in fact, larger than life. By contrast, guys who merely think they're larger than life wind up doing time.

Drinking American rye whiskey in an after-hours place, Garth Childress confides to Perry Rascoe, a beat-up, boozed-out newsie whom he trusts, that Frankie in Prison is *too clumsy. Too obvious. He's forgotten First Principle, that people don't mind being fleeced as long as you at least give the appearance of pulling the wool over their eyes. So that they don't really know they're being fleeced. Or at least have plausible deniability. That the snout in the public trough is only taking its fair share.* Childress signals for another. *Bottom line: Frankie in Prison is not sufficiently devious.*

He also forgot the FBI, Childress continues. *Forgot that FBI guys get promoted by putting away guys like Frankie in Prison. So not only do they have a natural antipathy toward guys like Frankie in Prison. They also have a vested interest in scuttling his ship.*

Childress sighs. *Frankie in Prison got lazy. Stupid. Sloppy. Clumsy with the phone. Greedy past Planet Saturn. It'll be easy enough to send him up. He's giving them their entire case. They'll never have to break a sweat.*

Neither will you, when it comes time to write your story.

Yes, Frankie in Prison has friends. Many friends. Many, many friends. Who warn him assiduously. Walk away, Frankie in Prison. Walk away clean. Walk away *now*.

Convinced he is both invulnerable and invisible, Frankie in Prison does not listen. His little bit of larceny is now an obsession. An addiction. A pathology.

Being far less interested in Frankie in Prison *per se* and far more in avoiding any scandal which will affect the Party, Roland calls in Frankie in Prison.

Truth be told, Roland warns him, *it's fine to be venal, Frankie in Prison, but you're overdoing it.*

For the record, this is Mayor Bill Roland, of the good-politician-is-the-one-who-stays-bought school, of the it-doesn't-matter-what-our-story-is-as-long-as-we-all-agree-to-it school, of the pol-who-tells-the-best-lie-is-elected school.

That Bill Roland.

And when Frankie in Prison does indeed overdo it, the hawk-nosed wiseacre Garth Childress is the first to recommend cutting him loose. *If it were done when 'tis done,* he quotes *Macbeth,* his favorite politician, *then 'twere well it were done quickly.*

Roland barely nods.

As which point Childress picks up the phone, makes a single, brief call, and knows that by morning everybody will be walking away from Frankie in Prison.

It's a miracle that Isaac Redmond, the Party lawyer, stands up for him. Well, he has a fee to earn.

Faced with a literal mountain of evidence against Frankie in Prison, US Attorney "Battlin'" Bob McAuliffe just shakes his head. *This isn't even a slam dunk,* he says. *This is a mail-in. Frankie in Prison has been heedless. Headstrong. Downright self-destructive.* He pauses. *The trial might take, what? Eight minutes?*

In court to be arraigned – the wood-paneled room smelling of old leather and pencil shavings – Battlin' Bob is suitably stern. *You're going away, Frankie in Prison*, he says. Although Frankie in Prison hangs his head, he figures he can skate on the charges.

He will shortly discover that he is very, very wrong.

With the counts in the indictment piling up like corn stalks at harvest time, Frankie in Prison asks "Red Nose" Redmond, *can't you just make all this go away?*

Against his will, against his wholly fictitious but highly self-serving self-image as the moderate, measured Spencer Tracy in *Inherit the Wind*, Redmond laughs out loud. *I'm your lawyer, Frankie in Prison*, he says, *not a magician. Not Penn or Teller. They have you cold on everything. Everything. The best we can do is hope that you get a fair shake at sentencing – which will hardly be easy, Frankie in Prison, because you left a phone and paper trail a mile wide. Trail? It's a trench. I hope that your health holds out, Frankie in Prison, that you don't die inside. You really don't want to do that.*

By the way, Frankie in Prison, he adds, *all the costs, and the fines, and my fees are cash up front.*

Hardly chagrined, Frankie in Prison proclaims his innocence so loudly and repeatedly, and with so much piety, that he actually begins to believe it himself – all witnesses, wiretaps, and writings to the contrary.

Furthering his own cause, Frankie in Prison creates a choir of well-wishers who sing his praises in the hopes of ameliorating the tsunami of testimony against him.

Of course, it doesn't help one iota, but an unintended and absolutely useless consequence is that the newsies can now write so-called balanced stories.

In addition, Frankie in Prison threatens a firestorm of countersuits for harassment and entrapment and what-have-you, until Redmond wisely counsels him to cease and desist. *They have you, Frankie in Prison, they have have have you*, he says. *It's so open-and-shut that it's shut before it's open. So the easier you make it for them, the easier they'll make it for you.*

Although it's contrary to his nature to back down from anything, Frankie in Prison, faced with that overwhelming logic, engages in a strategic retreat.

That doesn't help either, because they're really angry with Frankie in Prison. *Really* angry.

No, they're not throwing the book at me, Frankie in Prison says. *They're throwing the whole damn library.*

The federal judge, the dour Puritan "Maximum" Bill Bertrand, given to bow ties and long faces, makes it clear he's going to make an example of Frankie in Prison, a civics lesson about what happens when a public servant abuses a sacred trust.

The show trial is brief but bloody: the Feds have it all, the defense stipulates to everything, the judge is infuriated. The newsies follow the script to the letter.

Flagrant, Battlin' Bob says, *is clearly too mild a word for Frankie in Prison.*

Expiate the sin. Expurgate the evil. Nothing drives a story like a good villain, and Maximum Bill makes Frankie in Prison's trial a morality play of the first order.

Maximum Bill also knows that people love to see the dark side of themselves, then see it punished – the hapless, helpless child who's wet the bed.

Nearly snarling in the courtroom, Maximum Bill looks down at Frankie in Prison, clumsy, ham-handed, moon-faced.

Five years, fines, costs, fees. Frankie in Prison, newly crowned as the pol who's sold favors, which means every pol, neither contests nor appeals.

Among many other things that Frankie in Prison forgets is that the newsies are not his friends. They're not *anybody's* friends. They're bottom feeders who *love* burning anyone to the ground. So they *love* his story. *Love* making him the sine qua non of rampant political corruption.

They feed off his story for months.

Balance be gone, by the time they're done with him, there's nothing left.

Of course, Frankie in Prison's sentence initiates a series of public debates, in print and from the pulpit, about the worth of incarceration. For healing the body politic? Justice? Catharsis? Deterrence? Punishment?

As political profit center, long-term employer, patronage premium? All of the above?

Nothing like a good public debate to get the blood going, but none of it matters to Frankie in Prison, who's going away.

Getting his affairs in order, Frankie in Prison understands that Roland and Childress and all the others never forgive and never forget. So he's not merely burned his bridge to the Party, he's more or less taken it out in an airstrike.

Because he's committed the one unpardonable sin. He's made everyone look bad. He can never make that right. And so can never return. Permanent exile. Shoeless Joe Jackson and Pete Rose: banned for life.

You're going to be a straight arrow from now on, aren't you, Francis? gentle, kind Father Dave asks Frankie in Prison just before he's taken into federal custody.

Oh, yes, Father, Frankie in Prison answers piously.

You're a rogue, aren't you, Francis? Father Dave presses, having none of it.

Yes, Father, Frankie in Prison answers, chagrined, but not sufficiently chagrined to do anything about it.

While FCI Meinert is in the middle of nowhere geographically – ostensibly for security – politically it's at the center of the universe. Needing that north-central county to cement a win in Pennsylvania, the party in power sends a ton of money Meinert way – through a Senator, the Congressman, friends at the state and county levels – publicizing the tally sheet at every opportunity. Constructions jobs. Supply jobs. Corrections jobs. Teaching and medical and legal jobs. Light and power and water – it's a gold mine.

And it works.

With its long, low Modernist lines, FCI Meinert is one of the more humane prisons, or so it's considered in the Great Society, circa 1965. Lot of glass in the front building – shatterproof, of course, but plenty to let in the light and the forest. The surrounding fence, more formal than functional, is just a reminder, really, because FCI Meinert's inmates aren't going anywhere. Turn jackrabbit, they are warned before they arrive, and Corrections will add five years to your sentence. And you'll be going to a prison with walls, lights, and towers. More razor wire than a diamond mine. So as short-timers, men who count the days more than the years, they aren't running anywhere.

Frankie in Prison's first approach to FCI Meinert is hardly foreboding. There are locks and doors and fences, sure, but nothing grim or gruesome. No lights. No towers. No wall. It is, after all, Camp Cupcake, a minimum security facility for non-violent offenders. Bucolic setting, pine forest, deer nibbling the foliage, squirrels scurrying underfoot.

Frankie in Prison finds that he is indifferent to all that. Indifferent to the landscape, to the marked changes in season – green to gold, brown to white, and back again. A city boy, he never cares what birds are in the murmuring pines and hemlocks. He misses the Emerald and John Jameson. He misses Semple Street.

In processing, Frankie in Prison is arrayed in jewelry – more chains, he thinks, than a city snow plow.

Surrendering his personal effects, making a joke of it, Frankie in Prison discovers that the intake officers, while polite and efficient, are not in the least interested in small talk. Meaning that none of the charm that works so well for him at home works here.

Photographed, fingerprinted, issued standard prison gear, escorted to B Block, Frankie in Prison wants desperately to vomit.

When it's lawn-cutting time, FCI Meinert produces a whirlwind of dust and pollen. Afflicted, Frankie in Prison suffers from bouts of sneezing, wheezing, watery eyes. *I'm going to be the first inmate ever to die of green lung disease,* he grouses, missing concrete-clad South Oakland more than ever.

Warden Dickson peers at Frankie in Prison across his prison-gray metal-topped desk. He is an ugly man, squat, clean-shaven, humorless. Frankie in Prison immediately despises him, then realizes that that is perhaps the point.

We're in the lesson-teaching business, Frankie in Prison, the warden says. *You tarred us all with the same brush, every public official, everywhere, elected or not.* The Warden shrugs. *So we have some special lessons for you. As will become clear.*

I am here, the Warden adds, *to teach you those lessons, Frankie in Prison. And you are here to learn them. You will do so whether or not you want to learn the lessons, whether or not you like the lessons. You will do well, Frankie in Prison, never to forget that. So learn those lessons.*

Frankie in Prison understands that the entire administration – warden to white shirts to blue shirts on down – is *not* in the rehabilitation business. None of them believes in rehabilitation anyway. Instead, they all presume that every inmate needs to be straightened out. And straightening out begins with consequences – generally, the more severe the better. The more puissant the more powerful.

This is something that civilians – not the press, not the ACLU, not the rest of the tree-hugging do-gooders – will ever understand, Warden Dickson says. *But you will, Frankie in Prison. You most certainly will.*

That's lesson number one, Frankie in Prison. There'll be other lessons as well. That's all for today.

Frankie in Prison is also told by Warden Dickson, and everyone down the line, that since he has had troubling following rules, another great lesson that he will learn in FCI Meinert will be how to follow rules, *all* the rules, every single one of the rules, no matter how petty or arcane they may seem. *Because, Frankie in Prison*, he is told, *rules are rules, not meant to be broken*, never *meant to be broken. You are responsible for them, for following them, all of them.*

We will teach you how to follow rules, Warden Dickson tells Frankie in Prison in the manner of a school marm. Extra *rules. Because you were on the take, so flagrantly and so long. Special handling, Frankie in Prison. Special handling indeed.*

You made wrong choices, Frankie in Prison, Warden Dickson says. *We're going to teach you how to make the right ones.*

Speaking of being in the penitentiary, speaking of being penitent, Frankie in Prison has time to be penitent. Eons of time to be penitent. At work, in his cell, on the chow line, Frankie in Prison is indeed penitent. Exclusively about getting caught – and about his idiot lawyer who couldn't get the charges dropped.

Frankie in Prison quickly discovers that his fellow inmates are divided into two unequal parts: bad guys and screw ups. While the former, a much smaller number, are seriously evil people, the latter are generally banal and benign; addicts, addled, angry; illiterate, idiots, illegals. Never really learning coping skills – how to deal with appetite and occlusion – they are clumsy and quickly caught.

Like Willie White, Frankie in Prison's first cellie, an impossibly hairy, odiferous man who's in for price fixing and postal fraud – and figured that nobody was watching.

If there's one thing for which Frankie in Prison is grateful, it's that he's in Camp Cupcake, reserved for non-violent white-collar inmates who are not flight risks. At least at FCI Meinert he can enjoy the illusion of freedom – and not have to pass through multiple locked doors to move.

For the first time in his life, Frankie in Prison is faced with people whose power derives elsewhere, who don't care whom he knows.

To the contrary, the Feds despise pols like Frankie in Prison as inherently evil, fish waiting arrival in their nets.

The Feds being something of an occupying army.

It's the Whiskey Rebellion all over again, Frankie in Prison says. *No wonder the South rebelled.*

Ironically, Frankie in Prison finds an instant kinship with his fellow inmates. Because successful pols, like cons, instinctively see the weaknesses, appetites, or guilts in their fellows and can exploit them to their benefit.

Frankie in Prison quickly discovers that everyone inside is innocent, absolutely innocent, as-pure-as-the-driven-snow innocent. Why are they here? Their lawyers are incompetent. The Feds have it in for them. They catch a real Hanging Judge. Who is coincidentally up for re-election.

At first, Frankie in Prison expects gangs. But FCI Meinert is Camp

Cupcake after all. No one has the interest or the energy. They're doing easy time, will be out soon, don't need the hassle, or the heat, and have virtually nothing to prove.

If FCI Meinert has a motto it's *Lay Low.*

Frankie in Prison quickly learns that doing his nickel has nothing whatsoever to do with being corrected, or even about justice. It has everything to do with being punished.

To his credit, Frankie in Prison takes his trip to the woodshed like a man.

Frankie in Prison also learns, from hard personal experience, what it's like to be moved from B Block and placed in Special Housing, there to be caged like an animal. For the rest of his four years, eight months, and twelve days, he assiduously avoids such a fate. Although, Frankie in Prison, being Frankie in Prison, does fall once or twice. Make it twice – for tissues in the trash on inspection day and a shirt hanging outside his locker – and twice more because they want to (they don't need a reason; they already have a reason). Fortunately, for those infractions Frankie in Prison is merely placed on report.

Special Housing? For what? Frankie in Prison demands to call his lawyer.

Lawyer? Warden Dickson says. Lawyer? *Don't make me laugh, Frankie in Prison. There aren't any lawyers here. Just a dozen inmates ready to testify to what they saw you do. As in took a swing at a guard. That's five more years on your sentence plus transfer to maxi. So do yourself a favor, Frankie in Prison. Do what you're told. Do your bit and get out on time.*

At FCI Meinert, Special Housing is the euphemism for being locked alone in a cell for the better part of 23 hours. Showering while being chained to a wall. Walking about a small patch of asphalt behind a spanking-new chain-link fence.

If it's minimum security, Frankie in Prison thinks, *then they don't need acres of perfect greenery and a new fence. Well, the Feds do know how to spend money.*

After his week-long visit Frankie in Person has learned the value of following the rules, no matter how minor or arbitrary. Or nonexistent.

Of course, everyone has a job, and working in prison is difficult, depressing, and dispiriting, none of which Frankie in Prison realizes at first, until he sees that no one there is going to be charmed or hustled.

His first job – because he has to be put in his place – is cleaning showers on A, B, and C Blocks. Sure, it's dirty, and sure, Frankie in Prison hates it, but at least he ends each day smelling like Pine Sol. Frankie in Prison figures it could be a lot worse.

After his six-month review, Frankie in Prison graduates to the dining hall, which isn't so bad, except that he sincerely hates the food.

Waking up early every day, he lumbers off to the industrial-strength kitchen, lighting ovens, dumping sacks of powdered eggs into oversized vats, turning on the coffee urns. It's sweaty, wet work, but Frankie in Prison performs it well.

Even if he did not work in the kitchen, Frankie in Prison would be disgusted by the bill of fare. But seeing how it comes in and is processed, he finds it outright nauseates him.

Which actually works to his benefit. A porker when he goes in, with heart-attack-waiting-to-happen written all over his flushed map-of-Ireland face, Frankie in Prison sheds the avoirdupois like an ace – and so lowers all his bad numbers.

Meaning that when he walks out, he's far healthier than when he walked in.

Indeed Frankie in Prison's detractors – and he has many of them – expect him to become bloated on the high-fat, high-carb prison fare. To the contrary, cut off from his habitual carload of suds 'n' spuds, Frankie in Prison, slimmed down and svelte, drops 120 pounds and three suit sizes.

Frankie in Prison learns, too, he will only survive by being useful. Frankly, the administration couldn't care less what happens to him – they can always chalk up an early and unexpected demise to suicide, heart attack, or a particularly virulent and previously undetected cancer. Survivor that he is, Frankie in Prison learns the fine art of shutting his mouth and doing his job.

Frankie in Prison also doesn't care for badinage. Chit-chat. Small talk. No talk at all that doesn't add something to the balance sheet. Another account in the ledger. Additional tribute to the laird.

Talk, indeed all language for Frankie in Prison, all human interaction, exists solely to be saved, bartered, traded up.

None of that works at FCI Meinert.

Away, everyone misses something. Indeed, that's a large point of being inside. No matter how sanctimoniously Corrections officials bleat about rehabilitation, about any of the Corrections babble he has to endure in the weekly sessions with his counselor, a large dollop of punishment is plain and simple deprivation.

For many men it's women, of course. For others, it's liquor or drugs, although both are available inside, generally inferior, inevitably costly, but still there.

For Frankie in Prison it's neither. What Frankie in Prison thinks about, in his cerebral case file, is out. O-U-T. Out. More than anything, more, even, than palatable food, what Frankie in Prison misses most is South Oakland. Walking down the street, making deals, planning the future.

What Frankie in Prison misses most is the hustle.

One of the favorite games on the unit, at chow, in the yard, is discussing where they'll go when they get out. Predictably, many inmates talk about sand, sun, and surf. Miami. Maui. Santa Monica.

Not Frankie in Prison. All Frankie in Prison wants to do is go home. Back to cold, gray Wrightsville, South Oakland by the river, cracked sidewalks, all-night diners, ice in the gutters. When the other men – hair too long, shaves not taken, uniforms ragged and wrinkled – laugh at him, Frankie in Prison shrugs, then smiles.

Like everyone else inside, Frankie in Prison hates counts almost as much as he hates strip searches. Counts mean dropping everything and scampering back to the unit to be reminded of your name and number.

Jesus, Frankie in Prison thinks, as close to true prayer as he ever gets.

Frankie in Prison marvels at how spotless FCI Meinert is until he remembers that it's staffed by 1,100 inmates – all of whom have jobs to do.

Frankie in Prison despises the layers of gray institutional paint, the carbolic acid odor which does not quite mask the stench of vomit and urine and diarrhea. He hates the walls, the bells, the metal-upon-metal sound of locks and keys. He hates the endless, ill-fitting khaki uniforms. He hates the incessantly tasteless food just this side of rancid. He hates the inmates who never bathe because they're afraid of the showers. Or who hate water. Or who try to make themselves as obnoxious as they can.

Looking at the dull paint, Frankie in Prison wonders if this cheap, thick stuff is specified – or perhaps Dutch Boy is and Warden Dickson whispers something in Purchasing's ear, the bid is undercut, and they split the difference.

Of course, Frankie in Prison has no idea, but he certainly hopes so. For government exists to be fleeced.

Especially here, in backwoods Meinert, PA, where, out of sight is out of mind, and nobody, but nobody, is watching.

Put another way, who's going to come and look?

Put a third way, who's going to complain about it? The inmates?

Put a fourth way, he will be profoundly surprised – and greatly disappointed – if the warden doesn't get a piece of everything that passes through the gates.

Under the walls. Around the back.

Put a fifth way, after performing some rough calculations, Frankie in Prison finds the amount of money involved in running a prison is truly breath-taking.

No wonder it's *the* American growth industry, he thinks, with two million of his fellow citizens behind bars, growing every day, even at the border. Because prisons make money and generate jobs for every municipality they're in. And all this money, all these jobs, are magically transformed into votes. So despite the fact that for most prisoners all prison does is teach them how to deal with prison, and give them a record that will more or less ruin them for life, the system will never change and never go away.

Time on his hands, Frankie in Prison learns all the lingo for his current domicile: do a bit. Do a stretch. In the joint. In stir. In the slammer. The Big House. The Clink. On Uncle's Nickel. Away.

Away! he discovers has the greatest currency. As in, Frankie in Prison is going away for a while. And not just him – everyone else. Everyone stays away. Family. Friends. Constituents. Pols. Especially pols, who don't want to be spotted within a hundred miles of FCI Meinert. Which is why, on the third Sunday of every month, Frankie in Prison stays on the unit, playing pinochle with an undocumented Mexican marijuana mule named Octavio Vasquez, out of sorts and out of options, who thinks badly, rarely bathes, speaks virtually no English, and is awaiting extradition to some Latino country with bad water and worse leadership.

Attempting to communicate back home, Frankie in Prison finds that his letters and phone calls go unanswered. As he is damaged goods, he is studiously ignored.

Understanding the dictum that only true friends visit you in the hospital or in the joint, Frankie in Prison realizes that he has neither.

Finally, one idiot cousin, Herky from Altoona, writes to Frankie in Prison, asking if he can come see him. Since Cousin Herky is repetitive, inane, and tiresome at best, Frankie in Prison turns him down with such finality that Cousin Herky never asks again.

Considering that Roland, his supposed friend and mentor, has turned his back on Frankie in Prison faster than the March wind, Frankie in Prison later says *I would gladly watch him drown. And now would not be too soon.*

Doing his stretch, Frankie in Prison outlasts a succession of cellies, including Willie White, his first, and Vasquez, who got left holding the bag, literally and figuratively, when the FBI raided a crack house in Williamsport.

Then there's Bob Berko, a wiry, iron-haired, goateed White Supremacist who relentlessly preaches race hatred and repeatedly informs Frankie in Prison that the Irish are nothing more than albino niggers.

And Rose Jones, born Ron, a flaxen-haired transsexual meth head whose nose runs constantly and has virtually no short-term memory.

None, however, is more odious than a rogue phlebotomist named J.J. Boehmer who professes a love of blood, wets his bed, and never flushes the cell commode.

Beset by paranoia, Frankie in Prison is convinced that Warden Dickson is deliberately afflicting him with these misfits.

Truth is the process is entirely random, Frankie in Prison being blessed that way.

In Corrections hierarchy, white collar felons are considered worse than the lowest brain-dead gangbangers. Because the too-dumb-to-live lowlife never really thinks about what he does. Given the challenges of the moment, he simply makes bad choices.

But men like Frankie in Prison have plenty of time to plan. As such, Frankie in Prison's sole regret is that he was too close to the street. That his sights were too low.

Instead of macing painting contractors, he thinks, it should have been financiers.

There is loose talk – and that's all it is, loose talk – about the President pardoning Frankie in Prison. Or at the very least engineering a parole. Of course, the rumor eventually reaches Garth Childress, who, gifted mimic that he is, affects the President's bemused Midwestern bluster. *Let him out? Where's the bonus in that? Where's my political capital? Pardon the Crooked Councilman who done my friends in Wrightsville dirt? And have the newsies cry cronyism? This will not happen on my watch. On my watch Frankie in Prison will do his entire bit. Every minute of it.*

Good to their word, the Feds make Frankie in Prison do it all. Even though it's the other Party, and even though he merits parole, they don't want to endure even the hint of favoritism to a fellow pol.

So Frankie in Prison stands up for the entire five-spot.

Sentence up, it's time for Frankie in Prison's farewell chat with Warden Dickson.

No doubt a day you've long awaited, Frankie in Prison, Warden Dickson says. *You're leaving us.*

Yes, Warden, Frankie in Prison says, *yes, I am.*

You're a changed man, Frankie in Prison. You know that.

Yes, Warden, Frankie in Prison says, *yes, I do.*

For the better, Frankie in Prison, don't you think?

If you say, so, Warden.

Don't you think so, Frankie in Prison? Warden Dickson presses.

Frankie in Prison looks up at the Warden, at the cruel creases around his eyes. The shirt collar too tight. The diplomas and certificates hanging from his concrete block walls. The photos of Arthur B. Dickson in flaming orange hunting gear, holding aloft the head of a 12-point buck he's shot; waders on, fishing with his two look-alike sons; being awarded Federal Corrections Professional of the Year by former Vice President Quayle. The ceramic trout rising off the standard issue metal desk. The just-this-side-of-uncomfortable standard-issue gray couch and chairs surrounding a faux-wood coffee table holding outdoors and corrections magazines.

Yes, Warden, Frankie in Prison says. *Yes, I do.*

At discharge, Deputy Warden Higgins, a dour man in a three-piece blue suit and matching tie, wordlessly processes Frankie in Prison's paperwork. A man with enough government service points to warrant three retirements, DW Higgins survives all his Bureau of Corrections years as a dedicated bean counter – with no more humor or humanity than a Buick. Handling Frankie in Prison, he never looks up at him, never says good luck, never shakes his hand. He simply gives him Inmate 641-7743's paperwork and walks away.

Frankie in Prison's release is perfunctory. He signs for his personal effects – including an engraved money clip, a memento from Roland – and waits for the guard to open the glass doors that will return him to the world.

On a blustery March morning, Frankie in Prison walks out of FCI Meinert, out of the Great Society foyer, hearing the keys turn the lock one last time. Not looking back, he walks directly to the car arranged to take him to the St. Agnes halfway house, between Meinert and Wrightsville. Neither he nor the driver speak.

Riding through pine forests, Frankie in Prison finds himself relieved. He is grateful for the unencumbered sunlight, for the moist air outside the car.

Frankie in Prison is grateful, too, for the silence.

After a rare moment of introspection, Frankie in Prison feels nothing.

Sharing a small, second-story room with a quiet young man who'd posted child pornography on the internet – he claims innocence, of course, saying it was a mistake, or drugs, or a favor for a friend; the story keeps changing – Frankie in Prison watches six months of seasons, bags groceries at a 7-11, takes thrillers out of the public library, attends all required meetings, and largely keeps to himself.

Of course, having been away, and effectively erased, for five years, Frankie in Prison loses all his connections and clout. *Persona non grata,* he can't even get a City job raking leaves. Indeed, no one, but no one, returns his phone calls.

On Semple Street, all over South Oakland, everybody turns their backs. No wants to know him. When Frankie in Prison passes people sitting on their porches or their stoops, they get up and go in their houses. The silence is deafening.

Even Father Dave, having been transferred out of state, is no help.

To his chagrin, and surprise, Frankie in Prison has never heard of the woman who's taken his Council seat. Wife of a rich boy from the north end of the district, she isn't even a native. Frankie in Prison has trouble believing it.

He thinks about leaving, but has nowhere to go. Having neither the will nor the wherewithal to move out of Wrightsville, he moves into a small apartment overlooking the park. Filing applications all over town, he finally hooks up with Home Depot where he stocks plumbing supplies.

Apparently, Frankie in Prison thinks, the manager never reads the newspapers.

Thin, then thinner. Gaunt, even. Sallow. Having lost his hair, his cock-of-the-walk attitude, Frankie in Prison is almost unrecognizable. A husk of what he once was, lessons learned, he's survived.

Frankie in Prison is a shadow in an orange apron.

One day, an old-timer in gray pants and a light blue windbreaker wobbles down Aisle 13, looks, looks again, then walks over to a slight, slender man unloading a cart.

Hey, he says, sticking out his hand, *ain't you Frankie in Prison?*

Yeah, Frankie in Prison says, eyes lighting like an ember then going dark. *Yeah, I used to be.*

THE GREAT
McCLURE FIRE

▼

KAMLOOPS, BRITISH COLUMBIA

I give him a lot of credit: Jimmy trained himself not to shudder when he sees her – third-degree burns over 90 percent of her body, face so badly misshapen she can barely speak, fierce, unrelenting anger because he saved her. *For what?* she demands.

Of course, Jimmy has no answer.

Who would?

"I was lost," Jimmy likes to say. "I came to Canada to be found."

"Yeah," I grin, hooking my arm through his, "by me."

"I was always sold short," he shifts, puts his arm around my shoulders. "I was never asked who I was." He pauses. "You were the first one who did."

Sure, I asked. There was something about him, something very different, not only his core beliefs about hard work and war, but also his kindness and courage, his ability to see how we could make the world a safer place, one benzene trap at a time.

All of that was honed here, in Kamloops. You see, I'm a firm believer that place defines you. Re-defines you, maybe, if you adopt it.

At least that's what happened with my husband.

Put another way, it's good old American reinvention. Change your name, change your place, change your life. America. In this case, North America.

Now I'm no story teller, despite attending a four-week memoir-writing course at North Shore Community Centre. *Farm Girl of the Rockies*! But here's the story. The stories, really. 'Cause I can't tell you one without the other. Arc of two stories, a double helix. Not a bad simile from a Western Canadian sodbuster! Anyway, there are tragedies in life, and failures, but there are also triumphs. Muted, sometimes nearly invisible, indecipherable, but victories nonetheless. Sometimes you can't ask for more.

Let me start with Jimmy in his hometown, Tonawanda, New York, western edge of the state, near Buffalo, near the Canadian border. While he never said much about it, I gathered it was a town more or less like any other. Nothing special.

Here's Jimmy, 12 years old, walking home from Catholic school, messy hair, too-long tie, head befuddled by math and science. Quiet, obedient, child whom the Fathers would have picked dead last to be the class draft dodger.

By high school it had become clear that my husband-to-be, for all that he was, was not what you'd call a deep thinker. Avoided biology and chemistry and physics, took wood shop and auto mechanics instead. Worked with his hands. In the old days, he would've been shipped to a tech 'n' trade school. Nothing the matter with that.

Nothing the matter with his principles, either.

Fast forward to 1968. Largely apolitical, especially in sleepy little Republican Tonawanda, Jimmy lived with his working-class family, studied with all those priests. Riots and assassinations, Johnson and the war. Jimmy more or less ignored it all.

More or less. One night, after a good quantity of deeply mediocre gin, he did tell me that "in 1968 we thought the world was changing. Really turning a corner. Prague Spring. Paris Spring. Johnson was on the way out, so we thought the war would end immediately, if not sooner." Jimmy sighed. "Then the tanks rolled into Wenceslas Square. The de Gaulle government crushed the strike. Bobby Kennedy was murdered on television. Richard Nixon was elected. And the war raged on, worse than ever."

While Jimmy wasn't political per se, this started to eat at him, especially the war.

Other things, too. Photo from a cold, washed out Sunday morning. Jimmy, pale, glow-in-the-dark Northern European skin. Black hair. Limpid eyes. Dark suit, coming back from mass. Surplus pea coat, souvenir from a sailor who didn't make it. Jimmy stands before a welfare state that's failed. Lifeless trees, busted-up streets, torn-and-tattered homes of people who didn't matter.

Still, Jimmy didn't hassle it. But two years later, when four kids were shot at Kent State, Jimmy started asking questions. Killing our own children. Internal war crime. Like Vietnam, no one brought up on charges. No trials conducted, convictions reached, judgments meted out. Instead, body counts became national policy. Blood lust – death rates, napalm bombs, B-52 strikes – defined America's national character. Became an unwashable stain on the national soul.

Brought up to believe that his government would never lie to its own citizens, Jimmy began to think that America was no longer that country he was born in. And certainly not the country he wanted to be in.

The Great McClure Fire began – well, who cares how it began? Somebody flipped a cigarette butt and shouldn't have. Is that it? Does it matter? It began, that's all. How it began doesn't help. Doesn't help to find fault or assign blame. It happened. This is Western Canada. Fires happen. Fires follow drought as spring follows winter.

Fires happen.

In the fire hall – Kamloops Fire Hall No. 2, just north of the Thompson River – and in the field, firefighters invariably use their last names, sometimes a single syllable from their last names, for easy shouting. All of them, even auxiliaries like Jimmy. Not the first name, *never* the first name. Too soft, too familiar. Too much like Sunday school. Last name only, please. Very British. Canadian-cum-British. Tougher. More rugged. After all, this is the hard world of the outdoors, the dangerous world of fire.

So Jimmy, James Frederick Mainzdorfer – the original, longer German name got mangled at Ellis Island, but his family never bothered to fix it; they were already Americans, just keep moving, don't look back – was Mainz; more casually, Mainzers. After one too many Labatts, it morphed into Afterdinner Mainz. See how the Mainzails set. Mizzenmainz.

What passes for humor down at Fire Hall No. 2.

For her part, Jimmy's partner Laurel was Hitchens, or Hitch. Full name, Mountain Laurel Hitchens.

Mountain Laurel?

"My parents were hippies," she shrugged. "Alberta. Little commune outside of Calgary. Well, are there any big communes? They dipped candles. Sewed sandals. Sold them to tourists at the Stampede. Had five daughters – frisky kids, my parents, back in the day. Named us all for flowering plants. Hydrangea. Marigold. Azalea. Rhododendron. Lucky they didn't have sons. Would've been Jack-in-the Pulpit. Lodgepole Pine. Blue Spruce. Downhill from there."

Of course her name offered the opportunity for much hilarity at Fire Hall No. 2. Trailer Hitch. Timber Hitch. *Down the Hitch!*

When things really got out of hand, the Labbats flowing like the Thompson River, Mountain Laurel slid into Mount Laurel.

Oh, what grand natural wits!

Since Laurel refused to date any of them, married or not, they presumed she was frigid. Or liked girls. Neither was the case; Laurel just didn't mix pay and play. Iron Curtain, she'd say. Watertight door.

"Hell of a firefighter," Jimmy said. "Really tough for a scrawny little girl. Didn't have the heft of a longshoreman, but certainly had the swagger. And the mouth. Laurel could dish it with the best of them. Brave, resourceful, smart. All spit and sinew."

One night, sweaty and post-coital, Jimmy told me he remembered all too well being 19, confused, lost. That his family in Tonawanda – the family to this day I've never met – despite naval tours in both World War I and World War II, just didn't hold with Vietnam. *No goals. No one on the other side we can trust. Why get in the middle of a civil war?* He especially remembered his mother, hair in curlers, blue cigarette smoke hanging in the air, ratty housecoat buttoned to her chin, swearing that *I will* not *sacrifice my son for an idiot, unwinnable policy cooked up by a half-dozen nitwits in Washington.*

"I hear Tim O'Brien," Jimmy said, staring at the ceiling. "How he couldn't feature his father being asked at the hardware store *how's your son the draft dodger?* I figured that was a minor inconvenience compared to having my life on the line. Compared to taking part in a mass murder that was illegal, immoral, and absolutely pointless. And unlike O'Brien, I didn't think those guys in suits knew more than I did. Not at all. I knew what was happening and how it would turn out. Didn't want my ass shot off, or some other part of my anatomy. As Muhammad Ali said, 'I ain't got no quarrel with them Vietcongs.' It was their country, their conflict. Let them settle it. I didn't want to kill – or maim, or destroy – anybody trying to interfere.

"Having said all that, was my father angry? Sure, he was angry. He did his bit in World War II. Grandpap in World War I. That was then. Radical fascism run amuck. This was a senseless slaughter on no battlefields in the middle of an endless nightmare. It wasn't worth it. It wasn't worth anything. National interest is one thing. Maybe. But sometimes your country asks too much. This time it did."

So Jimmy gave his father the script – and neither of us ever knew if he used it. Told him to say that Jimmy went out west, which turned out to be true. Washington state. Spokane. Lumber mill. Why was Jimmy never home? Dad the steamfitter was supposed to shrug. *M'boy's got a life out there. Doesn't get a lot of time off. And Spokane's not next door. We'll get together one of these days.* Then his dad was to change the subject – Bisons, Bills, Sabres, something secure and safe. He was not to argue with people. He was not going to suborn their ostracism or their wrath.

For all that, for all his mother's disgust and distrust, Jimmy's family raised its collective eyebrows. Draft dodger? No, Jimmy said, not that. Just no skin in the game. He refused to shed blood – his or anyone else's – for such spurious goals. "Unfightable, unwinnable war, the bad versus the worse. My country isn't asking me, calling me. My country is lying to me, *stealing* me. I won't have any part in it."

As Jimmy told it, that more or less put an end to it. That and the fact he never argued, never lost his temper. Always treated them very well.

You'll never be able to come back, his mother shook her head.

I'll take my chances, Jimmy answered.

It began on July 30, 2003, and when it was done, done after 75 straight days of rage and fury, the Great McClure Fire burned more than 65,285 acres of timberland and 81 homes and businesses. It cost more than $3 million to *fight, more than $8 million in property damage, and caused the evacuation of nearly 4,000 people.*

Laurel had literally been in the center of the fire, in a clearing, digging a firebreak, when suddenly – is there any other way with a major fire? – a pine tree loaded with highly flammable sap, literally a fire bomb with roots, exploded next to her, hurling her 30 yards. After the fall broke both her legs, a burning tree limb tore through her PPE, sliced her helmet, thrust fiery wood and flaming pine sap into her suit. It was as if she had been bathed in a tub of burning gasoline.

Without hesitation, and at the risk of his life, Jimmy raced after her, found Laurel in the conflagration, picked her up, a burning rag doll, carried her out, saved her life.

Vietnam was simply kill or be killed. Jimmy wanted none of it.

He remembered a cloudy afternoon in high school, some army guy came to talk about the draft, about what he lightly referred to as *securing warm bodies.* Offended by the dehumanization, Jimmy also found himself thinking about his single-issue, non-replaceable warm body. Thinking that he didn't particularly relish having it dismembered. Or having it come back in a box. He even had a family precedent: his great-grandfather deserted the Kaiser's army during the insane slaughter of the 1870 Franco-Prussian War and made his way to America.

Knowing the draft board would soon be on his tail, Jimmy decided to jump the border. Easy enough to do from Tonawanda, where people drive to Canada for lunch.

"I'm not leaving," Jimmy told his family. "I'm being chased out. By lunatics who see the death toll rise every day – on both sides – and do nothing about it. I don't want to be part of a country that does things like this."

Although she hated the war more every day, his mother fumed, and his father settled into a silent rage. Sure, Jimmy still blames them for their lack of empathy, but I understand his parents' consternation and confusion. Of course, upon arrival from Germany, and away from the European wars, his family became more American than the Americans, patriotic to a fault.

His father even enlisted the day after Pearl Harbor, leaving his mother, a skinny, buck-toothed, 19-year-old war bride.

It's not that Jimmy saw it or smelled it first, because many people did. But as a lifelong firefighter, first in Tonawanda, then out here, he knew all the warning signs.

He had awakened to a glorious day. High blue Canadian sky. A few clouds. The air sweet and clean. Light breeze. Creation in all its glory.

Then it wasn't. There was something odd. Jimmy smelled smoke – slight and distant at first. Then closer and more clear. Stronger. More insistent. Heavier, somehow. Musty. No, he thought, this wasn't a picnic. A campfire. There was always a campfire, or a cookout, no matter how dry the season. A clogged chimney, maybe? Some outlaw burning leaves? No. Whatever this was, it was bigger, more ominous.

It was something, he feared, he knew, *far, far worse.*

The first time he saw Laurel, the first time he was allowed to see her, after the triage, after the race to the hospital, was many hours later, before the first of multiple surgeries, hours after he carried her, a burning, smoking ruin, out of the Great McClure Fire. Standing in the Royal Inland ICU, gowned and masked like a surgeon himself, Jimmy was allowed only five minutes, and that only from the doorway.

It was easy enough, a quick step over the Rainbow Bridge then request landed immigrant status. Well, it looked easy from the American side. On the Canadian side, given good old bureaucratic machinations and typical Northern stuffiness, becoming a landed immigrant was hardly as simple as the publicity promised. Luckily, Jimmy found a sympathetic counselor – a very pregnant, very sweaty woman named Trowbridge – who despised the American war even more than Jimmy did, if that were possible, and made it her mission to bring as many young Americans across as she could.

"Good that you can work with your hands," she encouraged. "As Canada moves farther and farther away from manual labor, you'll always be in demand. You'll always find work."

To that end, she hooked Jimmy up with a local plumbing contractor. Not Jimmy's training, but enough to put him over the top. Once his paperwork cleared, and not caring for Toronto – too crowded, too big, too expensive, too many Americans, too many politics – Jimmy wanted to go either east or west, the Maritimes or the Rockies. Literally flipping a coin one night he bought a Canadian Pacific ticket west.

There were switch yards and prairies, then the glorious Rockies. Banff. Calgary. Lake Louise. Kamloops. Time to get off. Time to look for a new life.

Time to find me.

Suddenly, there was smoke in the sky, in the houses, the sight and the silty, burning smell of it everywhere, like a storm.

The call came shortly thereafter, a barked, brief announcement. Jimmy acknowledged it, told us he didn't know when he'd be back, hoped it would be soon, kissed me, hugged and kissed Emmie and Petey, ran for his truck. Everything he needed would be in his locker at the fire hall.

Jimmy's the bravest man I know. Have ever known.

I don't know how long Laurel was in surgery or recovery. I want to say 16 hours, but that could be way off. I know that Jimmy wanted to be there the entire time, sat endlessly, disheveled and exhausted, on a hard plastic chair in the waiting room, until, finally, a nurse named Madeline Lorenzo had pity on him and told him to go home.

"There's nothing you can do here," she said. "You won't be able to see her for many, many hours yet, Mr. Mainzdorfer. Maybe days. And you need some rest, too." She paused. "I have your number. I'll call you."

Nodding, beaten, Jimmy came home, slept for 13 hours, showered, then sat silent through eggs over easy, wheat toast, and about six gallons of black coffee.

Jimmy got off the train as the dawn began to show wisps of color on the mountains – green and yellow and red against the brown earth and the blue sky.

Above the deep blue cold of Kamloops Lake, he saw caves and crevices like organ pipes punched out of the sheer cliffs. Bluffs painted purple, copper oxidizing green on rocks, pines standing sentinel along the ridges.

There was something else, too. Fire-scarred trees, thousands of them, entire hillsides covered in scorched, dead trees, black spikes in the pied black earth.

Used to be a lot of lumber yonder, a grizzled man with a stingy brown fedora gestured with his cane, *before the fires and the pine beetles got 'em. Used to be 47 paper mills here. Now there's but one. Still, eleven hundred cattle ranches out here BC way, quarter-million head, if'n you got a mind for ranchin'.*

Walking west, Jimmy found bungalows and small yards on flat streets dead-ending at rivers and hills. Edge of town, scrap heaps, torn-up yards, trailers. Wooden corrals, rusting cars, asphalt shingle roofs and blue plastic sheeting, brightly colored plastic children's toys.

A little red-haired man with a Viking beard offered Jimmy a job: carpentry, drywall. Sure, Jimmy said. The man had a sister – his virtual twin. The sister had a friend. Me.

Crunchy, he smiled when he met me, *like a bowl of granola,* and somehow the descriptive fit just right. Long, thin fingers, bony haunches, plaid shirts, work gloves; brown leather work boots, industrial-strength denims. I was two years out of high school, starting to farm for myself, plot of land I rented and later bought north of town, selling organic herbs and infusions. One clown called me Molly Manure, and the name stuck. I began selling my nostrums as Molly's Mixin's.

Name wasn't Molly, though. Still isn't. Marci Jo. Marci Jo Danbury. Canadians for a century. Farmers and shopkeepers. Harness makers. Salt-of-the-earth types.

Fire, an intractable enemy, takes no prisoners, offers no quarter. It destroys and kills.

In the awesome power of its destruction it inspires absolute terror in the women and men who fight it to the death.

They don their armor – heat-resistant suits, helmets, and masks; breathe oxygen. Yet for all their protection, countless firefighters die every year. Searing, solar winds, blinding black smoke, 1,600-degree heat that melts chainsaws and cracks boulders, ignites and explodes trees, creates 400-feet-high walls of fire, shoots smoke 40,000 feet – and higher.

They face a living creature whose fearsome might is known only to itself.

Three days later – it might have been less, but it's hard to remember – Jimmy got the call, and paid the first of many, many visits. Told to gown and mask again, he did so, unhesitatingly, and peered in.

Laurel, swathed in more bandages than a mummy, attached to more wires and monitors than a radio, was unconscious – had been since he carried her out of the burning forest. *Didn't matter that it was only five minutes standing 12 feet away,* he told me later, *I had to see her.*

She's in a coma, the doc explained, a tall, sandy-haired Scot named Ferguson. *No telling when she'll regain consciousness,* then paused to correct himself. *If.*

It was, as they say, a fine romance. Me, in my retro rags – Earth Shoes, gingham dress, granny glasses. Jimmy in his plaid shirt, bib overalls, steel-toed work boots. We didn't have very much, but we never wanted or needed very much. We had the rivers and the Rockies. And each other. In time, we realized we were compatible – and more. Didn't trip over each other in the bathroom, didn't fight, not ever, and liked the same things. Time to make it legal. Time to get married.

No, no church, that's not the way we rolled. Still don't. Instead, we did justice of the peace and your standard fire-hall covered-dish wedding. My family was fine with it.

And so Marci Jo Danbury became Marci Jo Mainzdorfer.

Of course, Jimmy invited his parents and brothers and sisters and aunts and uncles and cousins – half of Western New York state, by my count. We never heard from them. *Any* of them. I snarled. He said, why does the most negative answer have to be right? Which I thought was a display of the most remarkable equanimity.

Maybe the invitations, or the responses, got lost in the mail, he said.

All of them? I snapped.

Jimmy just shrugged.

Later, as things follow things, we sent his parents photos of their grandbabies. Similarly, no response. After a while, we stopped.

Jimmy never spoke about it.

Running every red light in Kamloops, Jimmy got to Fire Hall No. 2 and found everybody with their game faces on. Suiting up, he knocked back a paper cup of Gatorade and rode a yellow school bus to a military-style staging area outside of town. Spread out about him, invasion theater, trucks, water buffalos, bulldozers, ground crews, hot shots, hoses and oxygen tanks and fire axes.

"I need a 20-man boost over here," a white-shirted captain barked, and Jimmy, along with Laurel and four or five others from No. 2, lined up. Nodding, the captain checked off their names, and sent them out.

It would be 24 straight hours – 24 hours hacking through ground and brush to try to create a useless firebreak, to set back fires, to fight exhaustion and dehydration and sheer sweat and high winds and flying embers and the Great McClure Fire itself.

In the ICU, and for two weeks after, when things were still touch-and-go, Jimmy went to see Laurel every day, whether she was sleeping or sedated or barely sentient.

To a world of white – her bandages and sheets, gowned and masked nurses rustling in and out of her room. And blue – monitors, blinking lights, soft night lights.

When Jimmy came home, he stayed stone silent for a good two hours.

Before we knew it, we had our food moths. Emmie – Emma Antonia, after various grand units – and Pierre Baptiste. No, there's not an ounce of French blood between us, we just liked the name – and felt like practicing a little diversity out here in All-British-All-The-Time British Columbia.

Of course, we called him Little Petey for short.

Little Petey. It didn't take us long to find out that he was acutely autistic. Never hugged us. Never laughed at silly things. Never rolled the ball back to me.

The doctor at the clinic – a lovely woman named Srinivasan with beautiful dark skin, a caste sign, and a rich, melodic voice – was incredibly gentle and supportive. When I asked her about possible causes, she smiled sadly. "Unless you were a raging alcoholic or habitual drug abuser --"

I shook my head.

"I didn't think so. But unless you were, any discussion of how this happened is futile. There are so many possible causes, from genetics gone awry to benzene in the water. None of this will help you now."

"Doctor, I," I began, but Dr. Srinivasan held up her hand, then began talking about what we might expect from Petey in the near, middle, and distant future. About special programs and help for which we could apply. In all I was there for about an hour-and-a-half – the longest 20-minute appointment of my life.

On the way out, I thanked her and told her I legitimately felt better.

Which was true, but didn't stop me from crying myself to sleep for many nights.

Especially when Jimmy and I tried one program after another for Little Petey, and none of them seemed to help. Home schooling, and home farming, weren't much good, either, for I couldn't pay enough attention to him – and really didn't know how to work with him. An armload of books from the library didn't add much.

Neither did a kind, heavyset woman named Michaela who lived down the road and ran a home daycare. She meant well, but didn't know what to do with Petey, either.

"Let's keep trying," Jimmy said. "There's got to be something out there that's right for him."

"What if there isn't?" I asked.

"We'll burn that bridge when we get to it," he shrugged.

Hotshots!

The field commander gestured, and Jimmy, Laurel, and the others double downed, following the bulldozer, cutting the firebreak as the pines exploded and collapsed all about them.

Hoisting his Pulaski, that odd curved hoe-and-ax combo, Jimmy cut, while his line mates swung chain saws, and Laurel followed, her small frame buckled by the hurricane-strength winds, shoveling dirt to smother whatever fire might still be burning.

It's like corralling a thunderstorm!

They lasted the night, fought the smoldering fire in morning, tamping down the earth, feeling it with their bare hands, because embers can travel for miles, hot earth can be an inferno by noon, and flame tornados can tear trees out by their roots.

Nothing! Nothing left that can possibly burn!

They cold-trailed the fire scars, Jimmy's sweat dripping down his neck and into his soaked suit, feeling for heat, any heat, because tree stumps can continue to burn underground, causing murderous flare-ups and sudden, deadly sinkholes.

As soon as you disrespect fire, it will kill you!

Massaging the black earth, Jimmy remembered hearing of an Idaho fire that seemed contained on two acres – then grew to 15,000 acres by nightfall.

After all that, Laurel lived, the burn victim's burn victim. Jimmy – and a great team of BC health professionals – had saved her life. For which – and I don't blame her for this – Laurel was profoundly ungrateful. After all, the surgeries and the ICU and the rehab were hellacious. Her body – or most of it – was pools and ridges of scar tissue, especially her face, where the plastic of the mask had melted into her skin. With her lungs seared, part of her tongue bitten off and burned away, and face almost entirely immobile scar tissue, it was hard for Laurel to talk. Missing multiple fingers, largely immobile, at first it was virtually impossible for Laurel to accomplish anything on her own. Gradually, she was able to use a walker, then two canes. She still glowered.

Jimmy and I were fine living on society's margins. Hard by the Canadian Pacific tracks, we bought a house for the proverbial song. *Like* a song, actually, a rewritten line from "Heartbreak Hotel," *down at the end of Scrap Yard Street.* Yes, that's what we called it, when we weren't calling it Death Row, and the nearby trains Lost Soul Specials. With a yard full of car parts and scavenged trucks, Jimmy got into the spirit of the place by having cards printed up, Salvage Yard Blues: wrecker, mechanic, exile, end of the line.

We stay within our means. My farming goes well, herbs and home remedies, tinctures and teas. Farmer's Markets and church basements. I'm thinking of branching out into bees, too. Wildflower honey. Always the handyman, Jimmy built two small rooms onto the back of the house where I have my workbenches, pots, shelves, storage. Where Emmie comes to help of an afternoon when it's not too hot.

I'm at Molly's Mixin's farm or out there in my shed. Jimmy does odd jobs and auto work. I know him: he takes joy in fixing things, in fighting fires, even as an auxiliary. Both make him more aware of fragility, of damage and second chances.

Jimmy and I make our own schedules, work our own hours. Answer to no one. How many people can say that?

In temperate weather, we spend as much time as we can outdoors. Away from the city lights, where Jimmy can sketch the constellations for Emmie and Little Petey. *Cassiopeia!* he'll point, drawing lines across the sky. *The Great Bear!*

If we had a family crest on it would be *We don't want anything we didn't earn.*

On the line they toiled, Jimmy and Jonesy, Ritter and Clark, Hillman and Laurel, and many, many more, helmets and masks and thick PPEs, entirely unrecognizable, through smoke and fire, digging, cutting, gesturing, then gesturing some more, gesturing and muscle memory, gesturing and knowing what to do.

One day, barely awake, then coming around, uncomfortable and itching in her bandages, Laurel again blamed Jimmy. "It would have been better" – she swallowed; her voice a rustle of dry leaves she had trouble controlling – "if you'd let me die."

Jimmy just shook his head. "C'mon, Hitch," he said, "you know I couldn't do that." He paused. "We're soldiers. We don't leave troops in the field."

"Three-finger Betty," she held up one bandaged hand. He thought he saw Laurel smile, but with all that scar tissue he couldn't be certain.

After a time, Jimmy moved some of the detritus out and built a little beer garden in the back yard. Grilled some kind of critter, charged admission, sold beer. People took their ease of summer nights and Sunday afternoons. Illegal, of course, but no one cared about what went on behind Jimmy's Salvage Yard at the Canadian Pacific tracks.

Address? someone asked. *Confluence of big thirst and cheap lush,* I said.

Three days later – was it only three days? Jimmy wondered – they sat on the ground, spent, breathing hard, breathing heavy, just past the fire break, gulping air and Gatorade, too exhausted to talk, even to nod, washing their faces, leaving them wet, drinking, spitting, drinking, swallowing. Praying that the Great McClure Fire was waning, knowing it wasn't.

Knowing it was only a matter of time before they went back in.

Once she went to Buttermilk Skies Rehab, Jimmy went to see Laurel every week, Wednesday afternoons, like clockwork. While he never spoke about it – Jimmy's like that, like the Great Plains, given to vast silences – I know it tore at him.

Jimmy saw remnants of her blackened skin, but soon that, too, peeled off, leaving Laurel with little but scar tissue. With her muscles burned, and atrophied, she took physical therapy, but there was only so much they could do, could build on. Laurel's PT chief, a lanky Norwegian named Else with cornsilk blonde hair, translucent skin, and lake blue eyes, stretched and massaged and guided her. Little by little, Laurel could finally navigate the carpeted floors. After a month, some fingers whole, some stumps, some missing entirely, Laurel could painfully, painstakingly, pick up plastic packing peanuts, eat with silverware, type on a keyboard.

"Hey, Mainzers," she said, through thick lips, "I'm almost whole again."

The less said about winter in Western Canada the better. Fierce winds. Fiercer cold. Fiercest feet of snow. Day after day below zero. Nothing much else to do but lay around. Mend nets. Sharpen tools. Read. Correspond. Hibernate. Live off our pelts. Wait for spring. Make babies.

Having said that, for Jimmy and me, the replacement models were enough. Although a couple of extra farm hands wouldn't hurt. Let me think about it.

Spring. When the birds awake and the snow recedes. When the sun cuts in warm beneath the distant storm clouds.

When Petey, poor Petey, Petey, in his rigidity and his silence, goes back outside, mutely seeking meaning in the music of his father's auto body shop.

In the roar of the railroad, the trains howling like great steel coyotes, shaking the earth, making it feel as if our little house is going to be flipped off its flimsy foundation.

Suddenly the fire is everywhere all at once. An advancing army. Ordinance firing. Relentless. Walls of flame leaping from one stand of trees to another, superheated trees exploding as if they were bombs in the attack.

All is in vain — the hopeless ditching, the weak and vaporous chemical sprays. Nothing can stop or tame the fire and its deadly power.

Jimmy didn't see it, but there it was: the fire grabbing hold of tree roots and burrowing underground, deadly, invisible, suddenly springing up hundreds of yards away, with a ferocity previously unseen and unimaginable.

Losing the sun, losing daylight, Jimmy was suddenly surrounded in a curtain wall of black smoke. Even through his PPE, the heat was overwhelming. Blinded, disoriented, he was lost, trapped in concentric circles of flame, unable to find his way out. It was vertigo, plain and simple. Vertigo. And madness.

Drowning in a sea of vicious red and murderous yellow, Jimmy felt it grip him. All hands were lost.

It took her a while. Of course, it did. She wept a lot. Blamed herself. Not only for being clumsy – of course, she wasn't – but also, well…

"I'm being punished, Mainzers," she told Jimmy one day when he rolled her outside at Buttermilk Skies. Perfect late spring day, blue sky, patio overlooking the river and the mountains. Western Canada at her beautiful best.

"How's that?" Jimmy asked. Remember, my husband was never a deep thinker, but he was really bewildered this time.

"I was younger, Mainzers."

"Yeah, Hitch, we all were once."

"Yeah, but I was dumber. I got really wasted one night. Tequila, that sneaky Mexican'll do it to you every time. You know how that is."

"Been there."

"Right, Mainzers, I bet you have. Anyway, woke up with this real loser. Found out I was pregnant. I didn't want any kid, much less that creep's. So I took care of it. He never knew, which is just the way I wanted it."

"It happens," Jimmy shrugged.

"It doesn't just *happen*, Mainzers. I *made* it happen. I killed a human being. Now I'm paying for it."

"I don't think it works that way," Jimmy objected.

"No? What do you know about it?" Laurel pressed.

"Apparently not much. Sorry I said anything, Hitch. Really."

I get asked this all the time: why Jimmy? Of all the guys who came sucking around, why him? He's quiet. Solid. Patient. While he has the ability to change, Jimmy also has unshakeable core beliefs. Loyalty. Hard work. The resolution of conflicts by means other than violence.

Jimmy's also brave – astonishingly brave – hardly the coward he was believed to be. Because when he first came to Kamloops, before he signed up for the firefighting auxiliary, before his story got out, some people, happier in their easy answers and facile condemnation, never bothered to find out the truth. In short order, Jimmy became the straw man who made them feel good about themselves.

After all, now they had someone to hate.

At its worst, there was an ugly scene in a bar when Jimmy, branded a coward, called out for not standing up for his country, was noisily challenged to fight.

Never looking at his assailant, Jimmy just shook his head.

Look at this, the man said. *A Kraut who refuses to fight.*

The bartender, a bearded fellow roughly the size of Winnipeg, moved over. "Back off," he ordered. "This is a quiet place and you know it. Fighting him will solve nothing. A man's got to live with his own conscience. Besides, if you were so all-fired hot about Vietnam, why didn't you go and enlist? They would've loved to have you."

Jimmy never looked up, just rotated the Labatt bottle in his fingers. "I'm no coward," he said. "I wasn't then, and I'm not now. I'm just not a killer. I believe there's better ways to resolve conflicts than killing people."

"And when the Ruskies come over the hill?" the man demanded.

"When the Ruskies come over the hill, " Jimmy said, "call me, and we can discuss it."

What Jimmy didn't say, but could have, maybe *should* have, is that back home, before his number came up, Jimmy'd been a volunteer fire fighter. When the siren sounded, he ran. Shortly after that incident, he joined the Kamloops auxiliaries, the ones who get called up only for the worst of the worst – like the Great McClure Fire. Over the years, Jimmy's received more than his share of commendations for bravery. All of which he's shrugged off. Over those same years, he's saved more than a few lives – all at the risk of his own. When news of *that* got out, BC being a fairly conservative place, it tended to squelch all talk about *that Yank draft dodger.*

No, Jimmy's no coward. Hardly a coward. Laurel Hitchens can attest to that.

All about him, flying ash, flying embers, traveling miles on the superheated thermals, landing in trees and houses, reducing them to cinders in minutes, or less.

The fire jumping the road, jumping house to house, the worst part knowing that the Great McClure Fire was coming and standing helplessly before it.

"Hey, Hitchens," Jimmy said, trying, and failing, to beat her at checkers, "you ever going to that burn victims' support group?"

"Sure, Mainzers," a triple jump, "when the scars heal."

Does Jimmy miss America? That he never talks about it doesn't mean he doesn't miss it. But I don't think he does. He left too young, too green, to think much about it now. Canada's not that much different, and the language is the same, of course. Here, at least, there aren't constant wars that we have to protect our children from.

"No," he said one night, over Labatts in the backyard, "I don't miss the house I grew up in. It was nothing special. Neither was Tonawanda. Played-out little town, nothing much to miss. I miss it about as much as I miss going to mass.

"Besides, I like it up here. Different. Calmer. Cooler – socially, politically. Less materialistic. Less aggressive. It's not America Lite. It's different."

Jimmy paused. "I'm different.

"And it doesn't bother me that I can't go back. That means nothing to me. I've got everything I want right here." He looked at me and smiled. "All the rest of that was someplace else a long time ago. My family? If they want to see me that badly, they can visit me here. The Canadian Rockies are lovely this time of year." He smiled again. "Any time of year, really."

Sure, there was Bill Clinton's amnesty, but, as Jimmy put it, "amnesty?

That's the stranger who rides into town. They changed the rules once. Who knows if they'll change them again?"

Of course, he no longer had a family to speak of – they chose country over blood, which was their right – but that tore it with Jimmy. By then, he had no idea if anyone was still alive. And never bothered to find out.

Pressed about it at the Fire Hall, he shook his head. "Not interested. Not interested in what America is, what America has become. I'm happy here, with my family, pounding out dents. I've, ah, hammered out a life here."

Laughs all around.

"I'm not going anywhere. Especially not south of the border."

"Americans," a gnarled hotshot named Rollins waved, "are a warlike people."

"Yes," Jimmy agreed, "they are. Maybe that's why I'm not an American anymore. I'm a Canadian now. Have been for a good long time."

Of course, Jimmy didn't see what we did on television, the aerials, the scope of the Great McClure Fire, hill after hill ablaze, great plumes of orange fire retardant like a sudden sunset being sprayed all over BC. And the people, dazed, driving frantically away, swaddled in bedclothes, huddled with their belongs, waiting for the trucks and busses racing down mountain roads to take them to safety.

"I still feel 'em, Mainzers," Laurel waggled her bandaged stumps at him. "Still feel my fingers as if they were there. Phantom limb syndrome. Brain's funny that way."

"Yes," Jimmy agreed, "that ol' brain, she sure is funny."

"I think I've finally lost the nickname Yank," Jimmy said one lazy Sunday morning, the food moths snarfing pancakes, he and I in bathrobes, "although I wouldn't be surprised if they call me that behind my back. It's Canada. I'm always the exile, the outsider."

Well, maybe. Reinvention – isn't that the real American Dream? Maybe Jimmy just adapted to a new environment. He's a Canadian now, with a Canadian wife, a Canadian passport, two native-born Canadian children. Canadian attitudes.

Still, there are vestiges. People call him *your* American *husband,* as if he were a different species somehow.

Yet he's been here so long that some people swear they went to school with him.

Jimmy and Laurel and the rest slept on the ground, woke to a morning with a brown moon hanging in the west.

The air was smoke, the odor inescapable.

They had bivouacked some eight kilometers from the front line of the Great McClure Fire. By nightfall, the day's winds had died down a bit, and they began to breath a bit easier. Perhaps they could control the areas that had already burned.

Still, he was not afraid. While the devastation was palpable, there were many burned areas he had not yet seen, and while field reports told of enormous evacuations and losses, there were many not threatened.

Another day, he thought, two at the most, two days of ground sleeping and MREs before the field captain would clap him on the shoulder and say, you're out of here, Mainz, shift's over. You've done your bit. Nothing more you can do.

He and Laurel and the rest had a day, two at the most.

Of course, Laurel's parents were out of the picture – some kind of gray-haired hippies, living, well, who knew where? As were her four sisters, scattered to the four winds. So Laurel moved back to her bungalow – living room, dining room, two small bedrooms, big backyard – on an unpaved road out of town. With these and those and the other benefits, she welcomed a visiting nurse every day. Meals on Wheels, PT twice a week, other help – she was going to be all right. The National Health outfitted her house with a hospital bed, safety rails in the loo, a special ergonomic chair.

Jimmy saw her every week, and, unbeknownst to Laurel, built a little shrine to her at home. On a stand-alone wooden shelf in our TV room, between the Canucks and BC Lions banners, he put up a small framed photo of her, snaggle-toothed grin, sliver of a silver nose ring, heavy brown PPE, helmet in hand. Pine-scented candle, stone from the Sacred Mountain, small vial of ash from the fire itself.

As frugal as the summer day is long, the one luxury Jimmy allows himself is a Friday fish sandwich at Olive's Diner. *Catholic?* he was asked, as if Catholicism were some sort of suspect virus. *Lapsed*, he answered, *very lapsed* German *Catholic. Worst of both worlds.* Then motioned for the hot sauce to be passed down the scarred counter.

After he began showing up every week, and was asked why, he said that nothing tastes like Friday back home like fish sandwiches. When pressed *where home might be?* Jimmy shrugged and bit into the roll slathered over with tartar and Tabasco.

I should add that Olive's fish sandwiches were nothing to attract *Cordon Bleu* or *Gourmet* magazine. Just breaded cod, frozen around the time Lester Pearson was PM, deep fried in oil that's changed every five years or so, whether Olive needs to or not. On an Italian-style roll of uncertain age and lineage. In all, a minor vice.

"Hey, Olive," Jimmy said every Friday, sliding onto a stool.

Olive, a bone-thin woman with leathery skin, came to work every day in costume, net clutching her gray hair, pink waitress' uniform, cursive *Olive* stitched above the breast pocket that held a tightly pressed hanky.

"Hey, Jake," she answered.

Jake?

"Never could get my name right," Jimmy said, unperturbed as ever. "Don't bother me none. Long as the food's right."

"The usual?" she asked, already knowing the answer.

"The usual," Jimmy nodded.

Fish sandwiches meant meatless Fridays. Meant home. I was always glad that Jimmy had at least one pleasant memory of Tonawanda, no matter how small.

"The usual," Jimmy said again, and smiled.

When it was over, seventy-five days later, when the Great McClure Fire was finally over, it took Jimmy and me the better part of two months to scrub the smoke out of our house, out of the walls and clothes and carpets, out of the toys and cars and furniture, and the better part of two years to try to forget it, to try to forget the carnage it caused.

But outside, in the woodlands, the scarred, stunted landscape, the gnarled black trees, the impossibly scorched earth would never recover, never return.

Gradually, Laurel began to find herself, and with some job counseling applied for a part-time online teaching position, basic firefighting, advanced firefighting, continuing ed credits. Sitting out in her backyard, clinking Labatts, she shrugged. "I know all about firefighting, Mainzers," she said. "I'm a regular ace at firefighting."

"C'mon, Hitchens, lighten up. It's too nice a day to be bringing me down."

"It's nice money, Mainzers. No, it's OK money. But between that and disability – the province bein' pretty damn generous to its lame and its three-quarters-destroyed-in-the-line-of-duty halt – I ain't doin' so bad. And seein' as how I'm not havin' to waste a lot of jack on frivolities like a real smart wardrobe --"

"OK, Hitch," Jimmy swigged.

"What? So I can go out and see the entire room stiffen when Plastic Girl hobbles in with her two canes? No thanks, Mainzers. Plastic Girl doesn't need the barroom company all that badly. I can drink Labatts and Canadian Club all by my lonesome and no one will vomit when they see me."

"Hitchens."

"Time for you to go home."

"Hitchens, you're a tough woman to love, you know that?"

"I am," Laurel started to weep, "am't I?"

"C'mon, Hitch, it ain't that bad."

Laurel dropped her beer and cried into her cupped, bandaged hands. Taking both her hands in his, Jimmy squeezed gently.

"Laurel," he said, at long last. "Laurel."

If that fish sandwich was Jimmy's single luxury, his sole sin was the occasional binge. I understand: he gets weary of being responsible. And who knows how deep the scars go? He's had an enormous sense of gain living here in Canada. But his sense of loss? His family. His home. His native country. Although he never talks about any of it, that internal abyss must be overwhelming. Every so often he staunches the wound.

For Jimmy, the drug of choice is a case of Labatts, fairly harmless and highly infrequent. His version of a sweat lodge. Anyway, at least this is his self-medication and not heroin or bungee jumping or free-fall mountain biking.

Or some bimbo with whom he thinks he'll find safety and satiety. *Ha!*

Within a short time, Laurel had an army of followers and Facebook friends. "Best way, Mainzers," she told Jimmy one day. "As long as they don't have to see me," she flashed a pre-fire photo.

Scrolling down, Laurel showed him a Facebook friend – a smiling, moon-faced man on a beach, knee in the sand, scratching a collie's head. A quick glance showed the facts fleeting and vague – volunteer firefighter, single, aeronautic engineer, Cal Tech, Northrup. Nice words about her. For the time being some stranger was being kind to Laurel, which made her feel good about herself. "Hey, Mainzers," she waved her stumps. "I think I'm in love."

As always, her voice was thick and hard to decipher – half a tongue missing, all that scar tissue. But the grin, well, the grin was unmistakable.

"Good for you, Hitch," Jimmy answered. "Good for you." Then he paused. "I'm proud of you. I really am."

"As long as he never sees me."

"Give it time, Hitch, give it time. We're in the never-know business." Jimmy smiled at her. "You never know."

For Jimmy, mornings taste of motor oil and mauled metal, two parts engine exhaust and a dollop of ozone. All around it the sweet, sickly odor of benzene – benzene everywhere, a sickly frosting on a rotting cake.

My sorcerer husband; no one's allowed inside his auto body shop. But Jimmy's out now – picking up parts at NAPA – so I'll sneak you in for a glimpse in the twin sheds back of the house. Plastic sheeting protects his work area from the kids' swing set – two-by-fours, ropes, and tires.

He's made his separate peace out here, pounding out dents, doing motor work, rotating and balancing tires. Scrounging and retooling and reselling at flea markets. Even fixes the odd tractor. Hires out for farm work at harvest time. Plows snow in the winter, private roads up in the mountains.

Jimmy's got deft, quick hands, all self-taught.

Great reputation, all word-of-mouth: he can fix anything. Re-hang windows and doors. Refinish hardwood floors. A little plumbing work from his Toronto days.

Jimmy also works for barter. Trades for picked fruit, dentistry. Bag of apples, sack of potatoes. String of trout. Ten pounds of fresh moose meat – whatever's there. No invoices. *Never* invoices. What records there are stay in his small pocket notebook. It pays, Jimmy says, to stay unregulated, to fly beneath the radar. Between that and the National Health, the beer garden and Molly's Mixin's, we're good.

Jimmy's world is full of toolboxes and workbenches, sawhorses and miter boxes, tape measures and ball peen hammers. Jimmy takes pride in precision, finds passion in exactitudes.

Watch your step here. Gravel yard. Tires. Cars taken apart – right, that's a Fiat. Other one's a Ford, although you can barely recognize it with its engine torn out and its guts filled with empty oil and paint cans. Pile of spent car batteries and rusted radiators. If there's ever a run on either we'll be in hog heaven.

Wood forms and flotsam from patch work. What Jimmy can make out of nothing!

I get a kick out of the catalogs. The clocks. The red Snap-On tool cases. Everywhere. "There's a mess of 'em," he admits. "Just sorta growed."

Jimmy's careful with 'em, too. Tools cost money, and he needs them. Made boards with outlines to hang them all. Dedicated drawers for tire caps and screws and spark plugs, screwdrivers and wrenches, sandpaper and emery cloths. Mallets. Hoses and wires and spray lubricants. Rags and grease, dirt and oil.

And benzene everywhere.

Jimmy likes to come out here in the morning, in the silence, with just the birds for company, jays and cardinals and song sparrows. Traffic and distant trains.

He'll start a car, or try to. Sometimes these things take a while to turn over.

Coffee cup down, Jimmy starts his daily soundtrack, generally Scottish fiddle music or Irish bands. The air compressor starts up, asthmatic as an old pick-up. Sometimes he'll have a stack of tires to fill, balance, reset. Turning them gingerly, Jimmy'll check the treads. One'd been wobbling.

Done, he'll jack up an old Plymouth Fury, the patched workhorse living on faith and fumes, roll underneath, engineer an oil change, the old stuff black as sludge. "Miracle the damn thing still drives," Jimmy'll mutter, careful not to spill the oil. Cruising on his back, he'll spot trouble. Brake line is shot. "Take it to McGilley 'cross town," he'll call later. "Past my pay grade. My certification. Or lack thereof."

The secret, he'll say, is to set a rhythm, like a metronome, and stick to it. Work to it. Embrace it.

The rest of it – change an air filter, clean a carburetor – comes easy enough.

No, Jimmy, focusing on the task at hand, doesn't miss human company. The task, the craft, are sufficient companions.

Through it all, benzene seeps into the ground, and Jimmy, scrubbing the dishes every night in heavy detergent to get that odor off his hands, follows with liberal applications of Swiss hand cream, so that he can bathe his children and touch his wife.

As for me, I farm. And the more I farm, and the more I read, the more concerned I am about all the buzz words: global warming, carbon footprint, melting glaciers, plastic-choked oceans, especially the Arctic.

I started keeping a diary – gibberish, mostly, neither publishable nor profound. Just something to get the words out of me. Stuff like *The Earth is hardly inert. She's a living, breathing organism. She's Mrs. Newton: equal and opposite reaction. Push on her and she pushes back.* And so on.

In addition, I have grown increasingly concerned about Jimmy's work out back, the oils and solvents, the benzene. I knew he was careful, sure, but I was also convinced that he was not careful enough. That his drains and traps leached *muy malo hombres* into the ground water.

Rather than confront him head on – because that was a strategy that had no future – I had to figure out a way to get him to listen, and then to change.

I came at Jimmy through Petey.

"I've been reading," I said, casually, one night as we were doing the dishes.

"Uh oh," Jimmy shivered.

Can't sneak up on him, can I? The big lug knows every move I make.

"Our water may not be good for us," I began.

"I feel fine," he countered.

"Not the point," I said. "Your oils, your solvents, the benzene, they may all have contributed, well, to Little Petey."

"We don't know that," Jimmy said, fetching the dish towel and beginning to dry the dinner plates.

"Of course not," I said, beginning to stack. "But we don't know it didn't, either."

"OK," he kept wiping.

In a general way, I started to talk about water, about salt and sewage. About sloppy conditions and unregulated workshops.

"Marci Jo," he began, hanging up the dish towel to dry.

"I have to tell you, Jimmy, it's starting to frighten me, the poisons, not only here but everywhere."

"I can't do everywhere," Jimmy said, not unkindly.

"Right," I agreed, "neither can I. But I'm sure there are changes we can make. And, at the very least, we can listen."

"Listen," he said it like a question, but it wasn't.

I told him about the speaker coming to the Community Centre.

"I don't know," Jimmy demurred.

"Jimmy," I said in a way that he knew was important to me.

"OK," he shrugged. "I can't see much harm in it."

Bill Swiddens, the speaker from Blue Canada, an environmental action group, was a lanky 40-year-old in khakis. With a full head of brown hair, an easy smile, and an earnest manner, he exuded both charm and control. "Good-looking bastard," Jimmy grumped. "Full of himself."

"He hasn't even said anything yet," I squeezed Jimmy's arm. "Give him a chance, huh?"

To tell you the truth, I hadn't wanted to go, either, because professional environmentalists are usually too radical or too strident, but my friend and bee-keeping mentor Eleanor said Swiddens was all right. "No crusade," she promised, brushing away a few wisps of gray hair, sipping Ron Horton coffee out at the garden patch, talking apiaries. "Not over the top, like some of these guys. Practical." She paused for a word. "Soothing. Makes a lot of sense. Cute, too," she giggled.

Now Ellie's been faithfully married to Dan for 25 years and hardly wanted a little something on the side. But that never stopped her from looking. "I'm married," she'd smile, "not dead."

Making the rounds of BC communities, Swiddens was in Kamloops for a night, off the next morning to Whistler, two days in Vancouver, then Victoria. "Stumping for the gospel," he smiled.

Nice room in the Community Centre, cool, comfortable, windows on the world. Seats 60, usually draws 20-30. That night, something drew these folks, because there were more than 80. SRO, a dozen in the back. Not bad for a Thursday night.

Of course, I didn't know everyone there, but I recognized enough of them. Friends, customers, acquaintances. Farm folk, sure, to be expected. But also railroad people, school teachers, mail clerks. A couple of Main Street lawyers and a pair of undertakers. Most in shirt sleeves. Two with ties. Couple of sweat suits. Three, no, make that four old-style house dresses.

Water, coffee all around. Brief introduction by Marian McDermott, the NSCC exec, in blue jean skirt and One Proud Tree Hugger T-shirt. Presentation of credentials. Swiddens' gracious nod that we braved a beautiful spring night to be here.

Laughs and a smattering of applause.

Then he was on us.

"Man," Swiddens gestured, glancing around the room, "is a most arrogant creature. He believes he can alter Nature for his own benefit. And Nature will simply sit still for it. Without any pushback. Well." He paused for effect. "Sure. Droughts. Fires. Tsunamis. Rising water temperatures. Plastic eating the Arctic even as it melts before our eyes. We're reaping our harvest now. Conflagrations like the Great McClure Fire. A water supply poisoned by Canada's Original Environmental Sin – railroads that tore up the landscape – and its stepsons, salt, and solvents, sewage. And benzene. As Al Jolson used to say --"

A few nods from the 70-plus set.

"'you ain't seen nothin' yet!'"

Rueful smiles all around.

"The worst is yet to come because the damage increases geometrically.

Two-times-two-equals-four. Then four-times-four equals sixteen. Sixteen-times-sixteen equals 256. And so on. Worse by manifold factors."

"I've heard it before," Jimmy muttered. "*You've* said this before."

I shushed him.

"Because when you pour poison into the womb of Mother Earth it stays there. It poisons life. Poisons water. Poisons us. Poisons our children."

Jimmy felt me stiffen.

"Birth defects. Retardation. Autism. Even juvenile cancer." Swiddens shook his head. "The havoc we wreak on ourselves. The war we declare on our own children, born and unborn."

"Pretty strong stuff," Jimmy said, this time loud enough for Swiddens to hear.

"Strong indeed, my friend," Swiddens answered. "Strong indeed. Let me give you a few for instances.

"Let's take pre-natal first. Where life begins, right? Our population-based findings suggest that in-utero exposure to several correlated pollutants, common pollutants, including lead, benzene, and chlorine, vastly increases risks for autism."

"Right," I whispered.

"All those nasties should be highly familiar to folks like you, who live in a railroad community."

Nods all around.

"Benzene alone," Swiddens continued. "What a killer. Benzene leached into the water supply. Benzene from motor oil and gasoline. Benzene from plastics, resins, synthetic fibers, rubber lubricants, dyes, detergents, drugs, solvents, and pesticides." He paused. "For you farmers out there, especially pesticides."

Swiddens spread out his arms.

"We've poisoned our world. We've poisoned ourselves. Strip mining and mine acid run-off. You can't count the cancers in all this, plus all the cancers we cause ourselves, fighting ourselves, fighting everything."

People rustled in their seats. No one spoke.

"While, yes, alarms need to be sounded, because our world is going downhill fast, I don't want to be an alarmist. And I don't want to send out mixed messages, either. Why am I here? To discuss practical, incremental changes, changes we can all make. Are we facing a cataclysm? Sure we are. How soon is it? That's not clear – any sort of dating is not supported by all the evidence. It's not *not* supported by the evidence, either, if that's not too confusing."

A ripple of nervous laughter throughout the room.

"But sounding alarms, and demanding overwhelming change, all that comes at a price way too high, economic, social, especially political. No one's going to sit still for it. Support it. The cataclysm to the way we live would be devastating. Insupportable."

A farmer named Witherspoon, knit shirt, brown slacks, long beard, stood and blurted out, "isn't it coming anyway?"

Swiddens, genial, unfazed, said, "might be, sure. But there may be a way to head it off at the pass. Without the complete upheaval of everything."

"Upheaval?" demanded a man named Dinkins, a noted curmudgeon and habitual *Kamloops This Week* letter-writer.

I was expecting Jimmy to say it was time to go, but he sat still for it.

"What's espoused by our ex-patriot Canadian sister Naomi Klein, for one."

A ripple of disapproval went through the room, the growl of some feral creature.

"Right. I see that some of you have heard of her. She embraces a truly radical vision. End of agri-corporations. End of capitalism, really. Nearly a return to hunting and gathering as a way to save the world. Wants to tear up everything. No traction, politically or economically." Swiddens shook his head. "People love to bash big corporations. Sure, they do some bad things. But they also provide a great deal of food. Destroy the agri-corps and you have to ask how people will be fed. OK, sure, some populations are overfed. *Way* overfed. So what's next? Food rationing? There's a sure-fire vote-getter. Do you want *more* government? Deciding *that*?"

Laughter all around.

"It's radical, of course. Cataclysmic. Perhaps what she says is true, of course. Perhaps what she says is necessary. Perhaps the world requires that radical change."

I was struck, for all his force and message, how mild, how even-handed Swiddens was. And in that, how effective.

"But people will never willingly go for it. The political groundswell is not there. Not the political will, not the political capital. The fear is too great, and the money is all betting against it."

"So what's your answer?" This from a retired high school English teacher named Suzanne Phillips with a full head of iron-gray hair and a cardigan to match.

"Blue Canada stands for grassroots, incremental change. We use MADD as a model, abetted by the lightning rise of social media. We all remember the bad old days when people poured themselves into their cars and drove home."

Many laughs and head shaking.

"*When* they made it home and not in the hospital. Or jail. Or the morgue. MADD changed the world, one drunk driver at a time. We think that Blue Canada, and our partners around the world, can work us toward the tipping point where people are taking reasonable steps themselves, demanding that legislatures keep pace, and that large corporate interests act as Mother Earth's responsible husbands."

Swiddens paused. He had us and he knew it.

"Small, careful measures," he smiled. "Here's what we can start doing."

Afterward, I took Jimmy's arm. "It's too late for Petey, poisoned by benzene."

"We don't know that," Jimmy objected.

"Maybe not. But maybe yes."

Jimmy said nothing, but I knew what he was thinking.

"Maybe too late for Mother Earth," I said. "But maybe not."

"Maybe," he shrugged.

Jimmy, well, Jimmy knew when I'd gotten the better of him.

"OK, Marci Jo," he hung his head, a penitent, "I'll do it for you. I'll do it for my adopted homeland. I'll get better traps. Better waste disposal. I'll take out loans. I *hate* debt, but if you can live with it, so can I."

"Aw, thanks, Jimmy," I snuggled up to him, "but it won't be all that bad. I think we can afford it. I *hope* we can afford it. After all, you're a *Canadian* now, Jimmy, been one for a while. You're a made guy. We can do this."

He stared out the kitchen window at the sheds in the backyard. "One more benzene trap is going to save the world?"

"That's pretty funny, coming from you." I put down my Calgary Stampede coffee mug. "Jimmy Mainzdorfer, the pacifist. The one more guy you didn't kill in Vietnam. The one more life you saved in the Great McClure Fire. The one more benzene trap that might save a kid like Petey." I paused. "Might."

"Yeah," he shrugged. "I guess."

He didn't see my smirk.

All's well that ends well.

Maybe.

The wars. The fires. The benzene poisoning.

We travel on this planet and we make incremental changes. Laurel heals a bit at a time, inside and out. Petey gets into a special NSCC program, sort of Montessori-on-steroids. Only three hours a day, but it's a start. Jimmy's going to keep the benzene out of our ground water. I've bought two hives and a queen. Life is good.

However, Petey's always going to be Petey, and will be minimally prepared to deal with life. The glaciers will continue to recede. The Arctic – not so far away from Western Canada – will continue to fill up with indestructible, indigestible plastic.

Closer by, closer than we think, closer than we *want*, benzene continues to leach into the ground water, into the earth. And, hidden from view, snaking along root systems and sunken trees, the natural compost of the vast Canadian Rockies, the Great McClure Fire continues to smolder unabated, insidious, implacable, unstoppable, ready to rise up and strike at any time.

QUININE

▼

CANAL ZONE, PANAMA

"Colonel? We have a situation, sir."

That's how it began, on a sodden Sunday afternoon, Gamboa, Canal Zone, off-base officers' housing. Over a bucket of iced-down gin-and-tonics, the Old Man and I reviewing staffing reports, water clinging to every surface.

This was the peacetime army, an easy command, natives on one side of the border, shipping on the other, whores and criminals in the middle. Things went well as along as everyone stayed in place.

Billeted in two top floors of a three-story frame building, the Old Man was most at home in his large, open living room — eternally shrouded in heat, humidity, and cigar smoke. Although they tried, the ceiling fans were ineffective, pushing around the blue haze but never entirely dispelling it. Neither were the windows, open on three sides to the errant breezes. Clean and sober on base, on Sundays the Old Man liked his Fleischmann's — hardly top shelf, but readily available and able to get the job done.

"Never drink anything you can't pronounce," he liked to say.

Outside, the Gamboa compound was hedged by rainforest, a vast world of green jungle — royal palms with leaves large enough for roofs, swamp grass, ferns, vines tangled and thick. Above it, above the notch where the Chagres River runs into Lake Gatun, birds hung on thermals, and monkeys — howlers, tamarinds, capuchins — swung through the trees.

Situation. A code word. All language is, but some words are more charged than others. Situation. Something you never asked for, something you have to address.

Waving him in, the Old Man knew this was serious. Otherwise this soldier would not be bothering his CO off base – especially not when the drinking lamp was lit.

I turned: it was Sergeant Theo Kirkpatrick, lanky, buzzcut aide to Ben Anderson, fellow lieutenant, duty officer, Canalside HQ. The Old Man and I were both quizzical. Why send someone? Why not simply use the telephone?

And what situation was sufficiently dire to send a sergeant scampering up to Gamboa on a steamy, sleepy Sunday?

Trim, gray, with a manner as clipped as his white mustache, the Old Man was not without civility – and a sense of humor. "At ease, sergeant," he waved. "While I appreciate the attention, and the courtesy, why drive all the way up here? Couldn't this wait? And if not," he gestured at his desk, "wouldn't the phone have sufficed?"

"Yes, sir," Kirkpatrick allowed, "except that Lieutenant Anderson --"

"Good man, Anderson."

"Yes, sir. The lieutenant insisted that I brief the colonel personally. Ears only."

The Old Man turned a palm.

"The lieutenant's concerned about being overheard, sir."

The Old Man looked at me.

"Reasonable, sir," I nodded. "Who knows who listens in on unsecured lines."

Even assuming the locals weren't tapping our phones, Anderson's idea had merit. An army base is a sieve, information leaking everywhere.

"Go on, sergeant," the Old Man said.

"Edwards, sir, Private Travis."

The Old Man looked at me.

"PIA, sir," I said.

"Apparently. Go ahead, sergeant."

Clearly, concisely, Kirkpatrick, described how Edwards, a trained boxer, went off limits. When Edwards did not return to base by curfew, the MPs went looking for him. Discovering his whereabouts, they found he'd gotten into it with a *puta* and her *chulo*, and the girl wound up dead.

Despite the MPs' best efforts to extricate him, they failed. Situation is that Edwards is in some unnamed place and being held for ransom.

"How much?" the Old Man asked.

"Not known, sir," Kirkpatrick said, adding that the price was likely to be high.

The Old Man seemed unperturbed. "And if we don't pay them?"

"They said we will find what's left of our man in Lake Gatun."

"Thank you, sergeant, that will be all."

"Yes, sir," Kirkpatrick turned and left.

"Lieutenant?" the Old Man asked.

Colonel George Greggson Gardner; mother's family, the Missouri Greggson cattle and farming folks. Called Greg from childhood by his confidants and bridge partners. Trim, athletic, all spit and polish and spine, core of the peacetime army. After 18 years, he was looking at 20-and-out, "while I still have some years left," he said.

I was his adjutant and admired him. The Old Man liked army life, its rules and rituals and regularity. Unlike his predecessor, Tom Parsons, the Old Man knew how to control himself. Knew how to meet things with silence instead of an ill-tempered response. Never let his emotions get the better of him or said something he'd regret.

"Let me do some digging, sir," I said. "I'll have a brief for you at --"

"0900."

"Yes, sir," I stood, then paused. "I fear this won't end well."

"You make certain that it does, lieutenant."

Sickly and malarial, the Canal Zone's heat rose from the swamps and lakes and rivers in curtains of death and disease. In season, rain came in great cascades of water that crackled like gunfire and reduced visibility to zero.

It's all right to tell the story now. All the principals have passed, a piece of history that doesn't matter. A snapshot from the late 1950s.

The last of them, the Old Man himself, age 93, died peacefully in his sleep at his home, Chesapeake Bay, Eastern Shore, where he spent his last years, like Monet and his water lilies, painting watercolors of the hypnotic Maryland landscape, its variants of storm and sun, swamp and sea, seaweed and sand.

A soldier all his life, the Old Man enlisted on Monday, December 8, 1941, and never left. Anzio Beach, Inchon, he was army all the way, rising through the ranks, rotating in and out of domestic and overseas duty. The Canal Zone was his penultimate posting; Fort Jackson his last, quiet duty for a man who'd seen and done so much.

Quiet and moral, good at maintaining order and staying out of the way, the Old Man never cared much for policy or politics, liked parties even less. Never a striver or a climber, he was a professional, plain and simple. Member of a military family since 1862, when his great-grandfather skedaddled from the family farm to fight for Mr. Lincoln and the Union. Surviving Antietam Creek and the Wilderness, he served out west before coming home. His son, the Old Man's grandfather, saw action in the War with Spain, though he never much cared for Teddy Roosevelt, calling him a bully and a blowhard. "Never met a headline he didn't like," he muttered, "especially when it was about him". His son, in turn, serving under Black Jack Pershing, rode a trench in France and Belgium in what they called The Great War. When the Old Man retired, in early '63, adding two to his 20 to round out a tour in South Carolina, it was the first time in a century that a Gardner did not wear a uniform in service to his country. The Old Man had no sons, and his three daughters were not so inclined.

For his part, Slomanson – if that really was his name – simply vanished. I imagine that he spent a great deal of time in Vietnam, but that's pure speculation.

Predictably, Mark Stanley made captain, insisted on going to Vietnam, insisting on taking his tour of duty in the field, and died there.

Travis Edwards never made it out the Canal Zone.

I'm the only one left, Pat Rawlins – Bud Rawlins' boy – Massachusetts not Virginia Rawlins. Catholics not Presbyterians. Unionists not Secessionists. While I never made it past lieutenant, I never wanted to. I didn't need more military than that.

Is it all right to tell the story now? Has the statute of limitations expired?

No, because there's no statute of limitations on murder.

"Lieutenant?" the Old Man asked.

0900 on the dot, and we sat in the Old Man's office overlooking the

Canal. Tidy, windows open, the command center had cream-colored walls, wooden desks and book cases, photo of Ike, large American flag in the corner and smaller one on his desk. The humidity had already crawled under my skin like an unwelcome guest.

"Travis NMI Edwards. Twenty-two years old. Bad boy from out west. Oregon. Unwed, teenaged mother. Father absent and unknown. Golden Gloves boxer – with the busted nose to prove it. Juvenile delinquent. Given the choice by a judge, Edwards took the army to stay out of prison."

"We get far too many of those," the Old Man said.

"Undoubtedly, sir," I agreed.

"The courts dump these children on us," the Old Man said. "Post-adolescents who can't live with freedom. Who screw up. Who can't make it on the outside – otherwise, they would. Who like prison rules but want off-base passes. We're America's trash heap – and America doesn't really care what happens here.

"I know this Edwards – or too many like him. Never had a father so never learned to be a man. Depended on the army, but by then it was too late."

"Agreed, sir," I said, "Edwards tends to think with his one source of success, his fists. Never made for a soldier. Got him off the street in Eugene, but didn't help us. Brought an alien element into our culture. No guarantee it would work. Generally, the army and the soldier emerge unscathed. This time it didn't."

"Well said, lieutenant. Private Edwards' service jacket?"

"Already on your desk, sir."

The Old Man raised an eyebrow.

"The good adjutant always anticipates."

"Apparently so, lieutenant. Well done."

"Thank you, sir."

Reading quickly, the Old Man looked up. "Stockade three times in two months?"

"Yes, sir. DND. Refusing orders. Fighting. Good fighter, at that. While the army needs tough soldiers, it also needs soldiers who know how to take orders – and how to stay in their place."

"Well put, lieutenant."

"Thank you, sir."

"Dishonorable discharge?"

"Borderline, sir."

"Seems to have crossed the border this time, lieutenant."

"Yes, sir. FUBAR, sir."

"Start the paperwork, would you, lieutenant?"

"Yes, sir."

"We can execute it when he comes back. If he comes back." The Old Man paused. "Tell me about this place where they were holding him, this --"

"*El Perdido*," I said. "More or less translates as The Forgetting. In Panama City's worst slum. Think of Havana with social diseases."

Despite himself, the Old Man laughed.

"They indulge every fantasy, sir. And I mean *every* fantasy. You have the cash, they have the talent, willing and able. Of course, it's off limits, sir. *Very* off limits. Which is what attracts men like Private Edwards. Who ignore the four rules."

"You're joking, lieutenant," the Old Man objected.

"I wish I were, sir. Never go in alone, never drink the warm beer, never fraternize, never travel without someone to stand guard."

"Apparently," the Old Man said, "I haven't had enough coffee this morning."

"To call it an opium den is far too charitable. It's a warren of mold and mildew, mattresses and mayhem, every perversion imaginable. In a stage setting of paint hanging in strips, scavenged metal, standing water, urine and feces and blood smeared on the walls. *El Perdido* is right: it's easy to forget who you are, how to get back. There are places where you forget your soul. In *El Perdido* you forget your name."

"You sound like an expert, lieutenant."

"MPs called a few years back – before your time. One of our men OD'd; the locals had no use for an American corpse. We retrieved him without incident. Came armed, couple of Jacksons for the *chulo*, grabbed the GI, and were gone."

The Old Man waited.

"This time, sir, things got out of hand. Edwards was in whatever he was in, beat his very underage paramour to death. Now they want to be paid, because good talent doesn't come cheap, and because we want Private

Edwards returned alive and relatively unharmed." I paused. "There's blood on this one. It won't be simple."

The Old Man shook his head.

"Generally, we can make do with cash or gifts from the PX – liquor, perfume, cigarettes. But *El Perdido* is more complicated. Two reasons. First, the girls. I mean *girls*. Maybe 11. Maybe younger. They're merchandize. Property. Farm animals. Worth *mucho dinero*. Edwards cost them. Second, they didn't like his attitude. They want to make an example of him. Third, there's a hierarchy involved."

"I was afraid you were going to say that," the Old Man muttered.

"Early this morning I put in a call to Digby in the Governor General's office --"

The Old Man spread his hands.

"He's a good man," I assured him. "Discrete. Trustworthy. He filled in a lot of background. Why this *chulo* thinks he can play hardball with us." I took a deep breath. "Ostensibly, *El Perdido* is run by some *bandeleros* called *Hombres Muy Malos*, and they really are. Their ostensible leader is a pock-marked little squirt named Luis Rojas, one of *El Presidente's* bag men. Skims off the top, too."

"Of course," the Old Man said.

"He answers to *Los Pandilleros*, the murderers who run the rackets in Panama City. This group of cut-throats is headed by *El Largarto*. The Lizard."

The Old Man made a face.

"Cut off a leg, it grows back."

The Old Man shook his head.

"I wish it were as simple as the Opera Buffa it appears to be, sir, but it isn't. *El Largarto's* real name is Ramon Villaneuva."

Again, the Old Man shrugged.

"Who in real life is President Navarro's first cousin. Ernesto de la Guardia himself. *El Presidente*. Born in Panama City. Master's Degree in – are you ready for this? – finance. From Dartmouth. Speaks the lingo. Makes a great impression. Knows how to sweet-talk Ike. Already fought off one coup, allegedly sponsored by Fidel."

The Old Man closed his eyes.

"Digby says that Ike trusts him, as much as he trusts anyone south of the border, where alliances shift like tectonic plates. In any event, Navarro's our joe, and what's good for *El Presidente* is good for Ike. And what's good for Ike is good for us."

"Back to Edwards," the Old Man said.

"Yes, sir. While *El Largarto* is something of a psychopath, his rackets pay well. Since this is Panama, where the sun rises in the west and sets in the east, ships sail across mountains, and money flows uphill, Rojas *el chulo* kicks up to Villaneuva *El Largarto* kicks up to Navarro *El Presidente* for his Miami real estate and Swiss bank accounts. So this is going to be costly." I exhaled. "As far as Digby could ascertain, Edwards is being held in the jungle for a significant ransom – at this stage the numbers keep changing. Further, if we don't pay, *El Largarto*, meaning *El Presidente*, is threatening to stage a serious international incident."

The Old Man shook his head.

"Remember, sir, these people riot on demand."

"Let them," the Old Man said.

"Yes, sir, but that won't get us Private Edwards."

Before I could call Digby back, before the Old Man could think about what to do, we got an eyes-only telex from the regional commander at the Pentagon, cc someone at State, ordering us to stand fast until we meet with someone they were sending.

"Good," the Old Man said, although he would quickly change his mind. "At least somebody in Washington appreciates the fact there's a soldier lost in the field."

"Or this is something we can't handle out of petty cash," I said.

"I don't know that he has a title," the Old Man said, "and if he does, it hasn't been shared with me. I received this follow-up telex," he waved a piece of paper. "Seems that this fellow, Slomanson, is arriving at 1800 hours on a private DC-6. Just him. I think that spells clout, don't you, lieutenant?"

"Indeed, sir."

Appearing later in the evening, Slomanson was a flaccid man, 40, prematurely balding, sweat already soaking through his shirt. "Slomanson," he chuckled, as if we were all in on the joke. No first name, no title. When the Old Man asked, Slomanson simply shook his head. "No, not a consul. Here to help, that's all."

State? CIA? the Old Man prodded.

"Here to help," Slomanson repeated. "Here to make it all come out right."

"How was your flight in?" the Old Man asked.

"Oh, moderately crummy," Slomanson said, plopping into a chair.

Later, we took to calling him MC Slomanson, for Moderately Crummy, which was his answer to virtually everything. Or in military talk – milspeak – ModCrumSlo.

Round, flat face, which he mopped with a large, white handkerchief. Blue seersucker suit, dark knit tie, wrinkled collar – the inverse of the smooth, efficient spook, or state department apparatchik. Given Ike's notorious insistence on formality, Slomanson was a complete anomaly. Looking at him, we were certain that whoever he was, Slomanson must have been awfully good at his job. Looking at us, he seemed to carry a halo of sorrow – for the state of world affairs, for our predicament, for Private Edwards, unwitting progenitor of a possible major international confrontation.

With his husky voice, Slomanson sounded like a smoker, but wasn't. "Heat's something here, isn't it?" he wiped his face again, then said as if he were an avuncular country doctor, "let's see what we can fix."

"The situation," the Old Man began, but Slomanson cut him off.

"I'm not interested in the situation, Colonel," he said. "The situation is your affair. I'm interested in consequences. How Ike will appear on the front page of tomorrow's newspapers. Or *not* appear. What are you drinking?"

"I'm sorry," the Old Man said. "I should have offered you one. Gin and tonic."

"Tropical drink," Slomanson nodded. "I'll join you, if you don't mind."

"Not at all," the Old Man said, nodding to me.

As the Old Man had long ago dismissed the mess boys, I did the honors.

"Quinine," the Old Man said. "Wards off malaria, the various illnesses we get here. Good for the shakes and the sweats." He paused. "The gin doesn't hurt, either."

"Too bad quinine won't help with this one," Slomanson held up his glass. "This is my fourth, no fifth time here. Last time was three years ago, '56. Came with Ike – before him, actually; advance work. You weren't here, as I recall."

"No," the Old Man said. "Rotated in two years ago from Japan. That was quiet duty, too. We watched Korea. Hosted ball teams. Here, I inherited the post from Colonel Parsons. Staff in place – good men," the Old Man nodded at me. "Very good."

"Ike served here, too, in the '20s," Slomanson said. "Place hasn't changed much. Still beastly hot, still plenty of shipping, and, given the cut we give them, the natives still lay down. That's important because your man is more than just a wayward GI. That might work in Germany or Japan, where we don't have a lot at stake. But this is the Canal Zone. Another place we stole – like Hawaii. Stole Panama from Columbia, flooded 60 miles of jungle, destroyed countless natives and native villages, subjugated the rest, permanently placed an occupying army in country, held an entire independent state hostage. Might get somebody annoyed, don't you think?"

The Old Man said nothing.

"American imperialism," Slomanson said, "learned from our parent, Britain, the British Empire. Where the sun never set. Found its perfect apostle in the Sultan of the Strenuous Life. *Bully!* The world was his oyster, the Canal his crowning achievement. That photo on the giant earth mover – his toy. His monstrous toy. New leader for a new century – the American century."

Another nod, another drink, another face mop. "As you might imagine, such attitudes do not exactly play well everywhere. Especially in those lands blessed to be part of the new American enterprise." Slomanson shrugged. "That's the thing about grudges. Who knows how long they last? And how violent they become?

"This soldier may not matter to us, in a grand civic way, but they see it as part of a smoldering insurgency, the death of a thousand cuts. Private – " he fumbled.

"Edwards," I interjected.

"If we allow them to make Private Edwards one of the cuts, they'll play it around the world. We can't have that. It's a simple-enough fix. Costly, but simple.

"To Panama," Slomanson raised his glass, "unhappy host to a long line of rapists – Spain, Columbia, Uncle Sam. Uncle Sap. Uncle Squeeze – as by the *cojones*. We come around, everybody gets well."

"What happened to 'millions for defense but not one cent for tribute'?"

"Nice headline," Slomanson allowed. "Sure, kill 'em all. Nobody would care. Probably get medals from Navarro despite the fact that *El Largarto* is his cousin. Cousin but a loose cannon. But it's easier, cleaner, to pay them rather than risk creating martyrs to American imperialism and having the story on the front page of the *New York Times*. Put another way, we can't have anything like Caracas last May."

"That was Nixon," the Old Man said, "worst man in the history of the navy."

"Navy had nothing to do with it," Slomanson said, "and neither did Nixon. Poor planning, poor advance work. American Vice President, wrong place, wrong time."

"Still," the Old Man said.

"Privately," Slomanson said, "Ike despises Nixon, but he needs Nixon to placate the party's right wing. His price for the Presidency. Unctuous, endlessly self-serving, Nixon is everything Ike isn't. Be that as it may, after Venezuela, Ike wants things nice and calm. Quiet. Managed. Can't afford hostiles. Can't afford another Iran – not what we expect here, but you never know when things can get out of hand. Ike's still burning about that. Rightly so. We tried to make it go away. It hasn't, and he's still paying the price. Here, with the Canal in play, we don't need a GI as a public relations tool. So we're going to buy your soldier back. Call it Operation Quinine. There's payment for the dead girl. For Edwards' return. For *El Largarto*. For *El Presidente*."

Slomanson rose. "Whatever you do, keep the Ambassador, a drunk Republican banker if ever there were one, away from this. WASP inbreeding at its worst."

At least Slomanson was right about that. In the Canal Zone, the law was as you bought it. "Other than American pesos," my former CO, Colonel Nestor Parsons told me, "the only law they know is this." Parsons, a big-bellied, red-faced man ready for retirement, patted the Colt 1911 that he always wore, even to chapel. "Brown Betty, *la prima pistola Americana*. Made just in time – to subdue Panama's restless natives. Know what these *Yaquis* called it? The Yankee Fist." Parsons unholstered it to show me. "It's got a big, fat, slow-moving slug that knocks you down and keeps you down.

"I got a woman back home. Keeps me warm. Makes me feel good. But this one here," he holstered Betty, "she keeps me safe. She keeps the peace. Our peace."

Parsons was right. In the Canal Zone, the army was a government within a government. Certainly, there was civilian control, duly constituted, but by cash and coercion we made it work. Sometimes by the clear light of the glorious golden sun, sometimes by the deceptive light of the changeable ghostly moon. We distrusted – and circumvented – civilians whenever we could. Both the locals and our own diplomats – political appointees used to dealing with nothing more complex or combative than horticulture clubs. Hosting trade delegations, they spoke pidgin-Spanish, navigated cocktail parties. Felt important. Put on weight. Went home with swelled heads and fancy souvenirs. While we did the heavy lifting, including taking care of our own.

Panama being Panama, *El Largarto* was as good – or as bad – as his word. He simply kept the money – and Travis Edwards. Why? Why not? Why surrender his plaything?

It was night, and it was raining, and the isthmus seemed feverish. At the base, with a view of the Canal and Lake Gatun, ships' running lights splashed along the water.

"They've been paid," Slomanson chuckled, "paid well, so at least no riots.

"Not everything works," he shrugged, and the Old Man was silently furious. "We don't excuse. We don't apologize. We just write better copy."

"I've got a soldier in the jungle," the Old Man said. "That's not a matter of copy."

"I understand your objections," Slomanson said.

"How am I supposed to account for my solider?" the Old Man pressed.

Slomanson was good. Mild, controlled, unperturbed; he could have been discussing kitchen cleanser. "You can say he went AWOL. You can say he's MIA. You can say he drowned in Lake Gatun and his body was never recovered. You can say whatever you please, Colonel. It doesn't matter what your story is as long as we all agree to it. He's gone, and you're going to have to live with that. Cut your losses."

"I work to keep my men safe and secure and sent back home in one piece, proud that they've served their country. No one loves peace more than a solider, so, no, we don't want any trouble here, either. We like quiet. We like to keep it that way. But --"

"That's fine, Colonel. While we may be able to protect our men from the enemy, we can't protect them from themselves. Your man brought it on himself."

"Yes, he did," the Old Man said. "He'll be reprimanded. Perhaps discharged."

"He may well be sacrificed," Slomanson said. "We're dealing with – " Slomanson paused. "Who knows what happens when their blood is up? Unfortunately, a number of soldiers commit suicide. Consider your Private Edwards another one."

"Don't know as I like that," the Old Man said.

"Don't know as you have a choice," Slomanson said. "Don't know as I care."

"Are you," the Old Man began, but Slomanson cut him off.

"Soldiers are sacrificed for policy all the time, Colonel. You of all people should know that. We know that every army operates on acceptable levels of casualties. If it comes to that, your man will die so that we will continue to have good relations here and the ships will keep running. So that Ike won't have to deal with any SNAFUs."

The Old Man just glowered.

"You might even get a posting in the Pentagon out of this."

"I've been to Washington," the Old Man could barely conceal his contempt. "It's hot there, too. Like here, a city built on a swamp. I'm happy – happier – to be out in the field. Wherever the army sends me. Hopefully to keep my men out of harm's way."

Slomanson was finished. "You're being ordered to stand down, Colonel."

"Who are you to give me – " the Old Man began, but Slomanson cut him off.

"You don't want to ask that, Colonel. Just stand down. Save your career."

The Old Man began to say something.

"There are a lot of things we have to take, Colonel, and this is one of them. Like my old grandpappy used to say, 'you've got to eat a peck of dirt before you die.'"

Slomanson didn't know the Old Man. I did. He wasn't going to take a single bite.

Slomanson had gone, and we were drinking again. Gin and quinine.

"Perhaps we should improvise," the Old Man said.

"It would seem that way, sir," I answered.

Silence, broken by the sound of another two fingers of gin. Then two more.

"I like Ike," I muttered.

"Hell, I *love* Ike." The Old Man was livid. "I love Ike and the army and the good old US of A in that order. But this is a man down in the field. No matter how doubtful or damaged." He drained his glass – his fourth or fifth, I'd lost track. "And this is where a soldier never leaves his post. Where he disobeys his Commander-in-Chief. I don't care what kind of solider Private Edwards is or isn't. I'll be damned if I allow some stranger to tell me how to protect my own men. We will *not* leave him out there."

"Yes, sir."

"Call Stanley. Call the Black Squad. We're getting him back."

While every base had one, no one ever discussed the Black Squads. Completely necessary, completely off the books, Black Squads existed because when you put Americans in hostile environments, you need a way to protect them. Secretly. Silently.

Eight men. Separate quarters. Mess. Training. Drills.

A stocky scholastic wrestler, Lieutenant Mark Stanley relished his role as Black Squad leader. ROTC, Purdue engineer, student of military history itching to mix it up.

However, that was not what the Old Man wanted, and his orders were strict and explicit. "Do *not* go in with guns blazing, lieutenant. Go in as black as black gets. This is a simple extraction. You are *not* to kill anyone, although they do richly deserve it."

"How do we know where he is, sir?" Stanley asked. "And is the intel good?"

"Lieutenant," the Old Man gestured to me.

"Snitches drew us a map." I spread out a schematic of Lake Gatun and its tributaries. "These people would sell out their mothers, and usually do."

Stanley snorted.

"The double sawbuck was probably six months' income. And then some."

I showed Stanley the line our man had drawn down the Chagres River, two clicks into an unnamed jungle camp. "*El Largarto* has some kind of enclave there," I said. "He and his Merry Men – *Los Pandilleros*."

"Sounds like a joke," Stanley muttered.

"It's not, lieutenant," the Old Man said. "They're as deadly as deadly gets."

"*Hombres Muy Malos*," I said.

"This *El Largarto*," Stanley began, peering at the map.

"The worst of the worst, from what we're led to believe."

"Will he be there?" Stanley pressed.

"Not known," I said. "Keeps a tight grip on what goes on, so there's a chance."

Stanley started to smile but stopped when he heard the Old Man's voice.

"Another reason to maintain stealth, lieutenant. You do not want to get in a firefight with these murderers. And I don't want to lose anyone else on this one."

"Yes, sir."

"We've got to get this done *now*, lieutenant. Before the rainy season. We can deal with the locals. But we can't deal with eight inches of mud."

"Roger that, sir," Stanley said, never taking his eyes off the map.

Before the Old Man dismissed Stanley storm clouds had gathered over the jungle. Then it rained for five straight days. Because I knew the

Old Man would do little else until Private Edwards was safe, I stocked his Gamboa quarters with Fleischmann's and quinine. Most of the time, he stood, back to me, holding a highball glass, staring at the water pummeling the jungle. Finally, the weather cleared – and the Black Squad went.

Black rubber boat, black wet suits, black gloves, under cover of darkness. *Always* under cover of darkness. Even in broad daylight the Black Squad moved under cover of darkness.

Slipping off a rusty fishing trawler in Lake Gatun, they were wholly invisible as they headed toward the Chagres River, silent, save for a slight slip of water from their paddles. Silent, dodging the garish, multicolored running lights of the ships waiting to traverse the Miraflores Locks. Silent, masked in black wet suits and war paint. Silent, viewing the world through night goggles.

Unwritten Rule 101A in the *U.S. Army Survival Manual* is no plan ever survives first contact with the enemy. This one, no matter how cogent, was no exception.

When the Black Squad landed, Stanley ran the program by the book. Two men stayed with raft, six headed in. Two stayed at mouth of village, a half-dozen shabby huts, sounds of drink and sex, four headed in. Intel just right: two stayed at the doorway of the hut where Edwards was bound and beaten – beaten so badly that his left eye was swollen shut and his head was a purple basketball. Two entered, dirt floor, filth all around, untied Edwards, hauled him to his feet, headed out.

As he told me later, Stanley wasn't surprised that Edwards wasn't guarded. With the fix already in, who was going to attack an abandoned native village two clicks from the Chagres River? For the Black Squad, easy in, easy out, back on the river.

Except that they ran into a drunk *pandillero* staggering around the compound. Before they could cut his throat, he raised the alarm. Bullets started flying. According to Stanley – and I believe him – the Black Squad tried to leave without returning fire, thinking, rightfully, the locals could chalk it up to rum demons. No such luck. Bullets move like billiard balls, spinning all over the place. One nicked Willie James' rib, shattered, spun sideways, took a piece out of his side. Another winged Ted Ehrlich, slicing his upper arm. Of necessity, the Black Squad returned fire, just enough to cover themselves, Stanley hoping they could retreat with minimal damage.

You have to give the *Pandilleros* credit for being resolute. Although they couldn't see much, they really poured it on. So the Black Squad did, too. Had to. Of course, the locals were no match for them. In the crossfire, which got pretty thick, bullets shattered a lit kerosene lamp, which exploded. The palm huts went up in an instant, flames shooting 50 feet high, damn near igniting the entire jungle, except it was too wet. Nevertheless, the fire did burn something fierce, strong enough so that Stanley and the Black Squad saw everyone there, *los hombres armados* and their *putas*. It took about two minutes, maybe less, train fire with automatic weapons, easy as a carnival shooting gallery. No locals left alive.

No doubt all the ships saw the flames, but none called it in. Night in the jungle.

In five minutes the Black Squad and Edwards were back in the rubber boat, swift and silent, trawler in sight. When he came to, Edwards shook his head, spit blood, and smiled. Snickered, really. "Thanks for getting me, GIs," he said. "Got a little hairy back there." Edwards coughed, brought up more blood. "I know what's coming. Sick call. Two weeks D Block. I'll do that standing up – done it before. Then I'm going back."

"Off limits, private." Stanley kept up the rhythm with his paddle.

"Off limits my ass," Edwards rose to one elbow. "Those fuckers need payback. Big time. And I'm going to pay 'em back."

"Get the fuck down and shut the fuck up," Stanley said. "We're not home yet."

That was one debrief I didn't want to give.

"I'll get a full report from Lieutenant Stanley, sir, but the skinny is that it went south. While they did extract Private Edwards, the Black Squad had to kill them all. The camp burned down in the process."

The Old Man muttered something I couldn't hear.

"Our informants tell us that *El Largarto* was there. Died with the rest of them."

"There'll be hell to pay," the Old Man shook his head.

"Perhaps not, sir. Since the camp is not supposed to be there, it's all deniable. There're no witnesses. There's no proof we were there. To make this an incident *El Presidente* has to admit that this goes on in his progressive republic – and that he permits it." I paused. "He's already been paid. So he'll just have to take it."

"Slomanson?"

"Absolutely deniable, sir. It wasn't us. Rotgut rum. Squabble over a woman. All shot each other. Kerosene lamps, palm huts. What does anyone expect?"

The Old Man had iron in his spine – and stared down Slomanson. He, too, had to take it. He had to go back to Washington – and keep his mouth shut.

"You were under orders, Colonel," Slomanson objected.

"Not on the map," the Old Man said. "Doesn't have a name. Never existed."

"What if the *Times* finds it? UNESCO?" Slomanson was sweating again.

"Let them," the Old Man shrugged. "Some local party got out of hand. Rival drug gangs. Too many guns. Too many kerosene lanterns. Some weird religious ritual. Besides, Americans don't so such things. There're a lot of ways to walk it back." He paused. "Write better copy."

I suppressed a smile.

Slomanson tried to up the ante. "Do you know how vindictive Ike can be?"

"I don't know. And I don't care. Because Ike is never going to see this. You're to going to cover this, Mr. Slomanson, and you're going to like it."

Slomanson was taken aback. "Why is that?"

"Because you won't go back to Washington and admit you couldn't fix this."

"That won't placate Navarro."

"We've already paid him enough to offset the insult."

"Maybe not."

"Maybe yes. Make it very clear that if he doesn't sit still we'll kill everyone in his family, including the illegitimate daughter he's got stashed in that Zurich convent school, Zurich, so he can visit her and his money at the same time."

Slomanson ground his teeth.

"Besides, you can tell him we've done him a favor. *El Largarto* – who knows when he was going to get frisky? We got rid of him – now everyone else will get in line." The Old Man paused. "At least for a while."

Slomanson was silent.

"Ike never needs to know," the Old Man said.

"Ike pays me so that he *doesn't* know," Slomanson said. "Plausible deniability."

"We're finished here," the Old Man said. "Now get out of my office before I have you arrested for trespassing. Or shot for attempting to sabotage the Canal."

Slomanson, wiping his face, thought that the Old Man was joking. He wasn't.

"Lieutenant, assemble a detail to escort Mr. Slomanson off base. Immediately."

"With pleasure, sir."

The Old Man was one tough soldier, all right. He was going to send Edwards to D Block while he decided what to do with him. Court martial, no doubt, followed by a swift dishonorable discharge.

However, he had a change of heart when Edwards stood before him.

The picture of contrition, Travis Edwards nearly sniveled. "I'm truly sorry, sir. I truly regret my actions. I've brought shame on myself, my service, and my country. I'm deeply humiliated, and I've learned my lesson. I'm asking for a second chance."

No doubt about it, in juvenile court Edwards had learned how to manipulate language, people, and systems to escape punishment. In this case, he said exactly what the Old Man wanted to hear.

Not surprisingly, the Old Man turned to me. "What do you think, lieutenant?"

"I believe we should discuss it, sir."

"Right. Dismissed, Private Edwards."

The Old Man hit the intercom, instructed that Edwards be taken back to D Block.

I wasn't buying it. It wasn't only Edwards' general demeanor, but also what he said in the boat that night. Of course, Stanley told me. Of course, I kept it to myself.

Clearly, this was not going to go as planned. As anticipated.

Clearly, someone had to improvise. Handle the situation. Take matters in hand.

SOP was to take a standard GI knapsack, half-fill it with bricks wrapped in foam rubber, strap it on, and run the base's cross-country course. Hot or cold, rain or shine. Kept me in shape, cleared my mind. Did my best thinking there, following events to their presumed conclusion.

Setting out, I skirted the jungle, humidity hanging like muslin curtains. When the daily rain arrived, it showered straight down, rumbling like a train beneath the street.

In the Canal Zone I learned to think as the army thinks.

In the army, if something breaks, it's always someone's fault. Nothing just happens. Someone made it happen. And that someone has to pay the price.

The Buck stopped *there*, with the Old Man, and given Edwards' proclivities, it was likely to be bloody and public. For Slomanson, Edwards could disappear, drown, die. But the Old Man couldn't live with that, with betraying an American soldier. So the bad apple would be returned to the barrel – however briefly – and something would go wrong. Meaning a black mark on the Old Man's record. And that black mark, coming over direct orders from the Commander-in-Chief, meant the Old Man would never make general. Which would forever make him angry, bitter; a deserving man denied.

Even if Edwards managed to avoid his current travails, be discharged without wreaking havoc in *El Perdido*, get back to Oregon, he will not end well. There will be a woman. Paulie. Not Paula. Paulie. She'll be weak; thin woman, weak jaw. She'll be attracted to him because he's strong. She'll be afraid of him – as she was of her own father. She'll be comfortable in that relationship because it's familiar.

Edwards will be angry one day. Doesn't matter over what. Angry. Drunk. Worse, hung over. The worst dog of all. She'll say something. Or not say something.

He'll hit her, and, his blood rising, will hit her again. He'll break her jaw. Or her cheek bone – easy enough with those fists. Blind her. Cause a brain hemorrhage. Kill her. Either way, he'll go to prison, perhaps death row, depending on the jurisdiction and his defense counsel, neither of which will be top of the mark for Travis Edwards.

If not death row, he'll die violently. He'll get into it with the wrong people – the Bloods or the Brotherhood – who will beat him to death. Or shiv him. Or pitch him off the third-tier rail. Or the warden will have him shot trying to escape. Or have him shot attacking a guard. Or have him self-medicate with the wrong contraband. Or have him hung in his cell.

Taking care of him now was accepting the inevitable. Preventive maintenance.

As I passed the halfway mark, and began to feel it in my legs and ankles, I decided it would be wise to end the threat while there was still time. No charges that would land Edwards in D Block. Nothing fast enough even for a rushed and hushed court martial leading to too many lawyers, too many delays. Too much time for something to go wrong. No, Private Edwards required executive action, and he required it right away.

Heart rate up; breathing normal.

Hang himself in D Block? Too tricky, too difficult to control. Too many people around, too many people who'd have to be taken care of, now and in the future. Besides, the bellicose Private Edwards was hardly the suicidal type.

Accidental shooting on the rifle range? Same set of problems. Killed on the next weekend pass? Too many variables; hard to control the personnel, the area. Stabbing? Too messy. Accident? Hard to manufacture. Simply making him disappear, in the lake for instance, wouldn't work, either. Too many loose ends.

No, this had to be fast, and it had to be quiet, and it had to be close. On base.

Starting to feel it in my back.

Running path. Perfect. For all his faults, Private Edwards kept in boxing trim, including road work. Easy enough to ambush him there. Small tree branch. Step out of the shadows, hit him in the head, and again until he was unconscious and bloody. A third and a fourth time to finish the job. No witnesses. No fingerprints on the murder weapon. Fitting, too, given that he had beaten an 11-year-old prostitute to death.

Afterward, given Edwards' ability to make enemies, no one was going to look too hard for the killer. And if they did, they would never suspect someone without a motive.

Once Edwards was dead, I could dress it up any way that I wanted. Accident. Better still, died defending the Canal against attack. Vital interests of the United States. Give him a medal. Two medals. Ship him home. Leave it at that.

Where was the harm?

And the Old Man would receive his promotion, retirement, even internment at Arlington if he so desired.

"What do you see, lieutenant?" the Old Man asked.

A skilled water colorist, he was painting the jungle outside his Gamboa window.

"Leaves, sir?"

The Old Man smiled benignly as if at a slow child learning to read. "Four shades of green, lieutenant. Plus black and brown. And a splash of yellow. How the sunlight rests on the vines, darts in and out. You need an eye for detail, lieutenant."

To me, the Old Man's gauzy color wash resembled a good case of cataracts.

"Yes, sir."

Presuming that Gamboa did not have ears, we were meeting off base.

"A dead soldier is always a bad business."

"Yes, sir."

"Inquiries, lieutenant?"

"Yes, sir. Aside from his platoon, where should I start?"

"Are there no suspects, lieutenant?"

"Given Private Edwards' innate ability to offend people, his proclivity for terminating every conversion with a punch in the mouth, there might not be more than 400 men who wanted a piece of him. Assuming that's true, how much time should I spend?"

The Old Man put down his paint brush and wiped his fingers on a rag.

"He had a five-star way of making enemies, sir."

"Does the murder weapon tell us anything?"

"No, sir. Branch from a nearby tree. No fingerprints, none usable anyway."

"Waste of time."

"I can make all normal inquiries. If I find something, which I doubt, we can pursue it. Otherwise, we should leave it unsolved."

The Old Man drummed his fingers. "How many people know?"

"Very few, sir. We can contain it. Ultimately, nobody's going to care much."

"Don't we owe it to him, lieutenant?"

"Private Edwards was running at night. He ran into a tree. Call it an accident."

"Hard enough to snap his neck?"

"FUBAR. Saves disruption. Ties it off. We all move on. And," I began.

"Yes, lieutenant?"

"Create a legend. Make him a hero. Saved the Canal. Make his mother proud."

"You really are devious, lieutenant."

"Yes, sir."

"I'll consider it." He picked up his brush, dabbed it in water, then something green, and held it up. "Keep the remains, and everything else, under wraps."

"Yes, sir. Absolutely."

The Old Man spoke softly. "I'm of an age, and have an exemplary service record. I deserve – I've *earned* – an easy retirement. Two years and change to go. A murder on my base? Unsolved? Who knows where that will end? I don't need any screw-ups, lieutenant. Whatever you have to do to make it smooth, make it smooth."

"Yes, sir."

It was Ike's America, so we did indeed make Travis Edwards a hero. Invented a story about infiltration at the Canal. On patrol, took fire, returned fire. Gave his life to save his squad. I wrote the citation myself, arranged for the medal. I wanted a Silver Star, but the Old Man thought Bronze was sufficient to seal the deal, which is where we left it. Purple Heart, too, of course. Distinguished Unit Citation.

The Old Man's orders were explicit. "Send the coffin back sealed. Make sure it stays that way. Tell the military escort that, no, she doesn't want to see her boy one more time, not the way he looks now. Not after how he died. Tell her to remember him as he was. As he is. A true American hero."

It was early 1960, the end of an era, and the Old Man and I were preparing for our futures. With standing, status, and seniority, he was about to make general, about to rotate out of the Canal Zone. Choosing not to go to overseas, he preferred to run out his commission stateside, Fort Jackson, an easy-enough peacetime posting.

At the end of my four-year hitch, I wasn't so certain about where I was headed.

Vietnam was coming, and it didn't feel right. Maybe Ike saw it, sniffed it in the wind. After what happened to the French. Maybe we all felt that we couldn't make those mistakes. I know the Old Man didn't want it – a land war in Southeast Asia. We never foresaw what Kennedy et. al. would do. Their legacy, on and off the battlefield.

Leaving Panama before I did, the Old Man shipped stateside, stayed a bit longer for continuity and transition, and after 22 years mustered out. Taking his pension, he retired to the Maryland marshlands, to paint watercolors and dandle his grandchildren.

There to stay as far from the army as could possibly be. Never went to any reunions – never even answered the invitations. I knew the Old Man – he was neither angry nor standoffish. He had simply drawn the line. Never looked back.

Never answered my Christmas cards, either, any of them. Didn't stop me from sending them. I figured I owed him that much.

Not surprisingly, Stanley made captain. Easily. Could have stayed stateside. Went to Vietnam instead. Could have stayed in Saigon. Could have made major. But he wanted to be in the field. To be in it. He got in it, all right, and his gung-ho attitude got him blown to bits showing his men how to clear a tunnel. Barely enough of him remained to be scraped into a body bag and shipped back to Indiana for the funeral.

I never heard about Slomanson again, but I wouldn't have. You never do. I'm sure he wound up in Vietnam, one way or another. Back then, everyone did. I'd like to believe that like Stanley he got blown up. Saigon street bomb. I hope he never saw it coming.

Of course, I got wind of it. Mike Marquis poked his shiny head around my office door one chilly Washington morning, told me to check out the obits. "Gardner," he said. "General. You served under him, I believe. Your CO."

"I did indeed," I told him, ran the search.

As the obit told me, retired US Army Brigadier General George Greggson Gardner, age 93, passed peacefully in his sleep in his home outside Nanticoke, Maryland, Eastern Shore, Chesapeake Bay. In full possession of his faculties and serene at the last, he was surrounded by his family. Good. A blessing.

I thought about our last conversation, uncharacteristically about politics. "There'll never be another President like Ike," he said, sun already brilliant in the morning sky, the day's heat beginning to bake into HQ's walls. "A man's man. A real commander-in-chief. That kind of experience, that kind of balance, doesn't come along very often. This next election? Nixon looks like he's got the Republican nod – they do it by the numbers, and he's the next in line. Democrats? Johnson's the big name in the Senate. Between him and Rayburn in the House, and the Solid South, there's a lot of power."

I muttered something about Kennedy.

"Jack Kennedy? *Jack Kennedy*? The pretty boy? Joe Kennedy's kid? The playboy? The *very* junior Senator from Massachusetts?" The Old Man was aghast. "No. No way. No constituency. No power. He's not going anywhere. A political lightweight if there ever were one. Couldn't run a PT boat. Damn near got himself killed. Then had the gall to declare himself a war hero. Now he wants to be President? Doesn't have the focus. Not with all the whores in the District to keep him occupied for the next thousand years. And if they run dry, Hoover will see to it that there are more to distract him. He hates the Kennedys more than McCarthy hated Communists."

Of course, I never answered, never discussed the Kennedys with the Old Man, for many reasons, not the least of which was my own Massachusetts background. I have a dim memory of going to a Hyannis

Port pool party. Rose Kennedy, very regal, very toothy, sitting in a large chair, greeting people. Joe, I don't recall him there. Maybe he was having a tryst with a sweet young thing in the pool house. Who knows?

I do remember Jack, very youthful, very charismatic. Of course, there were a lot of women around him. There were always a lot of women around him. Various brothers and sisters – of no great import to me at the time. Cocktails, bathing suits, patterned cotton shirts. Nothing more profound than that.

My family was a distant star in their constellation. Railroads and real estate.

Like Jack, I thought about Congress when I was a kid. The Rawlins name wasn't a bad start, and I thought that the military might be a good credential. ROTC at Boston College – small, strong, Catholic. Close to home.

Like the Old Man, I considered the military for a career then discarded the idea – too rigid, too hierarchical. Besides, by '61 you really had to be strong about Vietnam to do well, and I wasn't. Everything about it was wrong. After I put in my four-year hitch, largely in Panama, where the army seemed to forget me, I declined the honor to re-up.

Georgetown law school – Catholic, familiar. Remained in the District, married the daughter of the Venezuelan consul – a beautiful girl named Paloma – but it didn't take. One reason or another, I never again walked down the aisle.

While I'd given up the idea of Congress --- neither the energy nor the ambition – I did work for the Massachusetts Delegation, research and editing, that sort of thing.

A chance meeting at the Jockey Club with a ROTC buddy named Alex Brome brought me to DOD. It was a good fit. My military background didn't hurt, and soon I began handling liaison work, knotty legal problems. Real estate entanglements. Missing supply items. Things that had to be moved under cover of darkness.

One day, the phone rang. Kennedy White House in the voice of Kenny O'Donnell, Jack's buddy. Knew him a little. He'd heard about my skills, discretion, military background. Did I want to come over?

Hell, yes, I wanted to come over. Jack, who didn't remember me, was the Sun King. And a pliant press made him shine all the brighter.

I wound up going all over the world, very-behind-the-scenes liaison between White House, DOD, outposts of the empire. Troubleshooting, smoothing, debriefing. Making things go away. Like Panama.

Of course, I went to Vietnam. More than once. Even for a war it was a mess. The most corrupt, disinterested, inept military imaginable. I tried to make that clear, but I was ignored.

It did not surprise me that when the President was shot I was dismissed in one of the first Johnson purges. Oh, he was effective, all right, master of the Senate, but I didn't care for his methods and detested him personally. None of that mattered, of course, because I was considered – by age, place of birth, background, religion – too close to the Kennedys. Fly too close to the sun, your wax wings melt.

When Bobby's people came looking for me a few years later, I respectfully declined. While I admired him, my fire had gone out. As it turned out, I declined to attend the wake, too. Such as it was.

Instead, I joined a nice quiet practice in McLean, Virginia. Enough real estate in and around the District to keep me busy.

I no longer drink gin. These days, I prefer something brown and burning, something that's been in the wood for a while.

Poplar Grove is a modest, two-story concrete block nursing home on a little bend of the Willamette River just outside Eugene, Oregon. In the late spring reeds grow high, dandelions run riot, and honey bees make hives in the crook of every tree. It's a pretty place, peaceful, a pleasant spot to spend the final years.

That's where I found Doris Casey, Travis Edwards' mother. Frail, tired, white-haired. Although it wasn't cold, she wore a sweater and a comforter, both power-blue.

It took me a long time to set it up, and a long time to get there. Understandably, the administrators felt that my request was odd and untoward, and it took some convincing to allow me to see the mother of one of the men with whom I had served so proudly, so long ago. Typically, the more they resisted, the harder I pressed. Finally, they agreed, and I made the trip to Eugene.

Treating myself to a business-class ticket, I eased the twinge in my knees from a little too much suburban DC touch football. Ought to know better at my age.

Why did I go? Conscience? Closure – that overworked idea? I don't think so.

Redemption? Expiation? A pilgrimage to salve my soul? I don't think so, either.

Maybe I was curious. Maybe I just wanted to make an aged mother feel better.

She sat on a cushioned wheelchair, in a small room, walls painted a noxious pink. Above her brown wooden dresser hung a shrine to her son, her only child – his long-faded service photo, the citation and medals we had created for him. How his actions in defense of the Panama Canal had protected America and saved lives.

When I sat down next to her I could smell her perfume and her powder.

"You knew my son," she said.

"I had the honor of serving with him, yes, ma'am," I said.

"My son died a true American hero," she said.

Yes, ma'am," I said, "he did. I never knew a better solider. He served his country wisely and well. You should be very proud of him."

As she looked at me, teared up, and said, "I am," I thought: I followed orders. I made it end well. I made it so an American mother lived peacefully, her wayward son became a good soldier, and a fine man received recognition and enjoyed peace of mind.

The good adjutant always anticipates.

RAVEN LODGE TOTEM

▼

HOONAH, ALASKA

Winter Solstice. Tlingit time – the time of both sides. Of greatest darkness. Of proceeding toward light.

Of greatest opportunity when light prepares to return.

Standing in the carving shed, the 20-foot red cedar log's sweet aroma filling the room, Michael Rhodes closes his eyes, breathes deeply, runs his hands over the wood, firm and fragrant, transmitter of spirit, exhaling magic. Not the White Man's trickery, but the marriage of dichotomies, corporeal-incorporeal, substance-spirit, temporal-eternal. Listening, Michael hears the spirits tell him how the transformations will emerge from the wood, as they always do, the murderous Dogfish-woman devouring a child, the screaming infant in her enormous belly; her demise at the hands of the steadfast Beaver, builder and protector of community; the fecund Bear, surrounded by berries and flowers, bringing life to all; the spawning Salmon, its eyes and hands human, its scales sharp, its womb full of roe, seeking the Tlingit way, past and future all at once; the cold and distant Moon, her face pale and edged with blue, fleeing from her sorrow and shame; finally, atop them all, beak high and wings outspread, the triumphant Raven; Raven the creator, Raven the storyteller, Raven the ultimate sustainer.

Considering the past that envelopes the Tlingit people like a second skin, Michael thinks of his great-grandfather, a shaman, a healer, a man who could foretell the future. Who could rid the Tlingit people of witches and bad medicine.

Opening his eyes, Michael lights traditional oil lamps, the oil redolent and smokey, shadows flickering across the room, all reminiscent of the old ways, before the White Man's electric, when his great-grandfather carved totems with stone and shell and shark teeth. Reaching beneath his work bench, Michael brings out his tools, as he always does when beginning a totem. Adze, rough, chipped, hard enough to cut stone. Chisel, bright and smooth. Hammer, worn and warm, wrapped in sealskin, softened with oil. Knives, blades glinting in the oil lights. Sandpaper, five different grades, for smoothing, burnishing, bringing life. Behind him, sealed, silent, standing sentinel, paints waiting patiently for their time, months hence, black and red, white and blue and green.

The Winter Solstice, the time the sun goes and comes, the time of beginnings.

It's the coldest, wettest winter anyone can remember. Even in my own memories of Hoonah, which go back to '35, I can't conjure a worse one. Storms, storms so heavy and so frequent that eagles fall from the sky. Moose shelter and hide. Even wolves, tired and frightened and ravenously hungry, skulk into the forest. Ashamed and chagrined, Sister Moon stays dark from one month to the next. With the ice and rain thick as pine board, and the darkness endless and impenetrable, the Tlingit people, all the people, all the clans, turn inward, turn toward themselves.

Some come to my place, Tlingit Beaver Lodge, but everybody calls it Pete's, for me, Peter Little Star, 85-year-old son of a Tlingit mother who skedaddled from what was then the Alaskan Territory near 90 year ago, wound up in New Mexico with the Pueblos, hitched up with my father, a Hopi, and died birthing my younger brother. Me being itchy, I wandered back here to my mother's people. Bought this place 50 year ago; one-story wood frame near the water; motor skiff tied to the dock out back. Been tending bar and selling my own sweet-'n'-salty smoked salmon ever since.

Good to remember that Pete's ain't nothing official, not part of the Tribe, or even my own Beaver clan. Instead, it's my own, a retread VFW Hall built 60 year ago and abandoned not long after. 'Cause I enjoy the work and the company, I stay open seven days a week, afternoons and evenings, as late as anybody's going to pay the freight. Good nights, I run four dozen people, all regulars, most coming a particular night or two.

Nothing special about Thursday nights except the four of them – Michael Rhodes and Tsuki Masuna; Thomas Howells and Rhea Bartlett. And two more, a witch – a real one, not a White Man's fantasy, but *naakw s'aatí*, a master of bad medicine named Doris Varona, and Erin Mitchell, a child, the innocent she destroys.

"Nearly drove off the road," Thomas says one Thursday, coming in out of the ice and the rain. "Had to hold on with both hands and fight the bus back on track."

"Two hands on the wheel?" Rhea asks. "First time for everything, huh?"

Thomas laughs but Michael doesn't. Looking down at Rhea, and Michael, Thomas asks where Tsuki is. Michael says nothing. Finally, Rhea says she's gone.

"What do you mean, gone?" he asks. "Gone as in –"

"Gone as in gone back to Japan," Rhea says.

Stripping off his wet slicker, Thomas sits down. "Michael," he begins, but Rhea answers instead.

"Not tonight, Thomas," she says.

"No, it's OK," Michael says, catches my eye, signals for a round. He begins, shrugs, begins again, stops, finally says, "sure, we all knew it. We knew it when she came here from Japan looking for her mother's people. Us. Tlingit people. She found us. Maybe she was part of us. But she couldn't stay with us. With me."

"It's not you, Michael," Rhea objects, rubbing his arm. "A lot of people come to Alaska looking for something – to find themselves, to find wilderness, to find whatever. So did Tsuki. And, yes, she found you. You found each other. And it was sweet. It was very sweet. But the darkness," she gestures. "And the weather. And the cold. Those are hard things to overcome." She pauses. "I told her that we all love her. I told her to stay. 'I can't wait out the winter,' Tsuki said. 'I can't wait out the darkness, the rain. Everything smells like wet wool.'"

"It wasn't the winter that drove Tsuki away," Michael says. "It was the moose hunt. I shouldn't have done that to her. She had too many nightmares about blood.

"I will feel this loss," Michael says. "I will feel this loss forever."

No, not forever, I think, for she will return. But I say nothing.

For endless loss is neither the Tlingit way nor the way of Tlingit stories.

Certainly, there is privation, and there is pain. But more important, like all Tlingit stories, Tsuki's departure is a tale of dichotomies, a tale of the resolution of such dichotomies as purity and impurity, of tension and resolution, of past and future.

It is a tale of two that becomes four, of the spirit beings of these four, Raven and Moon, Salmon and Bear, air and fire, water and earth, of yearning, of how they follow their own spirits, into the air, into the wilderness, there to seek their animas, to find self between animal sibling and angel spirit, between material and ethereal, to undertake journeys they can only take alone, later to meet and meld and marry as humans.

For the Tlingit way is about healing. About departing from one's self, and one's place, to be changed, to be transformed, to return.

First, however, these four, and the Tlingit people, require cleansing. She calls herself Doris Varona, a Haida woman, face wizened, seamed like a checkerboard, who brings an evil spirit to the Tlingit people, destroys a young woman named Erin Mitchell, and through her very presence breaks the nascent union of the four, and therefore must be excised so that healing can proceed.

So that in time Moon will return, will again rise, full-faced, to shine upon the air and the water and the earth; Salmon will spawn; Bear will return, laden with flowers and fruit; Raven will fly victorious; and union will once again be achieved.

How Raven Created Tlingit Lands

Creator and protector of the Tlingit people, Raven never possessed the Eagle's glory, or the Thunderbird's power, or the Hawk's grace. Instead, and out of necessity, he grew smarter, more resourceful, more careful and creative, more caring and concerned. So, from the crevices and the caves, the fissures and the depths, where life grows beyond language and logic, where dreams rise like mist from rushing streams, Raven assembled many waters, and many visions, to create the Tlingit lands and waters, the fish and flowers, for his people to live among and eat.

When I came here – that be about 1935 when I was 20 – it was the

Depression, and things were restless. I had to meet with the Tribal Council, six old men in plaid shirts and whipcord slacks sitting in a damp wooden shack. It was different back then, before statehood, before the Tlingit people were even recognized, much less respected.

When they greeted me, I said I was a half-breed Indian.

White? they asked

Who said anything about White? I spat on the floor. My father was Pueblo Hopi, my mother Tlingit Beaver. Half-breed. All Indian.

First Nations, one of them grunted.

First Nations, I said, is for some White Man on the government pap. First Nations is for some White Man taking money to call us something we never called ourselves. I'm an Indian. Plain and simple. Proud of it.

They asked me who my mother was. I told them my mother was Mabel Hightower. Of course, they remembered her.

Mabel Hightower, one of them said. Mabel Beaver Woman. I see the resemblance now. Must be 25 years. She just left one day. What possessed her?

I don't know, I said. Never asked. If I had, she wouldn't have answered. Maybe didn't know herself.

That about right, one said. I remember her. Even as a child she was contrary.

Some kind of married to my father, I said. Benjamin Little Star. Medicine being what it was, and us not getting much of it on the Res, my mother died giving birth to my brother when I was six. 'Bout six year after that my father died in a fall, and I went to live with an aunt and uncle. They sent my brother to a White Man's school back east. Never saw him again. Life was good enough but never felt like home, living in New Mexico, in Pueblo culture among the Hopis.

How was that? they asked.

I'm here, ain't I? I said.

Good answer, they smiled.

By the time I was out of the White Man's school, I said, I knew that life wasn't for me. Not just the Kiva and the stone carvings and the desert colors. More'n that, I hated being a Res Indian. Branded. Constricted. Undervalued. Underpaid. Underserviced. Got to where it felt like I couldn't breathe. I needed space. Maybe I just needed 200 rainy days a year. Every year. Mixed in with enough ice to get a man's blood going.

Despite themselves, they laughed.

Right. Res Indians are supposed to be quiet. Stupid. Mute as a cigar-store Indian. Another White Man myth to put us in a box. Anything to deny who we are.

The Council nodded.

Drifted a bit, did this and that. One day the idea got in my head that I should look for my mother's people up here in the Alaska territory. Worked my way up. When I couldn't find work, I rode the blinds.

Tough way to drift, one man said.

Not if you want something bad enough, it ain't, I said.

They nodded, then got serious. Can you prove any of this? Anything that says you should inherit what was hers?

No, I said.

The six of them turned to each other, talked a bit, then the head man, oldest by the look of him, said, we accept you as a Tlingit, Raven tribe, member of the Beaver clan. But we cannot give you property. You have to sign this paper saying you will not lay claim to any part of Beaver property because you cannot prove that you belong.

I ain't asking for nothing, I said, and I don't want nothing. I'm just here, that's all, and I'll work for anything I get.

Now we *know* you're a Tlingit, they said.

After that, I pulled shifts at the fish cannery, worked construction, did a fair bit of logging and 'jacking, avoided women 'cause they're only an expense, saved up, bought the VFW when the White Man discovered no Tlingit gave a damn. Fixed it up myself, even painted that Beaver on the far wall. Good Brunswick pool table. Cable TV. Oak bar. Found I could draw a beer and slap down a bag of chips with the best of 'em. Even smoke my own fish – keep it nice 'n' salty so they'll drink more. Only sop to the White Man is hard-boiled eggs 'n' Tabasco. Trick I learned off'n Seattle fishing boats. Keep 'em nice 'n' thirsty. Keep 'em buying beer.

Molson. We got Molson and we got Molson. You want something else, go up the road. It's cheap here 'cause I got a friend who brings it over the border. Another White Man's tax I don't pay – and pass on the savings.

Rather have 'em drink here, safe 'n' monitored, not driving into a ditch or falling into a snowbank and freezing to death.

Been running it more'n 50 year now and ain't lost no one yet. Don't plan on quitting any time soon. Ain't got nowhere to go – and nothing to do when I get there.

Tlingit Beaver Lodge – though everybody just calls it Pete's. Nothing official. Just my tribe and my clan. Just my heart and my soul. And my blood.

Confused, we first see the world in pairs, which double and become fours. And those fours are emblems of the Four Great Truths, the Winds, the Elements, the Generations, the Seasons. Uniting those Truths are transformations and marriages – water and earth form clay, married to air and fire they form pottery. The Tlingit people embrace the Truths, embrace the journey that material and spirit must undertake to achieve unity.

Breathing in air redolent with cedar and burning oil, Michael works, now carefully, now feverishly, wood shavings dropping silently to the shed floor. The totem is a living story, the spirits in the wood calling out to be freed, to stand in sight of the prescient world.

Michael feels the wood, hears what it says to him, hunches over with his adze, stretching his arms in long, delicate strokes.

Skin scorched dark, Michael's a throwback to the people who crossed the Asian land bridge to find Alaska. Perhaps, he often thinks, that's why Tsuki and I are one, a heritage of the vast silences of untouched mountains, fog pouring down the peaks.

Dark hair, dark eyes, hooked nose, Michael sings to the pole, working the edges of the wood. Chisel, knives, sandpaper will come much later.

Contemporary rather than traditional, Michael's totems are more colorful and creative than the stern, severe poles of the past. Facing bitter winds and impossible winters, men like his great-grandfather carved them with bone, stone, and shell, later ax and adze. Unlike the ancients, who mixed ash and fish eggs for black, iron oxide for red, copper oxide for blue, Michael uses latex, then varnish. Yet in the manner of the ancients, through prayer and song he imbues the animal spirit into the animal image, giving each totem not only a story, but also a frozen life of its own.

She has long black hair, tied back, hanging nearly to her waist. Soft skin, black eyes, non-Tlingit clothes, Tsuki stands thin, diaphanous, blue-veined, pale.

One of us and not one of us, and not merely because she is half-Japanese, like my own mother, Tsuki's Tlingit mother migrated many years ago, marrying a Japanese trader, exchanging rough-hewn Alaska for urban Tokyo. That's where Tsuki was born, she and her five sisters, yet she alone always felt caught between the two conflicting places. I know this because I, too, feel the tugs between cultures. Where I have been able to bury my Hopi half, she cannot, cannot conquer the contradictory parts of her changeable, Moon-like nature. Her celibacy and sexuality, her innocence and cunning.

The latter expresses itself in her work, Coldfire Cosmetics, Kabuki-inspired body paints. Bone white. Cold blue – robin's egg cut with ice. Pale green of frozen lichens. Gold, played-out and stark. Red, seemingly exsanguinated, appears lifeless.

Like the Moon herself, Tsuki, too, is not sufficiently steadfast, hiding, cyclic. Eventually, she will choose, will return, and Michael will also choose, to live with her changes, her perpetual transformations.

Small and quiet, with sharp, hunter's eyes, a wide, flat face, and high cheekbones, Tsuki Masuda paints herself Kabuki white, folds her tiny hands like origami, embraces her own tundra of silence.

Although she considers herself unlovable, Michael loves her, desperately, and wants her to stay. But the night after the moose hunt, she rises from their bed and stares into the incessant rain. Waking, he wraps them both in the large down comforter, tries to persuade her. But winter is too dark, too dank. The frame house is too damp and draughty. She is too distraught. At last, she says, "all I see is rain and night."

The next day – another day of rain and gray sunlight – Tsuki, wearing her signature Kabuki make-up but with icy-blue highlights, takes the ferry to Juneau, there a flight to Anchorage, there a flight to Japan.

Although the others are mystified, I understand. Some come to Alaska to discover themselves – through extreme conditions, physical challenge, endless silence. Some find there's nothing inside or outside; they return home or they perish. Tsuki felt that – that Tlingit call – but it wasn't sufficient. This time.

How Raven Created Time as a Spiral

Flying above the Earth and below the Water, as only he can do, Raven first saw the Fours, the four Elements – Earth, Water, Air, and Fire. Next, he discovered the secret of the fours – that the dualism of Man and Woman becomes a Union; that the dichotomy of Matter and Spirit becomes a Union. Finally, Raven experienced a marvelous Revelation, that with joining and co-joining, with past always part of present and future, time is not a flat line, running off endlessly into the distance. Nor is it a circle, spinning the same way for eternity. But like the Unions, like all Creation, Time has elements of both. Time is a spiral, repeating and changing, repeating and changing. This, Raven understood, is a powerful weapon, and so taught it to the Tlingit people to render them wise and comforted for all time.

Believing in happiness, the Tlingit people do not get lost in the White Man's distractions. Instead, they build true appreciation, satisfaction, joy with what they have. While the White Man overbuilds, overeats, over wants everything – then destroys or discards it – the Tlingit people live *in* Nature and within their means. The things that are given are things that are enough. Life is not about *more*. Instead, for the Tlingit people life is the soul's journey, forging healing, completion; souls coming home, returning safe.

Family legend has Thomas' great-grandfather fishing Icy Strait in a wooden boat like a large canoe. With the water relatively calm, and the fish plentiful, the Salmon clan, like many other Tlingit people, lived by and from the water.

Until the White Man came, setting up trading posts, using larger wooden and later metal boats, bringing money and demanding that the Tlingit people use it. At first, Thomas' grandfather, like the rest of his clan, rejected the White Man and his changes. But quickly, insidiously, the White Man and his ways subsumed everything around him.

Like many other Tlingit fishermen, Thomas' grandfather came to work for the White Man on his commercial boats and hated it. Hated the callous, disrespectful way the White Man treated the fish, how he took everything without regard for balance, without respect. How he treated him and his Tlingit brothers like ignorant savages; like farm animals.

Thomas remembers his grandfather, how gnarled his hands were, how simultaneously tough and tender. How quiet and caring he was. Thomas also remembers what his grandfather said, how the White Man despoils everything. Our water, our culture. Our totem.

Unlike his own father and grandfather before him, Thomas' father did not work on the water. Instead, he took the White Man's money to work in his canning factory, then, when that closed, drove a postal truck and worked construction. It was good enough.

Thomas, too, drives, albeit a school bus, and is the elementary school custodian. In the summers, he hires out for construction and carpentry. Tall, with long, nimble fingers, a strong back, and powerful thighs, he is good at his work.

Yet Thomas, too, feels his family's malaise, one that has its roots in something other than another long, rainy winter. "The White Man's materialism isn't doing it for me," he says one night. "I'm missing something. Maybe I want to return to the old ways. To the water. If not Icy Strait, then somewhere. I need a re-boot."

How Raven Created the Moon

Once, the Earth had two suns, each burning white, each filled with jealously for the other. In that time, Raven, too, was white, white as ice, white as the water of a waterfall, and flew about the suns, developing a great love for both. In time, he chose Sister Sun, and wanted to make love with her. Although she told him that her fire was real, and any act of love would be dangerous, Raven was not deterred. So fierce was his desire for Sister Sun that he did not — could not — heed the warning and embraced her. Her fire overwhelming him, Raven was scorched black — even as Sister Sun's fire burned itself out. While

Raven continued to fly, Sister Sun, once as bright and constant as the surviving Brother Sun, turned fearful, bashful, pained in her understanding of all that she had lost. Now called the Moon, now cold and sterile, in her shame, she flew away, disappearing, then re-appearing, forever an outcast.

I am honored that the four of them – Michael and Tsuki, Thomas and Rhea – choose my place to meet every Thursday night. Their own warming center, they call it, with pool balls and pulled salmon. Of course, they seem happy enough, two and two, each couple a classic mating, air and fire, water and earth. Raven and Moon, Salmon and Bear. If you ask me how I know their clans, I will tell you it is obvious.

What is less obvious is that each brings great discomfort that can't be healed. Tsuki, so pale, so small, huddled into her immense sweaters, says, "I can't wait out the winter. I have to go."

"We're heading into spring," Michael tells her.

"More rain," she says.

"You have to embrace the rain," Thomas tells her.

"That's just it," Tsuki says, "I can't. I don't want to. And I can't."

I want to go over and say something. I want to tell them that in Tlingit thought the whole is always greater than the sum of its parts. That to embrace the rain is to celebrate the marriage of water, air, and earth. That such marriages are life. And if you join them, Tsuki, with your hidden fire, you will create the double marriage of pottery.

Yet Tsuki is not alone. Thomas, chafing in his rubber boots and nylon parka, says that even though he's never left Hoonah, never spent even a night away from his native land, he still can't feel the culture. "I can't speak Tlingit," he says. "I don't know our own history. I've been stolen by the White Man, been banished to internal exile, even in my own tribal land."

Rhea, too, says, "when spring comes, when there's growth and light, I'm leaving. I'll camp alone in what the White Man calls the Tongass National Forest."

Pausing, Michael says. "I guess I'll be the only one staying. I'll be here, carving a totem for the new Raven Lodge. I, too, wish I had a tradition for this. A heritage. I don't. Instead, I have a pattern book. From a museum. Something the White Man found, collected, photographed. Loaned to us. Something no longer ours."

When Michael says that, I know he's lying. I just don't know why.

A short, wiry man with tightly packed muscles, Michael has large, calloused hands, a serious mien, and black hair tied in two long braids.

Before him, his father carved totems, Michael assisting him, running around his shed, fetching things. But Michael's father only carved a little, and only for himself, for totems had gone out of fashion – everyone had raced to reject the Tlingit heritage, to become like the White Man. Rejecting his grandfather's shamanism, and his father's adherence to the old ways of handwork and crafts, Michael's father instead went to pharmacy school to learn the White Man's medicine.

Although his grandparents continued to speak the old tongue, Michael's parents never had much to do with their history. Never put money in my pocket or food on my table, his father said.

Undeterred, Michael found other sheds, assisted through his teens years. By the time he had left the White Man's school, he was ready to apprentice. To be accepted, even to be considered, he had to show his work and drawings, and to demonstrate his spirit. And his willingness to move in, physically, to be a part not *of* the carving shed, but *in* the shed, to the point of taking meals and living there, sleeping on the floor. Because to be an apprentice is not merely to learn a craft or a trade. It is to replicate, replace, his master. Who and what he is.

It was the great master carver Henry Hunt who accepted Michael – an enormous honor, and Michael always treated it as such, remaining until the master said he was ready for his own shed. There was no clock, no credit hours; Michael worked under Master Hunt for five years – until he had learned everything he could from him, all the intricacies of the craft, of the art. Most important, of the spirit.

Raven, *Y'eil*, the Air we breathe, stands as our tribal totem because he is the greatest transformation of all, the death of carrion into the flesh and blood of bird into the fire of life into the very air itself.

By turns, all our clans reveal profound secrets of life. Earth, for the Bear, *S'eek*, is girlish, skittish, modest; she turns slowly to reveal only some of her secrets. Water, for the Salmon, *T'a*, is prolific, giving, endlessly replenishing her people. Fire, like the Moon, *Dis*, is most difficult to control, maintain, disappearing entirely when man tries to capture or define her. Moon: as soon as she's here, she's gone.

A short, stubby girl, rough, close to the ground, round face, dark skin, Rhea Bartlett didn't shave at all. An anomaly, because Asian/Native people generally don't grow body or facial hair, she did, in abundance, even, or especially, her woman-hair, thick, like a pelt, which reached from her thighs around her belly and up to her navel. Thomas, her lover, calls her his down comforter.

Always strong, always tough, even as a child, her early nickname, as a schoolyard seesaw champion, was Avalanche Annie. Later, as a virtually unbeatable, no-nonsense fighter, she was called Little Bear, a name she treasured.

Preferring sewing and sowing, what once was called women's work, Rhea emerged as a young leader of the Bear clan. While men from her lodge hunted moose and deer, and many joined the White Man's army, women like Rhea foraged, harvested, grew the little they could in the short, fertile season.

Becoming a greenhouse farmer, Rhea quickly adopted a number of the emerging technologies for producing hardy earth crops – cabbage, cauliflower, carrots. Although her friends teased her, calling her greenhouses Moose Poop Farms, undeterred, Rhea trademarked her own Greenolevio line and sold fresh vegetables in Hoonah, Juneau, all throughout Icy Strait.

Of the four, she has the most difficult time with winter, even more than Tsuki. "I feel so sluggish," Rhea says. "As the Earth herself sleeps, I feel like hibernating, like going to bed for three months and not waking 'til the glaciers thaw."

Conversely, Rhea felt the undeniable pull of the wilderness. "I can't resist it," she says one night after Tsuki left. "I feel it calling me. Almost as if Creation itself were physically pulling me. Not to nothingness. But through my human side to reach the animal. To lose myself to find myself and then return whole." Rhea pauses. "Come spring, come the equinox, when the fire rises in the Heavens, and the sun begins to show its strength, when the flowers begin to bud, and berries sprout, I'm going out."

While Thomas, her lover, says nothing, Michael says, "be careful out there, will you? Know when you've had enough. Know how to get back."

"I will," she promises.

This much I learned: the White Man is not a good husband of Mother Earth. Neither careful nor caring, he never bothers to seek for Truth.

Rapacious, selfish, when he came to Tlingit land he never saw us, never asked, never considered the Tlingit people. With statehood, when the White Man cemented his rule, we were invisible. Expendable. Natives who were simply more trees in the forest. Who were meant to have everything stolen or destroyed. Who had to have our rights and our lives, our language and our history returned to us.

The legend of the Rhodes family – a name, like all Tlingit names, assigned to them by the White Man – is that Michael's great-grandfather was a true shaman, not only a healer but also an intermediary with the spirit world. As a holy man who knew his tribe's stories and songs, his ancestors regularly appeared to him, as they might have appeared to Michael's grandfather, even to Michael himself.

No one today discusses that, however, because when the White Man seized Tlingit land he also forbade the old ways. Rather than go to war, the Tlingit people quietly acquiesced. As the change settled in, Michael's grandfather, son of a shaman and a true tribal elder, worked as a craftsman, a carpenter, a fixer of things. He, too, carved, but not regularly, not out of necessity, because gone was the need for clan totems. In his lust to eradicate Tlingit life, the White Man also forbade Tlingit clan houses, Tlingit lodges, insisting instead that the Tlingit people live separately, replacing large multiple-mate families with monogamy.

That winter, there was illness among the Tlingit people, and I alone knew the source.

I spotted her first in Anchorage, in a Kaladi Brothers coffee shop, where I had gone to negotiate some product for the Tlingit Beaver Lodge. She was unmistakable, if you knew how to look, and I did: lined, leathery face; long, wispy white hair; long black coat and dress like a shroud. To any outsider, she was nothing but an older Native woman trudging her way through life.

But I knew better.

When I heard her croaking spells to a young woman I was certain: *naakw s'aatí*, a master of evil medicine, creator of dangerous charms, source of sickness and spiritual contagion. As she whispered, the young woman seemed to be hypnotized. Neither was Tlingit – I was certain of that; Haida, maybe. Dogfish clan. Shark.

I thought no more of her until she showed up in the Beaver Lodge, shoulders hunched under a rain slicker, the young woman in tow.

Well, I thought, drawing a round of Molson, maybe I was wrong.

I knew wasn't.

I asked around; no one knew her or her people. Said she was indeed Haida, and no one had any reason to doubt her. Nor did they care to.

Said she was a counselor, that the young woman was on a spirit journey with her, that they were making their way from Anchorage to Vancouver, reasons not given – and protocol demanded that they not be asked. Said they had taken rooms in the Icy Strait Lodge overlooking the water.

Seemed normal enough, but I knew medicine women. They appear to heal you. Instead, they take your soul, leave your body lifeless as a sloughed-off snakeskin.

How Raven Created Man

In the time before time, water existed, water and earth, air and fire. In time, fish spawned in the water, fish alone the world's living creature. Raven, who can fly under water, found his friend the Salmon, convinced him to let him take some of his roe out of the water, out to the sun and the winds and the earth, there to form something not like the fish, formed not of a single element, but instead a wholly new creature, fashioned of all four. Respecting Raven's wisdom, Salmon gave Raven his seed to be placed upon dry land. Cohabiting with the earth, the sun, and the sky, the seed became Man, Man and Woman combined, strong and bronzed like the lichen-covered cliffs above the rivers and the canyons.

Once the Tlingit people lived as twin tribes, Raven and Eagle, and in those tribes resided many clans, each living in large clan houses, clan lodges, each engaged in multiple-partnered matrilineal communal life, their totem story carved prominently on a pole for all to see. While very much part of a clan, each person also had his or her own guardian spirit, *tu kinaayéik*, who helped and sustained individuals in many ways.

The animal and the anima, the tribe and the clan totems, the flesh and the spirit, the dichotomies of half and half – they all met in transformations, this way and that, cojoining many complex things. So arose the Tlingit people, the fluidity of maternity and of spirit like the fluidity of water, fire, air, and earth, all flowing one into another.

Cutting the *Miriam*'s motor, letting the fishing boat lie quiet and drift a bit on a rare, clear night, Captain Bradley, worn and weary and wearing waterproof waders and a torn plaid shirt, peers out at the night, listening. "If you starve in Alaska," he quotes the elders, "it's because you're lazy."

"The Tlingit people can't afford to be lazy" the mate Aiden says. "Especially not since the coming of the White Man."

Hearing the rushing, braying sound, almost like donkeys passing through brush, Bradley starts up again, heads into the darkness.

"How can he possibly see?" Rhea asks.

"By the light of the moon," Michael answers.

"What moon?" she presses. "There's no moon tonight."

"No moon you can see," Michael answers. "But it's always there."

"By the movement," Thomas points, "by the water. By the sound of the current."

"He can – " she begins.

"That's why he's been a boat captain for 40 years," Thomas answers. "Cousin to the water."

Standing, expectant, all wearing boots and aprons, they look into the darkness. All except Tsuki, sitting astern, her pale face closed like a fist.

"Here they come," Bradley says, then it's apparent to all of them, a herd of moose fording the narrows off Icy Strait. Taking out his Model 1911, he strides to the port gunwale.

"That'll stop a moose?" Rhea asks.

Sliding a round into the chamber, Bradley smiles tightly. "This is a .45 Colt. It'll stop an engine block. Squeezing the trigger is the easy part," he adds. "The hard work comes soon enough."

Gesturing for Michael and Thomas to be handy with the grappling hooks, and for Aiden to maneuver the boat into position, Bradley lets most of the herd go by. Finally, he sees the buck he wants. Aiming carefully, Colt in both hands, Bradley breathes, then fires, a single round, into the moose's great head.

As everyone on the *Miriam* involuntarily jumps at the deafening report, the sound echoes from the distant shore.

With its heart continuing to beat, blood spurts out of the wound into the dark water. As the moose turns, slipping into the deep, Michael and Thomas reach out the hooks. Seizing a third, Bradley digs the prongs into the moose's flesh and pulls hard. As the three men haul in unison, the moose slides over the low gunwale.

"Back us up and pull us away," Bradley tells Aiden, who knows to do it without being told.

So directed by Bradley, all six slip on latex gloves. Hoisting the carcass onto a large table, the four men begin cutting back the hide, sawing off limbs, slicing fat from the meat. Moving with great speed and dexterity, they are practiced, having been on Tlingit moose hunts since they were children. Handling the large saw, Bradley separates the head and the limbs. With a hack saw, Aiden cuts between ribs, giving more manageable pieces to Michael and Thomas. Using a hand ax, Michael further renders the meat into more recognizable cuts, while Thomas slices and trims and passes pieces to Rhea. Washing them with a hose, Rhea takes the butchered pieces to a second table where Tsuki is to wrap them in butcher paper for freezing and storage.

Yet Tsuki cannot. As the *Miriam* bobs like a cork in the wash of the moose herd, and blood continues to seep from the moose, the deck becomes thick with the sticky, sweet liquid. With the innards' odor and the offal's stench rising, covering the boat like a blanket, Tsuki, nauseated, gags, tries to fight back both her disgust and her tears, but fails, and vomits over the starboard gunwale. Standing upright, she vomits again, then collapses into the stern. Rushing over to her, wiping his gloved hands on his bloody apron, Michael begins to ask if she's all right, but Tsuki, weeping, waves him away.

As Tsuki sprawls in the stern, a headache nearly blinding her, the butchering continues for two more hours, the air rancid and revolting. As Rhea handles Tsuki's duties, Aiden and Thomas use the hose and a squeegee to clean the deck. Feeling the *Miriam* ease into her slip, Tsuki realizes that as Moon she cannot survive this much blood, this much fire. Yet her lover Raven, who can survive on carrion, is just fine.

He need not invoke the spirit of animism; it is already present in the wood. Being guided by the cedar itself, honoring his ancestors, Michael speaks aloud the mantra, and feels the spirit in all beings guide his hands. Feeling the transformations, he recognizes that it is all one. Matter and spirit. The ebb and flow of life.

Tlingit dichotomies. Dualism. Dualities. The totem freezing the portals between them, between worlds. We transform, we become other people, people we could not have imagined; that's the legacy, the lesson, of the totem. The lesson of our tribe, Raven, the changeling in all of us, mediation between who we were and who we will be.

We will outsmart the world. This is the Raven's tale.

How Raven Created Justice

As time spun on, Raven discovered, to his great dismay, that the Earth contained Evil, a great destroyer of all things good and sacred. Flying above the mountains and the sea, he wondered what might he do to vanquish Evil – if not to destroy it outright, then at least to ameliorate it, to reduce it, to render it less mighty. As such, Raven drew all the Tlingit clans together, Bear and Beaver, Salmon and Whale, and the rest, and instructed them in the righteousness of the Earth. And warned them that if any of them, or their clan members, turn on another, as Dogfish and Shark have, he will return, beat his great wings, enlist other clans against the renegades, and bring terror and destruction. So chastened, they returned home, there to lead the Tlingit people on righteous paths.

In his evil and his arrogance, the White Man said he would kill the Native to save the Man. In so doing, he cut off the Tlingit people's hair, changed their clothing, forbade their language – and washed out the mouths of Tlingit children who spoke their language in the White Man's schools.

Taking what they wanted, the White Man destroyed or discarded the rest.

Wary and watchful, the Tlingit people waited for the impatient White Man to depart. Growing, decaying, transforming, the Tlingit people knew that in the spiral of time there exists no stasis, neither past nor future, only movement, only transformation.

For time is not a line, one that discards the past and distrusts the future. Nor is it the White Man's clock-face spiked circle, for that hearkens only to seasons and is essentially meaningless. Instead, Tlingit time is a spiral, something that is always similar, yet always changing – a mystical marriage of line and circle.

Recreating this balance, the Tlingit people practice Potlach, tribal gatherings with gifts exchanged, debts forgiven, life cycle events celebrated – even more so now, as the Tlingit people restore their lives and language stolen by the White Man.

The young woman, Erin Mitchell, somehow wanders away, and is found four days later, naked, in a ditch about two miles from Icy Strait Lodge. While Doris Varona claims quietly, but publicly, that Erin was a troubled young woman whom she was trying to help, I know differently. I know the witch destroyed her. But what can I do?

I can go to the Tribal Council, but the conversation will prove worthless. They will ape the White Man, talking about a moral weakness afflicting the Tlingit people. But it's not; it's Doris Varona. They will ask for proof. I will say that I know. They will call me a foolish old man who believes too much in the old ways. They will say that if I really know anything, I must go to the White Man's police. So I can say nothing to them. I do not have the proof the White Man demands. I alone know we must be rid of her.

Further, if I go to the Tribal Council, not only will they take no action, they will also say I am slandering an old woman and deliver me to the White Man. Someone always does.

Because in this new time Tribal Councils are nice men. Welcoming. Committed. Congenial. Dressed like the White Man, working in a brick building with central heating and carpeted floors, like the White Man, they maintain Tlingit culture. They also keep the White Man's money coming. Which is a difficulty. Because while things need to get done, *should* be done, Councils won't do anything to compromise the arrival of the White Man's money. Perhaps they shouldn't. But they don't. They won't.

So I have to do something myself. Unlike the Tlingit people, the Pueblo people rose in revolt against the White Man. It may have happened 300 years ago, but time past is time present. Self-preservation is part of the Hopi people, so it is a part of me.

In time, Michael will finish carving the Totem, paint it, let it set and dry. At the summer solstice, at a great Tlingit potlatch, he will raise it before the Raven Lodge for all the world to see.

Now, as the snow begins to melt in the meadows, in the forests, and into the streams, it is time to fly. Time to go, to return. Time to reunite with Bear and Salmon.

And, in time, with Moon.

The night before they leave, Thomas and Rhea make love. As they sleep afterward, Thomas dreams of a long, flowering plant growing from Rhea's womanhood, miraculously bearing rich, green leaves and ripe, succulent fruit.

In two weeks, naked in the wilderness, Rhea will feel pine bristles scratch at her, cold stream water raise hackles on her skin, soak her immense tuft of woman-hair, ease her woman's urgency.

Know the depths, his grandfather tells him one night, one frigid night, when, with a belly full of Molson, Thomas skitters across the icy road home. Peering into the darkness over ancestral waters, he hears that crusted, gentle voice. Go farther, he says, deeper into the rain forest, into the rivers, into the rock passages, where the salmon spawn. There you will find yourself.

Following the flaming moon, the next night Thomas travels into untouched, unmapped land, uncharted places that have no names. Tlingit sacred lands, places of fog and mist, of mystery and transformation. A journey Thomas must undertake alone.

Undeterred by loneliness and danger, Thomas hikes three unbroken days, northeast into the mountains. You will know it, he is told, for it is marked by centuries of rock and lichen. It is the birthplace of the world, where spirit is transformed into flesh.

It is spring, and Thomas sees the gray canyon light reflect off the water. Here, Thomas knows, time is not a constant. Time can start and stop. Time can move backwards, freeze like memory, like water. Here, memory is time's echo. Here, it can pierce bodies and stitch souls. Here, time is not an arrow, not a spiked circle. But instead a spiral made manifest.

Walking into the interplay of light and dark, into spiked green hills with dark pines in shadow, black like Raven himself, Thomas stands beneath snow-bound iron peaks. Fierce, rugged, impenetrable, he gazes up at the bands of rock, the wisps of trees creeping up the steep slopes. Passing a 100-foot waterfall framed by 10,000-feet-high mountains, Thomas, standing a mile above sea level, is still encased in water.

High above, he sees the image of a human face on the mountain, the elusive Guardian Spirit of the forest. Bowing in respect and reverence, he feels the stillness thicken, sees an eagle land silently in a distant spruce. All around him there is stasis. Parched trees above a rocky shore. Aspen quaking, their light green leaves fluttering in river thermals. Evergreen sentinels, so still they are mirrored in water. As he stands, fog begins tumbling down the mountains, sacred smoke, the marriage of water and air.

Glacier cut, 500 feet deep. Above, the sun, very bright, nearly blinds him on the white snow, a washed-out band above the black line of crenelated trees. Lines of light and shadow march along the hump-backed mountains. White birches, juniper, spruce; long lines of iron cliffs, Ionic columns mottled by heat and time. Evergreens below, black earth a beard with a white cap across gray and brown rock. Sharp buckles on cliff faces, walls 90-degree joints then turning away. Spines of rock, like imbedded buttresses, run up the mountain sides. Twin concave cups in the unnamed mountain's side; snow collects, piles in the bottom. Racing clouds throw black bands across the sharp granite cliffs. Far below, Thomas knows there are epiphanies to come.

Sixty feet above the river, rushing green with white caps, Thomas passes lichens clinging to sheer vertical drops crowned by pole-thin spruce, shaggy barked and needled as if covered in Spanish moss. Black and gray, green and brown, the rocks and trees stand as a symphony of soft and hard.

Rock slide off the sheer surface; lichen and moss smeared on jagged edges of cliffs cut raw by water and silt. Suddenly, the river opens up to a wider, steeper canyon, spruces poking arrogantly at the sky, daring the winter ice to tear them down. Growing from sheer rock, pines seem fed by the air alone. Under the cliff, beads of rock jut out, as the force of the cataract rages, an immense power cutting through close rock sidings. Next to the falls the trees are spray-painted an eerie, nearly phosphorescent light green, moss desperately holding them. With spruce needles covering the ground, colors cut into the sandy brown rock, feral black, deep brown, slate blue, all whorled, as if time itself were gouged in two dimensions.

Etched by wind and time, the cliffs are black and brown, gray and tan: shale, limestone, dolomite. Truncated at top, sliced by wind in front, wisps of evergreens, scabs of snow. Ahead, Thomas sees the edge of the cliff, the endless waterfall. Peering farther into the water, steam rising above it, he feels the back of his hands, now rough like his grandfather's, now like fish scales, as he passes into the water unharmed

It is late, past closing time. I have made certain that she has had many Molsons, and she is tired. I smile and offer to take her home, to the Icy Strait Lodge. She nods yes.

It's easy enough. She's drowsy. When I seat her in my skiff, instead of my car, she looks quizzically me, and I assure her it's quicker this way. She nods, closes her eyes. I go out a bit, push her overboard. Sinking quickly, like stone, plummeting down into the dark water, she barely makes a sound. The current quickly sweeps her away.

The dogfish, the fierce shark with powerful jaws, is no match for the beaver with its great teeth. She is vanquished, drowned, dwelling in shame forever.

The next day, I am questioned by the White Man's police, an officious man in a beaver hat. This old woman has gone missing. Do I know anything?

I smile, a harmless-enough octogenarian. No, I know nothing. It was late; she was tired. Like everyone else; she walked out the door.

Do I know where she went?

This is Alaska, I gesture. People come and go. There are a million square miles to get lost in. She did say something about taking the plane to Juneau in the morning, then heading back to Anchorage.

Without her luggage? I am asked.

I really can't help you, I say.

I'm Peter Little Star, a half-breed Tlingit-Hopi. I tend bar and smoke fish and have never been drunk in my life. The worst thing people can say about me is that I've spent my life chasing shadows. Maybe that's so. But at least I've made my separate peace.

Closing his eyes, running his hand over the totem, Michael feels the spirits, the stories rising like smoke from the wood, the Dogfish and the child she devours, the triumphant Beaver, the Bear and the Salmon, most of all the Moon and her lover the Raven. The paint – a fine latex to seal the wood, then a coat of varnish on top of it – will emblazon the stories even more, giving rise to the Raven tribe, announcing to the world the dignity and worth of the lodge. Seeing ahead, it will be raised in three months' time, at the summer solstice, the day of the marriage of light and darkness, of the ascendency of the Raven, of the peace between the sun and the moon.

Raised at a great potlatch, a grand catch from Icy Strait, salmon and shellfish and sweet corn boiling; singing and dancing; forgiveness of grievances, of old wounds and older debts; betrothals and inheritances and memorials. A time of all times.

Opening his eyes, extinguishing his oil lamps, Michael walks outside, into the April darkness. The vernal equinox, the beginning of renewal, has passed. Time to fly.

His great-grandfather, the Raven shaman could fly, as could his mother. Smiling, Raven recalls how she transformed herself into a bird, a beautiful white gull, to fly over mountains, inquire of the trees, see to her sisters the bears.

Loosening his long braids, Michael feels them swell into wings, Raven's wings. With the wisps of beard at his throat filling out into feathers, night darkening his skin, his nose stretching into a Raven's beak, Michael struts, calls out in Raven's voice, flaps his wings, rises into the night sky.

There to seek his bashful lover, Moon. There to soar above the Earth, seeking both Bear and Salmon, insuring their safety, leading them home.

There to make certain that every clan is healthy, to stitch together the Earth's loose threads, the fallen pieces of Creation.

Flying, Raven foresees the Totem rising. Moon will return. The four elements will wed. The Tlingit people will stand transcendent.

REUNION

▼

KINGS POINT, NEW YORK

It's Arch Lohrber, your platter-pushin' pal here with you tonight, spinnin' the stacks, sendin' the signals, slingin' the sounds. So let's get started! Tonight's premiere tune – and what better? A sentimental favorite, something to set the tone, mark the mood, light up a very special evening. Bert Kampfert's classic "Wonderland by Night."

Long hair dyed a preternatural black, thick Van Dyke beard complete with curled mustache, enormous tinted glasses, and a simply hellacious brown, burgundy, and Kelly green double-knit suit, Lohrber was what passed for the evening's entertainment. Sitting at a long table, records and turntable before him, he deftly hoisted a 45.

"Real vinyl," I mused.

"Look at that outfit," Carole snorted. "Talk about blinded by the light. Who in the world is this fossil?"

"Apparently," I shrugged, "Doris felt we needed more than just *us* tonight. Quiet conversation and strong drink would not suffice. *Voila!* an era-appropriate DJ."

"This guy's no Jack Lacy," Carole objected. "Remember him?"

"Or Scott Muni. Of course."

"So gentle. Such beautiful voices."

Simply by chance Carole was the first person I saw at the 40th Bachand High Reunion. Completely unrecognizable – a pudgy, pimply girl had been magically transformed into a slender, smooth-skinned professional with the body of a 20-year-old gymnast. Wearing a modest brown suit and low-rise heels, she seemed so out of place that my first words were, "I'll tell you my name if you'll tell me yours."

Laughing, she complied,

Your surgeon's incredible, I nearly blurted.

Steering me toward the bar before we barely got in the door, she demanded, "can I get you one?" It was more an order than a question.

I demurred; driving that night, and so on.

"But the night is so young," she looked up at me.

"But I'm not," I answered. "Not anymore."

Laughing, Carole ordered a double Scotch straight up.

Not that anyone here is going to be all alone, not after a night like this, but just in case you are *alone and life is indeed making you lonely, here she is, England's favorite pet, Petula Clark, singing about that sure-fire cure for loneliness, "Downtown."*

I received the invitation as everyone else had – the 150 surviving class members, including those willing to be found – October 15, Melville Hall, United States Merchant Marine Academy, Kings Point, Long Island, New York.

I registered and in due course received the pre-event packet – green and white, our school colors. I took a breath and assiduously scanned the necrology, looking for Mandy's name. Not there. A relief. She was listed in the MIA column, of course, along with two dozen others. Perhaps they were the same as she: I knew that if she were alive she wouldn't want to be found. And if found, she would never answer. Because Mandy hated them, hated all of them, the people who so endlessly tortured her. Hated everything about Bachand High.

Most of all, she hated me.

But maybe, just maybe, she'd show up. Maybe time had healed those wounds.

If she was still alive – and I hoped so – maybe.

I came with three agenda items. A chat with Phyllis. I had always enjoyed speaking with her, and wanted to do so again. To see what we had to say to each other after all these years. To expiate myself with Mandy, whom I had hurt so badly – and regretted doing so for decades. A simple *sorry*; tell her how young and stupid I was. And to hook up with Becky. Sure, I had Katie at home, but our relationship was more inertia than emotion. Becky and I had flirted enough. It was time to take life to the next level.

As I drove the rental – a Chevy Volt, which felt like riding in an enclosed lawn mower – from LaGuardia, and glimpsed the remnants of New York's last World's Fair, I thought about that time: American optimism; my family's '57 Dodge, white and gold with outsized fins; old black-and-white movies on our old black-and-white television. And a secret girlfriend no one knew about.

Of course I lied to everyone about why I came. I've spent most of my life lying, one way or another, to others, to myself. After all, it was back in Bachand that I learned the two most important lessons of my life. Don't get caught. And always have your cover story in place first.

My cover story was curiosity, not connection. Connection meant vulnerability. So I crafted a believable persona, made it not Teflon but Kevlar, an impenetrable shell strong enough to withstand the blows I knew would be coming.

Meaning that the person who arrived at the Bachand High Reunion had buried the real Alan Gault, had kept him completely out of sight.

Here's a masterpiece of marketing, of branding par excellence. A simple English reed player becomes Mister Acker Bilk and blows a breathy, worldwide, romantic hit. Have a glass of wine with the wax, kids, and dig the soulful sounds of "Stranger on the Shore."

"Hey, Pirate Pete! You find Bluebeard's treasure yet?"

It was Gerry G., and I had expected this. Back at Bachand he had majored in mouth, mayhem, and madness. It got old the first day we walked in and four decades later hadn't gotten any better. Now, glass empty, he was on his way back to the bar.

"Clever as always, Gerry. You stay awake nights thinkin' up these things or does it come naturally? No, don't answer. Anyway, it was Blackbeard, the Pirate, who had the treasure, not Bluebeard, the wife killer, and no. I haven't."

"Well, Cap'n Ahab, keep tryin'."

"Bigger fish to fry, Gerry. Try not to walk to your car on your knees."

I had taken the Beach Boys literally. After six hours of school I'd had enough for one life. College seemed senseless – I had no idea what I wanted to do or how to pay for it. So I figured I'd hop the proverbial slow boat to China, or somewhere equally exotic, and think my way through to the next plateau, whatever that might be. Being from Long Island I'd always liked the ocean. And I really wanted to go away. I'd had enough of home. Enough of land life. Enough of Mandy. I wanted someplace – and someone – different. I just didn't know who, what, or where.

I also figured that sailing away would end the fear and the shame. Because Mandy was the girl I could never be seen with. Could never take home.

Enlisting in the Navy, I oiled engines, read a lot, kept to myself. Being an able-bodied seaman saved me from Vietnam. Another swell place for another lousy war.

As I crossed the Pacific – was it a dozen times? hard to remember – I kept thinking that I liked Long Island Sound. But I didn't like winter. It took a few years – the navy, a shipyard here and there – but before I was 30 I had drifted down to the Florida Keys, where it's always warm, and warmer. I was working on a fishing boat when I heard about a bait-and-tackle place for sale. I borrowed money, bought it, re-branded it, and made myself a fixture in the Keys.

"Alvin Gault is divided into three parts." Leonard, beery, blurry, barely remembering me, stuck out a meaty hand.

"Alan Gault," I corrected him. "Alan. Not Alvin. Alan. Al Gault. Al G's Bait 'n' Tackle 'n' Tours. Big joke in the Keys about algae. But easy to remember."

"You've changed," he weaved.

"Well, I would hope so, Leonard. I would hope that I've changed since I was 17. I would hope that the years have had some effect on me."

"You were – " he began.

"I would hate to be judged as that person," I interrupted. "It was a long time ago, Leonard, in a galaxy far, far away."

"Lazy," he persisted. "You were always lazy, always --"

"Actually, I wasn't. But I do wish you'd stop telling me about me. About the me you think I was. About the me you think is here."

Melville Hall was woody and clubby, just the thing for all these pretentious folks. Perched on the water, it was nautically themed, ship models under glass and framed Cutty Sark prints. Smacking of privilege and old money, of hazing and harassment, all it needed was the odd animal head to make it a cut-rate Sagamore Hill.

"Cool idea for a bunch of kids who opposed Vietnam," Gary smirked. Well, *that* hadn't changed since high school.

"Not everybody opposed Vietnam," I shrugged. "Some felt it was in the national interest to smack communism on the snout."

"They were wrong," he answered.

"Be that as it may," I began but found I was speaking to his back.

Cash bar, name-tag James, red vest and arm garters, obsequious, keeping all the near-sexagenarians well oiled, thanking them for tips stuffed into a dry tumbler.

Bay windows, view of the flagstone terrace, the water; beyond, the bridges, City Island, passing ships trailing lights across the dark Sound.

"Keys?" Moon-faced Douglas Davis demanded. "Key Largo? Bogie and Bacall? Bad, bad Eddie Robinson? *That* Key Largo?"

"Hardly," I countered, "but if it helps you to think that, Dougie, please continue unabated. Actually, *not* Key Largo. Actually, a lot of heat, humidity, and hard work."

I watched people turning in the widening gyre, glasses of wine and spirits, little plates of critter and *crudités*. Fueled by all the high-cal canapés and the cash bar, they were preening, gleaning, moving on – a verbal *La Ronde* prior to actions *très intime*.

A fair field of folk worthy of Weimar's George Grosz. Orange-haired men with trophy wives. Dowagers with hideous surgeries – bloated Botox lips; truncated porcine noses; jowls slipping their moorings, melting like something from *House of Wax*. Women looking younger than their 30-year-old daughters, faces tight and taut as drumheads. Beach balls stapled onto their chests.

I don't know which was more jarring: all those Sweet Sixteens become Little Old Ladies from Pasadena – or carved into superannuated Barbie Dolls.

It was Hubert's Freak Show: I stared, sickly fascinated, then turned away, embarrassed.

"Here we are," Joey ambled toward the cash bar, "in the hallowed Halls of Montezuma."

While Joey did play a good inside tackle in a single-wing offense, decent point guard, and solid-enough catcher, he was never the brightest bulb in the chandelier.

"Joey," I answered amiably, "those guys are the Marines. These guys are the *Merchant* Marines. Those guys fix bayonets. Hit the beaches. Raise the flag on Iwo Jima. These guys hoist boxes. Haul cargo. Lift a few at dinner."

"SSDD," Joey said, not breaking stride.

All those expensive suits; all those strivers. Timber wolves snapping and snarling, devouring a carcass. Fighting over money and jobs and power. And women.

Sure, the race belongs to the swift, but there's more than enough to go around. So why fight? Why compete? I never needed to have more than anyone else.

"Alpha male?" I said years ago to Becky. "I'm more like a Zeta male. Whatever happens is right. We more or less wind up where we should be anyway. So why raise our blood pressure along the way?"

"Wall Street?" I asked Larry, one of the 35 guys who'd gone on to become lawyers.

"Sure," he said, cadging his lone word as if it could be held against him in court.

"Three-piece suits?"

"Of course." Proud of himself, rocking back and forth.

"Thousand dollars?"

"Easily."

"I wear one to work, too, except it costs a bit less."

"Yeah?" he asked, not really interested.

"Yeah. Ball cap, blue jeans, fishin' vest."

Larry made a noise in his throat and shook his head.

"You feel good about yourself now?" I asked. "Better? That you make more money than I do? That you have a fancier house and a finer wardrobe? Who cares? I love what I'm doing and have all that I need. How many people can say that?"

Some can't. Our Class Beauty and Class President both fell in the same campaign. Noticeably beautiful, popular, and smart, they couldn't handle it. Couldn't handle their particular genius. Couldn't deal with the punctures and imperfections of the world.

A third, model-gorgeous, admitted before she died of leukemia that, like Mandy, she had had no friends at Bachand. I often think about that, about how something extraordinary – in this case, her stunning beauty – often exacts an impossible price.

Some say cancer is a kind of suicide, a subconscious war on the self. Is it? I have no idea. But the one who hated her beauty that drove other people away, died young. As did the other, pushed and pestered, poked and prodded, until she couldn't live with herself. Overdosed, intended or not. And Pres walked in front of a subway.

Tired of the noise and the heat, I wandered outside. Standing alone, slender and sour as always, Steve held something brown over ice and stared out at the choppy black water. I never had anything to say to him at Bachand and the years hadn't altered that. He had always returned the favor. Without acknowledging me, he began speaking.

"These inanities," he waved inside. "I think our time would be far better served discussing Howard's suicide. What drove my friend – that brilliant, gifted young man – to take his own life that way. What might it say about our generation. About America. About excessive expectations."

Still not looking at me – I was fairly certain that he knew someone was there, not necessarily me – he waited a moment. I had nothing to say, so I waited, too.

"But of course in all the one-upping chit-chat," he shrugged, "Howard's name hasn't been mentioned at all. Because Howard committed the one unpardonable sin. He left the party early. The gag was no longer funny. So he opted out.

"If Howard were here," Steve continued, "if Howard could speak, he would say, 'We were embryos, and the world was all before us. We were so eager. So sincere. We lived in a happy cocoon of post-war prosperity and privilege. In a peaceful village on Long Island. Where the best of the world was brought to us.

"'With that as our birthright we believed we could change the world. Fix it. What we didn't understand was that the world wasn't going to change. Wasn't going to be fixed. Instead, the world fixed us. We thought we were going to fly to the sun. When we discovered the truth, we crashed and burned.'"

Eddie. Eddie of toilet-paper-on-the-ceiling, itching-powder-in-the-jock-strap, tack-on-the-chair fame. Eddie, proud of the way he had cheated his way into the National Honor Society.

Tonight, Eddie was proud of his umpteenth marriage, of his umpteenth set of children. "Got it right this time," he said.

"We no longer have rutting seasons," Gary countered, muttering into his merlot. "We're like old stags, survivors sitting on the sidelines and watching."

I nodded at Linda, bouncing, prancing, flashing a body buffed by years on the tennis court. Wicked and wiry, she kept flashing that *noblesse oblige* smile she had perfected back at Bachand.

Of course, she was an exception. The rule was too many women stuffed into cheap ready-mades, bulges hither and yon from one too many desserts or late-in-the-evening adult beverages.

"Alan Gault. The Deep Sea Diver."

It was Ross, third runner-up for class clown, who apparently hadn't aged a day since we graduated. At least not on the inside.

"Wait. Wait. Let me guess. Red snapper jokes?"

"You always were too fast for me."

"It was never any contest, Ross."

"Very romantic," Billy came and took my arm. He hadn't changed much, either – full head of hair, albeit all gray, slight belly, a few facial lines, but, still, not much worse for the wear. When we were young, sure, we were fumbling adolescents, and *who knew?*

"Indeed, Lover. But my romance doesn't swing that way. At least not anymore."

"Oh, I know," he squeezed. "It never did. But a fella can dream, can't he?"

I laughed and told him it was good to see him.

Billy laughed back and told me it was better.

Hey, kids, aren't we havin' a gr-eat *time? Your platter pushin' pal sure is. All you hep cats and hot chicks! Here's the best brother-sister act of all time. Hot-as-a-pistol Nino Tempo and absolutely delectable April Stevens croonin' the classic "Deep Purple."*

I don't recall how Phyllis and I began our late night phone chats. It was after her father was out of the house – he drank or worked or tomcatted most nights – and my parents had gotten lost in their habitual knockdown-drag-out. Phyllis and I would whisper to each other over the phone. Art, music, theater. There was a kind of dreamy air to it – all we knew of the world came from idealized textbooks written to pacify not engage us. To make us docile citizens not to rile us up or get us out on the street. Or cause us to ask questions. Certainly not to protest anything. Instead to settle us down.

Of course Phyllis and I had drifted apart. We needed each other at Bachand, but she went off to the Seven Sisters and I joined up with Uncle Sam. It was impossible to call her from a ship, and by the time I mustered out Phyllis was long gone.

I realized much later that as much as anything at Bachand, I enjoyed our clandestine conversations and hoped now to see her, to see whom she'd become.

As with Mandy, I thought maybe, but no, there was no chance that Phyllis would come. Fetching her email address, I wrote to her the week before. "I won't," she answered. "There's nothing there for me." (Meaning, of course, that I wasn't worth the candle, but no matter.) "I want to remember everyone – you included, you sweet boy – as they were. It was a very special time. And I want to leave it that way. I don't want to change it. I don't want updates. I don't want cultural anthropology. I just want it where it belongs – in the past. Like a movie I once loved and don't want to see again. Because it won't be the same."

I cajoled, but no go. "Jack and I," she wrote, "used to belong to a little club, pot-luck-covered-dish suppers here on the West Side. Lots of pasta and salads and garlic bread. Even more laughs. *Way* too much wine. It was, oh, a long time ago, and we had a lot of fun. After a bit we left for various reasons – all benign. Children and work and so on. Last year, the West Side Fish and Chowder Society had a 30th anniversary, and naturally we were invited. Right day, right time, literally next door. At first, Jack and I were thrilled – *wouldn't it be great to see those folks, Jean and Joan and who knows who?* Some had passed. Others had become old and infirm. Jack and I talked about it. Then we talked some more. Finally we decided that we'd prefer to remember them as they were. So we graciously turned down the offer. The memories were enough.

"So, no, Al, you won't see me. I won't be coming."

Here's another arch comment from your pal Arch. Sarah Vaughan. Miss Sassy herself. A voice that could melt the polar ice cap or strip varnish off furniture. Her biggest hit made number seven on the charts – and its way into the classic repertoire for decades to come. "Broken-Hearted Melody."

These were songs of our era, but they were not ours – and he knew it. They were instead twilight. Soma. Lohrber's playlist suggested a gentle, perfect life. Small towns. Success. Certainly nothing real. Not the maelstrom we faced: war, riots, drugs.

"Hey, Beck."

There she was, older than I'd remembered, but who wasn't? While her red dress was at least two seasons – and 15 pounds – out of date, that was part of her charm. Always close to the mark, never quite on it. A woman perpetually out of focus.

"Hey, Big Boy," she took my arm. Becky always had cute names for me.

"Good to see you, as always."

"Always isn't often enough, you big hunk of man."

I smiled.

"You were always so popular," Becky said.

"Was I?" I asked. "I wish I had known that back then."

"You always were blind when it came to yourself," she said. "You were so – breezy. Gentle. Supportive."

"Gee, Beck, I wish I had known that guy."

"Did I forget to mention funny? Charming? Attentive?"

What I remembered, of course, was quite different. Their late-model cars. Personal charge accounts. Nights at the Copacabana. My borrowed '57 Dodge. Murderously dysfunctional family. Cheap nights at the drive-in.

"Did that husband of yours do the right thing, Beck, and divorce you?"

"You always were sweet," she smiled. "Actually, he had very bad back problems. Then they got worse. He's in a wheelchair now, Cutie, and never getting out of it."

I told her that I was sorry, and of course I didn't know.

"Of course not." She touched my cheek.

"Why don't we --"

"Later," she squeezed. "I promised Betty a good chin wag." She patted her sagging jaw. "And these days, it's getting pretty waggy. Later, Sugar."

"Later," I laughed.

"Ernest," I said, "as in the Importance of Being. How are you?"

Same shock of thick brown hair. Same serious mien. If we had had an official Class Scholar at Bachand, Ernie Foults would have been it. Rumor had it that he was a genius accountant, which didn't surprise me.

"Same blue eyes," he said, "good for a Brit."

"One-quarter Brit," I said, "my father's father. From the north, actually, so who knows how much Scot – or Viking – is mixed in there."

"Same smile," he said. "More quiet now, more grounded. Tell me."

"You can't be --"

"No, I am. I'm curious. Tell me. Florida now, correct? Keys?"

"Very good. Yes. Bought a bait and tackle shop. Learned the seascape, began taking people out on my retread Chris-Craft Catalina. Souped-up and ready to go."

The *Miss Mandy*, but I couldn't tell him that.

"I know a few good spots, how to cure hangovers, how to get out before the sun becomes overbearing. Keep a chest stocked with cold ones for the tourists."

"You don't get hangovers," he said, matter of fact.

"*Their* hangovers, not mine." I paused. "It's my little piece of paradise."

Where I can live with myself. I ran away, exiled from the Garden. From myself.

"Did you know Ted Williams?" he asked.

"Sure. Every fishing guide in Florida knew him. Like a lot of famous people, his bluster was all a defense mechanism. Ted was really very shy, very private. Very sensitive. People driven to perfection generally are. Having come from nothing, he could never understand why people wouldn't work hard – then harder.

"A good heart. Intensely loyal. Couldn't fathom why the fans didn't love him. Sad, that disconnect. Because he was a fine, generous man."

Pardon us while your platter playin' pal pushes back a tear. Rock-and-roller, crooner, Academy Award-nominated actor, this man left us way too soon. They don't make talent – or arrangements – like this anymore. Here's the great Bobby Darin's signature song, "Beyond the Sea."

As expected, Mead was a college professor – well, he pontificated in high school, would brook no interruptions, no adversaries, so the lecture hall was perfect for him. With an endless CV, and a chair endowed by the great-grandchildren of some robber baron, he could sally forth about anything. Tonight's topic: time.

"There are multiple theories of time," he rattled on in a Norman Mailer mumble. "One favored by Western secularists is that it's divided into discrete units. So that something that happens in one moment never affects or entices something in a future moment. There is no balance, in effect. A sterile idea, certainly.

"A second, equally valid view is that time is an organic whole. More

Zen-like, if you prefer. So that for some ineffable reason, Action A will indeed affect or influence Action B. No matter the distance in time. So that balance will be achieved.

"A third view of time – whether as linear, circular, spiral – is Deocentric. God is driving, controlling, leading all events, heading for redemption. According to this view, our actions are never our own, although we think they are. While we can and do affect what God will do with and for us, God's plan is not knowable. Good but not knowable."

I moved out of earshot before he started passing out ballots.

"You liking it, Sweetie?"

It was Becky, and she was at my elbow.

"I'm liking you, Beck."

"Me, too, Hon. Anybody else?"

"Ernie actually asked who I am. No one else has. They all presume I'm the same callow youth I was at 17."

"But can you perform the way you did at 17?" she smirked.

"Try me."

"Later," she moved.

"*Roberto!* Remember riding our bicycles to the movies? All those dreadful black-and-white horror films!"

Robert, now possessed of bright orange hair, jowls that covered the knot in his tie, and what appeared to be a store-bought frown, looked blankly at me.

"*Roberto!*" I said, with all the ebullience I could muster, "Vincent Price! *The Fly! House on Haunted Hill!* You swore you would never sleep again!"

It was clear that *Roberto!*, bored and embarrassed, didn't remember me.

I wondered if he remembered Vincent Price.

Nancy, slender, black sheath, wore the same so-damn-serious face she had at Bachand. Married, three children, therapist in Midtown Manhattan. Perching herself on one hip, cocking her champagne flute at me, she said bluntly, "you've changed."

"Well, yes, Nancy, thanks for noticing. I would think so. I would *hope* so. Time has done something for me. Including the fact that I'm no longer 17."

"What would you say to your 17-year-old self?"

"Good question," I nodded. "Gimme a sec."

After considering various obscene or insulting responses, including *what could a bait cutter possibly know?* and rejecting them all in favor or taking the high road, I said, "Well, Nance, I would say four things. First, be patient. Second, pay absolutely no attention to anyone else's opinion of anything, especially of you. Third, know that whatever you think you know now you'll be surprised in the future."

"That's for sure," she muttered.

"And fourth, know that you'll accomplish far more than you think you could."

"Wow," she said. "Pretty good stuff." Then a pause. "Do you believe all that?"

"Sure. Why not? It sure would have made life a lot better for me at Bachand."

"Well," she turned, "you've got me there."

"First time for everything, Nance."

"And the last."

And what I didn't say to her. I'd like to talk to that 17-year-old. I'd like to tell him a few things. About responsibility. About consequences.

I'd like to smack him one for some of the things that he did. Notably to Mandy.

Query: If a sin is no longer remembered by the injured party, does it still exist? Or does it continue to exist if only to modify the sinner's behavior?

What a great night, huh, kids? Arch Lohrber here with you, with all the hot sounds from New York town. Now a trio by the real, the original King himself – Nat "King" Cole. The man with the Chesire Cat smile and the mm-so-smooth velvet voice, "Mona Lisa," "Too Young," and "The Very Thought of You."

Of course, I couldn't ask anyone – that would have been too obvious.

Would have opened me up for ridicule or approbation – all those seeming adults reverting to insulting adolescents. But I could laugh and hint. *Oh, what was her name? You know? Mandy? Pandy? Panties? Whatever. You know, the class whore? The 70-cent spread?* I could do that. I could do that and survive.

She's a sped-up, choppy silent movie now, washed-out colors running too fast on the projector. Days and nights at the World's Fair. The wonders of technology, the generous paternalism of our corporate benefactors. Johnson's Wax and its movies. General Motors and its Futurama. IBM and its computers. Peace Through Understanding: underwater colonies and touch-tone phones and microwave ovens.

Such a skinny little kid. So happy. Glowing, even. Simply awestruck by our look into the future. She held my arm and snuggled.

Thinking back, it was perhaps the happiest, most optimistic I've ever been.

Our hair was long and plentiful, and time seemed endless.

It was another Saturday afternoon football game, Bachand, as usual, getting trounced by Mineola or Rockville Center or Port Washington, some gridiron power. Feeling paradoxically elated and slack, I was keyed up after all the standing and cheering but was too bushed to pursue any post-game parties. Against the odds, against all sense, Mandy and I found ourselves together, found ourselves walking back from the field, then walking back and forth in the alley behind her house, lonely, desperately needing someone to talk to. About what? I can't recall. Parents. Plans. Politics. Who knows? Suddenly we were holding each other, side by side, marching back and forth on the broken pavement. I remember feeling the heat of her body burning through her wool dress. Finally, we kissed, long and sweet. Without a word I hoisted her onto a trash can lid – there's no symbolism there; it was just a handy place – she drew up her legs and I came into her. It was fast and hot and very wet, and we held each other for a long time afterward, allowing our breathing to slow and the sweat to dry from our bodies. Savoring our secret.

"Bachand was all very innocent," Patty said. Patty of field hockey fame. Patty who bristled at home ec and went for architecture instead. Prairie School out in Wisconsin.

Even Mandy. Even the sex. That *sex. It was all very sweet. Very innocent. We were children. We couldn't dream there'd be any consequences.*

"Yes," I said. "Very."

Because Mandy was denounced as a scuz – no reason given, teenagers being teenagers – we hid. Ashamed. Mandy, too, because that reputation broke her heart.

All giddy and giggly and girly, she loved jazz, loved its freedom and surprise. Its wisdom and joy. I'd pump a dollar's worth of gas in the Dodge and we'd drive all over Long Island, Northern State to the Sunrise Highway, windows down, Symphony Sid on JZ, waiting for Dinah Washington and Lester Young. Mandy would smile, close her eyes, and curl up against the passenger door.

She felt safe with me. Comfortable. Never felt she had to speak. Never felt she had to be smart. She could be unafraid, unguarded, glad to be alive.

We played word games in the car. I read O. Henry to her, and she loved it.

She loved Long Island, too, driving all around, finding stuff she never imagined existed. One day, with money she cribbed from her mother's purse, we drove all the way to Montauk, just to see the ocean, just to stand in the shadow of the lighthouse.

She nibbled Wetson's burgers, guzzled Orange Crush and ice-milk shakes, but her favorite was bread and cheese, French-style, chunks torn off an uncut loaf accompanied by bites of Gruyere. She'd sit on the curb, chew vociferously, and smile.

I don't think I've ever seen a person so contented.

I wasn't. I felt that I needed to grow up. That I needed more. That she was too narrow, too small-town. That there wasn't enough there.

Then there was the white noise: she was the town whore. She had a *reputation.*

Aside from my friends' catcalls, I could only imagine how she'd play at home.

I parked that big-finned Dodge on a little sheltered road I'd found,

Douglaston or Little Neck, somewhere around there, low and narrow, overhung with trees and reeds, close to the water. We snuggled in the back seat and made love. Symphony Sid on the radio. Lights of the Throgs Neck Bridge blazing high above us. Long Island Sound a painter's palate of swirling colors.

We were sweet, loving teens. No future, no past. Simply the quiet present.

Until I went away. Until I wrote once or twice, wandered around a bit, found someone else.

Until I didn't answer her.

I've regretted it ever since.

About 10 years ago I began looking for her in all the usual places. Then the not-so-usual. I couldn't find her. Perhaps, I thought, she'd come tonight. Or leave enough of a vapor trail for me to follow. For me to make amends, if possible.

If she even remembered me.

Your platter-pushin' pal's takin' a break now. Men with our mileage surely understand.

"I've been painting by numbers for so long now that I've forgotten what a real brush stroke is," I answered Clifford. A family doc in Spokane, he was our sparky little shortstop. "My live-in live-in is a literal fish-monger in the Florida Keys."

"You're taller than I remembered you," he said. "Skin's darker, too."

"All that sun and salt air," I smiled.

"You get yourself checked for skin cancer?" he asked.

"Yes, thanks, and not a lick. All those good, recessive genes."

Maybe every high school class in America has somebody famous – or infamous. A self-made millionaire or a life-without-paroler.

Ours was a former dunderhead who majored in making animal noises when teachers' backs were turned – and who later made a fortune in land speculation. Then a very large fortune. Then did time for a spectacular oil-futures swindle in the Dakotas.

"Reggie," I said. "I read a profile of you in --"

"Right," he said, and walked away.

Right, I thought. Forgive me. I forgot how important you are.

"Well," our football team's starting center harrumphed, "I'm staring down the gun barrel of Social Security."

Solid in all the right places, he looked like he could still handle the snaps.

"Both knees," he slapped, "titanium. I set off airport security everywhere. I wish I got as much love back then as I get now."

"You ever try to talk to them now?" It was Murray, a balding, decent-enough chap who'd moved west.

"Who?" I asked.

"High school students."

"Not if I can avoid it. Why?"

"There's not much depth there. Not much profundity."

"I'm sure we were the same."

"Nah," Murray objected. "We felt we had to know everything. We felt *responsible*. They don't."

Richard Rodgers and Lorenz Hart – what a pair, right? What a couple of song slingers. Here's the Bronx's favorite bambino, Dion DiMucci, the catch in his throat and the tear in his eye, backed by the Belmonts, with his take on "Where or When."

Myra White – short and slender as ever, albeit with far-too-young multi-colored eyeglass frames and a turkey neck – stood to perform the ritual necrology before large framed photos of the departed. *The Grateful Dead*, Ross snickered.

I looked at Bobby Edwards – long face, shadow of a smile, thick brown hair. *Have a nice life* he had written in my yearbook. Had he? He had been a fine actor – our star, the best of our brief time at Bachand. Surely, we believed, he was bound for Broadway. Instead, he had squandered his talent on cheap dinner theater productions, got lost in the fleshpots of Lower Manhattan, died young of AIDS.

Nice life, indeed.

Accompanied by the predictable gasps and groans and shaken heads, Myra read the list of car crashes and construction accidents, cervical cancers and cardiac arrests, AIDs and ODs and suicides and all manner of ills. I was surprised by some, saddened by others. But, no, I did not hear Mandy's name. Hopefully, she was still alive, still flying under the radar, at least as broadcast by Bachand High.

When Myra said Jimmy Ehlers I lost it. He was such a happy, joyous, razzle-dazzle little kid. As Becky later told me, he died of failure to thrive. Of a lack of love.

My friend Jimmy died of a broken heart.

"Hey, man, I mean Whiskey Tango Foxtrot, right? *Right?*"
It was Freddie, fresh off the farm in his long braid and stained overalls.
"Right," I agreed.
"Right, man, Whiskey Tango Foxtrot."

Here's a little ditty you couldn't sing today. But that's what so great about living in the past. Take notes, girls. Here's how you make it. Jack Jones' "Wives and Lovers."

"Sure, it's a long time ago, Beck. But in many ways you've never left me."
We were in the hallway, halfway between the bar and the restrooms, in an odd, quiet moment.
Uncharacteristically, she was silent.
"Beck, I do believe you're blushing."
"Oh, you idiot. I hoped then. I hoped for a long time afterward. But the moment passed, Sweetie. We both wound up in other places and with other people."
"I was young. I was confused. I dated the wrong girls. I should have --"
"It all worked out the way it was supposed to." She paused, then touched my cheek. "You have to trust me on this."
"Always did, Beck. Always will."
Martini glass in hand, three olives on the bottom, she greeted Sherry, something of a visual artist. At least she and her surgeon husband thought so.

"Women?" Paul asked me. Paul, with his long hair, sloe-gin eyes, and lifelong slouch, considered himself irresistible. Perhaps he was.

"I'm retired," I lied, thinking of Katie, my broad-backed American mongrel back in the Keys. Makes a great lure. Baits a fine hook. Scales and guts 'em with the best.

"Hm," Paul considered.

Wasn't it always summer when we were young? Easy times, easy lives. What captured it better than Chad and Jeremy's "A Summer Song?"

"Alan Gault."

"Hey Jack."

My least-favorite high-school nemesis, someone I'd been avoiding all night. Bilious, bloated, bombastic. Endlessly obnoxious. He knew, well, *everything*, and was happy to tell you so. Standing by the bar, something tall and fizzy in his hand – Canadian whiskey ameliorated by soda water, I would think. Sliver of lemon plastered to the side.

"Still in Florida?"

"Still there."

"Bait and tackle?"

"And tours."

Jack sells cars – he was always interested in them and never got past that.

"Buy you a drink?"

"Driving tonight," I shrugged. "LaGuardia. Early flight back tomorrow."

"You always were a homebody."

"Always was."

"Hey, didn't you date Mandy or Pandy – whatever the hell her name was?"

"Nah. Wrong guy. I never got that lucky," I lied.

"I seem to remember --"

"Memory is notoriously tricky, Jack. You remember wrong. Why do you ask?"

"No reason."

"Whatever happened to her, anyway?"

"You interested?"

Jack signaled for a refill, three fingers of Windsor drowned in club soda.

"Jack, let us not confuse mere curiosity with actual interest. You brought her up. I'm just curious."

"Pam? Penny? Panties? Who can remember? You know who I mean."

"I presume so."

"Class slut. Heard – somewhere, who can remember? – that she wound up in some kind of clinic. Private rehab. Something. Lake Ronkonkoma? Maybe it wasn't. Somewhere. Who knows? Maybe I'm thinking of someone else. Anyway, gobbled too many pills. Or cut herself. Good old Gillette Blue Blades. Or took the bridge. Something. Anyway, she died. Or maybe she didn't. I mean, who cares? Just another high school slut. We're all going to die one day anyway, right? So what?"

"Right, Jack, so what?"

I could check further, make a few phone calls, but this was enough. For all his disclaimers, Jack was probably right. I felt it. For Mandy, it was the end of the line.

There was no way past it. No way to assess my part, if any, in the loss.

Mandy would forever stand as my snow leopard, my Lost City of Z, my Holy Grail. She was the journey that led me further into myself but had no conclusion.

The bandits didn't recognize the riches before them. They slashed open the sacks, and all the gold blew back to the Sierra Madre.

It's been a good one, hasn't it, kids? One of the best. This is Arch Lohrber signing off with something soft we'll all understand. Johnny Mathis' wonderful "Chances Are." If you're drivin', be safe, be sober. Have a great night – and for heaven's sake, get lucky!

It was a last walk on the terrace. I heard a rustle behind me and knew it was Becky come to say goodbye. I thought about her husband in the wheelchair.

"Is it later?" I began, turning to her.

She smiled.

"I --"

"I know," she said.

"Maybe --"

"We're different people now, Sweetie. You said so yourself."

"Don't we deserve a new start?"

"Perhaps you do, Sugar. But I have responsibilities. And feelings for Mike."

"So --"

"We'll always have Bachand," she smiled and was gone.

Three strikes and sit down, I remember Coach Keller saying.

It was worth another moment on the terrace, outdoors, near the Sound.

Mead's question stood: what is time? In the end, like good fishing, I found myself being patient. Recognizing that time is a flat line. Over is gone.

Perhaps Phyllis was right. Nothing that we do now can or will affect anything in the past. So it wasn't worth coming.

You can't erase it, change it, do it over again, do it right.

You can't.

I had come with three goals. None had worked. Time to go.

Hearing movement behind me, I turned. It was Mary Anne – fierce, brittle, uncompromising, at least back at Bachand. Opening a pack of smokes, she offered me one. I shook my head.

"You used to," she shook one out.

"Good memory. Yes, I did. Luckies. I loved them. It was so macho – all those war movies and all."

"LSMFT," she waved.

"Indeed it does. Or did."

She shrugged and lit hers.

"I did smoke for a good long time. 'Til a friend – a customer, then a client, finally a very good friend – died relatively young of lung cancer."

"One of yer fishin' buddies?" she affected a drawl – badly, I thought.

"Retired advertising executive. Brilliant man. Virginian. Made a fortune when the making was good. Came down to the Keys to fish and soak up the sun."

We were both quiet for a moment.

"If I take my glasses off," I gestured out at the water, "everything's a blur."

"Claude Monet," she said. "Turner. The Joshua Light Show."

"There's a blast from the past," I smiled.

"I think we've reached an age when everything's better with your glasses off."

"No more sharp lines," I said. "No more angularities."

It was her turn to smile.

"You were so tough," I said.

"So were you."

"So certain."

"Ditto."

"I remember that. All that clarity. Things were so black and white. *Very* black and white. Now, they're all gray. Or blurry," I gestured at the water. "Now, I'm not so sure about anything. Is that a function of this age or our age? Maybe both."

We looked out over the runny lines on Long Island Sound, the broken surface, the lights beyond.

"You used to write poetry."

"Nice that you remember," I nodded. "I used to write poetry."

"What happened?"

"Got it beaten out of me. Making a living. Being responsible. Being on time."

She grunted.

"Being on time's a killer. It'll ruin anything. Back at Bachand," I laughed, "you were the girl who wouldn't take yes for an answer."

"Belligerent, even," she nodded. "Sure. All those raging defense mechanisms. I was always afraid of being discovered as the class dummy. The weak sister."

"*You?*" I blurted. "How could that be? I thought I was."

She laughed. "I finally realized that I wasn't. Life's filed down that sharp edge." She paused. "Of course, 20 years of therapy didn't hurt."

"About as long as I've been running tours. Got us to the same place."

"Seems that way."

"Life's full of surprises," I said. "So are reunions. You're far more interesting now than you were then."

"Yeah?" she asked. "Why is that?"

"You seem that way. Life out there in," I fumbled.

"Fort Collins."

"Fort Collins," I repeated. "How did you --"

"I was going to the be the Wolf of Wall Street," she snorted.

"Ye-ow," I said. "I can see that."

"Yeah, I could, too. Then I couldn't. Didn't make any sense to me. I kept thinking about other things. Too many other things. So I sold out, went west, young woman, and opened a coffee shop."

"Hm," I said.

"Even enrolled in barista school. I mix a mean latte, dude. I mean a *mean* latte. Mary Anne with the shaky hands."

I laughed.

"Even won a couple of contests. Western bluebirds. Ponderosa pines." She wiggled her wrist. "Me specialty," she channeled Eliza Doolittle, "is an English rose."

I smiled.

"Shaky Hands Coffee. *What they done to your joe, these shaky hands.* Running the shop has been good for me. I've learned how to deal with people. How to listen to them. How to accept them for what they are." She paused. "Along the way, I've learned to accept me, too."

"Been there, done that."

"Bought the T-shirt," she smiled. "I sell them, too. Come out and see me."

"That's a thought."

She took my arm. "Well, do more than think about it, huh?"

Maybe, I thought. Then again, maybe not. Katie never asked who Mandy was. *Must've been a long time ago*, was all she said. Katie, my fine and happy fish monger back in the Keys. It all worked out the way it was supposed to.

Mary Anne took a last drag then flicked the cigarette into the dark water below.

I turned to look at her, then followed her eyes out to the water's black, broken surface. Wisps of fog began to gather on the Sound, obscuring City Island and the tops of the bridges. Even the freighters seemed to be going in for the night.

ROUGH SLEEPERS

▼

THE COTSWOLDS, ENGLAND

Dear Cat,

It's been a while since I've written, and I wanted to catch you up on life around here.

The early light is such a physical presence, Cat, seeming not to illuminate so much as settle on the houses and trees, on the gardens and rutted country lanes. There is, of course, that disagreement in physics about whether light is a particle or wave. As the morning sky is gray and pink, and the air is thick and heavy, it seems the former, light lying on the landscape – wrapping like a blanket or a comforter. A shroud.

Morning Star in the eastern sky today, bright and beautiful, unwavering; a beacon. I envied our Dover friends who see it above England's silver sea and Albion cliffs.

Later, St. Andrews Chapel, that sway-backed, dun-colored hut standing in a thicket of trees down Marlborough Mews. Today, the light at long late-summer dusk seemed palpable, dusty and purple, as if the Earth herself were exhaling it. A beautiful, peaceful sight, Cat, as the colors slowly leached from the sky.

It made me think of you, of our walks together.

The garden is pitiful; it desperately needs your green thumb, not my black one. Our small, autumnal English garden. Abandoned, overgrown.

The brick work has not suffered multiple winters well; cracked and worn, moribund and mortarless. Weeds abound; plants unloved have literally gone to seed. All those beautiful colors you coaxed from the earth now withered and faded in the weak and dying summer light.

th presbys r th best. come t th red door n high robie st. dole out fresh bread n hot soup n dont bleat so much bout saving our souls. guess they figure were too far gone. shelters r good too. hot. dry. clean cots. sleep in yer clothes cause you know. andy cross the hall with th men. we come here ever week or so when we want t get outta park. have a proper wash from rough sleepin by trees n under bushes like rabbits

Alex sends me those, the odd Baedeker from time to time, letters appearing unannounced, brown ink on yellow foolscap, torn from the pages of a notebook. No salutation, no return address. No beginning, middle, end. Neither date nor dateline; all information from context alone. Always fragments, always lower case. Content low, shock value high. I have no idea if the facts presented are real or fanciful. If current or ancient. Or if they're even from her, although the handwriting is a close approximation of what I recall from her schoolgirl years. While the narratives vary, the themes are constant: privation and relief. Hillary and Norgay, cold and wet, she and her stalwart tramping through the morbid, rainy north, then shucking their backpacks in a youth hostel, diving into hot showers, all soap and steam. Echoes of Keats and Shelley in sunny Italy. Dandling her feet in a fountain, latest beau buying her tea. Dip into their cash cache for beds, having slept in the same clothes and under bushes for weeks.

*in th alley. dark, dank. watcher stuff. watcher stash. bring enough t share. make **sure** you bring enough t share. never say no. never. t nothin. pavement always piss wet. trash always stinks. so does everyone. hit onna hash pipe helps. so does codeine clipped from th chemist 'round th corner. too many old men, filthy fingers, greedy hands*

She'll come home, Cat, sooner or later. I'm sure she will. She always does.

I ventured off to the village today. Cobblestones slick, sky heavy and overcast. Sun broke out for a moment, then scurried away like a frightened kitten. Stopped by Whitson's Bakeshop, unchanged since 1910. Or 1810, for that matter.

You remember it: rough-plastered butter-yellow walls, gleaming glass-fronted cases, old wooden pendulum clock *tocking* impatiently. Women in starched white blouses, crisp blue skirts; ruddy, round cheeks, toothy smiles.

The aroma was as overpowering as it was delicious: baking wheat flour and hot creamery butter. So inspired, I purchased a brace of scones, trotted them home, snuggled by our little wooden breakfast table, heated up the kettle, ingested a scone slathered over with butter and strawberry jam, knocked back a pot of scalding black tea. Simplicity itself, Cat; a bit of heaven here in the Cotswolds.

I often walk by Bruce Manor; I'm drawn to it. This morning, the way the sun hit the windows, or what's left of them, they seemed blind, glazed over. Impenetrable.

There's an endless, Dickensian family fight about the estate, or so I'm told; one side won't speak to, or sign off for, the other. *I'm not signing because you're asking me to sign.* Or some such. An all-too-familiar syndrome.

The result is that the Great House continues to crumble. I can see holes in the roof, pigeons roosting, streaks of tumbling guano, scars of water damage. This beautiful, irreplaceable piece of history evaporates a bit more every day.

rain n more rain n more rain still. by th river clyde. as if th waters r risin up an washin over th burnd n rotten industrial waste of th city. cold. boots fulla water. impossible t avoid th puddles. small lakes, gregory calls em, wherer th fishies? rain n sheets, water coverin th street corners, slidin cross th floors a busses. gregory finds a ten-bob note an we go t tea room. paki waitress sniffed n stared n shuffled but served us anyways

I walked a long way today, Cat. Put on the Wellingtons, strode down the muddy lane, into the woods, to the moors beyond. A Turner canvas in washed-out browns and grays. Black edges – and blacker holes like Hopper.

The smudges of green were dark and muted. Old-growth green. The green that survives time itself.

Thick wool coat, battered slouch hat. Water everywhere. Sky and rainwater all granulated and foreboding. Leaves slippery and rotting underfoot; mud sucking at my boots. Water of antediluvian proportions. Light barely in the sky.

Of course I thought about her, Cat. How could I not? Wondering if she's out in this. If she's sleeping in it. If she's surviving.

shelter where we find it. fields n thickets. under bridges. alleys n heatin grates. doorways n dumpsters. car barns n church basements left unlocked. cold floors where we lay unseen. huddled into musty greatcoats cribbed from shelters n soup kitchens

I thought of her as a child in our garden; a quiet, intent child. The Louis Agassiz of her age, you laughed, as she pulled at weeds and dissected dandelions. You waved off the incessant bees, sipped lemonade, slipped a bit into the shade. A fine afternoon, Cat.

Then I recalled her anger, her fits, her quick, prowling exits, only to return hours later, silent, dirty, slinking into the house.

Until one day she didn't.

It was a heavy rain, Cat. I felt weak and found my way back.

I keep fresh-cut flowers in her room. The rough-woven blanket on her bed that she always liked. Ready for her to come home at any time. We never know.

camped with th vagrants under a bridge. cold. fires verbotten, *so huddle fer warmth like soldiers. yeast infection. richard says he dont mind. course not. we stay in th museum to keep warm. tea tea and more tea. table scraps outside posh hotels on royal mile. no coughs. no keats yet. want to go south. shelley by the sea. byron, too*

It's a blue dawn this morning, Cat, the kind of light that you like, seeming to come from the land itself, then envelop the houses and trees. As I walk I can just see the outline of Bruce Manor up the hill. No hint of the strife.

letter openers. salt shakers. throw pillows stuffed down me trousers t make me look preggers. or in a big pocket i sewed in me coat. cadgin stuff. too far under th radar for th national dole, so me n muff were livin off th national steal. theavin. pilferin. shopliftin. liberatin. larceny great n small. food. meds. bedclothes n scarfs n hats. whatever we can use. whatever we can trade with our mates where were now, in th maze, th warren, burrowed outta bum mill cottages in south wales. pretty blowy here. boards on windows. no heat. got t heist water, use th loo down th bp. muff's pretty sick

Fog. For Dickens, avatar to his acolyte Conrad, the moral equivalent of the human landscape, life gone awry, moral compass boxed and broken.

It's a dark morning today, Cat; ghostly, deathly white.

The water wakes me, my skin and clothes clammy. Eyes burning, I stumble through marshy fields, trousers soaked to my thighs.

There is nothing familiar here, Cat. The world is a *tabula rasa*.

Our precious illusion of order disappears. Shakespeare's blessed plot dissolves into a world of wet winds and sodden ground.

For all I know it's all fabricated. That instead of being a Rough Sleeper she's enjoying a splendid fellowship at Oxford or Leeds, studying art, architecture, *anything*; like Hugh Lofting writing these inane fantasies, this faceless, interchangeable cast of characters, for her family's amusement. But I don't think so. Not our Alex. Too serious. Too real.

daniel is dyin so i marry him. dry, dusty office, city court, all proper. hes coughin blood, but his name wont die too. i will always be a part of him, n him a part of me. then silence on th moors. water, wind, trees rustlin. town tomorrow, t see daniel an wash dishes fr hot tea n day-old rolls. now i go in my bedroll n feel th silence. alone. apart

It's the equinox, Cat; light low on the horizon makes the bandwidth seem longer, sweeter, a deeper yellow. Time, too, not eclipsed, looms large.

Yesterday becomes today – is part and parcel of today with no segue or separation. Time, elongated, stretches languid as the light is thick and clotted, uncrystalized like clover honey. The shorter days seem paradoxically endless, with time and potential, even as sundowns come more quickly, one upon another, and the air suddenly waxes cold.

It's a scherzo, Cat, not a largo. Not a pastoral, or a romance. A joke. An interregnum. As notes and light and time stretch, and we banish thoughts of winter, of frosts and satires to come.

stowed away onna chunnel train. clothes sodden n surly from rough sleepin. edwards backpack stolen. last clean socks and kerouac. eurorail passes. folding money down me front, so i'm safe. french are french, he says. nasty lot. gimme eyeties any day

Speaking of satire, Cat, a distant memory appeared today, a wraith from the past. Henry Caldwell. Former colleague. Tall, bony chap. Cadaverous, even. Smug. Obtrusive. *Invasive.* Positively *lived* for gossip, the nastier the better.

Remember him? I wouldn't be surprised if you didn't. We came in that first great wave, the Swinging '60s, war raging, classes swelled by student deferments, money galore, humanities' stock on rise, five new faculty hired. The University, in its deeply humane and humanistic way, believed that, like gladiators, we could holler *Penguin Books at 20 paces!*, then duel each other until one or two of us were left standing as legitimate tenure candidates.

Didn't know what happened to him. Frankly, didn't care. But here he was, literally out of nowhere, tenured, some kind of endowed chair, come back, like Scrooge's underdone potato, the Ghost of Department Meetings Past, to haunt me.

Apparently to taunt me, as well; penance for my manifold sins.

Completely out of the empyrean he appeared on our doorstep, vile little valise in hand, seeking – nay, *demanding* – shelter from some imaginary storm.

-- You're hard man to find.
-- You found me.
-- It took work.
-- All the good things do.
-- You're a hard man to find.

-- I'm a hard man to find.

-- Why is that?

-- By design.

-- Why is that?

-- Why not? What would anyone from a former life add? Articulation? Authentication? Enlightenment?

-- Including me?

-- Especially you.

-- How kind.

-- Since you ask. Echoing the dictum, never ask a leading question to which you do not already know the answer.

-- Pause.

-- Or to which you do not want to know the answer.

-- I imagined you living the proper English country life,

-- You imagined wrong.

-- Wearing jodhpurs, playing cricket, riding to the hounds.

-- This is the best that you have to do with your time?

You would have liked it, Cat; a conversation guarded and arch, meant to conceal as much as it revealed. You should have seen him, the smug little professor, endlessly attempting to goad me, to have me rise to the bait. Oh, it was a proper sparring match, thrust and parry, feints left and right. As much about what wasn't said as what was.

How he did find me I still don't know. Don't know why anyone in our little tight-lipped village would give out the information.

Sat him for tea in the kitchen – a riot of disrepair, all wormy wood and decaying vegetable matter. He mooed over the rough-hewn wooden farm table, matching benches, counter tops, open shelves. Clay pots and tea cups. Rest of the house, too. He liked my line about it being furnished in Early Agrarian Nostalgia.

Sniffing about like a ferret, muttering about it being too primitive, he announced that the room hadn't had a proper wash, perm, and set since the Restoration. Horrified at the overgrown herb garden, the leftover tea and scraps of bread and jam, Caldwell was at his droll best when he pronounced, with no little air of superiority, "the entire house seems fungible. Arnold Lewis' Dead Flower Period."

-- How on earth did you find this place?

-- With wandring steps and slow. Catherine – no doubt you remember her – and I were bicycling about England generally, the Cotswolds specifically, and got lost. Found ourselves here quite by accident. A village so small that none of the houses have numbers, just names. Black Swan Hall. Bruce Manor. Logan House. Wold Cottage. And if one does not know or recall house names, or roads – which, unmarked, one similarly has to memorize – simply recalling the tenant will suffice.

-- Much the way I found you.

-- We felt our arrival was serendipitous and fell in love. We felt that the cottage, too, was Faulknerian, fecund, a growing thing. As simple – or simpleminded – as that.

-- Just so.

-- At the time we were quite at sixes-and-sevens, ready – no, eager – for a move, a change. We had enough money – a little, but enough – and nothing to hold us. The time and the price were right, the National Health didn't hurt, so we crossed the pond.

I remember it well, Cat, and I'm sure that you do, too. Empire. War. Depression. Nowhere firm to stand. Generations uneducated and impoverished. We, who were so naive, so idealistic, felt we could elevate everyone. We found instead that we were slipping farther into parochialism, nativism. Into the heart of darkness.

We kept telling ourselves the fable of Camelot, of a wonderful, benevolent American aristocracy. We found instead The Sense of an Ending.

We found our own history false. Our fantasies fleeting and futile.

We found a white moss blanketing the landscape, so thick we could not see the house or the road; we could barely see the shoes below our trousers. We had to stop and let it pass.

America was coming apart. The center, if it ever did, was not holding. There was no common parlance. No common ground.

America increasingly uncivil. America irrevocably headed for a race war.

American angry and unruly and insane.

We were on vacation, Catherine. We looked at each other. Simple as that.

-- A lovely place, St. Andrews-on-Wold.
-- St. Andrews? This is England, not Scotland.
-- An unrelated St. Andrew, perhaps.
-- A St. Andrew in exile?
-- An anomalous St. Andrew, I grant you, but St. Andrew nonetheless.
-- A *rogue* St. Andrew?
-- Could be. The Anglicans and their churches remain a mystery to me.

The years and the seasons have turned again, Cat. Nights and days and nights again. Still I stand my watch, Cat. I keep my vigil.

I watch for her. For our lost and wayward daughter.

livin n th fields, feastin on growin things, encounterin manure n marigolds. covered n yellow pollen blowin all over. hooked a pint of sweet brandy an nippin it all inna town. sunlight. birdsong. martin returnin with cadged muffins. findin me all askew like alsace

-- Nice enough little place here.
-- Thank you for your vote. I've been waiting decades for it.
-- Not what I meant.
-- No? Tell me what you meant.
-- Seems a big Spartan.
-- Your powers of observation astound me. Catherine and I like it this way. We like the chill. Damp rooms. Wearing sweaters. The sting of cold water on the flesh. It agrees with us. Or we with it. It all amounts to the same thing.

It is a cold cottage, Cat, rendered lethargic by two centuries of poverty and sleep.

One step down the road and an entire life changes. Was it random or directed, by happenstance or design? Chaos theory, Cat: the path of the butterfly, the dandelion seed borne by the wind. As the order we attempted to create fell apart something else arose to replace it.

It's a cold, windy landscape. Quiet, rural, green. The air clears the mind.

It's no Romance. I am not searching for anything. Quite the reverse. I'm not leaving the shire. I'm burrowing farther in.

-- Ours is one of a series of cottages on what used to be a large estate. Most were rented to tenant farmers, but of course they've all been sold off. Eaton Cottage. Whitcomb Cottage. Moraine Cottage. Bruce Cottage. Others, too, all sufficiently apart that we never see or hear each other except by design.

-- Desolate.

-- Ours is a bit different, but only slightly. Bruce Ford. Originally it was the gamekeeper's cottage. In St. Andrews I should say the gillie's cottage. The people who once lived in this house beat the bushes to roust the birds so the laird and his laddies could shoot them. Patrolled the estate's park lands, a euphemism for a private game preserve, his lordship's hunting lands surrounded by a solid stone wall, since fallen.

-- Pause.

-- Who knows how many starving poachers the Bruces hung?

-- Pause.

-- In the name of summary English justice.

-- Indeed.

-- You can just make out the Great House, Bruce Manor, through the tangle of trees and brush. See the slate roof? There's the southeast corner through the thickets, the gorse, the ground cover. Nobody lives there now, haven't for decades. Some sort of family feud – doesn't every family have one? Along with evil twins and maiden aunts?

-- All of the above.

-- Narratives about Bruce Manor abound, one cogent version being that the various family members can't – or won't – agree to sign off on the estate. Another is that they can't find all the heirs – too many ashrams or monasteries or rehab clinics. A third is that they can *find* the heirs but said heirs can't – or won't – agree to future use.

-- Pause.

-- You know the Scots.

-- Scots?

-- St. Andrews.

-- *The* Bruces?

-- Perhaps. More likely relatives. Refugees. Renegades. The record isn't quite clear, and there are many conflicting stories. One thing is for certain: they were farmers. In all likelihood they escaped Scotland – and with a certain amount of loot. Which may or not have lasted. One version is that they invested every cent in the slave trade.

-- Hm.

-- It was very legal and seemed like a good idea at the time. Eventually they needed the income from the farm. However, in the manner of the times, they didn't manage anything well. Nor did they rotate their crops – or if they did, not well enough. So that by the Great War, the Bruces had badly depleted the soil, thereby crippling the yield.

-- Not implausible.

-- There are tales of stock market crashes. Labor prices. Taxes. Ne'er-do-wells.

-- Hardly anomalous.

-- Then the peccadilloes. The last Lady of Bruce Manor had it off with the gardener. Ran off with the gardener. Was offed by the gardener. Take your pick. You know stories: they are unreliable. Lurid. Inconclusive.

-- Building seems to have good bones, though, to have stood this long.

-- Bruce Manor was built some 200 years ago. Perhaps more. The loss at Culloden and the subsequent diaspora may have figured into it. Family had some money then, and unity of purpose. If local legends are correct by the 1880s Bruce Manor was famous – infamous – for lavish, all-night parties. All-*week* parties. The Great House ablaze with lights. Three distinct orchestras spelled each other. Music at all hours. Champagne and oysters. Willful women. Willing servants. Debauchery deluxe.

-- Where can one buy tickets?

-- Then Bruce Manor went dark. War. Depression. More war. Family strife. Now the Great House lays derelict. As if an invading army had sacked it.

-- Pause.

-- I've seen it. Extensive water damage. Ceilings tumbling down. Walls reworked in mold and offal. We suspect squatters, but no one has the energy or the interest to find out. There's no reward for intervening. Some suspect that it will be taken by the National Trust – should the National Trust ever have the will or the money. Others believe that the house will simply collapse of its own excess. Like the family itself.

It's a cold, wicked, rainy night, Cat; you know the kind. Stocking feet by the crackling hearth. Scotch in hand. Heart breaking for all the wanderers like Alex, the rough sleepers in the woods and the fields. Lost and alone, sleeping in the rain.

Of course he wanted to stay, Cat. Move in. Of course I wouldn't let him, for fear of never being rid of him. Instead, I sent him packing to The Wayside Inn, which, as I discovered the following morning, he found perfectly acceptable.

-- My first nights in the village were there. A 200-year-old house re-imagined as a serviceable six-room hotel. Inn, really. The Wayside Inn. I presume you were comfortable. The rooms are clean. Water hot. Hosts unobtrusive, high on propriety.

-- Papered over with portraits of some rather severe-looking characters. Long line of hanging judges. A dour bunch at best.

-- In the old days, people were not given to perpetual smiling. A modern affliction.

-- I liked the breakfast.

-- Yes?

-- Tea the color and consistency of ink. Scones. Rhymes with stones. Only slightly softer and somewhat less tasty.

-- No one ever came to England for the cuisine.

-- Apparently not. At least not to St. Andrews-on-Wold.

In the rain the colors are rich, deep greens and browns, grays, black. Intense, dark, inviting. Color like the end of consciousness itself.

I have a memory of her, Cat, head popping up from the garden, hair like seaweed, as if she, too, were part of the growing world, had sprung not from us but from plant life itself. Perhaps that's why she chooses to sleep outdoors so much, why she seems to gather nourishment from the rain and the earth.

As a young child she took my watch, intently gazed at the incessant sweep of the second hand, and said, "around and around. Around and around."

"Yes," I agreed.

"It never stops," she added.

"No," I answered, "it never does."

gaudi church on acid. all th colors melted. boulevards sweet. some geezer picked me up, fed me coffee n croissants, pimped me out. it was ok. only a night or two. better'n bein' rousted n th park. havin' me backpack filched. hot bath n a scrub later, clean bed

-- You were denied tenure, as I recall.

-- You recall incorrectly. I did not stand for tenure. I simply let my second three-year contract expire, packed up my office, and left. That was 1971, and like Lot I've never looked back.

-- You were so ambitious for a time.

-- Perhaps I was; I really don't recall. But I do know that I found the requirements of the academy increasingly foolish. Pedantic. Inane. Inimical to what I wanted. So I decided that six years of living in Amherst were sufficient. Sentence reduced to time served. It was best to go. So I did, unheralded and unnoticed.

-- One day you simply weren't there. Like a tenant skipping out on a lease.

-- Well put.

-- Caused a minor flurry.

-- Very minor, I'm certain. I was hardly important. Or promising.

-- How have you made out since?

-- Quite well, thank you. We've been content here. Had a bit of an inheritance. Lived – not grandly but comfortably. We've never wanted much – so we were never in want.

It's gray today, Cat, all the color washed out of the cottages and the trees. Seems as if The Cotswolds are submerged.

Out early for a walk, I saw a young girl on a rise – backlit by a hazy sun. She was roughly the same size and shape as Alex; the same hair, a tangle of brambles. A briar patch. The Pre-Raphaelite look Alex adopted as a child. I felt my heart race and thought for a moment – but no. She wasn't.

Oh, Catherine. Catherine.

-- You've changed.

-- I would hope so, Henry. It's been a very long time. I would hope that the years have done something for me other than grind down my vital signs.

-- You don't say much.

-- No, I don't. What would you have me say?

-- Pause.

-- Let me put this another way, Henry. What are you looking for? Absolution? Expiation? I can't give you either.

-- Re-connection.

-- Why on earth would you want that?

-- Curiosity, then.

-- Well, then, I hope I've assuaged it.

I do recall those days, Cat. All that passion. All those senseless arguments.

-- You were ambitious. Combative. Contentious. Intemperate. Impatient.

-- Was I? All those dreadful things. Perhaps so. I'm surprised, then, that you'd want to look up such a fellow. In any event, I really don't recall. I'm quiet now. Contemplative. The lack of department meetings – the lack of a department – works wonders to smooth out the rough edges of character. If rough edges there were.

-- There most certainly were.

-- Thank you for coming all this way to remind me. But I'm no longer that person.

-- Where did he go?

-- I have no idea. When you find him – *if* you do find him – that headstrong 28-year-old, please let know. Or not. I don't know if I'd know him, or want to know him. Or if he would know me. Or if we could communicate.

Despite the promise of America, Cat, one can only re-invent oneself so much. If my life as an English gardener didn't quite jell, my premise was still sound. While the garden may lay in ruins, there remains much to recommend it. There are so many lovely shades of green here, light and dark, a landscape that suggests so many possibilities. Marvell, that genius: "a green thought in a green shade." All those ways to disappear.

The hedges and fences still enclose the garden, Cat, glistening this morning, in the spring rain's hard half-light. It's a proper cloister, Cat. It always was.

Since it was hidden, Cat, I know that we felt none of the rules applied. Innocence. Temperance. Liberty became license. She's our fault, Cat: we never reckoned the toll it could take. The broken or damaged spirit. The loss. The glittering smile that, in the right light, became truly frightening.

Alexandra. Our dark, brilliant daughter. That brilliance was her downfall. At best it was her challenge. She never quite fit. Now she's lost and not certain how to make herself found.

She chose a path of, perhaps not the least resistance, but one where she could write her own name. Neither outcast nor invisible, though some might call her so.

querulous n quarrelsome, she argues with us bout our laundry. hadnt done it fr weeks. hot sweaty sticky summer. when in rome bathed in fountains, peed in train stations. scraped up a couple euros, flounced down spanish steps like we owned em. iced tea at babingtons. loo so clean i could move in. peter a darling. attentive. had oodles of money, he said, but lost it. i don't believe him, but havin th grandest time, sleepin n friend's flat, dirtyin th sheets, eatin apple tarts an quince, leavin th windows open on hot nights, listenin t people yellin back n forth cross airshafts n down inna street

-- Still, you left.

-- I did not *leave* anything per se. It had nothing to do with the department, the profession, or even Vietnam, although the latter was reason enough. Oh, certainly, America was increasingly ugly. Angry. Dangerous. But, no, those were not sufficient reasons to leave. No, we came here, emigrated *here*, because we liked the sense of order, the sense of hierarchy. Of course, their history was just as bloody as ours – we're cousins, don't you see, as are the Germans and the rest of Northern Europe. But we liked the stasis – or what passed for stasis in 1971.

-- Pause.

-- I was 35, Cat was 33, Alex was six, and it was all fine.

We invented America out of nothing, Cat, it's what we do. Leave the Old World behind and adapt. Improvise. Create a world of *maybe*. That's where Americans excel.

We came here for disparate reasons. I for order and history. You for evolution and socialism. Certainly, the Brits had done their fair share, and more, but you felt it was a new United Kingdom. You were willing to overlook the bad in order to hope for something better. For something good.

So was I.

So we ignored the bloody conquests, the strait jacket of class, the self-righteousness, the imperialism. We told ourselves that America was irredeemably cursed: the twin evils of appropriating the Red Man's land, and the accompanying genocide; of enslaving the Black Man, and the perpetual apartheid. We had to leave.

We were young; it was easy to argue away or obviate the British hand in the slave trade. For us, Britain, not America, became the New Eden, the New Jerusalem. Britain was the solid past, the assured future. The hoary forest virgin again.

-- I preferred to be somewhere more stable. More ordered. More homogeneous. Less diffuse. Less imperialistic – or at least farther in the past. More diverse, although the old crowd despised the Irish and the Scots. Now there are Africans. Arabs. Asians of all stripe. Joke's on them. For me, if there weren't a majesty then at least there was an *order* to English life – that's what I wanted. Stratified, certainly, but also a semblance of propriety. Hardly the free-for-all, the senseless hodgepodge of America.

-- So goodbye Good Old U.S. of A.? For England with its empire? Its own immigrant, racial, and economic divisions? Ireland alone would seem an enormous disincentive.

-- A frequent discussion from the '60s, Henry: which country has clean hands? England certainly doesn't – and didn't. But weighing all the factors, we felt that we had a greater chance of dealing fairly with the future here rather than there. Besides, Catherine and I already spoke the language.

We're Americans. By definition we don't like limits, definitions.

America. Liberty. Clear cut the land, clear the title. Re-name it. Baptize it. Make it something else. Make it someone else. Devil take its history.

But Will Shakespeare had it right. The blood never fades. The damned spot is always there. Boiling and bubbling.

Reconciliation? Expiation? Salvation and redemption are very distant peaks. Life is a lot more like Macbeth than Martin or the Mahatma: jealous, ambitious, brooding, listening to all the wrong voices, answering blood with blood.

I tramped around the woods again today. Nearly lost a boot in the bargain. I thought – *delicious epiphany!* – this is us. Always in the suck and pull of history. The muck of modernity. The more we try to escape, the deeper we're drawn back down.

-- Nothing literary. Completely divorced?

-- Well, at one time I actually thought I'd write a literary study – something called *Six Archetypal Images*. About how everything in literature could be derived from six views of the physical world. A theory of mine I'd been developing since graduate school.

-- Derived from Jung, no doubt.

-- Not at all, but no matter. In any event, the study became increasingly diffuse, too personal, too much of this place, not sufficiently dispassionate. Not sufficiently scholarly or of the academy.

-- Perhaps because you were removed from the academy.

-- Very reasonable. In any event, taking it away from *me* became too much like work.

-- Is Donne's sphere one of your images? I recall how taken you were with that poem. His ride? The lone figure emerging from the sun?

-- I don't know. I hadn't gotten that far.

-- And?

-- I set it aside. I'll return to it one day. Perhaps.

-- Yes?

-- Probably not. *Sic transit.*

How vainly men themselves amaze, Cat. Simplify, Cat. Simplify. The small stone church at dusk, when the air seems filled with promise, suffused with quiet.

The garden, grown over, vibrant blues and greens.

Our Sage and Serious Spenser, Cat: we should reign over change. Cultivate our gardens, manage the colors.

Although I've seen her since then, of course, I always think of Alexandra as she was, a serious child with an infrequent smile and tangled hair. For whom time seemed as elusive as it was incessant.

-- Catherine.

-- Yes.

-- Something of a gardener, as I recall. Woodworker, too.

-- Yes. Those cabinets there.

-- Lovely. Quite lovely. Quite the artist. The filigree work is excellent.

-- Were she here, I'm sure she'd be flattered by the compliment and thank you for it.

-- And she is?

-- Not here.

What was I to tell him, Cat? That you suffer from an excess of High Seriousness? That at one point you decided to save the world one stripling at a time? In the manner of Blanche Dubois, by initiating them into manhood? Your mission? Your crusade?

That depending on one's view of carnality, you took upon yourself the noble-ignoble task of inaugurating-corrupting the village youth in the glories-trials of union?

And that upon your eventual – and wholly predictable – discovery, you enjoyed a certain level of opprobrium from certain parties? Some severe souls going so far as to denounce you as a succubus, Lilith herself, which they meant literally?

I could take their point. First, the resemblance: your long hair streaked with gray as if scorched by lightning. Vacant, slightly wild eyes. Hushed, conspiratorial tones. Dressed in what for all the world appeared to be gypsy shawls or slipcovers.

Second, you did act the proper wiccan. Sneaking around the village, hiding in the shadows, profligate with your favors, conjuring your spells.

Third, it's fair to say that we drifted apart. Then you drifted away. We're still on paper, as they say. You're out there, somewhere. Hopefully well.

I miss you, Cat, even as I think of Marvell, two Paradises living in Paradise alone.

-- You had a daughter, too.

-- I still do. Alexandra. Alex.

-- Scowled a lot.

-- Still does. First, it was at me. Now, at the world. At least did at last sighting.

-- Last sighting?

-- Rough sleeper, as we put it here. Left home. Acquired boyfriends. Tattoos. Not necessarily in that order.

-- Rough sleeper?

-- Vagabond. Homeless. By choice.

-- Oh?

-- On the bum, a proper English hobo, dirty, disheveled, cold on the frosty heath, sleeping under hedges, hither and yon.

-- You must --

-- I have never given up hope. I receive letters, which I accept as her umbilicus, however twisted. Her radio signals to the mother ship.

-- You must --

-- Apparently, she washes – when she does – in train stations; lives under bridges, in open fields, public parks; dumpster dives for restaurant discards, dines in soup kitchens, lives off the land.

-- How perfectly dreadful.

-- Life is choice and the consequence of choice. This is hers. She seems fine with it.

-- Her health? Physical and mental?

-- Not known.

-- You're a cold-blooded bastard.

-- The wound scarred-over years ago, Henry. I refuse to live in a hair shirt.

The facts as we know them, Cat. That Alex began sneaking out of the house when she thought I didn't hear her, roughly age 12. That she did it regularly. Then, finally, one day she didn't come back.

That Alex is out on the moors. Marshes. Fens.

That Alex is on a Grail quest – with no Grail. Peripatetic. Unsettled. ADD.

That Alex has a lot of us in her. Flying far below the radar. Invisible. Doesn't want to be found. Surfaces when she so desires.

That Alex is our very English daughter. Our very troubled English daughter. Smart. Impatient. Rebellious. All of the above, and who isn't at that age? A walker – those long strides down the path to the gorse, stick in hand, sack on shoulder. She always gave the impression of cross-country skiing, Cat, regardless of the weather.

Showing up at the oddest times, sometimes a man in tow, sometimes not. Sometimes sharing same living quarters, sometimes not. Nary any explanation or fanfare. Hardly a how-de-do. Simply a knock on the door, as if I'd been expecting her.

-- There are the tattoos.

-- Tattoos?

-- They began some time ago with a few cute little curlicues, Aztec or Arabian or Armenian designs tentatively poking about her forearms and calves.

-- Sounds innocent enough. These days.

-- That art morphed into the Arden Forest in all its shaggy glory.

-- Oh?

-- The *piece* – perhaps *pieces* is more accurate – *de resistance* is a Chartres-like endless landscape enveloping her entire back. Something like steamer trunk decals or refrigerator magnets: every whistle-stop where she can scrape together the cash she acquires something to help complete the vision – a vast jungle, a rain forest of varietals. Variations on a theme, the theme being the vastness and glory of the growing world.

-- My grandfather never went out in public without a coat and tie.

-- I glimpsed the masterwork just once, as she sunbathed in the garden. All across her back lay a large, vegetable growth, like the banyan tree in

Lahaina, or the Great Barrier Reef. A phantasmagoria, a riot of color and shape drawn by disparate hands.

-- One is at a loss.

-- Each a souvenir. Each a statement. With Alex, what isn't? It's as if the fleet's in port, and all the most incorrigible men are locked up in one ship.

Henry Caldwell embodies a growing American affliction, Cat. The curse of being comfortable. The curse of being Ibsen's Troll King – to thyself be enough. Never great. Never good. Simply good enough. The curse of being smart enough, of *not* having to work hard – and then not knowing how.

-- Conrad, another English convert, would have relished the supreme irony: I came here seeking order, stasis. The fine line between perfect and petrified. I found instead only disorder. Mutabilitie. I should have listened to Spenser. I should have stayed put.

-- Is that what he said?

-- It's what Dorothy says, about looking for your heart's desire in your own backyard. If my time in England has taught me nothing else, it's how much things change, societies, people, the works. How tenuous character is. How it depends on a balance of bodily experience and brain chemistry. How it is infinitely variable and utterly unpredictable. How we can wake up one day and be a completely different person.

-- Gregor Samsa. Kafka certainly got it right, didn't he?

-- There is great solace in these hills, Henry, in the rivers, in the gentle green and rolling landscape, in the houses, white and gray in the distance.

The mercifully quick conclusion of Caldwell's visit is not worth reporting, Cat. Suffice it to say that, upon garnering enough gossip, filling his vile valise, he left. Offered neither fanfare nor farewell. Just a hurried goodbye, as if his train were already pulling out of the station. Henry Caldwell vanished, leaving a vapor trail of disquieting memories.

A tough northeastern wind cuts something fearsome through the fissures in the cottage, Cat, and the rain batters the windows – so much rain for so long that it's beaten down the blossoms and transformed the garden into a quagmire. The power is already down – I'm writing this, like Keats, by candlelight – and I fear for the havoc the storm will wreak upon the water supply. Given how primitive all things mechanical are, given what leaches into the ground, I fear the worst.

Going to put the pen down now, Cat. Back in a mo. I see what appears to be two figures moving in the mist. Could be wisps of fog. Could be something else.

I can't be sure.

SOME GIRLS/IRISH

▼

MYKONOS, GREECE

"She was the belle of the ball," he said at last. It had been two years that he'd been coming to Gandalf's Grief Group, two years, and had said absolutely nothing.

Then Robert, tall and straight and steady, was all story.

As I listened to him, and wove in my own life, and my family, and the Wobblies, I began to fall in love with him, a dear and charming man whom I ultimately lost.

"When she – spelled Lilian, pronounced Lilly Ann – walked into a room, she *was* the room." Robert smiled. "And she loved it. She loved being seen, being a celebrity."

I never thought that Robert would speak, but Gandalf made that happen. It was part of his magic to get even the most reticent people to talk through their grief.

Gandalf the Grief Guy – real name Harry Thorsen. Sure, it was hokey, but maybe that's what we all needed to break the ice. To lay down the burden just a little.

All the New Age stuff – you could dismiss it as old wine in new bottles. Verities that always have, always will work. But maybe the old ideas needed that, to be dressed up like today. Emanating from a guy with a shaved head, exotic looks, a knowing mien. Psych degree from Stanford, two decades at self-help before re-branding himself. In Johnstown because his wife, engineer at Grumman, Ph.D. genius type, came for a job.

Some people hated group, didn't last. People whining about their losses, not listening to anyone else. There was one woman – mercifully, she tired of us, and the process, and left early. She didn't have to have the last word. She had to have *all* the words. Then there were others, like Robert and me, who stayed, in part because we needed the emotional buttressing, because listening to others helped frame the issues.

Gandalf's Grief Group met in the commons room of All Saints Church. *All* saints. I liked that, very lapsed Catholic that I am. Invite them all in. Why read anyone out?

It was one of those great, 19th-century, heavily wooded spaces. All burnished, hand-carved oak, indigenous flora and fauna. Really magnificent. If there had originally been any religious paraphernalia it had long since been removed. These days, the church sponsored various groups, hosted jazz services. Even had poetry readings.

We averaged fifteen people, give or take, mostly in our 50s, faded, like our clothes, a combination of loss and long days. We were weary and confused; bruised fruit. Gandalf knew we had untapped energy. He could make it active, alive. Current.

Standing in the center of the circle, he announced a topic, gave a brief precis, then deftly stepped aside and let us take over.

Some sessions were Open Mike: *What's on your mind today?*

Other times, Gandalf primed the pump. Overcame people's natural reticence. One was Some Girls, widowers speaking about their late wives.

So, Harry, Gandalf spun on one heel, *tell us about Ruth.*

A large, rumpled man – hair, suit, shirt – Harry was the picture of uncomfort. With everything ill-fitting, unclean, unkempt, it was as if he had fallen to pieces caring for his late wife. I had no idea what Harry did – Gandalf wisely preserved as much privacy as possible – but he spoke like a college professor. Not anecdotal or discursive, not hesitant or meandering, but lucid and exclamatory, as if he were lecturing on economic theory – and would brook no interruptions.

"Before she left me," Harry started, stopped, then started again, sweating, spreading out his hands as if he were pleading. "Before Ruth was swept under. Before she began to bark like a dog. Before the chemo stole her looks and her mind. Before the cancer spread, and shrank, and spread again. Before she became erratic. Before all that. Ruth had descended into utter irrationality. Her anger foremost and apparent, her eyes glittering, she denounced the postal system for stealing her mail. The gardener for ruining her lawn, destroying her rose bushes. The purchasers of our home for reducing it to rack and ruin." He shook his head. "Of course, none of it was true.

"Of course, I couldn't do or say anything. How could I? I was far too stunned. So I stood silent, smiling, supportive, as if I, too, shared her vision."

Harry wiped his eyes. "Ruth," he said, "was a noticeably bright woman from a family of noticeably bright people. Ruth was a Rhodes Scholar, or could have been.

"When she died in her sleep, she was 45 years old."

Harry collapsed into a chair accompanied by murmurs, head shakes.

Ron? Gandalf gestured.

As crisp as Harry was crushed, Ron wore a shirt with a starched oxford collar, cuffs turned up at his wrists, pressed khakis, loafers with no socks. Tall, angular, very square shoulders: could have been a model. Unlike Harry, Ron's words came with difficulty, infrequently, oases strung in the desert. As he spoke, and though people were patient, there was much stirring in the room. His hurt, his pain, were palpable.

"February," he said, "was Gwen's favorite month. Bright, sunny days. Cold. Brittle. Unforgiving. The way she was.

"The way the sun moved another notch in the sky," Ron gestured, "it was clear that spring was just over the horizon. Gwen was always looking forward: the warming weather would offer her absolution.

"She was a marathon talker, but everyone forgave her that. Because among the nonstop stream of memoir, fact, and speculation, there were nuggets, genuine nuggets, gleanings of gold panned in a stream.

"There was also an undercoating of anger, of venom, directed, misdirected, from her own storehouse of inadequacy. Nothing was ever good enough, at least for her.

"Gwen feared failure, and she feared darkness. She hated the long shadows of winter afternoons, how they gathered in corners and crept across rooms. She felt they were devouring her. Soon they did.

"She drank, then drank some more. At first, the drinking helped, an old family remedy. Then, predictably, it didn't. It just made matters worse."

Nods all around the room.

"Gwen maintained – preached, in fact – that America's enormous incidence of cancer was the result of people going to war against themselves. When she contracted brain cancer – silent, sudden, virulent – it was as if she had willed it on herself. As if she had wanted to take her own life. And this was the quickest, most effective way.

"As the cancer nibbled at, then devoured her brain, she retreated into stony silence, her face like a clenched fist, eyes a hateful black. Gwen, who could talk varnish off a table, spent her final days maddened and mute, angry, aggrieved, inarticulate."

Sitting down quickly, Ron buried his face in his hands.

As painful as it is, Gandalf said, *it's good to get it out. The bile that eats us. Irv?*

Speaking in an aggrieved tenor, Irv, in blue jeans and an orange Izod shirt, had text and subtext, an undercurrent that someone had done him an immense wrong.

"Ellen's eyes wandered, her head bobbed, and her words – what few there were – trailed off. A song from her childhood could bring her back briefly. A line or two of "Red, Red Robin," she was as vivacious as ever, then, like a wisp of smoke or shower of dandelion seeds, she got lost in mid-flight. At first, I could take her hands, and she would turn, and smile at me. Increasingly, even that failed to get her attention.

"All our stories end the same way," he said. "Or maybe just end in the middle."

Gandalf stood. *Who's ready for a new relationship? Who wants to discuss it? Grace?*

"Values," I said. "That's an important part of my story, because it was the value of everyday work that I found so attractive in Jeffrey. My late husband, Jeffrey Colter. Oh, I kept my name because I wanted to preserve my Irish heritage. But Jeffrey and I were partners in the best sense of the word. Could have been twins. Same broad, flat face, wide-set eyes. He was steady – he had the patience of a man who works with his hands. Farmers. Ranchers. You can't hurry things. The good ones transfer that to life.

"I was a social worker – still am. Jeffrey and I both worked long hours and had odd schedules. People in distress. Houses in distress. We relaxed together. Quiet time. Movies. Popcorn. Snuggled under a big old quilt my grandmother made.

"Jeffrey never smoked. One day he coughed, shrugged it off, kept moving.

"Jeffrey got sick. Then he got sicker. Overnight, he morphed into a mixed bag of needs. I went from being his soulmate to his hospice nurse. Jeffrey became the situation. At best, we talked. At worst, I could smell him rotting right there in the bed.

"I was in the room, and he was struggling. He was in a coma, but, clearly, he was struggling. Labored breathing. Chest heaving. I stroked his hair and held his hand. 'Jeffrey,' I said, 'it's OK to go. It's OK.' His breathing slowed down. Heart rate steadied. Fifteen minutes later it was over.

"When he passed, I didn't know what to do. Not out of grief – I had long before lost him as a partner. I mourned *then*, at that first diagnosis, because I knew that Jeffrey would never recover. That the man who was my husband was irretrievably gone. What was left was the husk of the man I had cared for. But I was lost.

"Ativan put me to sleep. Friends helped. So did group. Long walks. Work.

"Still, I had to get my bearings. It wasn't a matter of telling people the story, although I can understand how people need that. I really didn't. I came here because I thought this group might be helpful for me to re-set my priorities. While I don't recommend this – matter of taste – I found myself going back into my past. My family's past. My Uncle Jim. Jim Cavanaugh. The Wobblies. Labor. I read a lot about the Wobblies. Even got a tattoo to honor them."

I loosened my blouse to show the red IWW globe on my right shoulder blade.

Scattered applause.

"I thought about friends who have long-distance relationships – maybe twenty-five percent. Not for me. I don't know if I'll ever be as close with anyone as I was with Jeffrey, where everything we did involved or reflected the other. But I'm ready to try."

Robert, Gandalf prompted.

"It's two years," he said, "and I'm ready, too. Lilian was ill. Then she was gone."

He was reserved, a man careful with his words. With close-cropped gray hair, a lean, lithe body, Robert could have been a dancer. Distance runner.

"Like all of us," he continued, "I'd known loss before Lilian, but distantly. My parents were aged and infirm, and their twin passing didn't come as a surprise.

"I had one brother, six years younger. Didn't face many privations growing up. Given too much." He shrugged. "He liked to get stoned. *Really* liked to get stoned. Died young of pulmonary cancer. Was the dope a contributing factor? I have no idea.

"Did I know him well? Not really, given our differences in age and outlook. By the time he was much of anybody I was out of the house. What's more, I don't like to sit around. Never did. In college – his whole half-semester at Buffalo – he majored in loafing. Blowing reefer. And I can only imagine what else. Then he left. When he died, I didn't grieve. There are a lot of people, one way or another, who are no longer there. My brother was another one. Meant no more than that.

"Lilian was Southern, charming. Great conversationalist – she knew how to listen and how to remember what people said. What was important to them. She could have been a great politician had she the slightest interest in public policy. Or legislation. And the only ribbons she wanted to cut were on the properties we had bought, then sold.

"Southern, but decidedly postbellum. Post slavery. Her family came from Germany in the 1880s. South Carolina. Merchants when everything was family-owned, farms, stores, everything but the post office. Came with a good grubstake and bad English, proceeded to sell – whatever. At first, they settled on dry goods – pots, pans, shoes. Greatly in demand, very little spoilage. When one brother became a pharmacist, the family business shifted that way. They did well. Then did better.

"By the time Lilian came on board, her family was well vested – and invested – in Charleston society. She went to a private girls' school, then Finch College, a finishing school with books. Some books, anyway.

"Finch was wealth and privilege. Snooty girls with wardrobes and chauffeurs. Although she loved to deny it, Lilian more than fit in. She *defined* the place. Her textbook posture, social graces, ability to pour tea. Lilian was aristocracy. Royalty.

"She loved being the sun, having the planets revolve around her. You should have seen her with small-town politicos. They *always* took her calls. They liked her. Liked the way she would make them look good. Knew the regs better than they did. Made them know there was political capital to be made. And there always was.

"And money, too," Robert smiled. "Let's not forget that."

"We were 20 when we met – our families had mutual friends in New York City, and we were invited to a dinner in their apartment, something roughly the size of an airplane hangar, overlooking the Metropolitan Museum of Art. Of course, I didn't want to go. I don't know if Lilian wanted to or not. All I do know is that," pointing to me, "we were twins, too. Tall, thin. Fell hopelessly in love from that moment. Six months later we were married. Lavish, Southern affair. She just glowed.

"Neither one of us finished college. Finch was a holding pattern. I was pro forma at Penn, going through the motions, working in the family real estate business. Now that Lilian had her Mrs. degree, and I was making a living, who needed the sheepskins?

"She had smarts and style. Those people whom Lilian couldn't charm – anomalies, I grant you – she'd invite to dinner. And she could cook! Color, taste, presentation! All from scratch, all meals she knew our guests would love. What she could do with minced garlic and cayenne pepper. Pick you right up out of your chair!

"What a team we were. We started in Philadelphia, and, working in derelict neighborhoods, I made a pledge: for every unit of market housing I produced, I would produce one of affordable housing. Certainly, government subsidies helped. But it was hard work to keep costs down and quality up, then sell at a fair price to people in need.

"There was a bit of nomad in both of us, and we bounced around, Albany, Jamestown. Ebensburg, Somerset. Johnstown. We didn't intend it to be final.

"Lilian and I never read tea leaves. Held up a wet finger in the wind. Sure, real estate's a form of gambling. The stock market. Texas hold-'em. You watch where the money goes. Who's backing what with what. Once, railroads were the engine – pun intended. Mills. Mines. Rivers. Now it's Medicaid. Historic preservation. Health care and human services. Highways. We studied the financial pages. The demographics. Described a 20-mile radius around the locus of cash. That's where we looked for deals.

"We especially liked historic preservation because that kept the flavor of these areas. We'd research historicity. Old bookstores, barn sales, websites. Antiques – wash bowels, lanterns, household implements. Photos – people, places, things. Portraiture. Men in uniform. Families. Encouraged our purchasers to follow suit. We tried to extend the importance and dignity of the past. Of what and who came before.

"There were government grants for this kind of work, and for affordable housing. We were able to lever a great deal of money, and do a great deal of good.

"None of these were slam-dunks – or they would have been long gone before we arrived. We took risks, plenty of them. We lost a few – but gained more than we lost.

"Johnstown – Cambria City Historic District. Minersville. Moxham. Favorable federal loan-and-grant program. Lockheed Martin. Northrup Grumman. Lot of smaller folks. Good jobs, high-end support. They all need houses. Equity. Stability.

"We wanted to work 'til we were 80, like my dad." Robert paused. "We made it to 50, when Lilian died. Then I couldn't do it anymore. Grief and loss'll do that to you.

"Lilian's cancer, cervical, by the time they diagnosed it she was nearly gone.

"One memory that sticks is the last time I was with her before she went into the ICU. She had gone to the pharmacy to see about this med or that – she insisted on being independent. *Fly solo*, she said, red wool coat buttoned up to her chin.

"I don't know what the precipitating incident was – or even if there was one – but about a half-hour later I got a call. Lilian was causing a fuss, and could I come?

"When I got there, for a moment I didn't recognize her. Angry, emaciated. Splotchy hair dirty brown and gray, most of it burned off by chemo. Withered, wrinkled skin, voice a raspy whisper. Querulous, confused, *where are my meds?*

"I put my arm around her. She turned, started to snap, then recognized me. 'Oh, Robert', she said, buried what was left of her into my arms, and wept.

"Maybe that was too much for her. I've fought with myself about it for two years. Later that night she was unresponsive. I called the paramedics, who took her to the ICU. She never recovered. After slipping into a coma, Lilian died two days later.

"We were married for 30 years. Now I'm 52, ready to re-join life."

Afterward, in the gravel parking lot, I caught up with Robert. Said *nice night*, which it was. *This time of year is just lovely near the Conemaugh River.*

He asked if I was flirting with him.

"Flirting?" I laughed. "It's the Irish in me. The Wobbly. The Union Maid. Maybe it's just a long line of washerwomen and fish mongers who had to be tough to survive. I never was the English country gentlewoman. I was never good at meek, passive, submissive, wait-for-a-man-to-tell-you-it's-all-right. I was always an equal partner. If I wanted to call someone, I called, regardless of gender. I never expected to be wined and dined. Dutch was too clumsy – all that nickel-and-dime check-splitting – but I paid my fair share. I never held by pay-for-play, either, which is what a lot of what dating is."

Robert nodded.

"Flirting? I'm passing a few pleasantries and offering a caffeine boost."

It was an old-style diner, the kind they don't build anymore, red leather booths, green linoleum-topped tables. Ceramic cups and saucers from the Year One; waitress pre-dating that by a decade. She offered pie; we both thought ptomaine and passed.

"If you weren't going to speak, why did you come?" I prodded.

"I didn't know I wasn't going to speak," he said. "Didn't plan that. I was fascinated listening to other people. Just being there helped me. Enormously."

I nodded.

"Where do you come from?" he asked. "Twenty-five words or more."

"I'm Irish," I smiled.

"Right," he said. "You've said that."

"Starts with sand hogs and shanties. Staten Island, when it was a

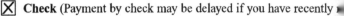

I ELECT TO RECEIVE MY PAYMENT BY:

 Check (Payment by check may be delayed if you have recently ▮

☐ **Electronic Funds Transfer (Please complete the section bel▮ an address change.)**

(This section MUST be completed if you have elected a taxable dis▮
See "PAYMENT ELECTION" in the attached instructio▮
this section is not completed and/or a▮

Depository (Bank or Credit Union) Information: (Deposits can▮

BANK OR CREDIT UNION NAME	
BANK ROUTING NUMBER (9 DIGIT)	ACCOUNT NUMBER

Account Type *(check one)*:

☐ Checking [You must attach a voided, original preprinted check▮ account holder(s).]*

☐ Savings [You must attach an account statement or deposit slip▮ of account holder(s) preprinted on the slip.]**

*If you do not have preprinted checks with your account, you ▮ bank document that contains the names of the account holders, bank, ABA routing number and your account number. Starter c▮ slips, direct deposit set-up forms and photocopies of a check w▮

**If you do not have your bank statement or preprinted deposi▮ provide a bank document that contains the names of the accou▮ name of the bank, ABA routing number and your account numb▮

pasture. My family dug the Battery Tunnel. Holland Tunnel. Queens Midtown Tunnel. Tough work."

Robert nodded.

"My father, Walter Mayo, wanted a shortcut. So he became a gangster."

Robert laughed.

"Rackets. Hustles. Things that fell off trucks. Bootlegging. A bit of boxing when he was younger. Well, what Irishman doesn't like to mix it up? Called himself Fatty Mayo, 158 pounds, a lot of potatoes for a little guy. That helped the family in the Depression. Then it didn't. When he wasn't in the rackets, he was a longshoreman, very big for the New York Irish. Things were fine for us in Staten Island.

"Then they weren't. Although no one will talk about it, we skipped just before some indictments were handed down – for him, or people close to him. Could've skated on them. Could've done time. Could've wound up in the marshes. That's how we got here, in Johnstown. Bethlehem Steel was a good place to hide."

"So I've heard," Robert said.

"As for me," I said, "back in the day there were very few jobs open to women. Teachers. Nurses. Secretaries. Shop girls. I didn't feature working the perfume counter or waiting tables or packing a lunch bucket, cooking and cleaning and living the life of laundry. I took the logical step up – social work. Went to college – first in my family, also first to get a professional job, one that required a degree. Two, in fact. Caseworker for Cambria County. I get a lot from my Uncle Jim, the activist, tempered by my Irish mother's desire to care for her family. I care for abandoned children, welfare moms, battered wives. Smoothing the square pegs of people to fit the round holes of regs. Housing. Medicaid and Medicare. Senior services. Child services."

"I get a lot from my father," Robert said. "We all have one formative influence, one real rite of passage that transforms us from child to adult. For my dad, it was the Air Force. Not an officer. Not a pilot. Just a T-5 who worked the repair shops. He took to the discipline, the regularity, the *rules*. There was a right way to do something, and he followed that. That's how he did everything. There's a lot of that in me.

"I can hear him to this day: *straight down the line.* I thought about putting it on his headstone. I didn't. Too many people would have thought it was a joke. It wasn't."

A week later we had a second date, a garish cheesecake place across town, near the flood museum and Point Stadium. This time, we had dessert, splitting two kinds of chocolate, white and bittersweet. The environs were plastic, the eatin' was great.

"I come from a hard-scrapple potato farm gone bust," Robert began. "My family was tough-minded. Hold on to the land. We could have been Oakies and penniless. But we were on the southeastern tip of Long Island. A million miles away from New York City. Until the socialites discovered the Hamptons. That little farm made us."

"We never had that luck," I smiled. "Or that luxury."

"We went to the ends of the earth. All the way to Philadelphia, where, luck not being the residue of design, my father took his grubstake and started buying properties in the shabby end of town. Which happened to abut the Liberty Bell. Suddenly the neighborhood was significant, and we made a fortune."

"I've never met a card-carrying capitalist before," I said.

"Slumming?"

"Penance."

"You Irish girls are all alike."

I pointed to his head. "Tough guy?"

"Right. Part of my left eyebrow is missing. I'm sure you think it was a polo mallet. Far more prosaic. Site inspection. Wasn't looking. Walked into a metal scaffolding. Taught me to wear a hard hat. Lucky it didn't take my eye out."

It was only a matter of time.

And intimacy.

We went out to dinner, riverside tavern, incline peeking around the bend, lights on the water, very romantic. Oysters, steak, all of it.

A wonderful chardonnay to start, then a cabernet that cost more than a Cadillac.

"Grace?" he asked. "Grace! Grace Kelly. Grace Jones. Grace Slick. Will and Grace. *Coup de Grace.* Graceland. Amazing Grace. *Say goodnight to the people, Gracie.* Too confusing. Too much Grace. Instead, I dub thee Irish. Arise, madam, and henceforth be known by that Gaelic honorific."

Robert was pretty looped that night. Charming. Alive. And pretty damn looped.

Did it give me pause? No. I saw it as necessary. Something he needed to jump-start his soul. I thought of this as one-time shock therapy. I was right.

We discussed how we should manage our relationship. How open, how distant? Joining for a few days or a week when the mutual need arose? Two domiciles – with a lifeline to each other? One old one? One entirely new, neutral ground, establish a space and m.o. together? Separate rooms? Nuptial vows? Merger not an acquisition?

"Well, Irish, what now?" Robert asked. "Make it one Irish stew? Or keep it separate, discrete? Separate check books? Separate families? Separate quarters?"

We decided. One house, his, which he signed over to me in his will. Some cousins, also in the family business, albeit on the East Coast, would inherit everything else. No clergy, no justice of the peace. No need for legalities. POSSLQs. All the banks and investments separate. Obviously, he had more to bring than I did, but I was still working, and our needs and tastes were simple, so it was fine.

Huddled in heavy sweaters and parkas, walking in the snow in a stand of ice-crusted pines, we made lists and compared them. Things We Can't Live Without. Books – With or Without Words. Chai Tea – Plenty of Cardamom. Wine – Early and Often. Meet in the middle as opposed to co-mingle souls, our souls being sort of set. Calcified.

"Sharing," Robert said, dodging a branch, "rather than swooning."

"With the time we have," I agreed, "let's have a good time."

Naked and coltish and giggling. Reminiscent of prom night, but with varicose veins, peripheral neuropathy, and rheumatoid arthritis.

"Yeah?" he asked.

"Yeah," I smiled.

"It's the – " he began, but I put my finger on his lips.

"It's the new normal. And it's just fine."

"Yeah?"

"Yeah."

I remember the first night he explored my body.

"What are you doing?" I asked.

"Running my fingers along your stretch marks," he said innocently.

"What should I do?" I asked, mildly offended. "Photoshop myself?"

"No," he protested. "You're perfect. You're exactly what you are. No artifice."

Then he kissed me.

"We have so much to know about each other," I said one morning, both of us in terrycloth bathrobes, steaming mugs of chai tea, sitting on the back deck facing the hills.

"Right," he agreed. "You first, Irish. What's the dumbest thing you ever did?"

"So many things," I sighed, "so little time. Skinny dipping in the Conemaugh?"

"That hardly counts."

"You're making this hard. OK. The summer I ate about 40,000 bugs."

"Sounds perfectly dreadful."

"It was, believe me."

"What made you do it?"

"Insanity pact. Mary Margaret Flaherty. Eileen O'Hara. Teens. Stupid. You?"

Robert smiled. "So dared, so challenged, I jumped off a bridge into the Schuylkill River. Broke more than a few bones. Wound up in a body cast."

"That was pretty damn dumb."

"No argument, Irish, no argument."

He liked my Wobbly tattoo, red ink on my shoulder blade. Then he noticed the glitch.

"I should have known better," I laughed. "Came into this whacko place. Tattoo artist wore a Clarabelle mask. Should've run then. Especially when I saw the lattice work in his eyeballs. *Stoned to the gills*, I said. *Get out!* Should have, but didn't want to make a fuss. Appear chicken. Of course he messed up – see it? The blotch where the globe's right line should be. Of course he took no responsibility, said that I sneezed, which was a lie. I was mad for a minute. Then I thought, no, this was fate taking a hand. Karma. The Wobblies, sure, but my Uncle Jim's part? Maybe. The story has so many layers of legend that it's twisted. So's the tattoo. Makes perfect sense."

Robert smiled.

"Lilian?" I asked. "Did she have a tattoo?"

"No. Lilian would never have gotten a tattoo. Considered her body holy, sacred. Would never have defiled it. Ironic, really. The cancer just ruined her. Made a mess."

"Not even on a riff?"

"OK, sure," he laughed. "She loved Southern culture. Had she gotten a tattoo, it would have been something Southern, the Old Rugged Cross, toes-in-the-dirt Dixie. Nothing to do with religion – wasn't religious in the slightest. But she loved that culture."

"You?"

"I never felt the need," he shrugged, "to avow or embrace anything in my flesh."

He did like his Scotch.

Sitting out back, looking out into trees, we savored the woods' earthy aroma.

Robert hoisted his glass in my direction.

"To you, Irish," he smiled.

Then I got a whiff of it.

"What is *that*?" I demanded.

"Laphroaig. Barley dried over peat fires. Sorry if it smells like Sterno."

"Sterno? *Sterno*? It's got a long way to go to smell as good as Sterno."

"I love you, too, Irish," Robert said. "Next week I'll find something suitably Irish – Bushmills or Jameson or some second-shelf swill. Now it's Scotland the Brave."

Things were fine. And then they weren't.

One beautiful spring day, Robert looked bad, said he felt worse. "Something I ate?" he wondered, then went on a super-bland diet for three days. It didn't help.

Robert went to see his doc, who took one look at him and sent him to a specialist at Conemaugh General, an internist named Ngwogu – a Nigerian with a soothing voice.

After a few tests, Dr. Ngwogu spoke with both of us. "I beamed the test results to the Mother Ship for review," he smiled. "They confirmed my diagnosis – unmistakable. I'm sorry to tell you that have pancreatic cancer. Before you request a second opinion," he added, "I already got you one. Dr. Stedman, at Hopkins. *The* world expert."

"Should I go see him?" Robert asked.

"You already have," Dr. Ngwogu said. "Teleconference. With your permission."

Robert nodded then turned to Dr. Ngwogu's computer.

"Data's right here," a big man pointed to an adjacent screen. "Numbers never lie. I looked at Dr. Ngwogu's results. Impeccable. I ought to know. Trained him myself. Most gifted resident I ever had. Helped design the protocols. Should've got the Nobel.

"In any event, Mr. –"

"Robert."

"Mr. Robert. In any event, Mr. Robert, I'm sorry to confirm my former student and current colleague's diagnosis. It doesn't have a happy ending. Bottom line is that this cancer in inoperable. Untreated, you have about three good months, six at the outside. Then not so good. Then very not good. Treated," he shrugged. "A bit more. Chemo will delay the inevitable, but not by much. And the chemo is magnificently unpleasant."

"Untreated?" Robert asked.

"Go home. Have a few parties. See a few sights. Later, hospice, with or without a morphine drip – but I recommend it. Pass peacefully."

"What do you think, Irish?" Robert asked.

"I think we need to think about it, Robert."

"Right," he said, rising. "Let's go home and think. Thank you, Dr. Stedman, Dr. Ngwogu. You've been very helpful and given us a lot to consider."

"I can't go through this again," I said in the car.

"No," he said, "*I* can't go through this again."

We were on the back deck, settling in to the setting sun. A merlot warmed us.

"It's my life," Robert was saying. "Or death, as it were. I don't want endless rounds of chemo-induced vomiting that will net me an extra six miserable months. I'd rather party a bit, travel, then just fade out. A little home hospice in a friendly place."

"To be continued," I drained my glass and marched off to bed.

It took a couple of nights, and more than a couple of bottles of good red wine, but we decided. No chemo. A vacation here in the states. Then off.

The three good months? Let me flip the postcards quickly. It was all art, or so Robert said. Our vacation began in New York City, the Manhattan high life. We went to small French restaurants and smaller theaters, the musty aromas of old wool and worn carpet – our Al Hirschfield days. We went sailing on Long Island Sound, two of us and a two-person crew, the aromas of salt air and steamers and lobster with drawn butter – our Winslow Homer days. Finally, we rented a cottage in the Berkshires, nestled in the black shadows of old-growth pines and mountain streams, imbibed the aromas of decaying leaves and distant skunks and fertilized farms – our Edward Hopper days.

Then it was back to black-and-white Johnstown – our Luke Swank days.

It was one of those solid gray Western Pennsylvania days, hardly any light, sky the color of gravel. Before long, rain began descending in sheets. "If you don't have seasonal affective disorder today," I said, warming the chai, "you'll never have it."

"It's time to go," Robert said. "I've grown to love these woods, these valleys --"

"This sorry, sodden landscape," I interjected.

"Dylan Thomas?" he cocked his head, as if hearing it. "Wilfrid Owen?"

"No, me."

"Not bad, Irish. We'll make a poet of you yet."

"I'm Irish, remember? It's in the blood."

"Right. Anyway, I want to go in light."

"Hm?"

"Mykonos. Sunlit. Hot. Roast my outsides – as my insides turn to toast."

"Robert," I protested.

"Would you come with me, Irish? I'd love it." He paused. "It won't take long."

"Robert."

"It's such a beautiful place."

"I'm sure it is." I paused. "Mykonos."

"Island in the Aegean. Parties. Tourists. Nude beaches. Ridiculously overpriced. Great place to die. Burning sun. Hospice."

"Speaking of which, Robert, who's going to care for you?" I paused. "Not to be clinical, but I had this with Jeffrey. I can't do it again."

"Way ahead of you. I'm in the process of hiring someone."

"Hm?"

"Registered. Professional. S/he will accompany us. And take care of me."

"Sold," I said, took his hand, and smiled.

Asked, advertised, acquired, 40-year-old male nurse, Morse (last name only, please), lanky, laconic, close-cropped reddish-brown hair and beard. Duly licensed, trained at Sloan-Kettering. Helpful, respectful, largely invisible – the perfect English butler.

It meant taking a villa with three bedrooms, three baths – Robert and I would stay together until he had to be alone. As always, he made all the arrangements – including a suitcase full of meds. Touch and go, Robert calling some Washington friends to make it happen. In the end, he had to sign more liability waivers than an NFL franchise.

A lovely place, in Chora, perched above the marketplace. I would have preferred something in the hills, above the fray, but Robert wanted the street – the sound and sweat and smell of it. White stucco walls. Inset wood. Blue accent tiles – someone loved this place. Back veranda facing gardens, plants, trees, and the odd grape vine. A lemon tree shaded us; the wicker chairs and hand-painted pots were warm and welcoming. It was heaven, even with the tourists, the bistros, and the bad, bad singing.

Robert even loved the *sturm* of fish and garbage. The *drang* of drunks and shoppers. He deliberately left the windows open; the noise, he said, was good for him.

"This is the real Greece," he said, "or at least it was. Back in the day, people came to get away from *everything*. To disappear. To stand in the sun and sweat. Then travel became easy and Mykonos became famous. Then everyone came here. Then the stores came, too – Versace and Louis Vuitton, boutiques and geegaws."

Of course, I was uncomfortable. I'm Irish, aren't I? We don't know how to approach life without Brits or bosses to fight, without cold-water flats or frigid farms, heavy boots and outsized sweaters. Robert relished it. "Makes me feel alive," he said.

He loved physicality – my flaccid skin, my fetid smells. "You're *real*," he said, "not prettified or perfumed. You're wet and wonderful. You've got nothing to prove.

"You've won."

"*We've* won," I corrected, then kissed him.

"Let's do Thomas Mann," Robert said, ouzo on the beach. "Let's pick up a boy."

"One of the real pretty ones," I agreed. "And both seduce him. Christopher Isherwood would approve. How wonderful."

No, we didn't. Not that we would have 20 years ago, but certainly not now.

Eschewing the Mykonos windmills, we drove to the Panagia Tourliani monastery, burning white in the afternoon sun, cool and dark inside. "All those men with their lust for spirituality," Robert said. "All I think about is you in that diaphanous night gown."

"With my sags and wrinkles," I laughed. "I've got more cracks and crevices than a Tennessee Valley reclamation project."

"Earthy," he said. "Tasty."

I laughed and loved him all the more.

Robert loved real life, real stories that had real endings. So he loved hearing about my Uncle Jim Cavanaugh, the rambler, roustabout, and rebel. The Wobbly.

When he was too tired to read, and too restive for TV, Robert asked me to tell him about Uncle Jim and his time with the Wobblies. "I'm going to be a piece of the past soon enough," he'd smile. "Might as well hear about one of my travellin' buddies."

I was happy to oblige. Often, sitting out on the back veranda, Robert fell asleep before I finished, but I kept on talking, more for me than for him.

Uncle Jim Cavanaugh, the Wobbly tough guy. No doubt family legend has more than burnished it over the years, but there's no one left to set it right.

He was actually my mother's uncle. Big Irish family, my mother was the oldest daughter of the oldest daughter, Uncle Jim the youngest son of the youngest son. He was my mother's age, give or take. Never married. Or maybe married. Or maybe married more than once. Or maybe married more than once simultaneously. No one knew. I get the feeling that he left a lot of his DNA out there.

Now the real Cavanaughs are Irish gentry, nobility, with a family crest. My mother's family was hardly that. They'd have to have taken a giant step up to get up to shanty. Related? I don't know. Bastards? Maybe. Plenty of those on the Auld Sod. Profligate son, exiled, fell into poverty and pig shit? I have no idea. Could have simply adopted the name – plenty of people did that. Or acquired it at Ellis Island from the next guy in the line. Or from an immigration clerk with a sense of humor. Or no sense of humor. In any event, these Cavanaughs were not wealthy.

Robert loved this little bistro by the water, indifferent house wine, fresh bread, olive oil, green salad, feta cheese – real Mediterranean diet. Tiny place. Never tired of it.

"I don' know how you can eat that," I waved at the feta. "Farmer cheese soaked in urine. More sodium than salt cod, which'll kill you."

"That's the trouble with you, Irish," Robert laughed. "You don't know good food when you taste it. Forty generations of boiled potatoes will do that for you."

"If Uncle Jim could see me now. Greek Islands. Amusing how the world turns."

"Look at how far we've come," Robert smiled.

"Or how deep our betrayal."

"C'mon, Irish. There are immense wrongs out there," he took my hand. "I know that. But the ills of the world are not our fault. I would change them, all of them, if I could. But I can't. I also know that we have done no harm, you and I. We have worked to make people's lives better, one way or another. Yes, we have reaped our just rewards, but the worker is worthy of his hire. Yes, others suffer while we live in plenty. And so, frankly, shall it always be. There are disparities in this world, Irish. Short of living good, decent lives, there's not a whole lot we can do about them." Robert paused. "Except enjoy a bottle of this truly mediocre local product."

Robert was woozy, distracted. "Hey, Irish," he said, "I can take a bit more of Uncle Jim."

"Sure," I answered, adjusting the pillows under his head.

He'd blow through Staten Island, short, smart, and sassy. Never afraid. First to hit the picket lines. First to hit back when union-busters came with baseball bats.

Uncle Jim was no Big Bill Haywood, no ideologue. He just thought working folk were getting a bad deal. Centuries of inbred resentment against English rule. Uncle Jim was no John Reed, no died-in-the-wool pamphleteer. Sure, he wanted to change the world. All the labor unionists did. It had replaced church. They all said the labor catechism. Preached the labor gospel — an injury anywhere is an injury everywhere.

I began to say more, but Robert was already asleep, the heat overcoming him.

Through it all, Morse was a ghostly presence. Despite invitations, took his meals alone. Companions? No idea where or with whom he dined. What gender he preferred.

He often sat in his room and read – St. Augustine? Stephen Hawking? Something esoteric about time or spirituality or both. And he wrote – notes? His own counter-theories? I don't know. A Rapidograph pen, a Moleskine notebook, a hand so precise it could have been typeset. No, I never read it, just happened to glance at it once – writing accompanied by graphs and charts. All freehand.

He was very attentive to Robert, as if keeping him clean and comfortable was worth the world entire. Often, when Morse adjusted the various medical drips, I'd go out for a walk – a glass of wine and a dash of nicotine.

"Uncle Jim," Robert waved his empty wine glass. "More Uncle Jim."

Anarchy. Action. Strikes. Seizing industries. Seizing states. Mother Jones, Joe Hill – these were the stations of the cross and the saints when I was growing up.

"Nice playmates," Robert muttered.

"Don't believe what you read," I said, watching Robert's eyes open and close.

According to family legend Uncle Jim's weapon of choice was a sawed-off pool cue. Quick, light-weight, effective. Easy to handle, easy to hide.

"Not a gat?" Robert snickered.

Uncle Jim avoided them. Guns went off. Guns got everybody's blood boiling. Guns got out of hand. Uncle Jim favored ducking. Dodging. Dishing out the pool cue.

"Black sheep?" Robert mumbled on the edge of sleep.

No. Wasn't even Black Irish. As my mother used to say, Uncle Jim was just Irish. Nobody knew how he got involved with the Wobblies – the hated International Workers of the World. How much after their 1905 creation? Hard to say, but everyone agreed he was at the McKees Rocks Pressed Car strike the following year.

If the state and local police were bad, the iron-and-coal police were worse. Wobblies came to the strikers' aid. The result: multiple shootings, a dozen confirmed dead, maybe 26, probably many more. Hard to tell. Lot of Ohio River available for dumping bodies. Funerals were held in 15 languages.

Robert was asleep, but I had to finish the story.

Uncle Jim threw a rock that killed a trooper. He didn't throw a rock that killed a trooper. You know how family legends go.

Dinner party overlooking the Aegean. Robert and I went in matching unisex outfits – muslin shirts (largely unbuttoned), tan cargo shorts (slung low), sandals (no socks; *never* socks.) The hilltop villa – belonged to Robert's friend – was awash in ex-pats.

There was the usual chatter – how *boring* America had become. How unnerved they were by the violence and racial tension; the crime, poverty, the banality. *It feels* so *Third World*, one bejeweled diva whined, accepting her fourth – fifth? – chardonnay.

It's all that man in the White House, a dyed redhead began.

No, a third objected loudly, *it's not that man in the White House. It's* never *that man in the White House. Presidents come and Presidents go. He'll be gone soon.*

The speaker, wearing a diaphanous, sleeveless top that revealed enormous swaying things, added, *I'm no apologist for him, but it's hardly his fault.*

"Apparently," Robert turned to me *sotto voce*, "she favors free-range bosoms."

"Too much of a good thing."

"She should put those things away before she hurts somebody."

"Amen to that, brother."

My money's there, a youngish man said, au courant in chartreuse Under Armor. *But I'm happy here. It's quiet.*

An out-of-focus short, dark woman took his arm. *As long as we stay away from the tourists. I didn't know there were that many Asians and Italians in the whole world.*

The first woman weighed in again, her bracelets shaking as she pointed a finger. *America is messy. Crowded. Noisy. Out of control. I have everything I want* here. *I* like *having servants. Why not? I earned them.*

Hear hear! Hear hear! glasses raised.

We've had first-world cultures since time began, a fifth woman, austere, with a mid-European accent, said. *What would you have us Social Darwinists do about it?*

A very young, very slender, very blond man added, *nobody's hands are clean.*

A broad-backed woman who had clearly had one too many was openly weeping. *Back in Ohio, on the farm, my family owned slaves. I don't know what to do about that.*

"America and her discontents," I said to Robert. "Time to let it go."

"I know her, Irish," he said. "She has a nice little time-share in Basel. Time for her to go there. With the surgeons, stockbrokers, and start-up owners."

"Maybe on the way she'll give her money to the Little Sisters of the Poor," I said.

It was a bad night. Robert needed to be cleaned, then given some sedatives. As he shifted in his hospital bed, he asked me to fill in more of the story.

The Wobblies changed over time and place, more Marxist, less Marxist, more anarchist, less anarchist, east more socialistic, west more anarchistic. But the central idea was always the same, one umbrella union for unskilled, non-guild wage earners.

Uncle Jim liked that. He was proud of his red Wobbly card, carried it with him everywhere. I'd love to have it, but its lost or buried with him. At least I have the tattoo.

When I realized how exhausted Robert was, I went back to our room and slept.

Morse helped, and so did the morning. By evening, Robert was able to walk to the car, and we drove to a cafe cut into a hillside. We ate grape leaves, drank wine. Got pleasantly sloshed. Watched the sun set beyond the trees. Felt the slight dip in temperature, the night winds nipping at our bare legs.

The best part was that we understood everything and didn't have to say a word.

The evening didn't last – they never do – and neither did Robert's health.

That night, Robert refused the morphine drip.

Morse objected, but Robert waved him off. "I want a clear head," he smiled at me. "I want to be able to see you. Not dream you. Tell me more."

He went where they sent him, walking – many of them did, hundreds of miles – sleeping in the open, foraging for food. Riding wagons. Hopping freight trains, hiding in box cars. Dirty, disheveled. I don't think Uncle Jim knew how many times he was arrested. Or how many beatings he had to take – or handed out.

Jail – without charge, without trials. Shootings. Lynchings. City, county, state police. Vigilantes. Militias. Pinkertons. Rigged judges, bought juries. Even if Uncle Jim faced half of what he said he did, it's a miracle he survived.

The labor wars were real wars. Especially out west. Joe Hill was executed by Utah firing squad. Thirty thousand came to his Chicago funeral. Uncle Jim was there. Or said he was. Frank Little and Wesley Everest were lynched – the latter castrated, hung, then riddled with bullets.

It was Robert's last day.

"Stay strong," he rasped, stark, slack, sweating. "Stay strong."

Taking me aside, Morse said I should leave. "He won't go if you're here."

I began to argue, then realized he was right. Taking Robert's hand, I said, "I'm going to go."

"I've had," he began, but couldn't finish it.

"Yes, you have," I smiled.

"Yeah?"

"Yeah," I squeezed his hand. "Yeah."

As Robert stirred painfully, Morse attached the morphine drip again. I went out back, traced the sun's path across the sky, and finished the story for myself.

Fought at every turn, torn by anarchism and internal strife, the Wobblies finally fell apart in 1924. But World War I, and the anti-Red prosecutions, had really killed it five years earlier. The Wobblies' 20-year run ended in indirection and exhaustion.

No longer young, too many broken bones, too many shifts in Wobbly policy, Uncle Jim left the movement. After that? My mother's surmise – a postcard, maybe – is that he ended up how he began, a longshoreman, but out on Puget Sound. The Irish, the sea-scent in him. Maybe not. My mother always believed that he made it into the '50s, the age of Ike and IBM and TV. And that he hated them all.

When Morse came out and shook his head, I broke down and cried.

I packed up. Wasn't much left and it didn't take long.

Morse took his leave. Morse went – wherever Morse went.

Robert, who had taken care of the details beforehand, had his remains returned. Two cousins arranged Robert's funeral, a non-sectarian affair in a Philadelphia suburb. They barely spoke to me, the late-life shadow-woman. Besides, they all had Robert stories from long ago. Johnstown and Mykonos didn't matter.

Afterward, I didn't come directly home. I needed to go somewhere else. Not New York, not Staten Island. That was another person who lived there all those years ago. Instead, I headed up to Canada, Quebec City, someplace foreign. Full of tourists, like Mykonos, but enough French food and red wine and a long-haired street busker to help me settle down a bit before coming back here. See what I wanted to do with my life. My house. Our house. The pretty, peaceful place that Robert loved so much.

I thought about going back to Gandalf's, but I wasn't ready. I couldn't listen. I couldn't speak. Time to be alone with my house, my work. The Wobblies.

One morning I took a cup of cardamom tea to the little deck facing the hills and allowed myself to think about Robert. About his life and about his death.

Robert had achieved something very rare. A great peace. He maintained his dignity, his sense of humor, his sense of self-worth. He did not let disease or circumstance define him. At the end, he had clarity. Surcease.

I had him for a short time. We had each other. I'm very grateful for that.

The Wobblies? I don't know. You have to believe in something. *Believe* believe. Even if you no longer believe. Even if you never believed. Even if none of it existed.

You have to believe in *something*.

SUICIDE WATCH

▼

SAN FRANCISCO, CALIFORNIA

He's done his homework. He knows that 245 feet above the water it's America's favorite suicide spot. From the time he steps off, accelerating to a top speed of 75 mph, it will take him just four seconds, and the impact will be like hitting concrete. His legs will shatter and his rib cage will splinter up through his lungs and heart, slicing his innards like razors. It will be akin to being blown apart by a hand grenade.

He also knows he has a 95 percent chance of perishing instantly. Should he happen to live past impact, he knows it's a virtual certainly that the freezing waters will induce hypothermia and kill him within seconds. Should that not occur, the murderous Golden Gate current will either drown him or hurl him out to sea.

All in all, there will be no surprises, no escape.

There have been some 1,500 people who have taken this journey before him. Fifteen hundred that we know about.

"Bobbi," David snaps his fingers like a band leader setting the beat, "Word of the Day."

"Misery!" she beams.

"Awright!" Jackson D applauds, then breaks into tobacco-induced coughing.

Howard, his face creased into permanent annoyance, shakes his head, more about him than her, but, truth be told, he can't stand her, either. For that matter, Howard can't stand Group, but he has to go. Part of his parole.

"As in what?" David demands. "Use it in a sentence."

"As in, 'you're a misery,'" she smiles sweetly, "often simply abbreviated into 'you misery.'"

"How charming," Leonid snorts.

"Aren't they all?" she asks innocently.

When the late-afternoon shadows cut across the lawns and trees, everyone sees the bright spots, the startling highlights in yellow and green. Hopper saw the dark. Black came first; darkness then light. David considers. Everyone wants to be Peter Pan. Nureyev. Everyone wants flight. Hopper wanted gravity. The downward pull, the darkness, the entropy.

Danny knew that.

Two years after I killed myself, Danny thinks, David followed my trail to San Francisco, trying to discover my life's narrative. At first, I proved impenetrable; David could see neither sense nor soul. He found the pain, all right; that was easy enough. He could parse that. But suicide?

This is San Francisco, and David wants to live where he can see the ocean. He can afford it, too, and daydreams about it, sitting at home, feet up, cabernet in hand, staring out at the sea. But he feels that such digs would be too self-indulgent. Would send the wrong message. But to whom is not clear.

Ditto a million-dollar fixer-upper in Mill Valley.

Tritto an ante-bellum manse in the deep East Bay.

He settles instead for something far more pedestrian, literally. A one floor walk-up in Oakland, faded Bob Marley posters on the wall, furnace perpetually on the fritz, plenty of hair shirts to assuage his guilt.

I would tell him that his furniture is so decrepit that no self-respecting Thrift Shop would take it, but he's not listening.

He's walked the bridge many times, the City to Sausalito and back again. Each time the wind tugged at him like an angry memory, a reminder of the sea near Norfolk. Eschewing the City view, he looked out to sea. This place felt seemed so right, so real. Hyper-real, like an acrylic painting.

Civilians wouldn't understand, he thought. Couldn't. He'd been through the valley of the shadow and had passed unscathed to the other side. It was time.

"I been gettin' loaded since I was eight," Andrea says, scraping a toe along the lines in the linoleum floor. "I was in third grade. One day I mistook my father's sacramental wine for grape juice. I had a couple of swigs before school." She shrugs. "'Hey,' I said, 'I feel a lot better than I usually do.'" Andrea lifts her head up and looks around. "It was all downhill from there."

David hears the murmurs, sees the nods, sees Arthur slump in his chair.

They come from Norfolk, a navy town, a town with rules about everything.

David could always live with rules, and the irony of people who broke them.

Danny couldn't.

As children, they were dressed as twins, coddled, chubby, charming.

Then there was Aunt Marion.

Part of his mosaic, David never flashes on it, as we do with memories. He doesn't conjure it up. Certain things don't trigger it. But that image is always there. Part of the wallpaper. Neither pleasant nor painful, simply there.

How cheerful, loving Aunt Marion locked herself in the garage one night, turned on the car, and asphyxiated herself.

David knows he carries her DNA in himself. An imperfection, like a predilection for arthritis or kidney stones.

He can fight it. Danny couldn't it.

In a classic case of transference, David hurls himself into often-quixotic efforts to save quintessential losers. People anyone would reasonably write off as wastes of time and resources. No-wins in spades.

David sees a 16-year-old girl in therapy. "We've known each other over a year now," he writes in the journal he keeps every day, "and her world is strange and blooming and awful. This weekend her best friend killed himself. Seventeen-year-old kid. They spent every week dancing together since they were six years old. He got into his top-choice college, and they made brownies together, and two hours later he went home and hung himself. She texted him in the morning to ask if everything was OK, because they always texted each other good night, and he didn't text her goodnight, and he didn't respond to her message in the morning either, because he was dead. It's such a profound waste. I almost can't bear it. It's Danny all over again. It's one Danny after another. Yet here I am, the person other people pay to bear such things. How can anyone bear such a thing?"

I often think of my brother David as having X-ray eyes, seeing through symptoms and syndromes to a person's essential goodness. Instead of losing ground in the negative, David immediately identifies the positive and begins to work on it. Of course, sometimes the scars run too keep – Tere Mercer was a notable failure, and the jury's still out on Peter – but by and large he's successful.

Those eyes, and David's clear and logical understanding of human behavior – a kind of genius of the simple – make him extraordinarily effective.

It seems higher, now that he's standing on the precipice. Higher, with that incessant wind pulling at his trousers, buffeting him about. More than once he has to reach behind to grasp the rail, to steady himself.

The water below is far away, slate blue. Behind him the morning traffic thumps over the expansion dams. Hidden, unable to be spotted by anyone, he has not drawn a crowd. Good. This is to be an intimate act. Small stage, empty theater. A sonata, not a symphony. He doesn't need anyone else.

"No," Arthur says, evasively, as if he's afraid of being overhead, "I didn't hate my parents. I still don't. They're wonderful people. Wonderful. We're best friends. Really. Still are. But I was nine when I felt the world wasn't right. And *I* wasn't right. That was very painful for me. I needed to stop that pain. I still do." He looks around furtively. "Three rehabs later, here I am."

There was no big split with the family, no dust-up. One day, quietly,

Danny moved to New York. Gravitating toward other visual artists, he wound up in The Factory. Where he discovered that, yes, Drella was a wretched human being, a real vampire.

Danny called New York the Burnt House, and for good reason. New York in the '80s was the world's most self-absorbed, most narcissistic city. Clamoring for fame, for self – for self-definition – everyone created characters, *personae*, to become famous. Outed, outré, outrageous – the more the better, the better to penetrate the permafrost, to banish the omnipresent ennui.

It was all worthless, superficial to the nth degree, but that was the point. That's what Drella taught. Everything was ultimately disposable – BIC lighters to human lives.

Danny got caught up in this rip tide.

Eventually, it cost him his life.

"The talk-show crowd and the rabble rousers miss the point," David writes in his journal, "perhaps deliberately. Substances are the by-product, the means, not the cause. They are the symptom. People are the heart of the matter. People with scars too rough to heal. Treat the psychology, not the addiction. Treat the hurts not the needle.

"Treat the despair not the drug."

He closes his eyes and breathes deeply. The blackness is good. There's nothing there, nothing outside, nothing inside. Surcease. No past, no future. It will be like going to sleep, but without the disquieting dreams.

The world is in pieces. There are no connections. I need it to end.

I can't be perfect. I'm too damaged.

Although David could have set up Group anywhere, he deliberately went downbeat, choosing a community center in what he calls the butt end of Berkeley, the heart of afflictions and affectations, the corner of macrobiotic and macramé. Windows, he knew, were distracting, so he deployed in an interior room, concrete block coated with thick yellow paint, beige plastic chairs with writing arms.

His training was short and sobering. Attending a mandatory seminar on the Berkeley campus, David listened assiduously, but after the speaker – a short, earnest man with long hair, cardigan sweater, and knit tie – said that just five percent of substance abusers who detox will be sober after five years, David lost the rest of the class, thinking of the destroyed lives, the lost children. Danny.

Looking back, page 41 in his dirty, dog-eared tan notebook, he found that was all he wrote from the entire three-hour session. Five percent.

Like the five percent who survive the Bridge, he thinks.

You could dismiss Danny as part of a cultural trend, poster boy for the '80s, but David doesn't think so. David thinks Danny was his own person, his own trend – although the primacy of the individual as opposed to the group is a fundament of David's mindset.

So, sure, although Danny took his own life in the '80s, and after that, when everything seemed to be falling apart and so many people died – Drella, '87; Basquiat, '88; Haring, '90; Wojnarowicz, '92 – David doesn't think that has anything to do with Danny. Sure, everything was breaking in pieces. Sure, limits were reached, and bypassed, and prices were paid. Hopper understood that – painting blackness, not shadow. Sartre spun nothingness. Milton described darkness visible.

But Danny, David thinks, was different.

Because the complete abandon of the '80s was The Masque of the Red Death. The Dance of Death. The true *tarantella* – the bite of the tarantula which brings with it madness then demise.

It was AIDS.

While that raged all around Danny, David doesn't think it affected him, held him captive. Because the signs were there beforehand. The tea leaves were in his cup.

We just couldn't read them.

Or wouldn't.

Scars may be dead tissue, but the skin around it isn't. It's very much alive, and it pulls; it moves with life. You constantly feel the tension, the tug between death and life.

The itch.

David hears that, hears despair tempered by redemption, but redemption is always thwarted. Salvation remains just beyond our reach.

Nothing can bring me back, David, I tell him, *despite your every loving, quixotic attempt to rewind life.*

Without another thought, without a wasted movement, he steps off and begins his quickening descent.

Group, a portrait in eyeliner and short skirts; cutters and coke-heads and emotional cripples. Self-haters so close to the edge they could feel the updraft.

Group is named for, well, it doesn't matter who it's named for. It's funded, and named, and nobody pays any attention to that. Never more than 10 at a time, because that's all David wants to handle. "More than that is unwieldy," David says. "More than that and people get lost – and they're lost already."

It's the Bay Area: Group is famous and furtive and has a serious waiting list.

David has considered starting a second Group, even a third, but his private practice takes up too much time. And Group takes up too much energy.

Danny threw one of his patented fits, rejected out of hand the micro-realism of Eliot Porter and f64, the timed and stroked precision of Ansel Adams, the pure portraiture of Richard Avedon. Instead, he embraced contrast, then grain, and more grain, grain for grain's sake, eclipsing such masters as Jo Brunenberg, Drew Sanborn, even Martijn van Oers' 1929 thrift-shop prints, finally Edward Steichen's 1904 Flatiron Building, which put grain on the map.

It was a big mouthful to chew, and Danny, being Danny, overdid it. Choked on it, his photos degenerating into babbles of black dots, impenetrable codes, images impossible to decipher. Hoping to pull viewers closer, to have them be the co-creators of the art, to share the secret, Danny's prints had precisely the opposite effect, pushing people away, literally and intellectually. *Love me or leave me!* he demanded.

They left.

It's depressing work, David thinks, shutting the blinds in his apartment, reaching for the cabernet. Very little fluoride for brightening. Little tunnel, less light. Trudging through the shoals of human misery.

Amusing how the numbers are the same, David considers. Standard deviation. Breakage. Bridge. Five years clean and sober. Five percent. That's all.

I feel like burning my notebook, David thinks.

"All my patients die," an oncology nurse tells him as she rotates into pediatrics. "I can't take it anymore."

It takes work to stay on that high narrow path, he thinks. Not to fall off.

It happens fast, faster than he had anticipated. He feels weightless at first. Then, as he plummets, the rush of air nearly asphyxiates him. It's not like I'm flying, exactly, he thinks. More like...

At first they call themselves the Lost Souls. One wag even wants to make up T-shirts, but Group nixes it. This is Berkeley, mind you, and even T-shirts are too formal. Too public.

Too regimented, Peter sniffs.

So it's Group, sometimes David's Group, because he started it, and they came, one after another. Somebody knowing somebody else. Misery loving company.

They came. Because they knew David was their lifeline, their last best hope. They had heard the chimes at midnight; they had peered down the gun barrel. Neither had frightened them. Group was more an intellectual exercise than mere rhetoric; they were looking for a viable argument against going gentle into that good night.

Because who says they want to be saved?

It's not like Danny hadn't tried, David thinks, making excuses. Like every artist, Danny had – perhaps I should say suffered – his phases. Soft focus, gritty realism, blanched and bleached-out vistas, tableaus like bedsheets. Drella really tagged him: he was famous for 15 minutes. Then he wasn't.

For a heartbeat the Met, MOMA, and the minimalists all liked him, *really* liked him, then they didn't. And, in the manner of wolf pack journalists, after fawning all over him, they turned on Danny for being too *him*, as they did with Basquiat.

There was everything. Then there was nothing.

"When I was young," David writes, "I didn't understand when adults called the death of my peers tragic, or wasteful. They seemed sad; of course, death is sad. But I couldn't understand then what now seems so obviously clear.

"If he had just waited, just a little while longer."

I admire David. He's trying. But he doesn't get it. David just doesn't get it.

We all need an exit strategy. We all need a time to go.

Bay Rescue finds what's left of him, and the news quickly dismisses him as another victim of Golden Gate syndrome. He came to San Francisco, found it more beautiful than he could possibly imagine. But he was still depressed, and got even more depressed asking himself how could he be depressed in such a beautiful place? Here at the end of the continent, at the end of the world?

With nothing to fill that hole, it was either the needle or the bridge. There was no middle path.

Civilians, he thinks. What could they possibly they know?

Who are they really? And why are they raining on my success?

There are two ways to rotate out of Group. Three, really. One is to move away – Montana or Manitoba or the Mid-Atlantic, anyplace where they herd turtles and nobody'll hassle them. Another is to conjure themselves cured and go to meetings instead. Or counselors. Or not. Depending.

The third is Tere Mercer's way, which is always the specter outside the door.

Despite the bad reviews, Danny did find an audience. Then he didn't. Challenged and engaged, they quickly became restive, moving away as abruptly as they had adopted him. Danny's once-packed galleries morphed into abandoned warehouses.

As Scott Fitzgerald famously said, there are no second acts in American life.

Although to give him credit, Danny moved to San Francisco and tried.

I was ambivalent – *The Simpsons* was sufficiently heavy lifting for me – but David liked dark fiction, the bleaker the better, adding "I prefer my nihilism with a side of hope."

Although it was hardly my intent – didn't even make it on the radar – I thwarted David's desire to have that hope in my life. Of course, he couldn't prevent my suicide – who could? Short of 24-hour lockdown no one can prevent anyone bent on destruction.

Nevertheless, David chose to spend the rest of his life atoning for his supposed sin. Looking to save others.

David became a lifer standing suicide watch.

David understands that behind the bravado trying to hold on to a viable persona is a daily battle royal. And like jazz, an artist never plays it the same way twice.

"Hey, Doc," Peter says, "I'm hearing footsteps. Or maybe I just think I'm hearing footsteps."

"Or you *want* to think you're hearing footsteps," David suggests. "Must make you pretty uncomfortable, doesn't it?"

Peter is noncommittal.

"That your comfort zone, Peter?" David prods. "Being uncomfortable?"

Well, David considers, Danny had to split the scene. The '80s were the last wild, cheap ride in New York City. Before gentrification came like the Black Death and ate everything. Before heroin took a bite. And AIDS gobbled the rest.

People grew up, got bored, got sick, got dead.

It was time to move on.

Two years after I walked off the Golden Gate Bridge, David moved out here to try to piece my story together. And to save others.

Picking only the hardest cases, he was perpetually setting himself up to fail. Take that young stockbroker – staid, then stable, then who knows?

Increasingly desperate, or despairing, he came to dread all those costumes, isms, ideologies. None of it could blanch his soul's blankness.

When he went back to the needle after two years, he copped the same dose. Which made sense, and didn't. Since his body wasn't used to it, the horse simply stomped out his heart.

David took that one hard.

Group was largely but not limited to high-end users, scions of wealth and privilege.

Why? David didn't have a cogent answer, other than to say that's where Danny would have gone – *should* have gone – had he gone anywhere, which he didn't.

"Better," Leslie says one rainy morning, "that we should have been brought up with no money."

There are nods and murmurs around the room. Bev gives out with a kind of moan of recognition, and Peter, clearly made uncomfortable by the topic, begins to tap restively on the chair's writing arm.

"Because we were raised in a world where we believed there were no consequences," she continues, "where we could buy our way out of anything."

"Right," Howard mumbles.

"We had no idea of failure," Leslie turns a hand. "None at all."

"Because we were given so much," Andrea adds, "we believed that we were worthless. That nothing we are, or do, could ever measure up."

"Once you're there," Leslie says, "the loneliness is overwhelming."

"Self-hating," Bobbi says, "stoned, stuck."

"*Her-o-in*," Peter starts to sing, then laughs in his hollow, haunted way.

Dramatically announcing that New York was dead, was nowheresville, Danny moved precipitously to the Left Coast, Sandy Frisco. Privately to David he decried what New York had become. "So much wantonness," he wrote, "so much waste. So much defeat, so much death."

Heading west full of high spirits and good hope, he set up shop in a tiny North Beach apartment, hung around City Lights books, began to worm his way in.

A year or two after David arrived it was San Francisco's famous summer of suicides. Drunks. Dealers. Drug addicts.

Makers of all manner of mayhem, David will never get them out of his head.

I fear that with their dangerous view of the bottom they'd seduce David with their bleakness – before he could save them with his wit and attention to detail, his innate goodness. Scorched Earth versus Bountiful Harvest.

Put another way, they were dangerous because they believed in darkness far more than he believed in light.

"She used to joke," Leonid retells the legend. "'Mercer. Rhymes with worser.' Right, David, there's no such thing as jokes. Tere, pronounced Terry. I know you thought for 10 seconds about naming this for her."

David nods.

He remembers the day she didn't show up for Group. No matter how bad she felt, no matter where she was, work shirt covered in vomit or not, she showed up for Group. When she didn't, they put out an all-points bulletin. Too late.

"Then thought again," Leonid continues. "Bad role model. *Very* bad role model. Heap bad role model. Dead junkies are *mucho* bad role models. Dead junkies who OD and choke on their own vomit while their babies starve to death next to them are the worst role models. Aren't they, David?"

There was no forgetting that. Family abandoned, money burned. Cold-water slum two steps ahead of the termites. What little her wasted body was worth she sold for bad drugs and worse needles.

"That was a tough day," Peter says. "Very tough day. No way for that to come out right."

I prefer my nihilism with a side of hope, David thinks but doesn't say it.

There was to be a show, Danny said. He had reached a new plateau, he said, a new vision. David took a look. The photos looked like fuzz tones on an electric guitar – blurred, blobs of black and white so abstract that the viewer had nowhere to stand.

Breakthrough? David wondered. Who knows? He was no art critic, and so much of success is luck, anyway. One favorable review, right place, right time.

But this seemed like a lot of work with no pay-off.

The textbook definition of all dressed up with no place to go.

David discovers that treating these people is like combat, like Panama; he will suffer a lingering case of PTSD, of malaria, preying on him, weakening him at the wrong time.

Their world becomes his world; he learns its trials and tragedies, its imprecations and imperfections.

In Norfolk people are polite and sedate by choice and training. They, and he, scrupulously avoid the worst excesses of contemporary life. Here, he's thrust four-square into an abyss of aberration, of life's worst impulses – and even worse responses. Of at-risk behavior, the stuff of daytime drama and penny dreadfuls, of freak shows and exploitation flicks.

"They have huge hearts," he writes. "You just have to get to them."

The yellow walls seem to yawn, but such is the nature of Group. Leslie fusses, as always, with her coffee, Cordon Bleu-level measuring and stirring. Arthur shifts warily in his seat. Jack Dawes mumbles to himself.

White noise, David thinks, low level. Not going to get any better.

It didn't stop him. It wouldn't.

Danny cried and cajoled, pulled every string that he could, got a show at City Lights, a room with *cachet*, don't you know?

It was so ill-attended that the exhibition evaporated within a week.

There was a second – his last, as it turned out – in some retrofitted firehouse down the peninsula. It, too, was more or less invisible.

One man dismissed the photos as "visual gibberish."

Another said, "it is ultimately not worth the journey, neither on the road nor in the eye. These images are the inverse of Rembrandt. For the Master there's light that illuminates dark. Here, by contrast, there's only darkness at the heart of darkness."

A third simply snorted, "hangovers."

It was no surprise to David that Danny answered his critics with silence. Then, abruptly, stopped shooting altogether.

Perhaps, David said at the time, that was his intention all along.

David reviews the players an hour before Group:

Leslie, nasal, fussy, pampered. Phrase of choice: it gives me a headache. David finds her amusing. Comes from department store money, flirted with Catholicism, traded catechism for cocaine. Near-fatal overdose sobered her up, chased her here.

Leonid, round little man, son of Chechin refugees, self-made lawyer given to prodigious benders, probity, cautious chuckles.

Howard, junkie; OK, recovering junkie. But once a junkie always a junkie. He knows that; the *world* knows that. Shaky, fastidious, spotless. As if everything weren't right the world would fall apart. *He* would fall apart. A life of eternal vigilance.

Arthur, wise and wary, *very* wary. Having been burned – badly, doing two bits in the joint for possession and trafficking – he did not wish to be burned again. Sliding into the room like a shadow, he eases into a chair, looks around, checks the perimeter, as if there were traitors in his midst and surely someone will ambush him again.

Andrea, who never stops talking and collects disasters the way other women collect purses or shoes. An army brat who moved more often than most people change their socks, she feels like detritus, something washed up on shore, entirely unvalued.

Bobbi, winsome, whiny, abused and ignored. Moderate make-up, black bras. She brings her *Child's Garden of Insults*, all the charming things her parents called her. David finds it a helpful device for Group when the conversation lags.

Jack Dawes, always both names, always dirty, disheveled. David is certain that there's black money there somewhere, he just can't discover the source. Increasingly delusional, David watches him deteriorating by inches. Soon, David will have to banish him for being unfocused and incorrigible.

Bev, the Great Mute. Bev, who doesn't say much at all. At first, the others dismissed her as a Valley Girl who thinks she's too good for them. 'Til they discovered that she has a serious speech impediment. Then they swore to protect her to the death. Let me see someone I can feel sorry for.

Peter, well, Peter. Peter, with his self-deprecating sense of humor and his tattooed face. While working in a head shop is probably two clicks above his pay grade, David understands that in a moment of joy, or inebriation, Peter had blue and red stars tattooed across the bridge of his nose, freckles racing in an alternate universe. Peter either felt very good about himself that day, David muses, or very rotten. There's no mediation about this. No middle ground. All or nothing. The most dangerous kind.

Danny's silence was disturbing.

David considered. Danny was like all artists, only more so. Perhaps all young artists – fierce, uncompromising – demand that viewers take the time. That they undertake the journey he makes. But Danny made a notoriously hot medium just *burn* – and like Icarus' wings, they melted in the heat.

"Dig it, Doc," Peter tells him one day. "Fast-actin' or slo-mo. Bridge be fast-actin'. Drugs 'n' drinking be slo-mo. But it be doin' yerself regardless."

Bobbi's *Child's Garden of Insults*. "No," she says, "it doesn't go away. Of course not."

Nods all around the room.

"It was so horrid," she says without self-pity. "So incessantly negative. It left such a bad taste, like the Cheshire Cat's ghastly grin, all that remains are the hurts."

"You telling it, girl," Jack Dawes says.

Arthur sits up in his chair.

"So that all authority becomes illegitimate," Leonid says, "or highly suspect."

"There are others," Bobbi says, "but here are the highlights."

"A is for act, as in you're lousing up the...

"B is for boar, as in you're as useful as tits on a...

"D is for damn, as in my sister and I were uniformly dismissed as damn brats...

"G is for galling, as in, name it, whatever we did, was galling...

"L is for lazy lout, as in what I was generally dismissed as..."

"Is there more of this?" Leslie demands.

"Shh," Andrea waves her off. "I like this."

You would, David thinks.

"Not much more," Bobbi says. "P is for philosopher, as in what I was incessantly told I would never be."

"Whatever the fuck *that* means," Peter says.

"Right," Bobbi says.

"S is for stinkweed, something else I was generally called.

"There's more," she adds, "but that's enough for now."

"Z," Peter demands. "What about Z? You left out Z."

"No doubt they were still working on it when I moved out," Bobbi says.

"That's some heavy shit," Jack Dawes says.

"This is what those rat bastards laid on a defenseless child," Bobbi says. "No wonder I'm fucked up."

"Whew," Arthur shakes his head.

"How many ways can you say hate?" Bobbi demands.

It was not so much later that Danny's letters slowed down, became more erratic, then stopped altogether. Apparently, David thought, Danny could no longer connect the dots of his own life. Could not find his own persona. His own central *raison d'etre*.

As David worked metaphors to describe his brother, Danny took the bridge.

Sure, David wants storm warnings, but because socialization demands that we hide most of who we are, they're hard to spot. David learns to deal with the quiet ones. With those best able to put up a calm, gentle exterior. Who can construct drywall like an ace. Who like a crafty landlord can hide the rot underneath.

Self-blame peeks around corners, David learns. You got to look for it.

"Homework!" David says. "Next Thursday, comics! Hulk, Spiderman, Watchmen. Batman. Let's talk about what you see."

"*Cooool*," Jack Dawes says.

"This is coming perilously close to losing its entertainment value," Howard complains.

David does a year or so of running interventions. Of picking up the pieces if any remain. "It's like using a desk blotter to mop up the blood," he writes in his journal.

He tires of such things, he writes, because he feels he's too late. "We need to catch them *before* they're at the edge of the cliff," he writes. "*Way* before."

"OK," David says, "superheroes. What do you have?"

"Secret identity," Arthur smiles.

"Save the world," Bobbi pumps a fist.

"Irony," Howard says slowly. "The difference between appearance and reality. The real me that nobody knows."

"Super strength," Peter flexes his biceps.

"Loss," Leonid says. "Krypton. Aunt May. The Waynes shot in front of a child."

"Self-control," says Jack Dawes. "That's the real message, ain't it, Doc? The Hulk. Got to keep all those bad impulses locked deep inside me. Lest they get out and *RRRRAAAA!!!!* ruin me and destroy the world."

"Is that what you see, Jack?" Leslie asks.

"It's us," Andrea says. "It's us in living color on cheap paper. These are people whose characters are not stable. Something they – and we – have to fight and build fresh every day. Smack those amino acids into shape and become a person. Strive for sense and sensibility. For sanity. For control. Because inside and out, the world is cracking and breaking, moving and crushing us like Shackleton's ice."

"Peter," David prods, "you with us?"

"Why did they never focus on the good things I did instead of constantly berating me for the bad?" he answers. "Or what those assholes considered bad?"

"That's a good place to stop today," David says.

Since pursuing Danny David has taken to weeping. Not every night, or even every week. But now and then, when things overwhelm him, and some unknown quantity triggers him, he will sit alone and let the tears stream down his face, lamenting all the hands lost at sea, all the souls abandoned and alone.

Peter's stories make no sense. They're all broken, as if logic had never existed.

So confused, David thinks. Like trying to stop a tsunami with a teaspoon.

"Fuck you."

Well, that's one way to put it, David thinks. At least you're not trying to charm me. It will take time to settle you out, Peter, to decipher you. To cut through clutter.

He looks at Peter, at the tattooed stars marching across his face. Some try to disarm me – I'm just as normal as you are. Some are in denial. Others just angry.

Welcome, Peter.

One way or another, David's dealing with raging defense mechanisms. To his credit, he's patient; he knows it will take time for things to settle down. To see what's really eating Peter, the others. What he has to work with. Which teeth he can save.

"That'll make it better?" he pushes Peter, who sits with his head down. "If you hurt yourself that'll hurt them? Or make them feel better? Because they're right?

"Or is the quiet of not-being better than the pain of being?

"Or maybe you feel better because you feel worse? That's a viable answer?"

David exhales. "Don't let me interrupt you, Peter. Pick one from Column A and one from Column B. Is this list too long? Is everything going to elicit a *fuck you* response?" He pauses. "I'll stop when you have something to say."

Sure, my brother wants to save everyone. But he also knows that 7/8ths of being an effective – forget good, settle for effective – therapist is knowing that you can't. And knowing that only people who *want* to heal actually will.

He also knows that character is constructed every day. Some days, the pieces just don't come together, don't coalesce.

Even then, like an iceberg, 90% of character is hidden even from ourselves.

"You ever have Demerol, Doc?" Peter asks. "Synthetic morphine."
David nods.
"It's like being the living dead. Like not being alive. Like..."
"Like not being aware," David says. "I've been there. The pain is better."
"That's what it's like all the time, Doc. I feel like I'm living in internal exile."

"Peter," David says, "you'll begin to heal when you realize that life isn't fair. Life isn't also *not* fair. Life just is. You've got to learn that. Got to *live* with that."

"There are moments made for us," David says to Group.
Arthur turns away. Leslie yawns. "*Zen zen zen zen*," Jack Dawes cackles. David ignores them.
"The trick is to recognize them, cherish them, and then, when they're gone, understand that they'll never return. And move on.'
"That's some deep shit, Doc," Leonid laughs, and the others do, too.

David understands that heroin – any drug, but Peter's was heroin, the nastiest jones of them all – is merely the embodiment of a cognizant dissonance, between the notes we play, the words we write, the images we make, and those we have in our heads.
David knows the Greeks understood that, too. Heroin as irony, the difference between appearance and reality, the ideal and the actual.
Heroin is the *imperfection* of the world.

"*Eros* and *Thanatos*," David writes, feet on the ottoman, cabernet in hand, "are not polarities but points on a scale. A zero sum game. If life is 15% then by definition death is 85%. Until the critical mass of one overcomes the other.
"So that the sense of an ending is not resignation but attraction. Certainly we want to deny that at the beginning, but the ending is always there, always sensual. We breathlessly lean in to the vampire's bite. Joyously

go off to war. Eagerly embrace the oblivion of the needle. It's not despair. It's *sex*."

If I save Peter, I'll save Danny.

Psych 101: the grief you didn't feel for me – perhaps the joy that the favored, infinitely more talented son was permanently out of the picture – transfers to Peter.

I know that David understands this. He understands, too, that stories are as much about deflecting, entertaining, as about revealing, truth telling.

Hiding, obscuring, fending off. Defending.

Especially for himself. Especially in Group, therapist serving as surrogate parent, priest, shaman. Doling out guilt, redemption, absolution, salvation.

"We have our work cut out for us," David smiles.

"We earthbound creatures who too fully feel the weight of gravity."

David stands at the Muir Lookout, Route 1, staring at the implacable gray Pacific. It's a thirsty fog that's swallowing everything, and David feels more than hears the ocean's thump and roar, the ocean that affords neither respite nor revelation. As the mist gathers around him, and his face waxes thick with moisture, David zips up his windbreaker. Time to go.

Maybe that's the trigger, he thinks. The last piece of crumbling internal edifice. More than synapses. Individual moments – they can't find a reason for them to hang together. No Aristotle: no beginning, middle, end. Through the ebb and flow of contact we hope to understand the present, predict the future, make sense of the past.

For Peter. For Danny, that pain, that dissociation, is the most intolerable.

That pain takes them to the needle.

And when the needle no longer works, the Bridge.

Tell it fast, tell it tight, he turns his back on the sea. You have to reject entirely the old story before you can embrace a new one.

Dodging SUVs and glancing at the roiling Pacific, David gets the call on the Great Highway. Peter's landed in SF General ICU. OD'd in the Mission District.

"Right," David sighs, "that's the place for it."

Turning the car around, he shuts off Sirius – "Lester Young, you'll be fine without me," he says – and thinks about Peter. Or *tries* to think about Peter, for my brother finds himself replaying for the umpteenth time our lives in exile, from Norfolk, from Main Street, from its mom-n-pops, coffee counters, and card shops; its fire stations, flea markets, and music stores. From summers with our kind and gentle grandfather, who always wore a suit and a smile no matter the heat. From our brilliant, absent father. From our lives as two chubby boys, two years apart, dressed as twins, novices in life, music, and baseball. From David speaking to a happy little kid named Danny who always seemed sunniest standing in his big brother's shadow, making up sidewalk games, hiding under his stingy fedora, who would now not ever come home.

Showing his ID, David finds Peter's room, nods at the nurses. Quickly reading the monitors, he is distracted by the green and blue lights bathing Peter's face, making the red and blue stars seem to fly into space.

The vital signs are low but stable, David sees, which is good. The breathing tube is not. He will wait to ask the attending.

The stars shimmer with Peter's breathing. The machine's breathing, David corrects himself.

Is Peter aware of anything? David wonders.

He knows you're here, I tell him, but David ignores me, looking instead at the man in the bed and thinking about how he could never save me. He sees that everywhere. David's carried that bag all his life; he will never put it down.

David doesn't hear me – can never hear me. By Peter's side he sleeps and revisits all the familiar dreams. Lost children, broken houses, dilapidated walls, his most sacred objects vanished.

Go home. I tell him. *There's nothing you can do. Peter's going to have to save himself. You know that. Nothing can bring me back. You know that, too, David. You can't save me. You could never save me. Go home.*

TRADE WINDS

▼

KAHAKULOA, MAUI

This is a story about dualities, about the powers of fire and water, about the songs of black sand and red blood, about meditation and remediation and memory past time.

It's a story about the black sand that eviscerates memory, all past, all meaning; how it dissolves both dreams and desire.

It's a story about the myths of fire and water, opposites more than attracting but depending on each other, opposites longing for unity, for surcease. For the twin myths of fire and water that *are* Hawaii, burning rock and boiling sea.

It's a story about Pele, and the price she extracts from men. About Kamohoali'i becoming a great white shark – by no accident Kamehameha's totem – bringing fire to the Islands, drawing Pele in her great canoe, Pele carrying fire in her womb.

It's a story about Kane, the bountiful god of life, and Ku, the fierce god of war – and the horrific toll he demands in human sacrifice.

It's a story about Kaneloas, the howling spirits; Heiaus, where blood flowed without surcease; Manas, kings and kahunas absorbing the blood and the spirits until they grew powerful beyond imagination.

It's a story about Kamehameha, who conquered the Islands, bathed in blood, betraying his own people.

It's a story about Haleakala, who gave her life to Pele, and Kilauea, who still burns in tribute.

It's a story about the blood that still shrieks today, at Iao Needle on

Maui and Pali Lookout on Oahu, where Ku broods over his troubled domain.

It's a story about the Trade Winds, about how they brought the Polynesians and the White Man to the Islands.

About how they brought Pele and Kamehameha, Makoa and Ira Mann.

It's a story about how the ali'i and kahuna read omens in clouds. How they see in the marriage of dot and line all of life. How they hear the cries of the great stone deities, read their anguish in mouths twisted grotesquely in eternal dread.

It's a story about Pele and the power of her volcanoes. Pele, whose very womb spews forth fire. Pele, handmaiden to Ku, himself hidden in the jagged mountains and the black sand, figured in a thousand black statues whose silent screams send forth evil that bursts through the crust of the earth.

It's a story about the power of fire and water, wind and time, of the Islands and the Trade Winds, of the chaos that is there, of the chaos that only the kahuna can calm.

The world is deep in Maui, in all the Islands, deep blue water, deep blue sky; water green and blue and black with a hoary fringe of white, an old man's tonsure. Where the Trade Winds brought people to wed the water and the land. To the sacred pools of Hana and the Iao Needle, to rocks scored by wind and scoured by sand, shards of rocks scratching at the sky.

To the waves that seep into the black rocks and roil the black sand, etch lines of years, cradle the fire sleeping within.

To the relentless winds and the endless flat ocean.

To the fire goddess Pele empowering them, Kamehameha setting forth in ships to conquer the Islands by blood and fire, to soak black sand in red blood.

To the trees that will twist away from the Trade Winds, as if they, too, understand the horror the wind will eventually bring.

To the ocean, soft blue ashore to steel gray horizon, halo of palm trees, brown exclamation points of Hana cliffs.

To Maui herself, clouds devouring Haleakala like some feral beast. Haleakala herself, silent, where the ali'i and the kahuna came for vision and prophecy. Came to learn the lessons of the earth and sky, the rhythms of the spirits, forward and back. Where the fog rises up like steam, 10,000 feet on a burning mountaintop desert.

Where Ira and Makoa, like so many before them, come barefoot in their pilgrimage, walking in silence. Crossing shelves of stone above fertile fields, they enter a world above clouds and sky, and sea beyond, where only kahuna can tread.

To peer down into the vast crater, the dormant volcano that is Pele's barren womb, the rock rich with iron, bathed in yellow light from clouds clinging to her black tortured cliffs, scraping the gorse and lichen, colors stark and moving before them.

To the House of the Sun, brittle dead volcano walls, moss climbing stubbornly on black rock, battling wind, rain, and sun. To trees mauled and stunted by the wind.

This is their story, Ira and Makoa, beginning in pre-history, in the Trade Winds, traveling across oceans, nurtured by conquest, surviving empire and exile, people displaced and dispossessed, in Islands of unspeakable beauty bathed in blood.

Finally, it's a story that ends in a treacherous surf off Maui's northwest coast, where two wounded men laugh and bleed into each other, no longer dualities but instead but two sides of the same man, their story informed far more by Carl Jung than Claude Levi-Strauss, not Trickster as mediator but Hero and Shadow as one.

As they discover, when you search for the Other what you find is yourself.

I should tell you something about myself, how I came to know these people and their story. My name is Jamie Hillier. James R. Hillier, Esquire. Law office in Lahaina, second floor, two rooms overlooking the harbor. Uniform of the day: sandals, shorts, Hawaii shirts tucked in only for formal occasions.

I did consider tending bar, but someone in Lahaina has to put in an honest day's work, more or less. Wills. Estates. Trusts. Land transfers. All relatively benign.

That's how I met Ira. Ira Mann. Ira Walker Mann, IV. Right here in Lahaina, where, clean and sober, he'd come to find a lawyer. Previously, the only reason why he came to Lahaina was to mix and mingle with the tourists, spread a little money around, find suitable, willing female accompaniment. Easy enough with all the collegians and clericals on vacation seeking a few hours of anonymous, unencumbered romance. No strings attached, nothing to bring back home. Or even to be mentioned back home. Perfect for Ira's drinking, carousing days, Ira being more or less monastic now, sails hauled in and tucked away, ship in dry dock.

Clean and sober 21, no, 22 years now. Steady. Stable. Decent chap. Keeps to himself. No more binges in Lahaina. No more binges anywhere. Relishes both his celibacy and sobriety. Relishes his role as a planter.

Ira also relishes his role as an inheritor of significant wealth, gathered and grown by great-grandpap, Ira Walker Mann, I.

It's a grand American story. Great-Great-Grandfather Seamus McMahon – sounded with all three syllables – left Ireland a young man, journeyed west to seek his fortune. And fortune he found, or at least his family did. Great-Great Grandpap did well enough. Settled in the western Pennsylvania coal fields. Ditch digger. Track layer. Intelligence and industry to burn. Smart and ambitious, he earned a battlefield commission from laborer to foreman after a rail slid down a steep incline, trapping four men beneath it. Quickly organizing a team to get the steel up and back in place, he personally hoisted the heaviest end, then carried a severely injured man up the hill to an aid station. Saved the man's life. More important, he saved the railroad time and money. Lauded by the track boss, McMahon was immediately upped to lead the section gang, then made a foreman.

At the same time, he saw which way the winds were blowing – fiercely anti-Irish, anti-Catholic. So in the best American way, he set about reinventing himself. Working on altering his accent, he moved his place of origin from County Cork to Sussex, changed and shortened his name to Steven Mann, joined the Episcopal Church, told everyone he'd come from England. As a strong, handsome, devout young Englishman, and a railroad foreman, he married well. Very well, in fact, into a comfortable Wrightsville family, dry goods merchants of standing and renown.

Steven's son, Ira's Great-Grandfather, used his family connections, read law, founded what became the family fortune. Hired on as a railroad lawyer, Ira Walker Mann, I, rose to corporate counsel, became a major stockholder in the era when railroads – and their investors – did very well. Appointed to the federal bench by President Taft, Ira Mann served with distinction. He also distinguished himself in the art of cultivating the right friends – very good friends – who were quite generous.

Suffice it to say, Great Grandpap, no more venal than the next black robe in the post-Gilded Age, amassed great wealth, invested it wisely. Mining. Mills. Railroads, of course. All the wealth that Wrightsville had to offer. Grew it. Protected it. Passed it down to his family in perpetuity via the kind of iron-clad trusts that allowed posterity to use the interest but never touch the principal.

Years later Ira, IV grew up, tall, charming, presentable. Also a wastrel of Kennedyesque proportions. When his profligacy resulted in an unwanted pregnancy, his father, Ira, III, unlike Joe Kennedy, Sr., refused to make the problem disappear. A hangin' judge not a fixer, Ira, III demanded marriage. A fast marriage. Then, amid a tsunami of charges and counter-charges, a faster divorce.

The resulting scandal, and flagrant substance abuse, added up to banishment from the shire.

Our wealth, Ira, IV said one day after his umpteenth departure from rehab, better we should never have had it. Because we were born believing we could buy our way out of anything. *Anything.* Just ask my sister. Oh, you can't ask my sister. Because she died of an overdose.

Then Ira did what he did best back then, went on a massive bender. Woke up here, out of a Bangkok binge. Was it Bangkok? He wasn't certain. Could have been anywhere. Suffice it to say, his dissipations, like Scott Fitzgerald's, were both legion and legendary. Blacked out for the better part of two months, he found himself on Maui with a pair of glasses and a monogrammed cigarette lighter on the night table – and no recollection whatsoever of who or what left them. Still has 'em, by the way, in case she – Ira guesses that's the gender – ever reappears to reclaim them.

Liking the romantic idea that he'd run to the end of the world – as long as the end of the world spoke English and did not require changing money – Ira remained.

Living in a rented cottage up an unpaved road, he stayed blasted most of the time. Then peered into the abyss – I don't know what the transformative moment was. He never mentioned it and I never asked. After all, his drinking days were over before we met. Suffice it to say, he had a vision of sobriety. So he stopped. Cold turkey.

Aside from liking it here – well, who *doesn't* like Maui? – he was also an outcast, an exile. While it was clear that he had torn it with his family, Ira did keep in touch with one brother – Matthew, younger, shorter, presumably smarter – who refused to take part in the family jousts. When their beloved grandmother died in Pennsylvania, all 14 surviving siblings and first cousins came for the funeral. Yes, they were all in the same place at the same time – for the last time, as it turned out – but you couldn't really call them together. Ira stood alone in the back of the church, and as the service ended, before anyone else stood up, he was gone. By the time they had carried Grandmama's remains to the hearse, he was on his way back to the airport.

That was many years ago. Could he return now? How bad *is* the blood? Pretty bad, it seems. Besides, a return would serve no purpose. Or so he tells me.

We're Americans; we're all exiles of one sort or another.

Put another way, Ira is something else washed up on the beach, blown here by the Trade Winds, like the Polynesians and the English and other Americans before him.

In his newfound sobriety, Ira decided – or was prompted by his brother Matthew, I'm not certain – that he needed a place to put his money. We met by chance – Trade Winds blowing again. I knew of an orchard on the northwest corner of the island that needed tending. Ohi'a'ai, Hawaiian mountain apples, something else the Trade Winds brought. I thought that Ira could stand to do something other than sit in a deck chair, nibble camembert, sip chamomile, and stare out at the sunset. Considering for a minute or two, Ira said he would take it.

I wouldn't have been surprised either way.

It's a *derelict* orchard, I warned him. It needs work. You won't be a gentleman grower. You're going to sweat. And you could easily fail.

I could use a little sweat about now, he shrugged. I'd actually like to get my hands dirty. Actually *work*.

And he did. Renaming it Mann Orchard, Ira put in 16-hour days, plowing, pruning, watering, weeding. At first, impatient, uninformed American that he is, Ira thought he would teach it a thing or two. Instead, it taught him. Time. Patience. How to care for living things. He began to see the trees – hundreds of them – as individuals, almost as prescient beings. He even named them and can tell you every name on the place. Along the way, he learned to love the aroma of growing things, of the buds and blossoms and fruits, of waking in the morning to the pervasive sweet, acrid odor of manure. He called it the perfume of promise.

At the Mann Orchard the wind sloughs off dips and depressions, tumbles down the distant peaks, beats about the clouds, shakes the crowns of trees white with dew and glinting in the early sun. The day will warm, the water will evaporate. The earth will breathe, like the rhythms of a body, with the growing seasons, the timing of heaven, of light and dark. Of rain. Ira learned to wait. To be patient.

Ira learned that we tie our heartbeats to the rising and falling of the ocean and the earth. Feeling the warmth of gestating things, the violence and gentility of birth, the sweetness and savagery of death.

After the first flush of his new venture, Ira found that farming was hardly as bucolic, as passive, as he had imagined. The trees required constant vigilance: mites, blights, birds, even the sun, he quickly discovered, were all his enemies. As were storms, price fluctuations, antiquated equipment, aging stock. Heavily invested, he saw that he constantly ran the risk of losing everything, which he nearly did a few years back, when only an experimental vaccine saved his orchard.

Then there was the stuff with which he had never wanted to be bothered, lawyers, accountants, taxes, labor, machinery. Still, Ira was stubborn, soldiered on. Did well, then did better. Perhaps it was a vestige of the Mann family luck.

He lived in the old caretaker's cottage – fire had razed the grand, 19th-century main house years before – one story, which he expanded, updated, upgraded. Fitted out in bamboo, teak, and rattan, he surrounded it with a long, low veranda – very much a planter's house. Spartan, cloistered even, Mann House, free of both affectation and ornament, was all he needed. Open to the elements, the Trade Winds, he did install ceiling fans for those hot, rainy nights when the windows had to be closed and the shutters drawn. Living with virtually nothing from his former life, the sole exception was a portrait in oils – how it was scavenged, I don't know – of his mother completed when she was a society girl, age 20 or so. Hair bobbed and shellacked, black dress, simple pearl necklace glowing, drawing all the light into the painting, *homage à Rembrandt*. And this ineffable glint in her eye – the portraitist's genius, whimsy, or desire, I couldn't say – knowing, sensual, self-sufficient, a genetic trait that destroyed one daughter and nearly ruined this son.

Every afternoon, the Trade Winds bend the palms nearly double. Every dusk, the sunset, startling in its deep reds and purples, washes light into the deep blue Pacific.

Ira learned to meditate, to empty his mind, to exorcise or eradicate the demons. Working to stop grinding about the past and worrying about future, he practiced twice daily, religiously, settling in after sencha in the morning, oolong at dusk. As he puts it, when he's got his mojo working, he feels at peace, appreciating the world as it is now. No mean feat.

After years of profligacy, he also relished quiet evenings of reading, Conrad a favorite. South Seas and exotic ports of call, of course, but also all those failures, exiles, characters full-to-the-brim with low self-esteem. Ira would have written about kindred souls in his journal, had he kept one, but he didn't; too much like work. So he read about them. *Lord Jim. Chance. Victory. Heart of Darkness. Nostromo.*

Joining the Growers Association, he quickly developed a reputation as a man of vision, a voice of reason and judgment. *Centered* was the word most often used.

Neither favoring nor choosing his celibacy, he nevertheless found being alone to be joyous. To his credit, Ira did not want to put in the time necessary to creating a decent, equal-partnered relationship. He'd had more than enough of the other kind.

I have no idea if Makoa was celibate or not, but he always seemed alone. How he lived – *where* he lived – were never quite clear, at least not to Ira and me. He was on the estate when Ira bought it, acting as the orchard's caretaker. Indeed, if it weren't for him during the fallow years all the trees might have perished. Dismissed by the agent who sold the orchard to Ira as *that dreamer, another native who has those visions, you know, every time the Big Island erupts. He's good with the locals, though, I have to give him that. I don't know where he finds them, and I don't care, but when the trees need to be picked he lines up an army of day laborers who do a great job. Very reasonable, too. Just don't listen to a word he says about myth or money and you'll be fine.*

In any event, Makoa lived somewhere on the grounds – he more or less faded into the dusk every night and re-appeared at first light, or thereabouts – seemed a good-enough fellow, knew and cared about the orchard, so Ira encouraged him to stay. Besides, at first, Ira was no grower, so someone had to lead him as he traversed the learning curve. Might as well have been Makoa.

With a broad Polynesian face, Makoa was short, taciturn, wiry and wary. Not wary, exactly. Guarded. Certainly silent and self-sufficient. With a palpable sense of loss – of what I couldn't say. There wasn't much he needed – or cared – to share.

If the adage is correct, that opposites – or in this case differing aspects of the same character – attract, or fuse, in very short order Ira and Makoa became as one. Just as just as light and dark combine to make dawn, and dusk, they were two bodies sharing the same love of – and reverence for – the trees.

Still, their differences were striking. To say that Ira was meticulous in his appearance puts it mildly, especially after his drinking days. Even in the field his all-cotton Hawaiian shirts and cargo shorts were always immaculately laundered, pressed *just so*. By contrast, Makoa was unruly, untidy, unkempt. Tattooed, his face was a fierce mask of dots and whorls, crystalline moments in time. To him, it was a religious obligation, the recognition that there is an inherent oneness, an inherent peace in the center of the soul – so important, so vital, he tattooed it in his flesh. Ira, for all his besotted past, was clear-headed, a rationalist. By contrast, Makoa was indeed a dreamer, a believer in signs, one of the kahuna – a practitioner of Polynesian magic and myth. Left to his own devices, pruning, planting, plaiting reeds, he sang the old songs, softly, to himself, in a language Ira did not understand.

I've told this story often enough to know what you're thinking. White Man/Dark Servant. Prospero/Caliban. Huck Finn/Jim. Lone Ranger/Tonto. But Ira and Makoa weren't that easy. They were more symbiotic, more a synthesis. Less polar opposites than two sides of same coin, a pushmi-pullyu that hadn't yet realized its twin nature.

While they always parted at dusk, Makoa slipping into the trees, at night Ira often spotted him, a shadow gliding along the shore.

By his presence Makoa posed the question which Ira was not equipped to ask: how far does tribal memory extend? Certainly, Ira felt his own family history strongly – name, inheritance, and so on. But never anything more than that, not nationally, certainly not mythically. Indeed, he knew neither the Celtic language nor Celtic customs nor Celtic myths – and cared about them even less. Time is now, he'd say, and what's here is here. Nothing more.

By contrast, Makoa did more than believe, he lived the idea that history and myth affect the present – indeed, they *are* the present. And if nothing else were presaged in his body, which he considered a kind of book, or tapestry, or living message; the past is a badge sealed in your flesh that you can never remove. Like your family, your tribe, your land, your past is something you could never lose, could never be stolen. *Head*, he would point, *heart*, he would spread his hands across his chest, *hands*, he would say, and I could see the white scars scored by years of outdoor work.

Looking at him, I saw the dots of the sun, the lines of the horizon. White caps on the sea. Lines of birds. The twists and turns of life. Hawks' beaks and sharks' teeth, the latter his totem, the shark, like Kamehameha, so beloved of Pele.

Like Pele herself, goddess of fire, like Kamehameha, usurper waging war, Makoa's time went back to outriggers plying the ocean at night, feeling the heave and pitch of the waves, the water blanketed with darkness, with the terror of fearsome gods and grotesque monsters. Sailing in a relentless search for better land and better lives, for peaceful nights and calmer seas, they came to the Islands in silence, in the rhythm of their strokes, in the singleness of their purpose.

Sailing in a time when blood expiated tribal flaws, they celebrated the blood and spirit of the sacrificed that added to the physical life and spiritual strength of the kahuna, the king, and the tribe.

Seeing that vast, blood-soaked past in dreams and waking visions,

Makoa holds his scarred and tattooed hands to the sky, calls out how he is a master of rainbows, reading the future in clouds, in moon shadows. Recounting his grandmother transforming herself into a hawk who dived off thorny cliffs to skim over the tops of jouncing seas; as she did, so does he channel divinations, predict rain, induce crops, exorcise beetles from apple trees.

Which clouds are clouds, and which are spirits of dog gods come to eat men? Rich with the four winds of magic, as the congress of gods appears to him spread out across the evening sky, Makoa sees how the spirits of the dead are transferred to others – through blood and incantations – through human sacrifice.

Who knows the bloody history of the Islands? he asks. In whispers? In dreams?

The First People had many magical powers, Makoa says, healing, growing, war. Cutting their enemies into pieces and burning them for Pele.

I remember, Makoa says. *I was there.*

As he was when they formed a 15-mile human chain on the Big Island, passing stones hand-to-hand, building an altar not to Pele but to Ku, god of war, whom they would worship and invoke before setting out to conquer the other Islands and unite all Hawaii under a single royal family.

As Makoa was when, emboldened by magic and the White Man's murderous technology, King Kamehameha held aloft the bleeding heads of the sacrificed, allowing their blood to wash down his arms and massive chest, enriching his royal power, rendering him superhuman, inducing his surrounding warriors to shout *victory!*

I remember, Makoa says, dreaming of a giant canoe crossing the sea beneath the cold, starry night and the relentless, burning sun. *I was there*

As he still is. Although blood sacrifices ceased 200 years ago, that hardly stopped a kahuna like Makoa from traveling on moonless nights to the ancient altars, there to induce the dark powers, to entice the ground, so drenched in blood, to release the spirits entrapped in her womb. To draw that blood like water, to defeat the chaos the renegade Trade Winds brought to the Islands, the murder and the blood, the butchery at the heart of their dreams.

So Makoa goes to Kilauea on the Big Island, for Pele's thunder and fire. And every Winter Solstice, on the longest night of the year, to Haleakala, Pele's dark and shrouded tomb 10,000 feet above Maui's broken shoreline, there to call on the entombed goddess not be extinguished but instead to bring back the sun's healing fires for the following year.

-- A good year, Ira says. A good harvest.

They are walking in the trees, Ira and Makoa, inspecting them before dusk.

-- Yes, Makoa agrees. Kane was good to us this year. Bountiful. I have remembered him. I have tended his shrine, have brought him offerings of oil and fruit.

-- Come sit with me on the veranda, Ira asks him. Tell me more about Kane.

Ira cannot see Makoa's fleeting smile in the fading light.

-- The White Man always needs to distance himself from Mother Earth. Come sit with me where the trees meet the sand and I will tell you.

Squatting beneath the trees, Makoa says that Ira must think about Kane, thank him for his gifts. That he must get used to being close to the earth, to feel its rhythms and its sweat, to consider his family totem.

-- Mine is the shark, the power and eternity of the sea, like Kamehameha the Great. Yours?

Ira says that he has no idea.

-- That is why the White Man wreaks so much havoc, Makoa says. He has neither tribe nor totem. No link to *land*. That is why he will pass from Mother Earth, as weightless as the morning dew, the hawk's feather, the clouds over Haleakala.

-- We're Americans, Ira begins. We all come from somewhere else. We are restless, rootless. Exiles. Not part of this land or any land. Only what we own.

Makoa breathes deeply, is silent, so silent that Ira fears he has fallen asleep.

-- The White Man does not understand, Makoa says sadly. You do not own land. The land owns you. Makoa pauses. This is another reason for your failure. Why you value so little and destroy so much.

-- I do not want to be that kind of White Man, Ira says.

-- Then you have to go back, Makoa says. To return.

-- To what? Ira asks.

-- Come with me to the vigil for Pele. Ask her to restore you to your totem, to your people's past. Then you can begin to understand yourself and the land.

-- When is that? Ira asks.

-- In two weeks, Makoa answers, on the longest night of the year, when the light is at her lowest ebb, when the power of heaven's fire is at her lowest, when Pele receives wishes for all returns.

Ira is silent.

-- It is a long night, Makoa says. A night of demons and visions. A night of sweat and chills.

-- I, Ira begins.

-- You have no idea, Makoa says, then pauses. If you accompany me I will take what the White Man calls no responsibility. This will be more perilous than you can imagine. Makoa pauses again. I hope that you will survive.

The two weeks pass quickly, the days waning, shorter and shorter, until finally Makoa is ready, albeit reluctantly, to take Ira to Haleakala, to Pele's tomb.

-- We must walk, Makoa insists.

Parking the car thousands of feet below the summit, Ira expresses surprise.

-- It is a pilgrimage, Makoa reminds him. Pilgrims approach humbly, through the self, not through an alien machine.

The night air is cold, at 4,000 feet, and gets colder as the two men set out in silence. Ira dons a second sweatshirt, then takes it off as a sheen of sweat forms on his body. For his part, Makoa seems impervious to the cold.

They walk on, in silence, night fog pinching them, undergrowth twisting away as if offended, or angered, by the intrusion. After nearly an hour, at 8,000 feet, Makoa turns to Ira and says that from here they must walk barefoot and in silence.

-- Do not speak, he says, but listen. There are mysteries here that you will not fathom. In the time before time only the most spiritually advanced ascended past this point. Only the true mystics. Makoa pauses. For others, it was too dangerous.

Ira nods, drinks from his canteen, some herbal concoction Makoa has given him, looks through the fog at a crazy quilt of stars.

-- They came with the spirits of the dead, Makoa says. You can hear them now, Ira, the ghostly, hurried footsteps of souls not at rest, warriors sacrificed to enrich the tribe, to feel the ecstasy of their final rendezvous with light.

The chill of the night air deepens, the path grows steeper, the stunted vegetation as sharp and brittle as the surrounding stones. The backs of Ira's legs ache, and his throat is dry and rustling, as he and Makoa approach the vast dark ridges of Haleakala, the great extinct volcano.

-- It was not always such, Makoa says. It burned, lavish and powerful. It was here the sacrifices were hurled in to the burning lava, strong, alive, ready to greet Pele in her lair, joyous to donate their strengths and souls to her and to Maui. Makoa pauses, spreads his hands about. Their souls never perished, he adds, but walk among us still. It was the ali'i who had the power to summon and speak with them, on this night to ask them to intercede with Pele, to win her favor, to return light to the world.

Ira looks down at the ruins of the implacable fire goddess, the rocks still scorched after centuries, the grass burned and uneasy, the souls not at rest. Huddling into his sweatshirts, he considers the placidity of the sky and the distant sea, the blood-soaked earth, the souls slaughtered to appease the goddess and enrich the king.

It is an odd moment, the clouds suddenly scurrying away, revealing the moon, enormous, bone white. Struck by the pallor of the landscape, the muted reds and browns, Ira turns to see Makoa, squatting, eyes closed, the backs of his hands resting on the hard ground, palms up and open. Realizing that Makoa is singing softly, Ira strains to hear the melody.

For the first time, Ira is frightened. Makoa, singing in English but in a voice not his own, sings of cutting himself and bleeding on Kamehameha's altar.

Ira, eyes closed now, hears the screams, smells the blood.

-- This is the truth found in spirits, Makoa sings, not in the White

Man's books. Not in the White Man's language forced upon us. The truth found only in stories, in dreams, in waking visions.

-- The truth written on the black sand.

-- The truth of the marriage of light and dark. Of Pele, of her white fire and her black fire.

Shivering as if feverish, Ira sees the world consumed by a fearsome conflagration. Against both his will and inclination, he begins to weep.

On Makoa sings, of his people, brought by the Trade Winds more than a thousand years ago. Ira sees it all, the winds and the ocean, seeing it as an endless tableau, a blood-drenched dream that he can neither evade nor erase.

Makoa sings of the warriors sacrificed to Pele, exalted because they, too, approach godhead, the gods who bring – and take – all life.

He sings of the great Loaloa Heiau, 500 feet long, 20 feet high, where the blood was ankle-deep and Maui sent souls to enrich Kane and Pele and Ku, the latter now figured as the fearsome maggot-mouth, who howled like the Trade Winds themselves, and whose tongue licked his subjects before their blood was taken.

He sings of Kamehameha, unspeakable, unscrupulous, relentless in war, and betrayal, who exacted an unimaginable price for opposing him.

He sings of Kamehameha, raised in the royal court of his uncle, who murdered his own cousin to seize the throne and declare war on the other Islands.

He sings of Kamehameha, who, in his own lust and greed, sold his birthright to British and American traders, who trained his warriors and gave him weapons.

He sings of the night before Kamehameha set forth with 1,000 men and 100 war canoes, standing aloft, his final sacrifice on the Big Island, holding aloft dead warriors' bloody heads, blood streaming down his arms, drinking their steaming blood, 1,000 frenzied warriors roaring *victory!*

He sings of Kamehameha's journey to Maui, to the Iao Valley, the sacred ali'i burial ground, where, before the vast 1,000-foot Needle, home to Kanaloa, god of the underworld, Kamehameha and his warriors fought so fiercely that they dammed the stream with the bodies of their dead enemies, their blood drowning the water, soaking the land itself.

Above them, the Iao Needle, shrieking, triumphant, its sharp peaks, its enormous combs of vegetation-clad rocks proclaiming victory. As the valley below regurgitated that offal forever, the very ridges twisted away like mummified beasts.

He sings of how neither the blood nor the souls are dead, but dormant, potent, ready to explode in fury, ready to unleash the energy loosed in slaughter.

He sings of how the blood boils up from the ground, unleashed in fire and fury.

Stop, Ira weeps silently. Please stop.

He sings of Kamehameha's pursuit of his rival Kalanikupule to Oahu, 10,000 warriors in 1,000 canoes, where hundreds of warriors were sent to their deaths 1,000 feet off Pali Lookout, their bodies torn by ravens and vultures, devoured by ants and animals, where the fierce winds still howl with the fallen warriors' tortured souls.

Seeing it all, the massive blood lust, the death of so many, the flight of so many souls, Ira becomes nauseated, terrified of the murder stalking the earth.

Makoa sings of Kamehameha's sacrifice of Kalanikupule to Ku, War Triumphant, his strength assumed by Kamehameha, now the bloody king of all the Islands.

Retching at the taste of human blood, Ira cannot see the moon or the sky.

Makoa sings of more human sacrifice, and more, to save Oahu from an epidemic, to propel Kamehameha to further victories, to infuse a new idol of Ku with the spirit of a warrior, buried alive to enrich Ku's ineffable power.

Finally, Makoa weeps as he sings the dirge of the destruction of the heiaus, the burning of the idols, the end of sacrifice, the cessation of blood.

Befouled by his own vomit, eyes blinded by tears, Ira cannot rid himself of the horrific images.

-- Are you all right, Makoa asks, solicitously, touching Ira's face and upper arm.

-- No, Ira says without irony, not really.

-- To be expected, Makoa says and waits.

Although it is still cold, and the dew clings to Ira like tree moss, there are streaks of red across the eastern sky. He begins to make out the shapes of plants and stone outcroppings. Across the vast crater he sees steam rise through the earth's sealed fissures. It is Pele answering, favorably, he believes, then shakes his head. A hallucination, he thinks, or a bit of fog blowing in the crater. That's all.

-- Where were you? he asks. *Who* were you?

-- Although we are both pilgrims, Makoa answers, I am kahuna. I, too, am part of the ancient ways. I, too, partake of the spirit world.

-- And the blood, Ira says.

-- It is part of who we were, Makoa says. Who we are.

-- And you think that all that savagery is right? Somehow it makes a difference?

-- It is Pele's wish that we come to her asking for her gifts. Makoa pauses. Now that dawn approaches you should eat something.

-- After all that blood I'm not hungry.

-- It was the White Man, Makoa says, transported here by the Trade Winds, who put the worm of doubt into the Islanders' minds. We never found it appalling – even questionable – until you told us it was. You with your firesticks and your firewater. You who seduced and corrupted us. You who stole our religion, our history, our language. Our land. Makoa pauses. You who demand that we be grateful. That we thank you.

Ira begins, then stops.

-- Witting and unwitting. We couldn't fight your guns. And we couldn't fight your money. And we couldn't fight your germs. No natural immunity to any of it. Gunpowder. Sugar cane. Smallpox. Measles. Cholera. Typhus. Syphilis. Everything we had, everything we were and wanted to be, was destroyed.

The streaks of red had become a band of light on the horizon. Fleetingly, Ira feels a moment of hope.

-- By the middle of the 19th Century, the surviving Hawaiians were displaced, their tribal lands stolen by sugar conglomerates. Communal farms became the White Man's cane fields, and an independent people became cane cutters – indentured servants and share croppers. That was Kamehameha's true legacy: his kingdom had become subject to foreign business.

Ira finds he cannot look at Makoa, but instead focuses on a flight of gulls far over the ocean.

-- Even that wasn't enough. The kingdom, insufficiently mortgaged to White oligarchs, was overthrown, replaced by a Republic, one owned by American businesses. But with war looming with Spain, and needing bases across the Pacific, five years later the American military seized Hawaii – and Guam and Samoa – rendering them all territories, all wholly owned vassal states. A half-century later, Hawaii became an American state, a supposed honor most natives despised.

-- My people have lived here for a thousand years, and, once again you're stealing it from us. Forcing us out because we can't afford it. You claim it's law and it's just, but that's just another form of the White Man's imperialism and theft.

-- It's a matter of law, Ira objects.

-- Law? What law? The White Man's law? You stole the land, then made up the law to justify it. Law? I'd laugh if the joke weren't so pitiful and painful.

-- And now you're trying to destroy our souls. But Pele will rise against you and defeat you. And Ku.

-- Yes, Ira, there will be another Kamehameha, a great, fearless, relentless warrior. And this time you will not own him. This time he will not do your bidding and murder his own countrymen to further your ends. This time he will destroy you.

Weak, exhausted, Ira asks if that's where the story ends.

-- It doesn't end, Makoa demurs, never ends, because history never ends. We're always living in the midst of it. Sometimes it seems to end, like Haleakala. Sometimes, it just takes a breather. Sometimes it rages on. Makoa pauses. Sometimes it takes many centuries to see light from a dead star. Or to feel the heat from a seemingly extinguished volcano.

-- Makoa, Ira begins, huddling into his clothes, watching the sun break the surface of the Pacific, do you think we could –

-- Staging area for Japan. R 'n' R from Vietnam. Now eyes on Korea. America does love her wars, Makoa continues, as if Ira had not spoken, the bigger, the grander, the better.

-- Like Kamehameha, Ira stretches, stands up.

-- They condemned him for his native practices, Makoa says, but there are statues of him today. Not because he embraced all the native arts and, in his butchery, ended centuries of inter-tribal fighting. But because he slaughtered his own people for the White Man. Because he was a tool of American money. And the American military.

-- Different now, Ira says, bending his back, smoothing his matted hair.

-- I bring my people's blood, Makoa says, their arms, their sacrifices, their wars. Yes, their atrocities. It's part of me, part of my people. Rising, Makoa gestures. But so do you, Ira. You bring empire. You bring greed, the kind of industrial agriculture that defeats indigenous farming, destroys crops, depletes the soil. Abandons it barren and bereft. You befoul the skies with jet fuel detritus and diesel oil exhaust. You bring theft and murder and oppression and hypocrisy. It's a peculiar delusion of the West that you're an endless series of individuals, lone wolves, not responsible for each other. That's as incorrect as it is insulting.

-- And in your drug addictions and cancer and heart disease you pay the price. And will continue to do so. Until you learn from history, and hearken to the spirits, and adjust your lives to live in concert with the heartbeat of Mother Earth and the breath of Father Sky. We may differ about their names, but that doesn't matter. What does is their reality. And your denial cannot alter or obviate that.

-- Think about what you've stolen, Ira. What the White Man has stolen. And the price you will have to pay to make things right. To give it all back.

-- I had nothing to do with all this, Ira protests.

-- Do you mean aside from your belief that you *own* land? Or is it your railroad money? How many were killed as your family created its wealth? Working on your railroads? In your mines? In your mills? How many lives were lost, forgotten, uncompensated? How many families destroyed? Have you any idea? I dare say not.

Ira says nothing.

-- Railroad money? That washes your hands clean? Is that money ever rid of its taint? Have you ever read the history of American railroads? How much blood there is on that money? Does it ever come clean? Is it ever washed away by changing hands or by time? All of it? None of it? Or is it poisoned forever like radioactive waste?

-- Or human sacrifice, Ira says.

-- Maybe that blood followed you here, and poisoned everything you've touched.

-- And maybe not, Makoa.

-- Right, Ira. And maybe not. But you think that because you smile and say *aloha* and *mahalo* and *bruddah*, and wave the White Man's paper, that you really care about us, that you're really one of us? You're not.

Ira says nothing.

-- You take, but you do not give. You do not offer. You do not practice reciprocity. You do not give thanks. You do not respect the sanctity of the land. In your slash-and-burn capitalism, you use it all up, move on, accept no responsibility. You blame changing markets or technology. But you never factor in human costs – even as you dismiss native sacrifice. Ultimately, you try Pele's patience.

Ira sees that full dawn – the sun blazing, the winds whisking the dew off the shards of spiky leaves – has risen over the sea.

-- That was your journey, Makoa said. Tonight was your penance. Your expiation. The spirits pray that you take these lessons to heart, and that Pele releases her bounty and accepts your contrition.

-- Where do we go from here? Ira asks.

-- To unity, Makoa answers. To love.

Feet up on my desk, dressed in his trademark cargo shorts, palm trees billowing on his shirt, equipped with cheroot and ginseng tea, Ira was as genial as he was firm. *No question*, he said emphatically. *Right down the middle. Equal shares of Mann Orchard, 50-50, Makoa and me.*

Let me see if I have this right, I demurred. In consideration for sweat equity --

No, Ira was emphatic. *Outright gift. In perpetuity. Assignable to his heirs. Assignable to anyone. I don't care. I want him to have half. I want us to be partners. Equal shares, equal say.*

Tie breaker? I asked politely.

Won't need one, Ira said. *Not now, not never.*

As the story emerged, Ira proposed the idea to Makoa after Haleakala, but Makoa, laughing, turned him down flat, reminding him we don't own land, land owns us.

-- All well and good, Ira allowed, but this is still America, and we live by American law. By American law I own Mann Orchard. I want to give you half.

-- Penance? Makoa asked. Peace? Parsing out the guilt?

-- None of the above, Ira answered. You've worked hard here, harder than I have. It's only fair that you have a true owner's share. OK, not owner. Grower. Steward. He paused. It will hardly right everything, Makoa. But it will be a first step.

Scam artist? I asked.

No, Ira said. *Absolutely not. You don't know. You weren't there.*

Can't argue with that, I allowed. Actually, I don't argue with much of anything these days – one must have a mind of Maui, and all. It's tough to argue in paradise. Got to *work* to get that blood pressure up.

So I wrote them a document, which they both signed, sharing equally in the land in perpetuity. Making up, at least a little, for wrongs committed.

Was it a senseless gesture? I don't think so. Miniscule? Maybe. But clearly it was a healing. It was a beginning.

Perhaps, I thought, preparing to file the amended deed, that's why the Trade Winds blew Ira here in the first place. Not to end the hatred and distrust, and the blood lust, and the reign of the angry, vengeful gods, of Ku and Pele, of war and fire, but at least to begin.

There's a coda to the story, one which none of the principals could have foreseen.

On a night that began like any other on the northwest corner of Maui, a sudden, unforeseen squall blew in, kicking up enormous waves all along the shore. As debris began flying out of the churning water, Ira didn't think anything of it until he caught sight of Makoa floundering about in the surf. Knocked down, and knocked down again, he was clearly distraught and disoriented.

Not hesitating, Ira ran down off his porch and, wading into the waist-high water, found himself knocked down. Struggling to stand up, he felt a sharp pain on his left thigh. Unsteady, buffeted by the waves, he put his hand on what he discovered was a serious wound – a sharp piece of rock had sliced open his leg.

Buckling, he first thought of returning to the safety of shore, then remembered Makoa, 20 yards off, similarly unable to stand. Shouting his name, afraid that his friend would drown, Ira fought the surging waters to reach him.

Knocked down, and knocked down again, his leg burning as the twin abrasives of sand and salt worked at his wound, Ira reached Makoa. Picking him up, holding him out of harm's way, he saw that Makoa, too, was wounded, bleeding. As he half-dragged, half-carried the smaller man to safety, Ira began to laugh. As the two wounds touched, and bled into each other, he knew that, yes, they had become true blood brothers, and that, yes, the Island had its requisite blood sacrifice.

Shouting over the storm, telling Makoa of his realization, he saw Makoa, too, laugh, come a bit to life, hug Ira in return.

That is where I leave them, embracing each other, wet and wounded, forever altered, bound in perpetuity in their journey of blood and earth; the shrill cries of savagery and blood sacrifice, of superiority and stealth, all stilled. Dualities accepted and reconciled, man and myth, land and spirit, past and future. Ku silenced but surely not dead, the warmth of Pele waiting in the dead crater of Haleakala.

For Ira, the remade Westerner, this is where the story ends, in brotherhood, in embrace. But for Makoa, Dreamer, inheritor of the kahuna, it ends very differently. It ends where it began, in the spirit world, with grievance, with Ku hardly appeased but instead gathering his forces.

With Pele churning beneath the earth's silent surface.

And with Kamehameha holding aloft a skull, blood draining down his arm, his warriors crying *victory!*

TRIOLOGY

▼

STONY CREEK, CONNECTICUT

DMV1579: R U?
November 21, 2018

DMV1579: U THR?
November 17, 2018

CBS3016: I desperately want to see you. One last time.
DMV1579: I don't think it's time to start talking about last times.
CBS3016: Not leaving Middle Earth on my own hook, D. Sooner or later we all start dealing with things. Sooner, here. Tying up loose ends.
DMV1579: Is that what I am? A loose end?
CBS3016: You know what I mean. Besides, D, it's to the point where I don't want to be in pain. And I don't want to be doped out of reality, either. It's also to the point when I wish I wouldn't be so out of place – Park Slope, you. And such a burden on Alan. The surgeries hurt, terribly, D, as does the chemo, but the other parts hurt worse. How much pain can we endure? How much can we lose before life is meaningless?
DMV1579: Claire.
CBS3016: It's not goodbye, my love. It's *never* goodbye. It's one world or another.
DMV1579: We've got years left, Claire.
CBS3016: Not years, D. Not even months. Maybe not even days. But know that as long as I'm here, you'll always be with me. You'll be with me

all the days of my life. My silvery thread, a line across planes of existence. No matter what, there'll always be you.

November 15, 2018

CBS3016: I weep uncontrollably for several hours every day. Alan can't bear it.

DMV1579: Claire.

CBS3016: Given all the damage they found, they tell me that it will be a long road to recovery – if at all.

DMV1579: Don't say that. Please.

CBS3016: It's hard to feel so helpless, so out of control. I get about an hour in the morning when I feel almost normal, save for the sensation that a tractor has rolled over me. Then sorrow and exhaustion set in. Writing to you, I can almost convince myself that I used to be a fully functioning person.

DMV1579: Claire.

CBS3016: I feel more trapped in this broken body than ever.

DMV1579: Oh, my love.

CBS3016: The weeping is taking over. I can't see the keys. Sorry to be such a mess.

November 1, 2018

CBS3016: Cancer, D. Cancer. Alan calls it death by a thousand cuts.

DMV1579: My love.

CBS3016: My world is getting smaller and smaller, D. More crabbed. I've got the heat on, all the time now. I'm dressed in two sweatsuits and a heavy terry bathrobe. I can barely move. Alan's bringing me herb tea. Too tired to write.

October 18, 2018

CBS3016: Missing you much lately. Thinking of you everywhere. In a Percocet haze. Alan makes sure I have plenty. And I do. Love them 'Cets. At least I can sit up.

DMV1579: Courage.

CBS3016: Full fall here, D. Makes me long for Park Slope. And for you.

DMV1579: For you, too. And of course in the frozen north fall is a distant memory.

CBS3016: Miss you. Did I just say that? It's the 'Cets. Miss you. Terribly.

DMV1579: Know that somebody in Minnesota loves you.

CBS3016: Achingly.

October 3, 2018

CBS3016: A little better today, thanks. Can sit up without it hurting. At least for a bit.

DMV1579: Good.

CBS3016: Been thinking a lot, though.

DMV1579: Uh oh.

CBS3016: Mortality. Diminishing horizons. You know. Dealing with it.

DMV1579: Barbara once said to me, "we'll have days and days like this."

CBS3016: Did you?

DMV1579: No. But it felt that way.

CBS3016: This doesn't. We've achieved a plateau. *The* plateau, D.

DMV1579: We're snakes, Claire. Our enemy and our teacher from our other Lost Eden. He gave us mortality – and so taught us the value of time. He taught us how to shed our skins. How to move on. We *have* to.

CBS3016: I've made my peace with that. Had to, really. Alan helps. So do you.

DMV1579: 'Til soon, my love.

CBS3016: 'Til always.

September 27, 2018

CBS3016: Remember that visit to Manhattan, D?

DMV1579: Sure do.

CBS3016: I didn't want to talk about it.

DMV1579: I do recall that.

CBS3016: It was cancer, D. The worst kind. Couldn't bring myself to tell you, hoping… I went into chemo last week. Alan takes me, dear man. I think I've vomited up a small, offshore island. Make that a large offshore island.

DMV1579: Claire.

CBS3016: Courage, D. You always were the weak one. I'll be fine.

August 10, 2018

DMV1579: Went to Cuban dance music last week. Seven guys from Miami. Blew the roof off the building.

CBS3016: Sounds like a good time.

DMV1579: They invited people up to the stage to boogie. I would have but I was in the balcony. I closed my eyes, imagined the two of us up there, you with your characteristic smirk and wonderful chiseled features. We were having the time of our lives.

CBS3016: The time of my life now is having the nurse fluff my pillows. So, my love, dancing will have to wait. A very long time.

DMV1579: The weather's a bear. Already. I miss the hell out of you.

August 17, 2018

CBS3016: I hope to be better soon. I'm not sure. But I do hope.

DMV1579: I would come and see you, but at least you have Alan.

CBS3016: At least. He is saying all the right things, D, but he's not you, my love.

July 23, 2018

CBS3016: I am here. I am not so well right now, but it will pass.

DMV1579: How not well is not well?

CBS3016: Had surgery for removal of chest, which went well. No complications, and a relatively easy healing period. However...

DMV1579: However?

CBS3016: They didn't like my scans. Then they really didn't like my scans. So last Wednesday I had a hysterectomy.

DMV1579: *What?*

CBS3016: It has not been such a tasty slice of dessert.

DMV1579: I would imagine not.

CBS3016: What was meant to be a relatively simple procedure (laparoscopic hysterectomy) morphed into something horrifically difficult. I've got a major slash across my belly instead of three cute little holes. Even dear, dear Alan is visibly worried.

DMV1579: *Please* take care!

CBS3016: Today I managed a major victory. Thirty minutes out of bed.

DMV1579: You go, girl!
April 23, 2018

CBS3016: I'm less fast now. Pre-op stuff to plan for. The op of pre-op, the surgery itself, is a chest reconstruction – a fancier term for a double mastectomy. I had essentially put it out of my mind. Now it's there.

DMV1579: Good heavens. Did I know about this?

CBS3016: No. I hadn't told you. Hadn't told anyone, really. Alan knows, of course.

DMV1579: Secretive, aren't we?

CBS3016: Not really, no. Just didn't want to discuss it. Docs – I've got a slew of them – didn't like what they saw. No jokes here.

DMV1579: Hardly.

CBS3016: These days it's a fairly routine procedure. I've got a great surgeon, but it's still surgery. I'm hopeful it won't be too bad and everything will go smoothly.

DMV1579: Everything? Another shoe going to drop?

CBS3016: Don't worry too much. The docs are making noise about this and that, but I figured I've survived worse that I didn't ask for, so this oughta be a piece of cake. Alan isn't so sure, so, please, keep me in mind that day. Good vibes, and all. There's something to a person sitting and concentrating, asking good things for you.

DMV1579: There is something, yes. Time has taught me that.

CBS3016: Longing mightily for Park Slope this week, D. Maybe transitions, or showstoppers like surgeries, always bring nostalgia. I won't make it back there this spring or summer, but maybe another autumn in New York. Winter, time of regression.

DMV1579: Permanent winter here in MN.

CBS3016: The sun finally shines here, brings with it robins.
March 20, 2018

CBS3016: I dream about it a lot.
DMV1579: About what?
CBS3016: Park Slope.
DMV1579: Our Lost Eden.
CBS3016: Yes.

February 8, 2018

DMV1579: Last time I saw her...well...

CBS3016: Yes?

DMV1579: She didn't know me. Or just ignored me, I don't know which. In the bakery line, haranguing the hapless clerk about an unfilled order. Elephant ears or bear claws. Gaunt, ghastly, the cancer eating her alive. Old, wasted. A husk of a human being.

CBS3016: How awful.

DMV1579: It got worse. She was always an angry, brittle person. Constantly at war with the world and with herself. Ultimately, it was a virulent stage four that ate her brain like Pac-Man. Not yet sixty, bitter, having lost the ability to speak. Silent at the end, she tried to stare down the world. Her face frozen in a kind of *rictus sardonicus*, twisted into this grotesque grin. She had a bright, hard smile, like a cold, clear February morning. Did she feel terror? I don't know. I think I would. In any event, she died mute, face wrinkled like dried fruit, eyes glittery, set for dubious battle, ready to fight or fly – or flay you. Her laugh, a hollow croaking sound, was a distant memory. She left one loveless marriage, many busted affairs, wholly barren, with neither progeny nor portfolio.

CBS3016: I'm sorry.

DMV1579: Thank you. But it was over a long time ago. Someone I used to know.

January 25, 2018

DMV1579: Speaking with Barbara became increasingly difficult. She was flinty, argumentative at best. As her cancer progressed she became increasingly irascible, then entirely uncommunicative.

CBS3016: Oh, D.

DMV1579: There was booze, too. Lots 'n' lots of booze. Self-medicating to the *nth*. Quarts and quarts of the stuff. She had endless mood changes.

CBS3016: How dreadful.

DMV1579: It was. I did love her, Claire, when she let me. She had been a good friend, and a lover, when I needed both.

January 24, 2018

DMV1579: At her zenith, Barbara really was wonderful. Made everyone happy just to be near her. Unfortunately, she collected mistakes the way other women collect purses. The lover who burned all her poetry. The charming man who picked her up on a subway platform. Why not? she reasoned. Why not a little adventure? A bad beating and a bruised ego later, she realized *that's* why not. And so on.

CBS3016: Perfect lover, D.

DMV1579: She was, really, at her best. Too bad her moral compass was boxed. Fancied herself a photographer, a woman of leisure, an artist who believed the world would beat a path to her lofty studio, a third-floor walk-up above a bar. Unfettered by community, convention, or church, she believed that getting laid, especially without a lot of time attached and virtually no commitment, was better than not.

CBS3016: Good night.

DMV1579: Of course, I couldn't get her off my mind.

CBS3016: Of course not.

DMV1579: Women are like that. *You're* like that. You know that you have that power over us. Something about taking it in and holding it. Somehow we can withdraw, but you never let go.

CBS3016: You can check out any time you like. But you can never leave.

DMV1579: Hotel California. Something like that.

January 23, 2018

DMV1579: No big message, Claire. Not getting misty, or feeling the year-end or cold-weather blues. Everything's fine. Just thinking about you, and missing you, and hoping that everything's working out all right for you.

CBS3016: You've been on my list. Of course, of course.

DMV1579: Of course.

CBS3016: Everything's OK over here, too. Alan's fine and I'm fine. Still, the holidays feel different, now that I'm here, and away from Park Slope, and away from you. It's hard to put into words, but I feel like turning 60 shifted a major thing in me. Everything about time feels different. Not better or worse, just different. Not about it running out, either, which was always the case when I was younger. Funny, D, you'd think that growing older would make the finish line loom larger, but the opposite is true. Life feels longer to me now.

DMV1579: Maybe aging is coming to terms with the boundaries of one's own skin.

CBS3016: I don't do resolutions – oh, how chic it seems now, to opt out of resolutions. But I did reflect on the year past and the year to come. Wrote myself a sealed letter to be opened in fifteen years. I would've had a good laugh reading my predictions for now from fifteen years ago. Who *was* that person?

DMV1579: :-)

CBS3016: Still, I worry about losing her. Do you lose your sharp edge when you get older, or do you just wander away? I was reading old letters the other day and admiring that young author, wondering if I could actually compete.

DMV1579: I'm sure you could.

CBS3016: I don't know, D. Honestly. I'm tired. Feel like I get through every day, but on auto-pilot. Not thinking, not igniting. I'd like to get that back. I'd like to get *her* back.

DMV1579: I'm sure she's still there. I'm sure *you're* still there.

CBS3016: We've got snow in the Connecticut woods. I was in bliss.

DMV1579: This is Minnesota. We get snow in July.

CBS3016: I hope, with great depth, that things are fine for you. We must see each other again soon. I'm going to try and come out. Somehow.

DMV1579: I hope so. I'll show you 8,500 of the 10,000 Lakes. We can ice skate through Flag Day.

CBS3016: 'Til soon.

DMV1579: 'Til always.

December 29, 2017

CBS3016: Hm?

DMV1579: Coping, thanks. Just found out that two old friends, out of touch for years but fondly recalled, died. In NY and FL. I had always hoped for some kind of reunion. One of was my best friend, age 14-15, the other a real pal in the '80s, a friend when I needed one. Tough time.

CBS3016: I'm sorry. Truly.

DMV1579: It's Ice Nine here in MN. Always is, it seems.

December 13, 2017

CBS3016: Train to New York yesterday.

DMV1579: Pilgrimage?

CBS3016: Had to see a doctor in Manhattan.

DMV1579: Everything OK?

CBS3016: Mostly.

DMV1579: Mostly?

CBS3016: Next topic, please.

DMV1579: Visit the 'hood?

CBS3016: No. Manhattan only. Couldn't go to Park Slope. Too many ghosts.

DMV1579: I feel the same way.

CBS3016: Got out at Grand Central, took the subway uptown. When I got out, there was a group of musicians playing, and a woman jerking in a violent kind of dance. Guitarist in fatigues; sax player in thick gloves and arctic parka. Dancer in billows of black, wrapped in a knitted corset of cream. She had eyes painted on her eyelids, and her movements seemed like the shudders of an old ecstatic. A dervish. I thought they were burning incense somewhere, or dope, then I realized it was in her clothing and coming off in auras as she spun on the platform.

DMV1579: Contact high.

CBS3016: The music, well, I admit to being young once. The guitarist raked a pick across the strings, strangling out something guttural, which the drummer echoed, pulling his tom across the floor so that the legs gargled against the concrete. The sax player screeched Albert Ayler outtakes.

DMV1579: You whip out that iPhone and take videos? How can I live without them?

CBS3016: The sounds slowed, then swelled. The dancing wasn't beautiful, and the music wasn't good. Yet it was the deepest, best kind of good. It had heart – the way nothing has heart in a train station, just frozen fingers and worries about dinner. They didn't have a case out for money; they weren't selling anything. I wanted to know them.

DMV1579: Of course you did.

CBS3016: Because it felt like the purest exercise in joy, and the joy was contagious. That a group of people should decide, around a dinner table (here I'm sure it was wood, not particle board, and they'd hauled it off the street, or from a thrift store, into their shared kitchen) to do what they do, in a train station. To push the limits of dance, and music, and beauty, and to do it for nothing.

DMV1579: :-)

CBS3016: People came, and people went. I felt a strange solidarity with them, on the edges of a circle described by the whirling woman. I began to rock back and forth, then I realized that my toes were numb. Neuropathy at 60.

DMV1579: You and me both, sister.

CBS3016: As she spun, I saw her drop something from her sleeves. A few turns later, another. A cardboard square with some writing, some colors. Onlookers picked them up. It was clear that the cardboard squares were not a mistake. They were not dropped, they were placed. They were gifts.

DMV1579: Nice.

CBS3016: People started to collect them, regarding them with the hungry curiosity of anyone who knows that something is valuable without caring about what it actually is.

DMV1579: :-)

CBS3016: Suddenly, as if they'd heard something no one else could, the musicians left. Cardboard squares lay scattered across the subway tiles. They were CDs.

DMV1579: Wow.

CBS3016: I'm tempted to try and find that woman. Just to know something about her. Who is she, how did she get here? But I'm going to leave her alone. I don't want to spoil her magic with names and addresses and wrench her from dream to reality.

DMV1579: I love you. You are very wise.

November 8, 2017

CBS3016: Yes, please re-build my heart a bit at a time. Send me good news.

DMV1579: I will.

CBS3016: With love.

DMV1579: Flirt.

October 25, 2017

CBS3016: You've been much on my mind lately.

DMV1579: Well, you're always on my mind.

CBS3016: How did the move go? How's living there? When will you return my heart?

DMV1579: All these questions. Answers: Fine. Cold and lonely. Never never never.

CBS3016: I'll tell you what: each time you do something remotely good, write me with evidence. Then I'll get my heart back piece by piece, since I'll know a bit of it is in anything good you do.

DMV1579: Deal.

CBS3016: All the love.

DMV1579: Back atcha.

October 22, 2017

CBS3016: Autumn in CT. I can't hear the thump of the sea, but I know it's there. The woods – well, they're lovely, dark, and deep. Full of squirrels, chipmunks, raccoons. Deer. Ornithology of all type – jays, sparrows, finches – too many to name.

DMV1579: Robert Frost. Charlie Parker. I think winter's set in already.

CBS3016: Nobody asked you to move to MN. Anyway, went to NYC yesterday. Autumn in New York. Wish we could have shared it in high school.

DMV1579: That's a very long time ago.

CBS3016: Wish you could have been here.

DMV1579: So do I.

CBS3016: You're so far away.

DMV1579: Where life took me.

CBS3016: Where you took you.

DMV1579: You weren't there. Park Slope wasn't getting any cheaper. There wasn't any reason to stay. Besides, I had a good opportunity in Minneapolis.

CBS3016: Still, you could have moved closer.

DMV1579: Could have. Maybe it was just time for me to get out of New York.

CBS3016: I want to see you.

DMV1579: I want to see you, too. Very badly.

CBS3016: New York?

DMV1579: Halfway? Fort Wayne.

CBS3016: Just where I want to spend a long weekend. Garden spot of the Heartland.

DMV1579: Not even for me? Johnny Appleseed's grave.

CBS3016: Can't miss that!

DMV1579: Fort Wayne Philharmonic.

CBS3016: Be still my heart!

DMV1579: The Fort Wayne TinCaps – formerly the Fort Wayne Wizards.

CBS3016: Huh?

DMV1579: Midwest League. Class A baseball.

CBS3016: You embody romance, D.

September 29, 2017

CBS3016: Looking out at the woods now. The air is cool and a breeze has just moved in. I can almost smell the ocean. It's really lovely here, D.

DMV1579: There's no ocean in MN. Just prairie. Lakes and prairie. And no you.

September 15, 2017

CBS3016: Minneapolis? Really? They ever get summer up there?

DMV1579: It's a 48-hour virus. Actually, it's quite lovely. The lakes and all.

CBS3016: Sounds nice.

DMV1579: It's a good move for me. Out of New York. Copy supervisor for a nice agency. Good shop. Nice gig for a guy my age. Hard to cobble together decent money from part-time work. And people aren't so quick to hire folks our age anymore.

CBS3016: And pay for benefits!

DMV1579: Right. Not huge money, but enough to live on. Enough in a time of diminished needs and expectations. Enough for a ticket out of New York.

CBS3016: I know how that feels.

DMV1579: It's good here. Pace slower. Well, anything's slower than New York.

CBS3016: Even CT.

DMV1579: I was lucky to get it. Friend hooked me up. Get to work with some kids.

CBS3016: Like forty-year-olds.
DMV1579: Right.
CBS3016: Good luck.
DMV1579: Thanks.
CBS3016: It's very far away.
DMV1579: Yes. Yes, it is.
June 1, 2017

CBS3016: I see that life is a question of adjusting to what you get – not what you wish you got. You can't always get what you want.
DMV1579: Thank you, Ms. Jagger.
CBS3016: :-)
DMV1579: Adjusting. That's the ballgame.
May 15, 2017

DMV1579: The more baggage you bring, the less able you are to move forward.
CBS3016: I don't want to move forward. I want to move back. With you.
May 8, 2017

DMV1579: Happened again. Walking by a parking garage. Saw a woman from behind – your hair, your build, your stance. For a second I thought... but no.
CBS3016: Hopes dashed again.
DMV1579: Mark Knopfler wrote, it's your face I'm looking for on every street.
CBS3016: Damn, I miss you.
April 29, 2017

DMV1579: Out of the corner of my eye I saw someone with your walk. Turned happy, expectant. It wasn't you, of course. Wishful seeing.
CBS3016: I drink alone at bars .
DMV1579: I would, too, but I'd miss you too much.
CBS3016: Catch me up on things, and I'll pretend you're here, sipping along.

DMV1579: I'd go on the stoop now and do the same, except it ain't the same.

April 10, 2017

DMV1579: Went out today. Didn't please me. It wasn't the same without you.

CBS3016: Looking out at the woods here in Stony Creek. Full of nostalgia and strange whispers from the trees. My heart feels sick. Sick enough to leave Alan. Chuck it all and come back to Park Slope. But I do love him. And even if I didn't, I wouldn't want to break his heart. He's too kind for that. Maybe I could pretend it's Italy in the 1880s, spend a few months in the land of everything-is-so-expensive, come back, and somehow make amends. Paper it over.

DMV1579: Really?

CBS3016: Figured I'd keep it in my back pocket. Mind if I share your residence?

DMV1579: Anything to get you back.

March 25, 2017

CBS3016: The job search, well, Connecticut ain't all it's cracked up to be.

DMV1579: What is?

CBS3016: It's looking increasingly that I am coming up empty handed after having gone for the golden arrow, flown too close to the sun, attempted to hold the ocean in my hands only to find myself with dripping socks.

DMV1579: At least you've maintained your sense of humor. Or the absurd.

CBS3016: Not a single interview from the 16 massage therapy positions I applied for. Too old. Too uncredentialed. Too *something*. I'll try again, but at our age I'm already disillusioned and exhausted.

DMV1579: Can't say that I blame you. Thought that all your experience might do the trick for you. Doesn't help to say been there, done that, retooled. Way of the world.

CBS3016: I had this clever Plan B where I would use my skills and just do the health club scene, but this, too, turns out to be disillusioning and exhausting.

DMV1579: Cold comfort, but we've all been there.

CBS3016: When I investigated Plan B more thoroughly, I found it will require years of working for somebody else to become capable enough to do what I already know how to do. Years of slave wages. Years of toting that barge, lifting that bale. I simply don't have it in me. I won't. I can't.

DMV1579: Cold comfort II, at least Alan's making a living.

CBS3016: A good living. But still...

DMV1579: Still...

CBS3016: I know I have skills useful to all sorts of industries. Office visits. I'm excellent at talking to people, discerning where they hurt, how to fix it. I also know what I really want out of my work and what makes me feel alive – connecting with people, fostering greater awareness of wellness and their bodies. And I know that this is possible in lots of places. But I don't know how to find them. I'm not in *my* place, and I don't know where to go, what to do, how to start.

DMV1579: No matter what anyone says, staying in one place, and being known, makes all the difference.

CBS3016: Old school.

DMV1579: Sometimes it's the only school. The *chi* of land, of place.

CBS3016: :-(

DMV1579: Separate what you like to do and what you *need* to do to keep body and soul together, put food on the table, have liquor on the shelf. Pick an industry and pursue it. Conferences, contacts, cold calls, trade associations. Don't give up. As a famous counselor put it, getting a job *is* a job.

CBS3016: I need help. And soothing. And whiskey. Gimme two out of three and we'll call it square.

DMV1579: Booze? You gotta show up here for that.

CBS3016: Any time?

DMV1579: Any time.

February 17, 2017

DMV1579: There are days – and this is one of them – when I feel as if a piece of myself has been torn off and is living in Stony Creek, far, far away.

CBS3016: I bet you say that to all the girls.

DMV1579: No. No, only you. Forever you.

February 2, 2017

CBS3016: I was thinking of you this weekend. Thinking of slipping away, coming back to see you. But schedules just didn't jive.

DMV1579: Anything to get you back.

CBS3016: Damn.

DMV1579: You can say that again.

CBS3016: Damn.

DMV1579: About right.

January 15, 2017

CBS3016: Surprise! We're leaving.

DMV1579: What? Where? Your lovely apartment?

CBS3016: Park Slope. Alan says we've been priced out.

DMV1579: Say it ain't so! Where you going?

CBS3016: Going where the wind don't blow so strange. Where life is cheap and expectancy is short.

DMV1579: Thank you, Robert Hunter. Queens?

CBS3016: And coffee ain't five bucks a clip.

DMV1579: Where might that be?

CBS3016: Actually, Alan got a great job with the CT M.E. lab. Great end-of-career move. His cousin found us a great deal on a house. Estate sale. Woody *cul-de-sac*.

DMV1579: Sounds like a horn player. Or a utility infielder. Now batting, the shortstop, Number Twenty-Five, Woody Cul-De-Sac.

CBS3016: LOL

DMV1579: I bet Alan suspected something. Feral. Smelled me on you.

CBS3016: That's your guilt. Nascent paranoia. He never did. I *know* that.

DMV1579: K

CBS3016: Will you stay?

DMV1579: For the time being. Price is price. And it won't be the same without you.

CBS3016: It's still beautiful.

DMV1579: Indeed. Just a lot less beautiful without you.

November 23, 2016

CBS3016: I was riding the bus, not fifteen minutes ago, having had a belt or two of tequila, composing an email to you. I had to put it away, though. Started to weep.

DMV1579: But we're here. Cosmically linked. Stardust in the bones.

CBS3016: Man, do I miss you. You're a part of me in ways I couldn't have imagined. This is an ache I'm going to have to live with. I'm happily married. I love Alan. Yet...

DMV1579: Maybe it's New York; subset, Park Slope; the madness of it.

November 3, 2016

CBS3016: It's lovely here today.

DMV1579: Yes, it is.

CBS3016: The birds, the bees, the trees outside my window – just lovely.

DMV1579: Glad you like it.

CBS3016: I'd take my laptop into the park with me, but I don't want to sully the beautiful moments outdoors. I just want to *be* there, not use it as a backdrop.

DMV1579: What a beautiful place to live.

CBS3016: I don't ever want to leave.

October 10, 2016

CBS3016: I wish you could come over here right now.

DMV1579: No more than I do.

CBS3016: I can see Prospect Park. I love looking at it in the dark. The rolling tree-tops, barely visible in the moonlight. So beautiful in their quiet consolations.

August 1, 2016

CBS3016: Mourning doves this morning. Red cardinals and song sparrows. It's still cool in the mornings. Dew glistens on plants and little grass patches.

DMV1579: You make it sound so lovely.

CBS3016: It is. The sun will scorch it later, but right now Park Slope is paradise

July 3, 2016

CBS3016: No, Alan doesn't know. Doesn't suspect. Not a thing.

DMV1579: How do you know?

CBS3016: He's a wonderful man, and I love him desperately. But he's also the most obvious man in the world. So I know.

DMV1579: K

June 21, 2016

CBS3016: Alan's out of town. Let's have a candlelight dinner. Room full of candles, burning, aromatic, everywhere. Shadows, dancing, undulating, igniting our desire.

DMV1579: I'll have a chilled chardonnay there in an hour.

CBS3016: Make it a half-hour. Make it 10 minutes. Make it *now!*

DMV1579: You're on.

June 12, 2016

DMV1579: You're like a ballerina.

CBS3016: People have called me a lot of things over the years, D, but hardly...

DMV1579: You have a lightness combined with sinews. Light enough to soar, tough enough to make those leaps.

CBS3016: LOL

DMV1579: You're sinewy. Chewy.

CBS3016: I used to see you, with Barbara, with Alan, and wondered – for *years* – what this might be like. What *we* might be like.

DMV1579: And...

CBS3016: And, well, the interface of dreams and reality, they're never the same.

DMV1579: No, they're not.

CBS3016: I'm sure you've wondered what this would be like.

DMV1579: :-)

CBS3016: Let's put it this way: I never thought you'd pay *any* attention to me – ever. You were Barbara's lover. Rachel's before that. Discrete, I know, but everyone knew it.

DMV1579: I try not be *too* obvious.

CBS3016: Now that I'm getting all this attention it's a little weird. More than a little.

DMV1579: You did bring it on yourself, remember.

CBS3016: I always wished you were interested in me. Not bold or brave enough to pursue you, but...

DMV1579: So as any editor or ad manager would ask, why this story at this time?

CBS3016: Tired? Bored? Bio clock long overdue? I don't know. Time to take the plunge. Maybe nothing more than that.

DMV1579: So what *are* you doing after the orgy?

CBS3016: Maybe *over*thinking ruins the experience for many people.

DMV1579: Maybe.

CBS3016: When you actually break down the many layers of a sexual relationship...

DMV1579: Sounds *way* too much like work.

CBS3016: On days when I feel vulnerable, or question my balance, I can't help myself.

DMV1579: Four Tops.

CBS3016: All told, dear one, you have no idea how much more at ease I am having told you what I did. You would make a good mother. Men can be – and some are – much more nurturing than women.

DMV1579: Father Damian. Gimme a sec whilst I rustle up my Roman collar.

May 29, 2016

CBS3016: Let's get together. I miss you.

DMV1579: At the very minute you wrote I went through a pang of missing you, too.

CBS3016: Joined forever at the hip, I suspect.

DMV1579: Perhaps we were lovers in previous lives as well.

CBS3016: I'm sure we were. Anyway, please let's get together.

DMV1579: Come up now. We'll leave the windows open.

CBS3016: And have Singapore Slings afterwards.

May 15, 2016

CBS3016: When lilacs last in the dooryard bloom'd...my sun porch windows are all open, the aroma filling the entire apartment.

DMV1579: Whitman again. Lucky you, facing the street. I face the alley in back. I get everyone's trash.

CBS3016: The aroma is fabulous. Mine, not yours.

April 28, 2016

CBS3016: You are exceedingly sweet.

DMV1579: Let me be honest, not arch. Not my habitual terse. Yes, I am. It's the result of years of working on myself, of consciously putting others, and their troubles, before me and my desires. I am proud of myself for doing that. A friend – well, maybe not such a friend – called it a pathology. Call it what you will, I consistently think that there is no higher service – rent to be paid on this planet, if you will – than doing what I can, even if it's only a kind word, for other people.

CBS3016: I may bother you at times, being repetitious or boring or obvious.

DMV1579: No. Never.

CBS3016: But I value you in so many ways.

DMV1579: As I do you.

CBS3016: I'll never leave you. And I'll never leave Park Slope, which I love so much.

April 10, 2106

CBS3016: We have so much to say to each other.

DMV1579: Yes, we do.

CBS3016: You *listen* to me. Alan doesn't. He pretends to, dear man, but he really doesn't. You do. Thank God for you, D. My love and my savior.

DMV1579: I love it when you talk dirty.

March 23, 2016

CBS3016: We're passing notes back and forth like schoolgirls.

DMV1579: :-)

March 3, 2016

CBS3016: I'm thrilled and gratified to count you as my lover. My privilege, believe me. You are a jewel (gem, if you think jewel is too feminine. I don't – but I'm not you.) In my way, I can only say thank you for your vast friendship. I value it all.

DMV1579: :-)

CBS3016: Of course you're smiling. Smiling boyfriends – their kind words and encouragement – are the best thing in life. They give me strength to keep on. I have a wonderful husband whom I love. But it's been a long time between smiling boyfriends.

February 15, 2016

CBS3016: It was wonderful.

DMV1579: Yes, it was.

CBS3016: I love Alan. I truly do. He's a good man. And a kind man. But he doesn't know. And he doesn't get it.

January 12, 2016

CBS3016: You and me and Alan. We have *so much* to say to each other!

DMV1579: Indeed we do. And so much *not* to say.

CBS3016: I'm blushing.

DMV1579: We had a *Potemkin* moment the other day, Claire. The sunlight glinted off your glasses, turning them opaque, obscuring my view of your eyes. There's a visual like that in Eisenstein's film: I saw only what your glasses reflected, only what was around you.

CBS3016: It was you, my heart.

DMV1579: If it was me, it was you inside.

December 28, 2015

DMV1579: You love it when you flirt with me in front of Alan.

CBS3016: I do love him, but he just doesn't get it.

DMV1579: Why should he? He trusts you.

CBS3016: He trusts you, too.

DMV1579: It would never occur to him not to. It would never occur to him to ask why you keep finding excuses to have me over.

CBS3016: No, it wouldn't. He's a wonderful man. But he's not you.

DMV1579: He thinks I'm his best friend.

CBS3016: You *are* his best friend. You're my best friend, too. Only in a different way.

DMV1579: Right. That's not what I meant.

CBS3016: Sure you did.

DMV1579: Our European Romance.

CBS3016: Our Continental Scherzo.

December 15, 2015

CBS3016: Sex with you is...daunting.

DMV1579: Never heard it described that way, exactly.

CBS3016: It was a true out of body – *extasis* – experience.

DMV1579: We'll have to have a very long time to talk about this.

December 3, 2015

CBS3016: Furtive, guilty pleasures.

DMV1579: All the protocols, the rituals, of keeping secrets; the baggage of betrayal.

CBS3016: Fraught with time and space, freighted with odors and stains.

DMV1579: And desire.

November 25, 2015

DMV1579: Let's be honest.

CBS3016: For once.

DMV1579: Sure, for once. You love Alan.

CBS3016: Yes. Yes, I do. He's a dear man. So, yes, I do.

DMV1579: But you also love conning and cuckolding him.

CBS3016: Do I contradict myself? Very well, I contradict myself. I am large. I contain multitudes.

DMV1579: Walt Whitman. How 'bout Hank Williams? Your cheatin' heart? Or garden-variety low self-esteem? Or…?

CBS3016: Stop, please. I'm tired. Leave it at I love you both – in different ways.

DMV1579: Fair enough.

November 18, 2015

CBS3016: Canine and feline.

DMV1579: ???

CBS3016: Alan's canine. Loyal. Straightforward. Stalwart.

DMV1579: Stalwart?

CBS3016: You know what I mean. He called me his best friend.

DMV1579: You are.

CBS3016: I know that.

DMV1579: And I?

CBS3016: Are feline. Elusive. Self-absorbed. Self-possessed.

DMV1579: If you say so.

November 10, 2015

CBS3016: Alan really likes you.

DMV1579: I really like Alan.

CBS3016: Even though you're sleeping with his wife.

DMV1579: The right hand doesn't know that it has a left hand.

CBS3016: He can't get enough of you.

DMV1579: How flattering.

CBS3016: Nor, apparently, can I.

DMV1579: Even more flattering. And alluring.

CBS3016: So, apparently, you have seduced us both. In a manner of speaking.

DMV1579: In a manner of speaking. I did see *Cabaret*. Read the book, in fact. Christopher Isherwood. *Berlin Stories*. A minor classic.

November 1, 2015

CBS3016: How do I love thee? Let me count the ways.

DMV1579: No, allow me. You held me fiercely 'round the neck. Said in hushed tones that you'd always wanted to do this, with me, since the first time you saw me. Then you took me, fiercely, hurriedly, insatiably, until you were indeed sated.

CBS3016: Lothario!

DMV1579: Don't worry. I'll respect you in the morning.

CBS3016: Oh, I don't care about that. As long as you love me in the morning.

October 25, 2015

CBS3016: I love Alan – you know that. It's just that everything about him is boring and predictable. He has a marked absence of passion and spontaneity. He has his routines and is content with them. He isn't a Swiss watchmaker, D. He's a Swiss watch.

DMV1579: So along came Jones.

CBS3016: In a manner of speaking, yes.

October 20, 2015

CBS3016: Claire Brevard Stanton, actually. The Brevards are old money. Old *old* money. Nineteenth-century New York railroad money. Alan's family, the Stantons, are parvenus. Only society doctors – when such a thing existed – for a century.

DMV1579: Well, ex-*cuse* me!

CBS3016: A little pro bono. Precious little pro bono. Just enough to keep up appearances. Just enough to let them show their faces at Ladies Aid dinners.

DMV1579: That explains everything.

CBS3016: Right. And the Vrabels?

DMV1579: Not *those* Vrabels. Unrelated Vrabels. Working-class Vrabels. Common enough name. Means sparrow. But this being Ellis Island America, could be a corruption of something else. I don't know. I've thought about changing it. But I always run out of interest and energy. Doesn't seem important enough for the hassle.

CBS3016: That's me all over: slumming.

October 13, 2015

CBS3016: It was wonderful.

DMV1579: Yes. Yes, it was.

October 8, 2015

CBS3016: Shall we be lovers, then, marry our fortunes together?

DMV1579: The question is as sudden as it is disarming, Paul Simon.

CBS3016: Pleasant luncheons, conversations in the park.

DMV1579: Sounds like you've done this before.

CBS3016: What makes you think I haven't? Now it's the directness of age, D. I'm 58. You're 56. There's nothing left to say. No horse play. No clever pick-up lines. Life at our age is so obvious. There's only one place to go, in our era of fading ability. It's sex. Sex or nothing.

DMV1579: The, ah, proverbial offer I can't refuse.
September 29, 2015

DMV1579: You're finding ways to run into me.
CBS3016: Yes. Yes, I am.
DMV1579: Mrs. Robinson, I think you're trying to seduce me.
CBS3016: Yes. Yes, I am.
DMV1579: How do you know I'm seducible?
CBS3016: A woman always knows. *Always* knows.
DMV1579: And you know about me.
CBS3016: Oh, I *know* about you.
September 20, 2015

DMV1579: What I most like about you is the way you tell every story in hushed, breathless tones, as if each narrative were fraught with enormous import. Arch, knowing, as if it's the tip of the proverbial iceberg, as if every word conceals great ironies and truths.
CBS3016: Do I?
DMV1579: Oh, absolutely.
CBS3016: How entertaining for you.
DMV1579: Sure is.
September 18, 2015

CBS3016: You've always been around. It seems as if I've known you forever.
DMV1579: No, not forever. Ten years, maybe. Maybe more.
CBS3016: Some days it seems like a thousand years ago.
DMV1579: I had just moved here from Sandy Frisco, where I had been working on a now-defunct magazine called *American Continent*. Alan and I met at a committee for the library. We hit it off.
CBS3016: All those dinner parties. All that earnest committee work. You used to come with...
DMV1579: Rachel.
CBS3016: Right. Rachel. Later Barbara. But first Rachel. I remember her well. Anorexic little thing. All those ear piercings. I always wondered how all that metal didn't tear the ears off her head.

DMV1579: She was a convenient place to hang out. Not much of a thinker. Not much of a conversationalist. Didn't much care for sex.

CBS3016: Sounds fab.

DMV1579: She seemed like a good idea at the time, Claire. Rachel was never demanding, never said no. Never really said yes, either. Enjoyed being admired, needed, with a man. Sex was a small price to pay. A little pushing, a little poking, a little wetness, a brief clean-up – and *voila!* A relationship.

CBS3016: You make it sound so carnal, so mechanical.

DMV1579: It was. She was. She was the path of least resistance.

CBS3016: And...

DMV1579: It fizzled out. You know.

CBS3016: I do indeed.

September 15, 2015

CBS3016: We've got to stop meeting like this.

DMV1579: Who is this?

CBS3016: Claire. Alan gave me your address.

DMV1579: Alan gave it to you?

CBS3016: Well, no, Damian. Actually, I stole it from his computer.

DMV1579: Aha.

CBS3016: Liberated it. Nice running into you this morning

DMV1579: Nice morning to be run into. Just beautiful.

CBS3016: It's a beautiful neighborhood.

DMV1579: Park Slope is.

CBS3016: I love Park Slope

DMV1579: It's got everything. Age. Charm.

CBS3016: Good bones.

DMV1579: Right.

CBS3016: I was born and raised here. I *belong* here. I never want to leave.

September 10, 2015

WINTER DAWN

▼

DAVENPORT, IOWA

The sun rose, a grimy yellow through the mist and naked trees, a cold, lifeless dawn spread out across the gray sky.

Not much there. Not much to understand. I know.

Please don't get me wrong, Ms. Beltran. I realize you have to conduct these interviews, case histories, the kind of family gleanings that might help make your job easier or my wife more comfortable. I understand that. And I'm grateful for it. I'm just not used to it, that's all. I've spent most of my life listening to other people, so I'm really not used to talking. So, sure, I'll try to give you what you need.

I'm sure you've heard this a thousand times, Ms. Beltran. Grania was fine – more than fine, really – until she wasn't.

Oh, sure, she was a bit forgetful – but at our age who isn't? And there's the absent-minded professor aspect. She was always so busy with her tests and her papers, her lectures and her students, that sometimes she lost track of simple details. But that's to be expected, right? Mind somewhere else and all that.

Then one day, unexpectedly, she lost it in class, and, understandably upset, had to leave. After that, it was a quick departure from her department. A matter of days.

We thought – well, we must have been in denial. We thought that she was just overworked, and that a little rest would make a world of difference. We even talked about getting her reinstated.

The rest helped, for about five days, until she got lost driving. Stopped for a very long time at a green light, Grania was approached by a police officer, who took one look at her, took her out of her car, and called me.

Then she was incontinent. Then she couldn't bathe or dress herself.

Then, well, you know the three questions: was she falling, wandering, hurting herself? No, yes, and no. That *yes* has me here today. Because, yes, she needs to be watched 24 hours a day. That's far more than I can provide at home – even with help. I know that you know this: Grania is better off here, in a locked unit with 24-hour care.

Life is loss? Well, perhaps you're right Ms. Beltran. Although that's a cheerful thought, isn't it?

Right. Best to be prepared.

Family. Grania and I have one child, a daughter, Brianna. She's 40 now, lives in Cedar Rapids. Hawkeye born and bred. No, never married, but has another common-law. How many is this in her voyage of serial monogamy? I really don't know. Maybe this one will last. Maybe not. I don't know that, either. Anyway, this one gave her a baby – or maybe she took her from him. I don't know. Anyway, Grania and I have a granddaughter. Beatrice, but they call her Beanie, a happy, healthy little two-year-old girl. We're grateful for her.

I would be lying if I didn't tell you I worry about Brianna. She's so ill-equipped. So short-sighted. So self-absorbed. She just kind of bumps along. As if she sees no future, refuses even to consider the concept. Well, maybe none of us do until the future ups and smacks us on the snout.

You know the drill. First, re-orient. Grania would say something completely incorrect – *I never had any babies*, for example. When I reminded her that we have a daughter, she'd laugh and nod and say, *of course, how silly of me. Old Forgetful Jones.*

Next, of course, go with the flow. Who knows *where* those radio signals originate? She'd been a gypsy dancer – fluttering her fingers as if she had castanets. She'd been a Hawaiian cane cutter. She was a WAVE on Omaha Beach. Of course none of it was even remotely accurate. Nevertheless, I would agree with her and proceed with the conversation. As far as it went.

For as quickly as it switched on, it switched off, and Grania was an entirely different person somewhere else.

It was like spinning a radio dial.

No, no, I'm OK, thanks. Thanks for asking. I'm OK. Really. Sometimes, well sometimes it's hard, but I'm OK.

Winter Dawn. Nursing home. Skilled-care facility. People incapable of doing for themselves, far too difficult for aging family members. Dementia and other infirmities. The things we never thought we'd think about.

We tend to lump them all together, Ms. Beltran, and day-to-day for the families diagnoses don't matter much. Dementia, senility, Alzheimer's – all I know is that in lay terms her brain is more or less melting. Losing function. Memory, our most sophisticated human trait, goes first. Along with language. Then fine motor skills – fingers, hands. Finally, eating, even breathing. The brain, clogged, rendered into mush, can't remember how to function. Ultimately, the signals to the heart stop.

No, Ms. Beltran, it's hardly pretty. Not pleasant. But it's what Grania's going through, although she doesn't realize it because she can no longer remember who or what she was. Barring an unforeseen, undiagnosed miracle, she will never recover, never get better. I know that our task is to make her safe and comfortable.

When she can no longer speak, how much will she understand? We're not certain. The important thing is to keep her in the circle as long as we can. Look at her, smile at her, talk to her. Hold her hands. Don't let go – physically, emotionally, spiritually. There's *always* someone there – even when it seems there isn't.

I like the fact that Winter Dawn is out of town, past the last tract houses. What became of the old Adler farm, or so I'm told. Summer corn and sorghum. I can see the corn stubble out there, pushing up through the season's first snow.

This is a nice facility, Ms. Beltran. One story for a reason? They can't navigate stairs? And the falling risk? I get it. The things we don't think about until we do.

Clean, bright. Well, a Winter Dawn.

I hope you don't mind me looking. Nice family, Ms. Beltran. Beautiful children. Books on aging. MSW from ISU. No, I've never been to Ames. Never had any reason.

And those lovely photos – family camping trips. Nice. Canoeing in Minnesota. Rafting on the Colorado – that must have been fun. Those times are irreplaceable.

I can see it out your window, Ms. Beltran. As the winter sun sets early, and darkness embraces the land, I can see the desolation, the uneven surface, icy tufts on the snow.

Dementia is like watching a house melt – or be torn apart by an explosion. Here's a door left standing, a lone window, half a wall. The rest is missing. Bit by bit, things evaporate. As soon as you figure out what's here, it's gone.

Then the shadow crosses over you, and you realize that you, too, will pass. No, it's not frightening. It's very calming, in fact. A sign, a bit of precognition, that it's time to think about things, get them in order. While the walls are still standing and you can.

One of the last conversations Grania and I had, before she began to slip under, was one of our typical contretemps about life – one of the philosophical discussions she loved so much, generally over black coffee and the Sunday *Des Moines Register*. I know what you say, I said, and we agree to disagree. You say that when one says *however*, it obviates everything that's said prior to it.

As you no doubt remember, I added, I beg to differ. *However* alters. It ameliorates. But it does not obviate. It does not cancel.

So be it. We disagreed.

I kept Grania at home as long as I could. Bathed her, fed her, dressed her, combed her hair. Finally, it got to be too much. The house had too many hazards – everything from the stove to open doors, light sockets to the medicine chest. Between child-proofing and constant cleaning, things became too challenging.

Sure, it's very quiet, very lonely at home. Thanks for asking. Sure, I'm rattling around in a big house, far too big for me. Sure, at some point I'll have to clean it out, and sell it. Takes time, though. And energy. It'll be quite a chore. What's the line about vainly fighting the old ennui? And inertia. Easier to stay where I am. For the time being.

Forgive me for smiling, but, no, my daughter can't help. Won't? I don't know about won't. Probably not. But certainly can't. No, I'm on my own.

Son-in-law? I don't know that I have a son-in-law. What day is it?

I'm also not ready to dispose of her stuff – perhaps the school would want her books and papers. I have no idea. I do know I'm not ready to go through mine. Most of what I have would have to go and, no, I'm not prepared to do that right now. No.

An earthy aroma of early spring rose from the ground this morning. The cold leached up like ice melting.

Six-month review? I think things are going well with Grania, yes. You tell me.

I do like the way you hold her hands. You are very loving, Ms. Beltran, that's obvious. You seem to be telling her everything that we're saying. Like Annie Sullivan and Helen Keller. Grania seems to understand. Perhaps she does. Perhaps that's only wishful thinking on my part. But she seems comforted, not agitated, which is certainly comforting to me.

Grania used to be able to process large amounts of information – that was the historian in her. Whole oceans of facts and theories and personalities dancing on the proverbial head of a pin. Then like an aperture, or a sudden cataract, her field of vision, of understanding, became constricted, her retention became smaller and smaller and increasingly small. Within a year or so I'd read to her, little things, and she couldn't remember them from one minute to the next. I could repeat myself, verbatim, a dozen times, and she'd retain none of it. Finally, I stopped.

Yes, thanks, I did try to make her room as cheerful and familiar as possible. Photos of the two of us – a memorable vacation on Maui. Have you been there? Oh, you must!

Pictures of our daughter Brianna and our granddaughter Beatrice. A vacation we took with another couple – rented a lodge in Colorado, got snowed in. Huge fire in the fireplace, the four of us huddled in enormous wool sweaters, sipping whisky toddies, playing marathon bridge games. Had a wonderful time!

And our marvelous three-story gingerbread house, circa 1880. Yes, it took a *huge* amount of work to restore it to that pristine condition, and we're very proud of it. The sun room, a porch which we made into the 365-day room. The kitchen. And of course her third-floor office – the wide-angle shot makes it look bigger than it really is. Unfinished attic we finished – insulation, skylights, the works. She loved it up there.

I love the view from her window here, by the way – the sun on the cornfields. It's nice. Bright. Cheerful.

Well, we used to eat at Olive's Diner on Locust Street – have you ever been there? Oh, it's worth it, Ms. Beltran. Coffee in real china mugs. Eggs over easy. But instead of home fries – why send the money to Idaho? – Olive serves these wonderful hard-fried corn fritters, griddle-fried not deep-fried, stove-top like home fries. Crispy and crusty. Locally sourced corn, as they say these days. Means they buy it from Bill Stoddard right down the road. Sweet corn, not feed corn. *Never* feed corn. Never blue or red corn. Yellow sweet corn. Fried in real butter, just a hint of sugar in the batter, served with hot sauce and cinnamon. Can't beat 'em!

For that non-caffeinated afternoon pick-me-up I still enjoy Olive's strawberry milk shakes. The secret's in the preserves she puts up herself. Extra sugar, I bet. Olive never scrimps on the sweets!

No, I don't know how long I've been going there. Probably from the first day I opened up on Locust Street. I do know that the diner pre-dates me. Olive started it when her husband Dick was in the navy. Action in the North Atlantic. WWII. I remember him well – always wore a dark windbreaker, veteran's pin on the collar, tie, tan fedora. Called them his walkin'-into-town clothes.

Dick worked as her counterman, mixed a mean soda before sodas came pre-mixed. Now Dick, Jr. and his boy Tommy help out Olive, who's up there in years but still makes a mean batter! Three generations. Nice little Iowa family business.

Nothing special about it, Ms. Beltran, except the food. Nothing fancy. One item, though: in back of the counter there's a signed picture of young Bob Feller, from over in Van Meter, slicked hair, leather jacket, big smile as if he owned the entire world. Or at least the American League, which he did for a while.

Well, yes, I'm still right up the street. Perhaps you've seen it. Fred Mitchell Agency. Storefront right there on Locust. No? No matter. Strictly one-man shop. Mom-n-pop without the mom. Rotary, Chamber of Commerce. Use the front window to advertise the community. Boy Scout week. High school basketball. 4-H competitions. What folks around here spend their lives doing. I try to support that.

Insurance? No, you can't insure anything. You can't stop time. But you but can make the inevitable bumps a little smoother. So, no, insurance is not a panacea. Not even a guarantee. Just a little help at the right time. While people want to avoid risk, life *is* risk. We can anticipate it. Balance it. But we can't stop it. We have no antidotes to it – and anyone who tells you otherwise is selling you a bill of goods. When – not *if*, but *when* – you get hurt, it won't be too bad. But you can't stop it.

I try to be non-invasive. Help people protect themselves.

No, I'm not retiring, not yet. I'm not ready. Besides, I don't know what I'd do. Sure, I could sell the agency – I have a lot of good accounts and even more good will. But I don't know what I'd do with myself.

Forgive me for smiling, but, no, living with, or near, my daughter Brianna is not an option. And I'm not ready to play canasta all day at the Golden Age Club.

What I found with Grania, before she slipped under, was that I had to take her, do for her. When I smiled and made her feel comfortable I could get her to do anything. But if I showed anger or frustration, she'd sense danger and refuse.

You know, Ms. Beltran, like everyone else in Davenport I hear the trains howling in the distance. Americans are fidgety. We've always had a romance with trains. But trains aren't inherently romantic. They're loud and jerky and frequently uncomfortable. It's just that trains go somewhere else. That's how we got here. How we live. Not by family. Not by land. Somewhere else.

Grania's somewhere else now, Ms. Beltran, isn't she?

Have you looked outside? Perfect early summer light. If life has taught me nothing else, it's to be happy with simple daily pleasures. They're all gone too soon.

I do like your line, Ms. Beltran, and I've used it with my clients a lot. When they point to their gray hair, I tell them, "don't think of it as gray. Think of it as silver. And you've won." They all smile. So thank you for that.

Sure. Grania always thought of herself that way, as a winner. She was always so demonstrative, so articulate. So *solid.* From the first time I met her.

How *did* we meet? One of those chance encounters that changes everything. I was working in radio in New York – I'll tell you about that another time, if you have the time and the interest, and I wouldn't blame you if you had neither. No, I wasn't an actor. I was a sound engineer. A sound engineer is not the low man on the totem pole. He's the part of the totem pole under the ground that holds up the rest of the totem pole.

Anyway, in radio none of us other than the execs and what they called *the talent* were making very much money, so we ate very frugally. I usually grabbed lunch at the Automat – Horn & Hardart, all those self-serve soups and sandwiches for nickels! Once a month, on payday, I'd treat myself to a nice meal at Schrafft's. One day, there I was, with all the wait staff and white tablecloths and all, and there was nowhere to sit. With the clock ticking – I had less than an hour – I spotted an empty seat at a table. It didn't hurt that on the other side sat a very lovely young lady. I asked if she minded, she smiled and said she didn't. Three months later we were married.

Grania always joked that we were introduced by a bowl of creamed cauliflower, which was about right. Well, that was a very long time ago.

These days her memory is like a snow squall on the prairie, a white out that obfuscates some things. Confuses others. Reveals yet others. It's always a challenge. Always a moveable feast.

Well, for all of us memory is less a flash than a series of flashes, a mosaic perhaps, things always there, a tapestry.

Memory is also as flighty and fickle as a jaybird.

I have what Grania doesn't: time. Time to let the dust settle. Let the noise abate.

No question about it, Grania was – listen to me, talking about her in the past tense. Well, she isn't what she was, so maybe that's correct. Anyway, Grania was an intellect from a family of noted intellects. She enjoyed it, the conferences, the papers, the journal articles. She found it all very challenging, very satisfying.

I was always happy for her.

You know what? She asked me the other day who those people are on her wall, what that house was. I knew that was coming, sooner or later, but still --

Yes, thanks, a tissue would be handy. Thanks.

I don't know if Grania knows me any longer – I don't think so. How could she? She doesn't even know who she is. No, there's no recognition. Not even a flicker. I'm pleasant, and, as a living creature she obviously enjoys the physical warmth. I think that's all there is. She's so blank when I see her.

Does it hurt? Since you ask, yes, Ms. Beltran, it's like a knife in my heart. How could it be otherwise?

Yes, thanks, a grief counselor would help. I don't see how it could hurt. Or give me any more pain than I already have.

I do love autumn – that blazing bright yellow light, stunning red leaves, cold blue sky.

I'm not morbid per se, but I often dream of death. How could I not? There are so many people I know who are card-carrying members of the Absent Friends Club.

Oh, no, they're not imaginary people. This isn't some made-up story, Ms. Beltran. They're very real. They embody the ravages of cancer, heart attacks, diabetes, and strong drink. They're people who were here, and are still here, one way or another, flitting in and out of our lives. Traces of who we once were.

I thought the other day about a fellow. I was 18, he was 19. Meaning that he was impossibly old and surely the most sophisticated man in the world. He had grown a mustache, which made him look so distinguished, so continental. I wondered what had happened to him. So I did a little detective work. He had married. Fathered children. Begat a business. And after a brief illness passed from Middle Earth, age 55.

That's the Absent Friends Club, Ms. Beltran. You think you know something about life. Then you hear about Charlie. Or Bob, who was pulling weeds in his backyard, yanked at a tough one, tumbled, split his head on a rock. Just like that.

We move, don't we, Ms. Beltran, through seasons? From fall, with its loss and redemption, to winter, with its death and anticipated rebirth.

So, no, thoughts of mortality aren't frightening. It's not resignation so much as serenity. Eternity. It seems normal, natural. It's all around us.

Loss presses on you, Ms. Beltran. It's an emptiness, a weight.

A legacy.

No, thanks for asking, but, no, I don't feel any guilt about what's happening. I realize that some people do. But I don't. I realize that it has nothing to do with me. That it's entirely organic and far beyond anyone's ability to create or control.

It would be the same as if she got cancer. That would hardly be my fault, either.

Sometimes I look at Iowa and see a landscape that appears like a time-worn photo, blacks and reds faded, leaving only yellows and blues. Green with no depth, no dimensionality, no shadows. Something still and quiet and past. Looking at it, we forget all the movement, all the haste and hurts that happened just before it was snapped, before time was irrevocably stopped. All we have left is the washed-out moment.

Autumn is not tragedy. Not a fall. More a depletion. A sigh. A retrenchment.

Just as the dull blue light of winter is not death. It is more dormancy. Because there is light. There is dawn.

No, I'm not from not New York City, where Grania and I met. I'm from way north of there, Lake Placid. Like many people did back then, I lived on a small family farm – a few maple trees, chickens, milk cows. Potatoes, corn, beans. That sort of thing. With the short growing season, things were pretty much hand-to-mouth. My dad also hired out to meet ends meet – and sometimes they didn't. The one luxury we had was an old radio set. I loved it; I loved *sound*. In northern New York there seemed no future in it.

After high school I went in the service. My time was sandwiched between wars; it was just before Korea, and America wasn't so eager to fight, at least not for a while. I was stationed in Germany, and as luck would have it was assigned to the Signal Corps. I had all the latest equipment and learned everything there was to know about radio.

Mustered out, I went straight to New York City. With my background it was easy to get a job. It didn't pay much, but I was young and didn't care. Back then it was easy to be poor in New York City. Besides, I loved radio. So there I was.

Yes, thank you, Ms. Beltran. I did meet with the grief counselor. She was very helpful. Carmella Cortez. You know her? I'm not surprised. Davenport is such a small town.

I will work through the grief. Get an early start on it. Because this – she, Grania – is not going to end well. And I can't let that become my *raison d'etre*. My permanent shroud. I have to allow myself to breathe. I can't let it define me.

Quick, funny story. There was an older woman waiting to speak with Ms. Cortez. When I told the woman that she looked familiar, which she did, she glared at me. "I'm a happily married women," she snapped.

Well, nerves twitch even in dead limbs.

Dusk seems thick, doesn't it? As if the ebbing light is indeed a particle heavy with weight. Or, alternatively, as if the light waves are infused with dust.

A couple of other members of the Absent Friends Club. Together, they illustrate the idea that life is active. You have to *want* to live. If you give up on living, life goes away. In both cases, both of them were perfectly healthy. Yet when their significant others died, so did they. Closed up like plants and passed.

That's why I worry about a cousin – one of Grania's cousins, actually. Jonathan used to be Mr. Outward Bound. Motorcycles. Motor boats. Mountain bikes. He was a man born for movement. Now all he wants to do is sit in a chair.

Given what I've seen, I don't think he's long for us now.

You know this as well I do, Ms. Beltran: memory, like life, is hardly static. It's fluid, malleable, changeable. Memory's a slippery slope. Spongy. Subject to both whim and weather. It's frightening, really, because we are only the sum total of who we were. Who we *think* we were. When that disappears, well, who are we?

So Dr. Kevorkian's question stands: when are you no longer you? When is life no longer worth living? When is it time to say goodbye while you can still understand?

Radio? Are you sure you want to hear about this? Stop me when it becomes tiresome.

I was a sound engineer, as I mentioned. Worked for various stations, worked free-lance. Even worked a bit with Rudy Van Gelder out in Englewood Cliffs. Was patient, had good hands. All those crackles and hisses and buzzes – I could wipe 'em clean like Windex on a bathroom mirror. Balance everything from multiple horns to multiple sound effects. I may have been in my twenties, but I was a seasoned veteran. And I loved it.

It was work, sure, but it was also fun. The pay wasn't great – but was good enough for a guy with no responsibilities. I was young and single. I didn't own a house in Westchester or a Duesenberg. I rented an efficiency apartment, rode the subway.

And I was wonderfully anonymous. I could walk down the street and never be bothered. I mean, who wanted to be Alan Ladd? He was always pestered. Always told he wasn't as tall as he seemed on the screen – which he wasn't. He was never allowed to be alone. Or normal.

It was a great medium because listeners had to be co-creators. Had to make up all the scenes in their heads. Radio incited their imaginations. We may have supplied all those glorious voices and terrific effects, but our listeners supplied the brain power.

We also presented good, crisp dramas. Articulate characters, clear stories, clear resolutions. Nothing fuzzy or messy like life. Nothing confusing. Nothing inconclusive.

And radio was clean. The whole family could tune in.

I always imagined the people listening, women in aprons and housedresses in the kitchen, dads in the living room, sweater and tie, pipe and newspaper. Entire families around the dining room table. A quieter, more civil time.

While we were good at our work – there's no doubt about that – I was always amazed at what people really *believed*. Oh, I don't mean *War of the Worlds* – Mr. Orson Welles being Mr. Orson Welles, things got out of hand. No, I mean they really believed Bob Bailey *was* Johnny Dollar. Or Truman Bradley. Great voice. *Great* voice. Hell of a nice guy. But when he went on TV's *Science Fiction Theater* – a room full of junk, like that pie pan with an ice pick in it! People thought he *was* a Nobel Laureate. They thought he knew all about science. What a hoot!

You'd be been amazed at our working conditions. Some places were so crummy that I was afraid I'd be electrocuted if I touched a wire or a dial.

Sure, they showed photos of nice studios, but not the cheap ones. *Never* the cheap ones. Man, were they cold in the winter and hot in summer! Some were little more than broom closets. Egg cartons as soundproofing would have been a step up. And try to find a chair! We were lucky that so many of the shows were short. So we could get out and sit down somewhere. Have a smoke and a sarsaparilla.

Part of my job was to edit out all the extraneous noise – street traffic, elevators, doors slamming. You name it. All of us, we worked hard and we worked long hours. Well, we were hungry. We were afraid we'd be replaced. We *had* to show up. There were multiple Boston Blackies, Charlie Chans, name it. The brand, the character, was more important than the people. Unless you were a big star, and there were very few of those, everybody else, especially in the technical end, was hired help. Which was fine. It beat working in a factory or a coal mine. And I never liked farming!

Sure, the top guys ate at the Algonquin, and we ate at the Automat, as I said. But it was better than army chow or a breadline.

Who did I know? Who didn't I know? Bob Bailey. He played Johnny Dollar from his head and his heart. Really sold it. A real gentleman off the air. If he saw us eating anywhere he'd always grab the check. Didn't want to be thanked. Just who he was.

Sid Greenstreet as Nero Wolfe – he sort of waddled through his part. Charming man, perfect manners, but never prepared. Listen to the old tapes. He's always a beat behind the action, sometimes two beats. Always sounds like he's groping for the right rhythm of the line – the right way to lead the action. No wonder that show didn't last!

Boris Karloff – I loved that voice, sugar crystals in butter. A kind, gentle man.

Howard Duff had a wonderful voice, was terrific as Sam Spade. He had the right mix of verve, nerve, and tough. He was better than Bogart, in my book. I never cared for Bogie's lisp and the affectations that, for me, always bordered on self-parody.

Who else? Dick Powell, a hugely talented man under-sung in his day and under-remembered today. He was a terrific singer – and terrific as Richard Diamond.

Bill Conrad had a weight problem and a great voice. Played so many roles. He was the first Matt Dillon on *Gunsmoke*. He wanted the TV role, but the network wanted someone more photogenic – taller, more rugged. They got Jim Arness, who made history. Bill was bitter, very bitter. But that was the business, and, frankly, he should have looked in the mirror. He should have known better. Truth be told, he was dreadful as Cannon. Well, most television is dreadful.

Inner Sanctum. It was a gas doing that one. All those weird sounds – and weirder voices! *Suspense*, too. *Another tale well calculated to keep you in.* The effects guys on that show were legend, deservedly so. One guy actually stabbed himself in the hand – ice-picking a head of cabbage – and kept on going. That's dedication!

Jack Webb – oh, on TV he got lost in all that clipped dialogue. And his hatchet face. But if you listen to his radio work – *Pat Novak, Jeff Regan*, especially *Pete Kelly's Blues* – you'll hear something entirely different. Listen to that velvet voice.

Dragnet, of course. Jack Webb owned the show, owned the part of Joe Friday. Brilliant guy, visionary, really understood drama, pacing. Made a perfect transition to TV. I did some work with him. He was a complete professional – and demanded the same from everyone around him. He was tough, but a true gentleman. Didn't have to flaunt his genius like Mr. Orson Welles.

Right. *The Shadow*. It's hard to believe he was only 22 when he began, in 1937. Half-a-dozen others played that part, but it was Orson who had the power to cloud men's minds, as anyone who ever worked with him knew. Half blarney, half bologna, he busted every budget – not to mention every pair of trousers – he ever had, then blamed everyone else. Genius? I don't know. I don't know what genius is.

Sure, he was vastly talented, there's no denying that – least of all by Orson himself. He did have a great voice. A fabulous voice.

At the very least he was a genius at self-promotion. You always knew it when he was around. And, to give him credit, he always surrounded himself with first-rate talent, people who'd make him look good, from sound engineers – just listen to *War of the Worlds* – to set designers and lighting assistants to wonderful actors – Joe Cotton and Aggie Moorehead and Ev Sloane. You've probably heard Ev 1,000 times but never knew it. He could bend his voice like salt water taffy. He could be anyone.

What I remember most about Orson is his bombast, body odor, and bad breath. One too many assignations. Well, he was the most seductive man I've ever met. One look into those endless eyes, one purr from that magnificent voice, and women simply melted. Then, great sleight-of-hand artist that he was, when he'd make that rose appear, they were his for the taking.

And he took!

He was such a show. He'd come dashing in at the last second – we were always *sure* that someone else would have to read his part – pick up the script, ask who his character was, and dive right in. No prep, no pre-read, no rehearsal. *Never* rehearsal. *Bang!* He could sight-read like a demon. Shakespeare, Sherlock Holmes, the Shadow – he'd just become the character. Just like that. Could read *anything* – first time through. He'd just nail it, any part, any time.

Then he'd dash out, over to some other studio. *Pardon my dust!* Damndest thing I've ever seen, riding around NYC in an ambulance, one performance to the next. What a mountebank!

Was Mr. Orson Welles a team player? Sure. Just as long as *he* was the team. All Orson all the time.

I worked a bit on *The Lives of Harry Lime*. There was Orson, by then a tubby, unshaven, sloppy man. If people could have seen him. Well, they did, finally. A fat fool shilling cheap wine and guesting on laughable TV shows.

Winter's coming, which always make me sad. Everyone says it's the light, which I think is a way of talking about death.

So it is with dementia patients. If the circuits are broken or blocked, even temporarily, they can't begin anything. If they can't see all the moves, can't see the end, they can't start. Far too overwhelming. It's the same with the rest of us, too. It's just that we can instinctively see where we're going and what we have to do. They can't.

How did Grania and I get to Davenport? After that chance encounter in Schrafft's?

Grania was living at a residential hotel for young women – very proper, the only way her parents would let her come to New York. At the time she had a two-year secretarial degree, and had found a job at *Mademoiselle* copy editing and retyping stories. It was long hours with a gnawed blue pencil and an ancient Underwood upright.

But Broadway was cheap, and the bright lights dazzled, and Schrafft's had those scrumptious menus – pineapple criss-cross pie, corn souffles, even corned beef and cabbage! For a girl from North Dakota, it was heaven!

Grania and I were married at City Hall. Sure, two could live as cheaply as one, and we did, but we were also pushing 30. Past it, in my case. Time to put away childish things. We had had our fling with New York. It's a hard place to live over time. There is a lot to do. But the lot takes money. And we didn't have much. We didn't see our futures there. It was time to be different people.

Do I feel sorry for myself? For leaving New York and radio? Not at all. Nature of the beast. Technology is a ravenous, shape-shifting beast. Voracious. Ever-changing. Like high-button shoes or adding machines, which went away, so did radio – or radio drama, at least. I was privileged to play a very small part in the Golden Age.

So as radio began to wither, and as Grania began to tire of clerical work, we decided to leave. We were both glad we'd come, but were both ready to make our separate peace with the city. A competitive, combative place. And loud. I've been noisy and I've been quiet, Ms. Beltran, and believe me, quiet is better. It was time for something smaller, more silent, more like home. Which for her was the prairie.

But North Dakota was a bit *too* step-down after the City That Never Sleeps.

And there was her family, which could be a bit suffocating. They never saw her as a 30-year-old married woman. She was still Little Granny, the skinny high school kid scratching out her homework at the dining room table.

She had family out here. And the ghost of Bix Beiderbecke. It was a good town. A good place to stay. Close enough to North Dakota so that she felt at home. Insurance? My grandfather was the first agent in the North Adirondacks. I never thought I'd follow him into the business, but a few night courses did the trick.

I never thought about this at the time, but these days I think that if you could say both our names in the same sentence, and have neither one of us embarrassed, I'll consider my life well spent.

North Dakota. No, she didn't know Teddy Roosevelt – we're not *that* old, Ms. Beltran. But, sure, she knew the Egstroms – the state population's very small, and it seems that everybody knows everybody else. She remembered Norma quite well – great voice, even as a girl. Very ambitious. Grania always smiled when she saw *Miss Peggy Lee* on TV.

The Egstroms more or less disowned Norma, at least at first. They could never understand how she could run away like that, a teenager. How she could leave them. How she could leave the *land*. Because that farm meant everything to them.

Anyway, when it was time to go we went, Grania and I. We were still young, or young enough, and figured we'd give Iowa a try. Over the years we became people we couldn't imagine we'd be when we were age 30.

No, we never kept in touch with anyone from New York. Either one of us. Closed the door. Another part of our lives. It was easy to leave. To be gone.

Sure, it's cold out this morning. The ground is colder than the air. I could feel the cold rise from the earth.

That stark yellow light knifes along the ground, across the frozen ground.

What did Grania do? By the time we moved to Davenport, Grania had decided to go back to school. She had that two-year secretarial degree, but, figured, being a fast learner, she'd go learn something. Went to Iowa, in Des Moines, for a college degree – and couldn't stop. No, the commute wasn't so bad – an hour each way. B.A., M.A., Ph.D. in history, specialty 19th-century Europe. Metternich. Congress of Vienna. All those insane alliances, endless wars, bloody rebellions. Look at France. Monarchy. Republic. Monarchy. Couldn't make up their minds.

Even for a professor she was noticeably smart. I ran to keep up with her. Well, I tried. Faked it well. I'm sure she saw through me, but was far too much a lady to let on.

She was an intellect from a family of intellects – albeit farmers, because that's how they could make a living. But their old farmhouse was full of books. And they read entire libraries! She got a job teaching at colleges around Davenport. Every year or so she gave seminars in her office at home. I'd be pouring over actuarial tables or liability claims, papers all over the dining room table, an old radio show on – there's a station out of Moline that plays old dramas – and I'd hear them tromping up and down stairs.

The winter light is clear, brilliant, like a guttering candle. Perhaps it knows that it, and the year, are dying.

You don't really want to get older, Ms. Beltran. Just like you don't want to get cancer. Or Alzheimer's. It just happens.

How *do* you cope with a long-term death sentence?

I marvel, Ms. Beltran, that faced with so much devastation, so much loss, you can remain so cheerful. So optimistic.

I would think that it would feel like walking uphill in snow. A friend was an oncology nurse. One day she couldn't take it anymore – all her patients died. So she switched over to pediatrics. And had a grand time!

You've seen Grania. She's suffered a complete loss of speech. As we knew she would. First, it was uncompleted sentences. Then word fragments. Then gibberish – just growls and mutters. Now, nothing. Just a tight, frozen smile. Her skin stretched taut across her cheekbones. And those glittering blue eyes. A vestige of humanity in her otherwise ruined face.

It was one of our last days at home, a bright, sunny winter morning. With the air clear and cold, and the sky a deep blue, I buttoned her pea coat up to her neck, put on her round wool hat – a multicolored soft fez. That coupled with her sallow skin – it had been turned inexplicably pale by her anti-depressants – gave Grania a slightly Asian cast. Wu Li, she called herself, and why not? Character is entirely a construct anyway. And with so much already slipping away, why not simply change?

I'm not great at metaphors, Ms. Beltran, never was. Not my forte. But I often think of Grania as a snake or a lizard. Oh, not in a bad way. Just the way she's traveled through these phases of her life. Like shedding a skin. She replaces one life with another. Leaving hardly any trace – certainly no memory – of one to another.

Me? I'm a regular Iowa Hawkeye now.

Well, no, I'm not. I never will be. I've just learned protective coloration. I've learned to bury the past – however benign, or not – and move on.

Bury the dead by the side of the road and keep pushing on.

It's the American way.

But Iowa's taught me a lot. It's taught me that life is not a lark, not a radio show, not even pay-for-hire. Life is growing into the role we *have* to play. We were *chosen* to play. The job we *have* to do.

I lost two close friends to cancer last fall. I am watching other friends die by inches. It's a tough time, Ms. Beltran. Soon they will join the Absent Friends Club.

I know times will get better, Ms. Beltran, it's just the waiting that wears me out. Because everything feels different all the time, and it just keeps slipping farther away. Every year the concrete hardens a little more. Sometimes now I think age, more than any other divide, may be the strongest, the fiercest to overcome. We are so good at forgetting.

A friend wrote to me, "of the ways to use an evening this was perhaps not on your list. Enhanced by the loving presence of others, and in celebration with us of the surety you feel, know that we support and understand you. Without the depths, it is harder to understand the heights. It is a new day.

Iowa still prays. We never know what we will find when we travel there, within and without."

You know, Ms. Beltran, every year I have a moment of real panic when I believe with perfect surety that winter will never leave. That the land will remain permanently frozen.

Then I recall the rich, fertile soil, fecund even, the crops, the corn, plates piled high with food, the cornucopia of our farmers' markets.

I see those winters, Ms. Beltran, I see them both: the glitter of the ice on the fields; the glitter of Grania's icy smile. I hear the dual silences. I see you holding her hands. I see her mute.

There is death and dying all around us, Ms. Beltran. But there is also life beginning beneath the earth. I see Grania. But I also see Beanie, a little girl whose life and future I will surely not share. But I will take comfort knowing that it, and many others, exist. Hopefully for the good.

The sun *also* rises, Ms. Beltran. It may be winter, but it's also winter dawn.

AFTERWORD

▼

SPOOLS OF NARRATIVE

As I thought about this book, 10 years and more, in and around other projects, three ideas kept recurring. Exile, loss – not only of place but also of self, and the overwhelming desire to re-connect – with people, places, the past. Sometimes, as in these stories, these concerns are linked to aging, and death, sometimes not. But they are omnipresent. They're always there.

We're Americans, and however ill-defined our sense of ourselves as a people, we do feel we're a people in a place. We may not draw our *chi* from this place, but we certainly have a feeling of being *here*. At least for a time.

But what if, for one reason or another, we are torn from this place? What becomes of us then?

Similarly, the characters we create for ourselves – what if we lose them? If we lose each other? Are they not the worst sorts of exile?

And do we not want – perhaps more than anything else – to re-unite?

If either exile or loss occur, and failure to achieve reunion, do we then use narrative to buttress ourselves? Re-create ourselves? If so, must that narrative be true? Or do we need only that which will comfort and console us, propel us through one day and into the next?

Exploring such questions in these 16 disparate stories, I tried, as with any credible story collection, not to render *Reunion* a hodgepodge – regardless of deliberate stylistic variances. Instead, I conceived of the book as variations on a theme. A couple of themes, really, all tearing us from self, from place. All thwarting reunion.

War is certainly one theme here, for we never seen to lack for that, for its victims on both sides of the battle lines. Ecological disaster is another. Aging and death, too. Broken families and wayward children. The past. Failure: personal, political, national.

These themes, these concerns, have long been with me, allowing me to consider them over time as deeper histories, longer plot lines, more definitive conclusions. As such, *Reunion* is hardly a book I could have written in my 20s or 30s. Simply, I hadn't lived or experienced enough. Traveled enough. Lost enough.

Where did I find these people, these places? Sometimes close to home. Other times, when I traveled. On the road, a story, or the germ of a story, will rise unexpected and unbidden from the landscape. Inspiration comes as she will. There is no enticing or cajoling it. Forcing it. It arrives or it doesn't; there's accounting for it.

Panama, yes; Florence, no. Kamloops, yes; Santa Fe, no. And so on.

To answer a frequently asked question, no, I never plan my epiphanies. I never say, I will go to Rome and find a story. That's not how these things work, at least not with me. I go to places because I go to places, and things spark. Or they don't.

It's the same with the past, or pieces of the past, the lens through which we see, understand, define ourselves – Americans, our country, our culture. Although many try to obviate the past, it invariably affects us, who we are, what we do. To assume otherwise is puerile – even in a Twitter-obsessed throwaway society that seemingly has no memory. Not to instruct our young about the depth and dignity and vital importance of what went on before us is shortsighted – and arguably criminal. (That is no doubt why they feel they can so blithely or heedlessly cancel or alter it at will and with impunity. Orwell's Memory Tube indeed.) However, as figured in *Reunion*, past and present narrative lines invariably intersect and inform each other, with varying results.

Stories live within stories, time is fluid, and sometimes things are best told backward. Why? perhaps because Americans are a rootless, edgy people, uncomfortable, never sated or satisfied, perpetually moving about. In some ways, that desire to move is our greatest strength; it's what brought us here. In some ways, though, our rootlessness is our greatest weakness, the thing that makes us ignore far too many people, far too many narratives, both here and around the world.

They, the others, know, as we should, that past and place are real and always affect the present. It's a peculiar American delusion that they don't. They always do, a scar that moves across the skin.

As is narrative, the stories we tell ourselves, the stories that are defining. That are the basis upon which we create moral action.

Without narrative, especially in exile, we are nothing. For stories change us, not the other way around. Stories, like bisecting planes, interstices in time, affect other stories, sometimes illuminating, expanding; other times obscuring, rendering oblique.

In *Reunion*, while each story is a discrete unit, nevertheless, as in *Ghost Dancer*, there are internal links – President Eisenhower, for example, appears more than once. So does Jack Kennedy. Suicide, murder, the armed forces, the death or disappearance of loved ones. There's an interrelatedness of things, as life continually teaches us.

While some of the narratives may appear disjointed, they aren't. Some end, some don't. Some seem to have lost a reasonable sense of temporality; they haven't. Instead, time, like memory itself, changes. So does narrative. Here, fictional techniques attempt to capture such multi-faceted, multi-temporal experiences.

Taken that way, life and art are part of a single continuum. To presume otherwise is foolish. Therefore, to separate any from all, to say that one life or one art, is fit only for a certain person or group, is antithetical to life and art themselves.

As such, the very idea of cultural appropriation is fraudulent.

Nevertheless, to answer the charges. First, *Reunion* is a work of fiction. If there are representations of real people, places, ideas, as in all fiction, I use them only as springboards for imaginative leaps. They are just that – fiction – and nothing more.

Put another way, good fiction is always reality-based, but reality that's been rounded off, cured in a second barrel to soften the sting, to hammer out life's myriad loose ends into a reasonable Aristotelian beginning-middle-and-end. It's our human gift, to make sense of the world in this way.

Second, history belongs to everyone or it belongs to no one. Narratives. Interpretations. Should Edith Wharton not have written about New England farmers? John Steinbeck about Oklahoma refugees? Asserting that they shouldn't have is as absurd as saying that John Milton shouldn't have used the Hebrew Bible.

Or that Will Shakespeare shouldn't have written about a Venetian Jew.

By contrast, diversity means not that I will jealously hold on to my turf, however I define it, but instead that all narrative belongs to all of us.

Put a different way, just as American jazz is a little bit of everything, so is literature. Or it is nothing.

Perhaps literature's best defender was the late Toni Morrison, who, when pressed about the issue of one writer writing about a man of a different race, famously said, "he has the right to write about whatever he wants. To suggest otherwise is outrageous." (She, of course, wrote tellingly and well about White people in *Tar Baby*.)

What's only slightly less outrageous is to assume that the stories in *Reunion* are formulaic, that I somehow produced them by rote. The very idea is laughable, for many reasons, no less than that a standard element of authorial method is surprise, not only for my readers but especially for me. Wander off the trail, plunge headlong into the woods. Watch the river cut new, unexpected channels. Akin to finding stories in strange locales, all the stories in *Reunion* invariably took me in unplanned directions. No sooner had I what I thought was a finished outline then invariably the story itself took over. New characters, new situations, new denouements appeared out of nowhere. Like a runaway train, it was all I could do to hold on, to keep from hurtling off.

Truth be told, even unexpected stories elbowed their way in. Convinced after many lists and iterations that *Reunion* would be 14 stories, at a point near the finish line, two completely unplanned stories simply showed up and demanded they be included. I found that I couldn't deny them.

Similarly, I found various characters and situations more active than I had originally anticipated. Some were written during the pandemic – a topic I assiduously avoided because I wanted it to settle; it was too new, too fresh, to consider with any depth. Put another way, I saw the nomenclature but not the architecture of face masks, social distancing, sheltering-in-place – and isolation, substance abuse, anxiety, and depression – for effective fiction. I'm sure all of it will ignite one day; right now, it's wet kindling.

Still, I found myself writing about more nights than I had previously planned, and many characters more willing to bend – or outright break – the rules. Executive action, ends justifying the means, and all. Was it a pandemic-related sense of frustration – something desperate, somehow a way out of the box? Could be. Could be long-held beliefs about action itself. Or our American fascination with outlaws. I honestly don't know. Psychology's notoriously tricky, especially one's own.

If I were pressed, though, I would say that there are a couple of touchstones, a few standard points that managed to withstand the intuitive onslaughts. For example, what would my scribblings be without at least one visit from Wrightsville's venerable Mayor Bill Roland and his crooked cast of political miscreants, so basic, so transparent, so venal? Our old friend Damian Vrabel? Dressed up in different frocks the neighborhood tavern as church, or at least as confessional? And so on.

And over and over again, the theme of exile. Of loss. Of passing. Along with the irresistible attraction of damaged characters – far more interesting than the whole ones. Just as the edges of life are far more interesting than the center.

And the idea of reunion, of trying to get back something we had and lost, or had never had and wished we once did. The rosy glow of lost opportunity, real or imagined.

Perhaps there's always been some sort of exile as first cousin to the American experience. After all, we all had to be exiles to come here – to be forced from or to turn our backs on our ancestral lands. Since then, we've needed a place, needed to be indigenous. But we haven't been here long enough, either for roots or rust. (Perhaps that's why the rest of the world doesn't trust us very much. We have neither the grounding nor the gravitas. Further, because nowhere is naturally our place, we believe that everywhere is our place – and we're willing to take it.)

Restless, impatient people, Huck Finn to Sal Paradise, Americans often discover themselves elsewhere, on the road, domestically, globally. Exile as romance, Mark Twain to Jack Kerouac, Walt Whitman to Henry James, Ernest Hemingway's inebriated ex-pats to Woody Guthrie's hopeless migrants coming with the dust and going with the wind, American vagabonds, restless to get here, restless to leave. Exile and loss, return and reunion, and the failures thereof, old as *The Odyssey*, fresh as Facebook.

The search continues; it's hard to know when to stop. In *Reunion* the stories themselves told me. Until they told me they were finished, they changed every day. If they didn't have their own internal kill switches, I'd still be the writing the first one. Along the way, I made them as fresh and perceptive as I could. Then set them aside.

The world has changed. The writer has changed. The stories are documents, snapshots, spools of narrative longing for completion.

Abby Mendelson
March 2021

CPSIA information can be obtained
at www.ICGtesting.com
Printed in the USA
BVHW042212240721
612597BV00007B/56